Days of Rage

Days of Rage

A Novel

Mike Shepherd

iUniverse, Inc.
New York Lincoln Shanghai

Days of Rage

Copyright © 2007 by Mike D. Shepherd

All rights reserved. No part of this book may be used or reproduced by any means, graphic, electronic, or mechanical, including photocopying, recording, taping or by any information storage retrieval system without the written permission of the publisher except in the case of brief quotations embodied in critical articles and reviews.

iUniverse books may be ordered through booksellers or by contacting:

iUniverse
2021 Pine Lake Road, Suite 100
Lincoln, NE 68512
www.iuniverse.com
1-800-Authors (1-800-288-4677)

This is a work of fiction. All of the characters, names, incidents, places, organizations, and dialogue in this novel are either the products of the author's imagination or are used fictitiously.

ISBN-13: 978-0-595-42572-3 (pbk)
ISBN-13: 978-0-595-86901-5 (ebk)
ISBN-10: 0-595-42572-0 (pbk)
ISBN-10: 0-595-86901-7 (ebk)

Printed in the United States of America

Prologue

Sirens screamed as the night time sky above Southern Illinois University turned smoky red. Old Main was burning. Curtains of fire burst through the windows of its seven-story cupola-topped center tower. Arching geysers of water were swallowed by the flames.

Firemen battled the blaze up close, some from the end of elevated ladders, until the roofs collapsed with a crackling roar, sending a mass of glowing embers skyward. The hellish heat forced them to retreat. It had become a lost cause. A young bearded man, whose glasses reflected the fire, stood among the watching crowd, grinning ever-so-slightly, and under his breath he muttered, "Burn, baby, burn."

The cause of the fire was unknown, but many suspected it was started by members of SIU's antiwar movement. They were in the habit of burning draft cards and American flags.

On the heals of the fire another incident sent shockwaves through Little Egypt. Fishermen found a body floating among the lily pads in the shallows of Horseshoe Lake near Cairo, Illinois. The following day the woman was identified as Gretchen Witherspoon, last seen alive participating in a demonstration in Cairo in protest of racial inequality in this small city situated at the confluence of the Ohio and Mississippi Rivers at the very southern tip of Illinois.

A political science graduate student at SIU, about fifty miles to the north, Witherspoon had been active with the Southern Illinois Peace Committee, which had joined forces with the black United Front of Cairo to draw attention to the blatant segregation and discrimination. The town was deeply divided along racial lines.

Witherspoon hadn't drowned. The Alexander County coroner determined she had been strangled. In other words she was murdered. Had she been murdered because of her activism by Cairo's white supremacist as everyone suspected? The local police, some of whom were accused of being white supremacists themselves, seemed to be dragging their feet in investigating the murder. Would it, too, go unsolved like many of the murders of other civil rights activists in the South?

Chapter 1

Mick Scott got out of jail the day after he had been arrested for rioting at the Democratic National Convention in Chicago. He hadn't intended to be involved in the massive and violent antiwar demonstrations. He had only become involved as a result of getting a ride with a van full of peaceniks while hitchhiking from San Francisco, where he had been discharged from the military after serving thirteen months in Vietnam as a combat correspondent for Armed Forces Radio.

He had been swept into the melee by the serging crowd just as he stepped out of the van in Grant Park. A Chicago cop had clubbed him on the head and he was hauled off to jail in a paddy wagon along with several bloodied protesters.

Mick wasn't quite as gung ho as he had been when he left for the war. Witnessing casualties and losing buddies can sometimes dampen ones enthusiasm for armed conflict, but he was still convinced the war was winnable as well as justified. He still believed the United States remained committed to stopping the spread of Communism in Southeast Asia, but the American mass media's interpretation of how the war was going had begun to turn public opinion against it. So much so in fact that the Commander-In-Chief, President Lyndon B. Johnson, following a commentary by Walter Cronkite on national television maintaining that the war was not winnable, announced in frustration, and almost in tears, that he would not seek re-election if that were indeed the case. LBJ was reported to have said off camera, "If I've lost Walter Cronkite then I've lost the American people."

Cronkite's remarks were made in direct response to his gloomy assessment of the Tet Offensive of 1968, despite the fact that the Allies had dealt the Viet Cong a devastating defeat. They were nearly wiped out. Only the persistent infiltration by the North Vietnamese Army (NVA) into South Vietnam kept Ho Chi Minh's dream of one Vietnam under the Communist flag alive.

Mick was now on his way to O'Hare to catch a plane downstate to Springfield, the last leg on his journey home. It was a relatively short flight, two hundred miles south of Chicago, and as the plane descended the final few miles, he could see the silver-domed State Capitol looming on the horizon, and the white obelisk of Lincoln's tomb in Oak Ridge Cemetery; landmarks that distinguished Springfield from other ordinary-looking central Illinois towns.

After landing the plane quickly emptied, except for Mick; he just sat there in a daze, still stunned by what had happened in Chicago, and in Vietnam. It had all happened so fast, at least that's how it seemed to him now. *In* Vietnam, one year felt like ten, and suddenly it was catching up to him.

Mick felt tired and old, and a little sad too. Not so much because of what he had done—he hadn't been a soldier—but because of what he had seen as a correspondent. He had had to put all that into words, things that words couldn't really describe.

When he had glanced at himself in the laboratory mirror of the airplane in mid-flight he'd hardly recognized himself. His boyish freckles were no longer apparent, his eyes looked gray instead of blue, and there were speckles of gray in his sandy blond hair.

"Sir, this is Springfield, your stop," the stewardess said gently shaking Mick from the trance he had been in.

"Oh, yeah, sorry. Thanks," he said, and he disembarked.

Chapter 2

The red and blue neon beer sign at Tommy Seno's Tap beckoned Mick. He had often thought of the place while in Nam, as one thinks of a long-lost buddy. It was an old fashioned tavern with high, ornate tin ceilings, and smoke-tainted black and white photographs of boxers and baseball players on the walls. And what respectable Illinois sports bar didn't have a poster of Dick Butkus in those days—the consummate Chicago Bear? The Cubs were on TV, which sat on a shelf above the door that led from behind the long mahogany bar into the kitchen where Mick guessed Mama Seno would be preparing pizzas and spaghetti.

Tommy Seno, a stocky, muscular man in his mid-thirties greeted Mick with a smile, handshake and frosty glass of Pabst Blue Ribbon Beer. "Well, I see you made it back in one piece."

Tommy didn't take anything too seriously, unless an umpire blew a call, then he'd yell, "God damn, this game is in the tank," and he'd call his bookie and complain.

"Hear the women over there are pretty nice lookin'," he sais.

Tommy was known as a ladies man. He had those Italian good looks, except for the boxer's nose. He resembled Rocky Marciano (whose autographed picture hung on the wall behind him), especially through the shoulders and arms, but that didn't frighten Mama, who was hollering at him from the kitchen for allowing the tomato sauce to scorch while he watched the game. Tommy sauntered back and he and Mama began arguing, loudly, in Italian. Mick smiled. Things hadn't really changed that much in the year he was gone. Mick looked up at the TV. Yep, the Cubs were losing.

As Mick and the other two customers—older guys whom he did not recognize—nursed their beers waiting for Tommy to return from the kitchen, someone came in who Mick recognized, despite the long hair and a beard. It was Jan Sanders, a guy he had gone to junior college with. The last Mick heard Jan had been drafted by the Marines and was in Vietnam.

Jan recognized Mick too. He walked straight to him and they shook hands. Judging from the way Jan limped, he hadn't made it back unscathed.

Tommy came out of the kitchen, shaking his head and mumbling to himself. Mick asked for another beer and whatever Jan wanted.

"Same-same," he said.

Tommy set them up and went back down to the end of the bar to watch the game.

"Thanks," Jan said. They touched glasses.

"So where ya been, Mick, haven't seen you for awhile?"

"Nam. Just got back. Heard you were over there too."

"Yeah," Jan said, and he took a long drink of beer.

"So what brings you to Tommy's?" Mick asked. I know you're not into sports, didn't used to be anyway."

"Pizza, Man, I've got the munchies bad."

They looked at each other and grinned. Having the munchies meant Jan was stoned on grass. His soft blue eyes were glazed and a little red, and Mick could smell it on his clothes.

"Wanna smoke one?" he asked Mick.

"Uh, well, yeah, sure. But where?"

"Out back. Finish your beer and we'll go."

They drank up and went out the back door to the alley. Tommy didn't seem to notice them leaving. His eyes were riveted on the baseball game.

Out back was a grove of what were commonly called stink trees—or "ghetto palms" as Mick called them—growing between two small, brick garages. Together they formed an alcove into where Jan led the way. It hid them from the glare of a street light. He lit a large joint and handed it to Mick, who knew what to do, he had smoked pot overseas.

"Won't Tommy be suspicious about us coming back here?"

"Nah," Jan said. He's got a 'don't ask, don't tell' policy going on like a lot of the bar keeps around town do. So many people toke up now, it's pretty much tolerated. Just don't ever try to smoke it in there, though, like some idiot did the other night. Tommy tossed him out the door like a bucket of dirty mop water."

"Understood."

After two or three tokes apiece, the inevitable came up.

"You wounded over there?" Mick asked Jan.

"Chunk of shrapnel took out a piece of my calf."

"Where were you fighting?"

"Con Thien, but I don't wanna talk about that crap, Man. That's the past, I'm only interested in what's happening now."

"So what is happening now, Jan?"

"Carbondale, Man, that's where it's at. I'm going to school there on the GI Bill."

Mick knew about Carbondale, deep in southern Illinois, in the Bible Belt. It was supposed to be quite hip though; an oasis in conservative Little Egypt, as the region was known as in part because it included the towns of Cairo and Thebes, and was relatively close to Memphis, Tennessee.

"You should come down," Jan said. "Use the GI Bill. Get something out of that fucked up war. I'm renting a house there. Could use some help with expenses."

"I'll think about it, but right now I'm too fucked up. This is some dynamite shit."

Jan grinned then he sucked the joint down to a nub and they went back inside and got two more beers. Tommy didn't seem to notice they had been gone.

Jan ordered his pizza to go, unbaked, gave Mick his phone number, and left.

The following day Mick started the paperwork that would lead him back to school on the GI Bill at Southern Illinois University, then he made arrangements with Jan to meet him down there in the fall where they'd split the rent on a house.

Chapter 3

The tension in the air in Carbondale was heavy as the humidity of its late summer weather. Southern Illinois University had become a hotbed of dissent surrounding the Vietnam War. The Students for a Democratic Society, the SDS, were active in protesting it with numerous, riotous demonstrations. They burned draft cards and the American flag, while flying the Viet Cong's as if they were of that army; the army of Uncle Sam's enemy—the South Vietnamese Communists.

They met periodically, late at night, at a table at the very rear of Mr. Natural's Health Food Store, in the dim light—a dark-bearded man with glasses; Stuart Bolshinsky, leader of SIU's SDS, and someone else whose face was shadowed by the brim of a straw hat.

"The files you seek are locked in a cabinet whose combination I've yet to learn."

"How will you find it out?" Stuart asked.

"My fingers and ears are capable of detecting the faintest of a click."

"These files will reveal a definite link between the CIA, the Vietnamese Studies Center and the university?" Stuart asked.

"Yes, and once we've leaked the information in the form of photographs of the files to the press, the Center will be shut down; all of them, nationwide, and the pro-war propaganda on the respective campuses will cease. The American press is our ally—Ho Chi Minh's ally. They are turning students and the American people in general against the war, which in turn will persuade American politicians, particularly the President, to withdraw US troops unilaterally from Vietnam soon."

"But not soon enough," Stuart said angrily. "Nixon must be persuaded to get out now. The antiwar movement needs to be shifted into a higher gear. Burning draft cards and flags isn't enough. Buildings must burn," Stuart growled through gritted teeth. His eyes, magnified by the glasses he wore, looked mad.

The time then came for Mr. Natural's to close, and Stuart Bolshinsky and his shadowy companion left stealthily through the back door, and in the dark alley they went their separate, secretive ways.

Chapter 4

Mick felt strange walking across campus among the hordes of students, most of whom were younger than he, even the ones with beards. But now and then one passed by whose eyes betrayed them, revealing something no amount of hair could hide; something Mick had seen before—the "thousand yard stare"—peculiar to those who had been to war. Or maybe they were just plain stoned. He laughed to himself. Could be a combination of both, like with Jan. Jan was stoned most of the time.

He grew his own weed in the back yard of their house in Carbondale, camouflaged by wild flowers and bamboo, which to Mick's surprise could be found in abundance in southern Illinois. Its leaves resembled those of a marijuana plant. It looked like a jungle back there, especially when Jan's black cat, Jazzpur came prowling through.

Jan got Jazzpur stoned too, along with Mick once in awhile. But mostly Mick liked to drink at The Club uptown, a Vietnam vet hangout where he could rap about the war. Unlike Jan he was still interested in it. The damn thing was still going on of course, and GIs were still dying. It also was being discussed quite a bit in his Communications curriculum classes, as well as in the Current World Affairs class he was taking.

Mick had decided to continue in the vein of electronic journalism—not wanting his experience as a radio reporter in Nam to go to waste.

His professors weren't aware that's what he had been, except for his creative writing instructor, as a result of an autobiographical composition he had written for the class. He had expressed in it his support for the war, which didn't seem to be the prevailing sentiment in academia, in the Communications curriculum anyway. The professors were quite outspoken against it, and they assumed that all of their students were too, showing no interest whatsoever in contrasting opinions of which Mick had plenty. But he kept his views to himself until in one of his classes the tape of Walter Cronkite's famous and damning assessment of how the war was going was played. It was based on his erroneous perception of the Communist Tet Offensive of 1968. Cronkite ascertained that as a result of the offensive the war had become a lost cause and that we should try to negotiate out of it. Mick stood up and disputed Cronkite's assessment. It caused quite a row, not so much with the professor, but with some of the other students in class who only knew about the war through network TV, *Time, Newsweek, Life* and *Look* magazines and the *New York Times* which, along with other nationally-prominent rags like the *Washington Post* was available at the library. All of these sources were mediums with anti-Vietnam War slanted perspectives, a perspective that most journalists seemed to have.

Mick, who had witnessed the Tet Offensive first-hand, contended that it had been portrayed by the American mass media as an Allied failure simply because a few Viet Cong commandos had managed to get into the US Embassy in Saigon the night the offensive began. He set the record straight. He had covered one of the most ferocious battles of the offensive at Tan Son Nhut Air Base. At first the Air Force security police guarding the sprawling base on the northern outskirts of Saigon were caught by surprise because of faulty intelligence.

An attack had been expected, but not quite on the scale of the one that occurred. A large enemy force caught security undermanned, and they quickly breached the perimeter before Allied forces, with support from armor and air, beat back the attack and eventually defeated the Communists forces soundly. It was that way all over South Vietnam that night, as it had been a nationwide offensive, but by sun-up the next day scores of Viet Cong lay dead on the battlefields, including the grounds of the US Embassy. It had, in fact, been a stunning defeat for the enemy despite what the American mass media had reported.

Mick and a smug little myopic dude with long blond hair worn in a pony tail got into a shouting match over it, the debate centering not on the pros and cons of the war itself, but about the role of the media in reporting it.

"Knee-jerk reactions like you just saw only serve to undermine the war effort and the morale of our troops," Mick argued.

"Granted, there may have been an intelligence failure, but the fact is in the end the Tet Offensive was disastrous for the enemy. Hell, we could win this war right now, if Westmoreland would get the additional troops he's requested to go after the NVA, especially in their sanctuaries in Laos, Cambodia and the DMZ, but instead, just because some numb-skull talking head says the war is unwinnable now, it probably won't happen. No newsie should wield that much power when it comes to military affairs. They're journalists, not generals!"

To which Mick's adversary responded, "It's the responsibility of journalist to report things as they see them. It sounds to me like you're advocating some kind of censorship, Dude!"

"Not a bad idea in certain situations. What if say, Walter Winchell would have broadcast something similar about the Battle of the Bulge, or Tarawa, when there was a lapse in intelligence; they'd a hung him for treason."

"There is one big difference Mr. Scott," the professor interjected. "That was a war in which the United States itself would have been in danger had we lost it. If the Communists win the Vietnam War they would be of no direct threat to us. We have no business interfering in Vietnam's internal affairs. It's a civil war."

"You don't see the spread of Communism as a threat to our way of life?"

"Not at all Mr. Scott. Vietnam is 10,000 miles away."

"So then why did John Kennedy say that Americans must be willing to pay any price, bear any burden, oppose any foe to assure the survival and success of liberty in Vietnam."

The professor cleared his throat and looked at the clock. "That will be all for today. Class dismissed."

It was four o'clock and time for Happy Hour at the Club, a long, narrow, relatively dark place whose lighting came from the small front window and a variety of beer signs hanging on the dark paneled walls. A circular Budweiser sign with a miniature team of Clydesdales pulling a beer wagon round and round hung over the center of the bar. There were red vinyl booths along the wall and stools at the bar, and in the back there was a small game room just big enough for a handful of people to throw darts at two boards. There was a juke box of course, and a TV. Being Friday, the place was already hopping by the time Mick arrived, and as usual, Reggie Rodriquez was in the game room throwing darts. They had met only two weeks before, but that wasn't the first time Mick had seen him. Late one night, soon after he had arrived in Carbondale, he saw Reggie rolling through the drive-up window of a hamburger joint. Not so unusual, except he was in a wheelchair. After receiving his order he wheeled down the street as if he were driving a car. Mick watched as a cop pulled him over, put Reggie, along with his chair in the car and drove off.

Mick, still steaming by what had transpired in his last class, bought a cold one and slipped into the last empty booth in a dark corner at the front of the tavern and tried to cool off. It was the first confrontation he'd had about the war since coming back from Nam, notwithstanding being clubbed on the head by a cop at the Democratic National Convention.

Drinking fast and furious he quickly quaffed the first beer, went to the bar for another one and sat back down. Soon, Reggie, who had finished his dart game, saw Mick and he maneuvered through the crowd to the booth.

"Hey, Man, what's happening?"

His voice was gravelly and loud, and he laughed, which Mick noticed he did often.

"Ready for another one?" he asked Mick.

"Sure, but I'll get it."

Before Mick could get up to get them both one, Reggie had spun his chair around and was on his way through the crowd again to the closest end of the bar. One of the tenders, John, a big, muscular fellow with a red, well-waxed handle bar mustache, placed a tray on Reggie's lap and sat two bottles of beer on it. Reggie rolled back, this time with a little more difficulty as the place was now packed, and it had gotten so noisy with the juke box blasting the two of them were forced to shout.

"I wish you would have been in my last class today, Reggie."

"Oh, yeah, why's that?"

Mick told him about the confrontation he had and Reggie just laughed. "Fuck 'em if they can't take a joke."

Reggie didn't seem to take anything too seriously, not even what had befallen him in Vietnam; an AK-47 bullet in the back in the horrific Battle of Ia Drang three years before. Besides rendering him paralyzed from the waist down, it had also caused one of his big brown eyes to wander, making it difficult sometimes to tell who or what he was looking at, and Reggie knew that and he played games with it.

"Hey, Mick, check out that chick over there."

"Where?"

"By the door."

Mick looked toward the front door."

"No, Man, not that door." Then he let out with an uproarious laugh.

Reggie often made light of his handicap, sometimes calling himself a gimp. Perhaps that's what kept him so buoyant, for having to sit in a wheelchair for the rest of one's life would certainly weigh heavy on the mind, body and soul. The thought of it weighed heavy on Mick's mind. He tried to imagine what it would be like not to be able to walk; not to be able to feel the extremities below the waste as was Reggie's case Mick assumed. Not to be able to-

"Hey, Mick, check her out. No, I'm serious this time. That blond chick who just came in the front door. That's Trudy, the townie, she's hot to trot, Man, you could score. I'll introduce yous two."

"Reggie!"

The woman spotted him right away and came over and gave him a kiss on the head. She slipped into the booth opposite Mick, and when two other people slid in after her as there was no place else left to sit, or even stand for that matter, Trudy wound up sitting next to Mick.

"Hi, I'm Trudy, the townie," she said, introducing herself to Mick, and she glanced at Reggie and smiled. Mick thought she resembled Cher, the singer, but with blond hair.

"The one and only," Reggie said smiling affectionately in return.

While Reggie conversed with the others who had sat down in the booth—another woman and two men—Trudy and Mick began to talk, a little clumsily at first. She asked the basics like, "where ya from," "who's your favorite group," and "what's your sign?"

"Springfield, the Young Rascals, Scorpio," Mick replied.

"Scorpio," she repeated smiling, and she lifted an eyebrow and made a clicking sound with her tongue against her teeth.

"The sign of sex," she said bluntly.

"Really?" Mick responded. "Since when."

They both laughed.

"And death," she added. "Ruled by the planet Pluto. It's one of the water signs. Scorpes have a strong feminine side too." Something Mick didn't particularly like hearing, but he liked hearing Trudy talk. She had a sweet, southern Illinois accent. Carbondale was closer to Memphis than Chicago, sparing her of that annoying upper-Midwestern twang, which Mick was sure that he had, being from the plains of central Illinois.

"What's your sign?" Mick asked Trudy.

"Aquarius," she said with apparent pride.

"So what are Aquarians all about?"

"Compassion mostly."

Reggie laughed. "That's why she's hangin' out with a gimp."

"Reggie's a Leo. I guessed it the first time we met," Trudy said. "Ruled by the sun; noble and proud with lot's of heart, like the lion, and light of heart too; buoyant, gregarious and generous, and sometimes a little obnoxious when he's had too much to drink."

"That's me," Reggie said laughing. "Who wants another beer?"

"It's my turn," Trudy said.

Mick stood up to let her out, and as she brushed past him their eyes met closely and she smiled. His eyes followed her as she made her way through the crowd to the bar. Her tall, slender, but well-shaped figure moved gracefully and she left behind a trace of perfume that Mick recognized as patchouli oil, which was what Chelsea wore.

Chelsea was the last woman Mick had been with; in August in San Francisco, the night he got back from Vietnam. He had met her in Haight-Ashbury while wandering around half-drunk like a tourist wanting to see what real hippies looked like up close, and he literally stumbled upon one sitting on a curb—Chelsea, and she got him stoned on hash and they wound up body surfing together on her waterbed. Those waves had long-petered out and Mick had become marooned on dry sand. It was high time now for him to get wet again.

He laughed to himself about his lewd, double entendre musings. But he was serious about his intentions. He intended to live up to the Zodiacal characteristics Trudy said were peculiar to Scorpios, excluding the death aspect, unless he died doing it with Trudy, who he fantasized about while watching her walk to the bar. Her long blond hair flowed like golden silk down her back which Mick's eyes followed to her hips. While waiting for the drinks she moved them subtly to the music; a slow, jazzy, sensuous tune that featured a sexy saxophone.

When she returned with the beers and sat back down in the booth Mick cozied up to her right away and she responded in kind. Soon they were kissing and oblivious to anyone else around. They had become acquainted fast, which was the trend in this day and age of fly-by-night sex. Mick asked Trudy if she wanted to go some place else more quiet. His place was what he had in mind, but Trudy had other plans.

"My place would be nice," she whispered close to Mick's ear. They got up and went outside. Mick took a deep breath, and at once the cool, autumn night air intensified the high he felt from the alcohol.

"Ahhh, what a rush," he sighed.

The sidewalk was crowded, and they stepped back against the front of the bar to avoid being swept along.

"Where you parked?" Trudy asked.

"I walked tonight," Mick said.

"I'm parked over there." They walked across the street to a yellow Volkswagen bug. She unlocked the door, let Mick in and they drove away. Alone together for the first time, they both became a little shy and conversed somewhat nervously, again engaging in small talk; about how crowded and noisy the Club was, and how much fun Reggie is to be around and so on, until after about six blocks west of Illinois Avenue they turned up a long, worn, gravel lane to the back of a wooded lot where a little green trailer sat, lighted by a lamp on a utility pole. It shown amidst a sugar maple tree whose bright yellow leaves, some falling, gave off a dried, musty smell, the smell of autumn.

"Home sweet home," Trudy said.

This was her home away from home in Carbondale. Her parents lived on the outskirts of town, but being devout, church-going folk they weren't hip to her lifestyle, so she had moved out her senior year in high school—the year before. She was only 18 and worked as a waitress at a diner. John the bartender didn't care if she wasn't 21; she looked it.

As soon as they stepped inside the trailer Mick could see that the place was strictly astrology motif. Psychedelic green, purple, blue, pink, orange and yellow black light posters of Gothic art representing the twelve Zodiac signs adorned the walls. And the mystic, new wave music Trudy put on lent to the cosmic atmosphere.

"Have a seat, Mick," Trudy said, motioning to the couch. She lit a stick of incense and candles, went to the kitchenette and came back with two glasses and a bottle of wine, sat them down on the coffee table, opened a small wooden box and produced a joint, assuming that Mick partook. They smoked and drank and Trudy spoke of astrology of course, and of how compatible Scorpios and Aquarians were, especially when the sun is in such-and-such and this planet is aligned with that one and it's in retrograde. The thought of all of it, along with the wine, pot, incense smoke and new wave music made Mick's head swim. He sat back and Trudy placed her hand softly against Mick's cheek. "Let's go where it's more comfortable," she whispered.

She took Mick's hand and led him into the bedroom where they undressed, laid down and after much creative foreplay made love until they were both satisfied—as satisfied as two people who were drunk could be. They then fell asleep, and in the morning Mick slipped away without waking Trudy and walked home, in the crisp autumn dawn, his favorite time of year, when the Sun is in Scorpio, the sign of sex.

Chapter 5

Mick had never voted before, not having been old enough, but now that he was eligible he welcomed the opportunity. The Vietnam War had made him more politically conscious, knowing it was the politicians—particularly the president—who committed the country to such things. He wanted a say in deciding who that might be.

In the months following the riotous Democratic National Convention the presidential campaigns became more contentious, but not between the two main parties so much as within, especially among the Democrats who saw their platform splintered in Chicago by the Vietnam War.

When things finally settled down after the Windy City's streets had been cleared of demonstrators by the cops and Illinois National Guardsmen, Hubert H. Humphrey—with LBJ now out of the picture—survived as the party's candidate.

Lame duck president or not though, Lyndon Baines Johnson still called the shots in Vietnam. October 31, as Mick prepared to go out on the town for Halloween, traditionally a big party night in Carbondale, he heard the radio news of the bombing halt imposed by LBJ and it flat pissed him off. Mick knew, having been in Nam as recently as July, that the Communists were on the ropes as a result of the Tet Offensive, and the ongoing bombing campaign, called "Rolling Thunder," had taken it's toll on North Vietnam's infrastructure and morale.

"If Westy had been granted his additional 250,000 troops for search and destroy, and the bombing continued-, God damnit!" Mick threw his half-empty beer can against the wall, which freaked out Jan's cat Jazzpur who had been sleeping on the bed, and he dashed down the stairs. When Jan heard the disturbance he came upstairs to check it out.

"What's going on?" he asked Mick.

"LBJ halted the bombing of the North."

"Good. Maybe that'll put an end to this fucked up war."

The two didn't see eye-to-eye regarding the war, but they never argued about it as Mick always deferred when it came to their difference of opinion out of respect for Jan who had been in combat as a soldier, and not as an observer like Mick. Mick turned off the radio not wanting to hear anymore about the god damn bombing halt.

"So, who you dressed up like, Jan?"

Jan smiled, which was rare. "Timothy Leary, Man; turn on, tune in, drop out," he said, loosely quoting the infamous acid-dropping, former Harvard professor, and self-appointed guru of the counter culture.

Jan looked the part: beard, long hair, bandana, white, pajama-like cotton shirt and pants, loop-toe leather sandals and a tote bag hanging from his shoulder on a leather strap that was made from remnants of an old Persian throw rug he had bought at the Salvation Army.

"And you?" Jan inquired.

"A hobo." Mick had been shopping at the Salvation Army too. "Original huh?"

"Yeah, but lose the watch. Here, Mick, wanna try some of this?"

Jan pulled a little piece of paper with small purple dots on it from his bag.

"What is it?"

"Blotter acid, Man. Just put one of these little dots here on your tongue and get ready for the ride."

He tore off a piece of paper around one of the dots and offered it to Mick.

"No thanks. Halloween is spooky enough without that shit," Mick said, declining Jan's offer. He had heard how scary acid trips could be for some people.

Jan shrugged his shoulders and put the piece of paper back in his bag and went downstairs leaving Mick to put the finishing touches on his costume.

Mick liked celebrating Halloween, because at midnight it was his birthday. He had spent the last one hunkered down in what amounted to a fox hole made by an exploded enemy mortar shell at the horrific Battle of Loc Ninh, the battle in which Mick had been grazed across the upper forehead by a Viet Cong bullet; a wound that still hadn't completely healed, because a Chicago cop had clubbed him smack dab on top of it at the Democratic National Convention in August, having mistaken him for a demonstrator.

The scar wasn't all that bad, really, but Mick covered it with his hair anyway, not wanting anyone to ask about it. He didn't want to have to divulge that he had been given a Purple Heart for such a minor flesh wound, when guys like Reggie were confined to wheelchairs, and Jan was limping around like an old man.

Mick had been invited to a party being thrown by people from The Club, mostly vets. He expected to see Trudy and Reggie there, and he did, and they appeared to be together, judging from the way they acted, like a couple on a date. She stood beside him with her hand on his shoulder, dressed like the Aquarian woman. He wore the costume of a lion, symbolic of his birth sign Leo, Mick supposed, and his wheelchair was decorated to look like a throne.

Mick was surprised to see them together like that. He didn't know they were a couple. Reggie had introduced her to Mick at the Club and then let them be as if he were fixing them up. And Trudy had left the Club with Mick without hesitation, and they had made love at her trailer. Did Reggie know? If he did he didn't seem to care as he seemed friendly enough flashing Mick the peace sign, the sign of the times. But Trudy, while somewhat friendly, seemed a little standoffish. Perhaps she felt guilty for what they had done.

"Hi Scorpe," was all that she said, but with a smile.

Watching them, he couldn't help but wonder if they could, if Reggie could do what Mick and Trudy had done, being paralyzed from the waste down.

"None of your god damn business," Mick swore to himself, and he went about mingling and drinking and smoking the endless joint that was floating around, which more often than not was handed to him by a dark haired woman with big blue eyes who appeared to be dressed like a gypsy, or so Mick thought until she apologized for not dressing up for the night. In reality she was a little hippie chick who had crashed the party in order to, "… connect with the vets," she said.

"It's surprising how groovy you guys are," she said, "I mean like this is dynamite pot."

"Vets smoke the best," Mick said, having brought some of Jan's primo, home grown weed to pass around.

"Were you in Nam?" the woman asked.

Mick didn't really want to think or talk about Vietnam this night. Hearing about the bombing halt had made him angry and he didn't want to be angry; not on his birthday which began at midnight, but he answered her question anyway.

"Yeah." Then he tried to change the subject. "What's your name?" he asked.

"Kathy."

But she wouldn't let him change the subject.

"Must be pretty bad over there, huh?"
"Yeah. So where ya from Kathy?"
"St. Louis. Did you kill anyone?"
"Not that I know of."

Mick had only fired his weapon once in Vietnam, an M-16, at the enemy lines the night the Tet Offensive began at Tan Son Nhut, the sprawling air base on the northern outskirts of Saigon.

He had gone out there to report on the attack, but when the Air Force security police he had ridden to the battle with in a jeep came under intense fire, he, as a GI first and foremost, was forced to put down his tape recorder and shoulder the rifle to help defend their position which had become a shallow ditch. He had squeezed off a few shots randomly with no one in particular in his sights. So Mick truly did not know if he had killed anyone or not.

"What branch were you in?" Kathy asked, continuing with her persistent line of questioning.

"Air Force."

"Oh, the bombers. Drop any napalm?"

"Me? No, I wasn't a pilot."

But Mick had flown on a bombing mission over Dak To, strictly as an observer. Napalm had been used, being an important weapon in close air support, and quite controversial because it was at times difficult to control being made of a highly volatile petroleum jell. On impact it exploded into a fast moving fire storm.

The tone of the conversation had changed, and Mick knew where it was headed.

"I saw a photograph in a magazine of children screaming as they ran down the road from a Vietnamese village after it had been hit by that shit," Kathy said, her eyes peering up intensely at Mick's as if he were responsible. "Seems like an awful lot of innocent Vietnamese people are getting hurt by that war."

"That's right," Mick shot back. "Thousands were executed by Communist forces at Hue because they chose not to side with them when the Tet Offensive began."

Mick could feel his temperature rising.

"But I thought you said you came here to connect with vets, not to pick a fight."

"You're right. I'm sorry." Kathy smiled and put her hand on Mick's arm.

"Hey, would you like to go to another party?" she asked.

Mick looked around. This one had gone a little flat, or maybe it just hadn't quite gotten started yet, being relatively early, and Trudy and Reggie were being kind of lovie-dovie so he didn't feel comfortable about talking with them right then.

"Sure," Mick said. "Why not."

"Wanna walk?" Kathy asked, "it's not too far."

Mick waved to Reggie and Trudy, who smiled, and he and Kathy left.

It was a blustery night. Most of the leaves had fallen from the trees by now, and some of them were blowing across the street making skit-scat-scittering sounds. A dog, a large sounding dog barked, sending chills up Mick's spine. Halloween was in the air.

"So where's this party?" Mick asked.

"Bucky's dome."

"Bucky's dome?"

"Buckminister Fuller," Kathy said incredulously. "Surely you've heard of him. The world-famous architect? He's a design professor here."

"Oh, you talkin' about that brown thing at the corner of Forest and Cherry."

"That's the one."

Coincidently Mick lived across the street from it. Soon they were there. He looked over at his house and in one of the windows Jazzpur sat puffed up and looking perfectly Halloween; yellow eyes glowing like a jack-o-lantern's. Kathy noticed him too.

"Far out," she said.

Mick looked at the dome. He had grown accustomed to seeing it every day going to and from campus, but tonight, being so stoned, its globular, multi-faceted, brown shingled facade appeared as a large exotic mushroom growing in the moonlight, with classical music emanating from inside.

He followed Kathy through the door. It appeared so much larger from within, and at once Mick felt as if he had stepped into another world.

The interior was lighted by sconces, and a singular moon-like globe hanging from the center of the ceiling directly above a large round table containing a punch bowl where people, dressed in a wild variety of costumes, milled about. Mick wondered if one of them might be Fuller.

Suddenly he realized Kathy had left him alone, so he made his way to the punch bowl for a little social lubrication. As he ladled a glass of it, not the least bit concerned about what it might contain, any kind of alcohol would do, he thought he heard someone faintly calling his name. He looked around and spotted Jan standing off by himself. He nodded at Mick and smiled. It was nice to see a familiar face; one that wasn't made up or masked. Other than Kathy's, Jan's appeared to be the only one that wasn't. Oh, yes, and his. Mick had dressed like a bum, but he hadn't put any makeup on, except for a couple blackened front teeth. He sauntered over to Jan.

"What's happening Timothy?" he asked, referring to the guru Leary, who he had dressed up like.

"Everything, Man, everything is happening everywhere you are when you're hip to being there."

"Well, I guess that pretty much covers it," Mick said. "So, which one of these creatures is Fuller?"

"Oh, Bucky's in Boston," knowing such because Jan was in the design program. "His assistant is throwing the party. That's him over there, dressed like Raggedy Ann."

"Okay."

"So what brings you to this party, Mick, I thought you were going to the vet's?"

"Some little hippie chick. That's her at the punch bowl."

"Oh, Christ, that's Kathy, she's in design too. What the fuck was she doing at the vet's party? She hates vets."

"Said she wanted to connect."

"Connect an electric prong to your dick, maybe. All that chick wants to do is pick fights about Nam, especially when she's drunk. I've seen her in action before. Oh, shit, here she comes, I'm gone, Man, I don't wanna talk about that fucked up war with her when I'm trippin', or any other time for that matter."

Jan quickly got lost in the crowd as Kathy, who looked drunk, came straight up to Mick and got into his face about what else, Vietnam, and she sounded like the Communist broadcast propagandist, Hanoi Hannah. Mick had heard her many times on the radio overseas.

"You imperialist air pirate, warmongering pig. How can you drop napalm on innocent children and kill old women and men?"

Mick hadn't done either; most GIs hadn't, not intentionally anyway, but that was the rap put on them by misinformation coming out of Hanoi with a little help from the American mass media in general, unwittingly or otherwise.

"How can you justify poisoning the countryside with Agent Orange, and turning Vietnamese housewives and teenage girls into whores for the pleasure of marauding GIs who murder their husbands and fathers!"

She was all over Mick like a yapping little dog, and he backed away not knowing what to say, and soon he found himself backing out the door, which was then slammed in his face by the woman who had invited him to the party under the pretense of wanting to connect. Connections like this, Mick didn't need.

Soon Jan came outside, having seen what had gone down.

"I told ya, Man, don't let people know you were in Nam. We ain't welcome around here. I found that out the day I got back, in the airport in Frisco when some bitch spit on my shoe."

Jan turned and limped away to their house across the street. Mick stood there alone, stunned by what had just happened—stunned by the suddenness and the violence of it. He shivered with anger that guys like Jan, who should have been welcomed home as heroes for fighting for the freedom of others, were being treated instead as villains by snotty little pip-squeaks like this Kathy who knew nothing about the war except what she had gleaned from the press.

Chapter 6

After Nixon was elected president in November, and the fall semester wound down toward Christmas break, the antiwar movement began to pick up steam nationwide. Antiwar dissidents at SIU were especially resentful of the presence of military recruiters on campus where they had set up shop in the student center. Mick happened to be there one day when protesters formed a circle in front of the main entrance, started a small fire on the sidewalk and began tossing their draft cards onto the flames, while chanting "hell no, we won't go!" Soon more people, including women, gravitated to the demonstration and it became ever-larger and louder and four or five campus cops showed up, and there was pushing and shoving and shouting.

Mick distanced himself from the ruckus as he did not want to get swept up in it like he had done in Chicago.

The cops soon lost control of the situation as the crowd, now numbering nearly a hundred, Mick guessed, surged toward the center of campus. Then out of the crowd a man lept up on the edge of a fountain with a bullhorn and began shouting something about Nixon, but it wasn't exactly clear what he was saying. Whatever it was, it worked the demonstrators into a frenzy. Soon dozens of Carbondale and state police arrived, with bullhorns too and demanded that the crowd disperse immediately or face arrest. Most did, and the ones who didn't were put into paddy wagons and were taken away to jail. The demonstrator with the bullhorn climbed into a tree and directed his diatribe at the police who eventually pulled him down and drove off with him too.

The demonstration hadn't gotten bloody like in Chicago, but it showed how widespread dissent had become, even on campuses in the Midwest. It was sparked by a handful of young men burning their draft cards. Hell no, they didn't wanna go, but neither had Mick. In a sense he too had been a draft dodger. He went to Vietnam because his grades in junior college had slipped below an acceptable level, making him vulnerable to the draft. He dodged it by joining the Air Force hoping to avoid Nam, but he was sent there anyway. So, he was in no position really, to criticize others who were trying to avoid it as well, albeit illegally.

What upset him most, though, was the anti-GI tone of it all, like what Jan had experienced at the airport in San Francisco, and the episode Mick went through with Kathy, the hippie chick, at the party at Bucky's dome.

GIs were simply doing what their country had asked them to do; to help the South Vietnamese defend themselves against Communism, enemy of democracy, enemy of individualism, in other words freedom, as corny as that may sound. Freedom's not corny to those who don't have it.

Why weren't people protesting North Vietnamese violations of the Geneva Conference of 1954 when Ho Chi Minh's Communist forces were mandated to stay above the 17th Parallel—the DMZ, the demilitarized zone—which they now used as a staging area to launch assaults against South Vietnam. And they were infiltrating the South with men and supplies in support of their southern comrades, the Viet Cong. They were in essence invading South Vietnam, again in violation of the Geneva accords, one soldier, one rifle, one truck towing one artillery piece at a time in a never-ending military parade down the Ho Chi Minh Trail, around the DMZ, through Laos and Cambodia.

Yet it was US policy not to go after them in their sanctuaries outside of South Vietnam because LBJ didn't want to agitate the peaceniks who would accuse him of widening the war, which in turn would be bad for him politically. Is that what this war was really all about, Mick wondered, the politics of an American president?

Chapter 7

▼

Mick went home to Springfield for Christmas—home only in the sense of town. His parents had been killed in a car wreck when he was 15. His Aunt Jenny, an alcoholic widow, had taken him in until he graduated from high school, but she continued to keep a room open for whenever he came home from the service, and now college. He could come and go as he pleased through the back door and up the stairs.

Aunt Jenny spent all day drinking and smoking cigarettes in the front room, shades pulled down, staring at the TV. Her eyes were always red, like her nose, and her face was wrinkled and ashen, but with a yellow tint. She had her booze and cigarettes delivered by the drug store, along with prescriptions for her back pain. Mick gave her a fruit cake for Christmas a couple of nights before the Day, kissed her on the cheek and went out. He started off at Tommy Seno's Tap hoping to see old friends and people home for the holidays from the service or school.

He especially hoped to see Tim White who had been due back from Nam in November. They had gone to high school together.

"Hey, College Boy," Tommy said, pouring a Pabst Blue Ribbon from the tap assuming that's what Mick wanted. Mick never had the heart to tell Tommy that his house beer sucked.

The place was busy, but Tommy moved at the same old leisurely pace from the taps and coolers, to customers clamoring for drinks, to the cash register and back and forth carrying on conversations mixed with wisecracks all the while. He was the consummate bartender.

The customers were lined up at the bar or sitting at the tables. Some were playing foosball or sliding pucks down the long shuffle board. Mamma Seno was in the kitchen, black hair done up in a bun, wearing the old country style black dress and shoes and black stockings with white apron, preparing pizzas to be carried out unbaked, the house specialty popular all over town. And naturally she was barking at Tommy in Italian about something, which he naturally ignored.

Mick spotted a mutual friend of his and Tim White's in the crowd.

"Hey, Billy!"

"Mick. What's happening, Man, how's school?"

"Okay. Tim get home?"

"No, Man, didn't you hear? He's missing in action. Door gunner on a chopper that never returned."

"God damn."

Mick's enthusiasm for partying dampened momentarily as he thought about how Tim's mom and dad would be taking it, not knowing the fate of their only son. Missing was better than killed though, Mick thought, at least there was still some hope that he'd be found alive, even if it were in a prison camp.

"Hey, there's a band playing at a new place uptown," Billy said. "I'm going there after this beer. You should come."

"Huh? Oh, yeah, live music sounds pretty good. Where's it at?"

"Fifth and Monroe—Tony's Place."

"Okay, I'll meet you there."

Mick drank up, waved to Tommy and left. On his way uptown he decided to drive past Tim's parent's house. Maybe he'd stop in for a quick visit; give his regards. They always seemed to like Mick. Before he and Tim went into the service the old man threw a party for them. Tim's dad was fun to drink with, like one of the guys.

He turned onto their street. It had been snowing much of the day. Mick could hear the snow packing beneath his tires on the bricks as he slowly drove up in front of the house. No Christmas lights were on this year, just a lamp in the living room window.

Mick pulled over to the curb across the street and looked at the two-story, plain white frame house. Should he go in? What would he say? He turned the car off and just sat there in the silence as the snow began to fall again. Soon he saw Tim's dad come to the window and peek out as if he were expecting someone, then he turned, looking downcast and disappeared. Mick drove away, but before he went to Tony's to meet Bill he stopped at another place he used to go to occasionally, Two Brothers' Lounge. It was a Friday night and the white-collar after-work-crowd—state government and insurance workers most of them—were there. Mick was still conservative at heart, and he liked looking at the secretary types in short skirts and high heels. Most of the men wore suits, white shirts and ties, loosened, which made it easier to turn their heads when the women walked by.

Standing off by himself, Mick happened to glance at himself in the mirror and he was surprised to see how long his hair had gotten compared to most of the other men there. Then he realized he had tucked his jeans into his boots because of the high snow, and with his brown leather bomber jacket and turtle neck sweater, Mick stood out in contrast to the others, and he felt a little self-conscious about it. He drank the rest of his beer and left, but before going down the street to Tony's he ducked into an alley to smoke a joint of some of Jan's shit he had brought up from Carbondale. After having seen himself in the mirror at Two Brothers' surrounded by all those bureaucrats Mick realized how much Carbondale had rubbed off on him, on the surface anyway. But inside he was still pretty much the same, that conservative-at-heart who liked the way women looked in high heels. The blond one in the suit at the little table by the juke box had nice legs. Mick thought she had been checking him out. He thought about going back, but not stoned, not there, he had been paranoid enough.

The band at Tony's, a popular local group called Fat Tuesday, rocked hard and the Friday night, hip, home-for-the-holiday crowd cheered them on incessantly.

In the crowd Mick spotted Billy again, and he looked to be feeling no pain, grinning from ear to ear, glasses halfway down his nose, holding his bottle up to the band. It was so noisy Mick didn't even try to talk to him, instead he found a place to stand at the very back of the room near the rear exit door. But people were coming in and one of them was the blond woman, the one with the nice legs he had seen up the street. She bought a drink and squeezed in next to him. Occasionally their shoulders brushed when they moved to let someone by. Once they turned facing each other close enough to be dancing, and Mick realized how pretty her hazel eyes were. She smiled.

"I saw you at Two Brothers', looking at yourself in the mirror." She laughed lightly.

Mick smiled. "Oh, yeah, I was noticing how much different I looked compared to the rest of the guys there."

"Yes, you did, like I look different here, in this suit and heels."

"You look nice," Mick said flirtingly.

"Thanks," she said. "So do you. I get tired of seeing the suits," she laughed and glanced down at hers, "even mine. On weekends I'm much more casual.

Sometimes I don't get dressed at all, I mean, well, you know what I mean, I don't, never mind."

"No sweat, I know what you mean," but Mick couldn't help but visualize her not being dressed at all, and he felt aroused, and when the band came back he asked her to dance.

"Okay," she said.

They sat their drinks on a ledge near where they were standing and went to the area where other people were dancing in front of the band. It was crowded, and they danced close even though the song was a fast one. She moved well; gracefully and in control, unlike some of the others on the floor who were thrashing about as if possessed. She smiled sensuously, looking Mick over from head to toe, apparently liking the way he moved too. After another song they returned to their place which had gotten even smaller, forcing them, if that were necessary, to stand very close, face-to-face as if they were slow dancing. Mick slipped his arm around her waist pulling her hips up against his and they kissed, lightly at first then long and deeply, and when they came up for air she whispered in his ear when the band stopped between numbers, "These shoes are killing me, I need to take them off."

"Go ahead."

"Not here."

"Where?"

"The Hilton. Know where that is?"

"Yeah."

"Meet me there in twenty minutes. My name is Sue, uh, Sue Smith. Just ask the front desk which room I'm in." She gave Mick a quick kiss on the cheek and left.

Mick nursed his beer; he had twenty minutes. No, half an hour, he'd take his time, be a little late. This was shaping up to be a pretty nice Christmas. Mick felt the glee, he was high, but then when the band started playing *We've Gotta Get Out of This Place*," by the Animals, a favorite song of GIs in Nam, he was reminded of his friend Tim who had been reported missing in action. Mick thought about what kind of Christmas he'd be having, maybe in some god-forsaken prison camp. For the moment he had forgotten about Sue and their rendevous, but only for a moment. He could still smell her perfume; it must have rubbed off on his clothes when they kissed. Man, she could kiss. He wanted more of the same and then some. And if he did get some he'd consider it a Christmas gift to Tim.

On the way to his car Mick could see the top of the Hilton about six blocks away. It was the tallest building in town; a 31-story tower with the top three or four stories built outwardly forming a bulbous-like rim all the way around. "Prick of the Prairie," some called it. An amusing metaphor considering why Mick was going there, and despite trying not to, he felt anxious about it, which he didn't want to appear to be. There were times before when he had gone on a hot date thinking he had a sure thing and it didn't turn out that way; wrong time of month, or she had gotten too drunk and threw up in the car, or she had gotten a case of the oh yes, no, please, yes, yes, no no's.

Mick walked up to the front desk and asked what room Sue Smith was in.

"2715."

The elevator went up fast and deposited Mick directly in front of Room 2715. Then his stomach caught up. He took a deep breath and knocked on the door. It opened as far as the chain would allow. Sue's face appeared. In the hall light she looked a little older than in the bar, thirty at least, nonetheless she was very pretty. She smiled, unlatched the chain, invited Mick in, shut the door behind him, put her arms around his shoulders and they kissed, passionately like they had done at Tony's, and Mick felt like he was in the fast rising elevator again.

Embracing, they danced around the room past the bed where Mick tried to stop, but she led him to a table that contained a bucket of champagne on ice. "Let's take our time, Darling," she said, handing him the bottle which he opened with a corkscrew. She poured two glasses of the bubbly and they clinked glasses and drank, eyes locked on to each others as they sipped the champagne. Then Sue sat her glass down and removed her jacket. Her light pink blouse was unbuttoned enough to see the cleavage of her sizeable white breasts, and the lacy top trim of her black bra.

He kissed them, and she moaned with pleasure while running her hands through his hair. She pushed Mick's jacket back off of his shoulders and off of his arms, and undid his jeans. Mick sat on the edge of the bed, took his boots and socks off and pushed off his jeans, underwear going too, then he peeled his sweater off, while Sue removed her blouse and suit, and Mick was surprised to see that under it she had worn a black garter belt and black stockings. Extremely aroused, as this was one of his secret fantasies, he stood up and pressed himself hard against her, and he lifted her and she wrapped her legs around his hips, and they rolled onto the bed with her on top. She unfastened her bra and let her breasts fall to his lips. And then she moved down his body kissing him all the way until she reached what she was looking for. Her hair felt like a scarf of silk on his abdomen and thighs, and her mouth felt even softer. And then they made love in different ways that tested Mick's relatively fertile, lascivious imagination, and in the midst of it all Sue managed to say, "Oh darling, darling, I don't even know your name."

"Tim."

"Merry Christmas, Tim."

When he awoke in the morning Sue was gone.

Mick went back to Carbondale earlier than he had planned. It had been just too damn depressing staying at Aunt Jenny's; with her drinking all day, cooped up in the house, watching soap operas, as the world turned outside.

Chapter 8

As the world turned into 1969, with Richard Nixon sworn in as President, the war began to change, and the antiwar movement continued to pick up steam, even though Nixon indicated he might have a plan for getting us out of the quagmire the previous administration had gotten us into. This would entail turning the fighting over to the South Vietnamese while the US attempted to negotiate a peace.

Meanwhile, in February the North Vietnamese Army launched a countrywide offensive in the south, hoping, it was speculated, to force Nixon to show his hand in regards to his new war strategy, while producing American casualties which would give impetus to the anti-war movement in the US, but the enemy gained little militarily except for media and dissident attention. Ironically it was reported by a captured Communist soldier that the February offensive had caused the morale of the VC, which had already suffered greatly because of the Tet Offensive of 1968, to sink precipitously. More than 1,000 VC defectors surrendered to the Allies during the first week of the February offensive, thinning their ranks even more.

The offensive also violated an agreement, albeit vague and unwritten, by which Hanoi, in return for Johnson's bombing halt of October '68, would refrain from such aggressive actions.

This pissed Nixon off and he retaliated by bombing the North Vietnamese Army's southern command headquarters in Cambodia with B-52s, sending a message to Hanoi that he would not be shy, as the previous administration had been, about going after Uncle Ho's forces outside of South Vietnam despite knowing he would surely be accused by the dissidents and the media of widening the war. In fact the media did accuse him of such when they got wind of the bombing, and it didn't take long for the dissidents to start raising hell in Carbondale again.

An antiwar group called the Southern Illinois Peace Committee (SIPC) had recently been formed, and while the Cambodia bombing certainly did not sit well with the SIPC, a faction of the more widely-known Students for a Democratic Society (SDS), they became especially incensed with the announcement by the university that it had accepted a million dollar grant from the US Agency for International Development (AID) to establish a Vietnamese Studies Center at SIU.

AID was known to be funding a variety of social service programs in third world nations, including an SIU mission in Southeast Asia to train teachers. It had also been rumored that AID served as a front for the CIA, but university officials insisted that the Center would in no way be involved in any clandestine activities related to the war. Its activities would be strictly academic, compiling a library of Vietnamese books and periodicals, in addition to providing one of the first Vietnamese language classes in the US, writing a dictionary and history of Vietnam and sponsoring speakers and lectures.

However, some of the administrators hired to run the Center were known to have been associated with a University of Michigan project funded by AID. The project had supposedly been initiated to train South Vietnamese police in counter-insurgency tactics, which of course aroused the ire of the SIPC, and they demonstrated violently against the opening of the Center. And like the demonstration Mick had witnessed last semester, the one that began with the burning of draft cards, this one spread fast, again overwhelming the relatively small police force which had come to quell it.

Mick saw something at this one that infuriated him; a Viet Cong flag being waved above the throng. A cheer went up and that was all he could take. He turned away and headed up Illinois Avenue to the Club before doing something stupid, like kicking the guy's ass. But then he'd be arrested for rioting again, like he had been in Chicago, and he'd spend the night in jail for infringing on someone's constitutional rights.

Shaking with anger, Mick held his breath, counted to ten and stepped inside the Club. As the door shut behind him the sounds of the riot, which had grown fainter with distance, were replaced by the murmur of patrons inside who were oblivious, obviously, to what was going on up the street on campus, just six blocks away. But the image of the Viet Cong flag had stayed with him as he walked up to the bar and ordered a glass of beer from John. He quaffed it in three long swallows and got another. Calming down some, he looked around and saw Reggie in the back tossing darts with someone Mick didn't know. There were only about 10 other people in the place, a couple making out in a booth and the rest sitting on stools at the bar.

Reggie saw Mick, and after his dart game he rolled up to where he stood at the end of the bar by the door.

"Hey, Mick."

"Reggie. What's up?"

"Sure ain't me," and he laughed of course, but Mick wasn't in any mood for jokes.

"What's wrong?" Reggie asked.

"There's a big riot going on."

"Riot? Where?"

"On campus," Mick said.

"Again? Those bastards. Can't they give it a rest?"

"Not till we're out of Nam," John chimed in as he brought Mick and Reggie a beer. "It's on the house." He winked and went back to watching the nightly news until Chet said goodnight to David, then he turned the TV off and plugged in the juke box, but before anyone could play it the muffled sounds of shouting and sirens could be heard. Mick went to the window and peaked out through a neon beer sign. The demonstration had moved off campus and up Illinois Avenue. John and Reggie came to the window too, followed by several patrons. And then, right in front of the Club, as if it were planned, knowing the bar was a Vietnam vet hangout, one of the demonstrators unfurled an American flag while another put a cigarette lighter to it.

"Not on my watch you don't," Reggie growled. "John, hold that fuckin' door open."

John obliged and the noise of the riot rushed in. Reggie rolled to about ten feet from the door and turned around. His wandering eye no longer seemed to wander. Both were intensely focused on his intended target. Mick could see it in his eyes—Old Glory.

Neck bowed, jugular vein swollen, muscular shoulders, arms and chest bulging out of the tank top he wore, Reggie reared back in his chair and let fly out the door, bounced off the walk and plowed headlong into the crowd, and in one-felled swoop, just before the flag caught fire, he snatched it out of the demonstrators' hands. Others tried to get it back from Reggie. John and Mick charged out after Reggie and waded in. There were fisticuffs, and the cops came swinging billy clubs, and again Mick took one directly on top of the scar on his head causing it to bleed all over his face and clothes, like in Chicago. And like in Chicago he was arrested, along with John and Reggie whose wheelchair was put in the trunk of the squad car after he had been unceremoniously deposited in the back seat clutching the flag in his arms. A cop yanked it from Reggie's grip and tossed it back to the demonstrators, and the three were driven away. Looking back through the window of the squad car Mick saw the flag being torched.

"It's their Constitutional right," the cop who was driving said to Reggie through the rear view mirror.

After they were booked on disorderly conduct, and a nurse at the jail cleaned and bandaged Mick's wound, one of the officers, a guy about their age, explained, apologetically.

"Sorry boys, but we had no choice. It's the law. They're protected by the Constitution."

"Those draft-dodging, flag-burning pinko motherfuckers are protected by the Constitution?" Reggie asked with a sarcastic laugh.

The cop pushed his hat back on his head, put a foot on a chair and rested his arms, crossed, on one knee.

"Fraid so," he said. "You guys are vets, right?"

The three nodded and the cop smiled. "Me too, and as US servicemen we swore to protect the Constitution. Specifically, they are, we are, protected by the First Amendment; freedom of speech, freedom to assemble and so on. You know that."

Mick did, but at the moment he didn't want to admit it.

"I'm going to let you guys go on your own recognizance with a notice to appear in court next month. If the arresting officer doesn't show then the charges will be dropped. Let's see." The cop looked over a calendar.

"How about March 26, I'll be out of town that day." He patted Reggie on the shoulder. "You guys are free to go now, but Reggie, please stop going through those drive-thru windows at MacDonald's in that chair."

Reggie laughed. "Yes, Sir."

John called a cab. He needed to get back to the Club having left unexpectedly.

By the time they got back the demonstration had fizzled out, but the faint smell of tear gas lingered, causing Mick's nose and eyes to burn. Through the tears he saw on the walk charred remnants of the flag.

Luckily for John one of the patrons had taken the initiative to tend bar in his absence, which had been about two hours. The place had become packed and rowdy and celebratory because of Reggie, John and Mick's heroic actions—primarily Reggie's. Four men picked up his wheelchair with him in it and sat it on one of the tables. He looked like a Roman soldier in a chariot who had just returned from battle, as did Mick with the blood on his shirt and bandaged head. John, who had somehow managed to keep his handle-bar mustache in perfect shape despite the fray, (it would take a pipe wrench to muss that heavily-waxed thing) went back to tending bar, and for the rest of the night the three were heralded by the Club's patriotic patrons as heroes, even though despite their effort the American flag had burned.

Chapter 9

Curious as to what the Vietnamese Studies Center was really all about, when the smoke had cleared after the demonstration, Mick went there and introduced himself to the director, a Mr. David Gordon who happened to be standing at the receptionist's desk when he walked in. They shook hands and Mick's felt small in his. The man was a tall and slender, but big-boned with coal black curly hair and thick black eyebrows. His eyes were dark and piercing. He wore a white, short-sleeved shirt and khaki pants. In his left hand he held an unlit pipe. When Mick told him he was a Vietnam veteran Mr. Gordon smiled and invited him into his office to talk.

"Please, have a seat."

Mick sat down in a chair in front of the desk the director sat behind. He lit the pipe and Mick immediately recognized the tobacco as cherry blend.

"So what brings you to the Center?" Mr. Gordon asked.

"I'm interested in learning more about the history of Vietnam, and our involvement in it," Mick said. "I figure since I participated in the war I should know a little more about how we got involved in it."

"What did you do in Nam, Mick?" he asked between puffs on the pipe.

"I was an Air Force reporter for Armed Forces Radio."

"Interesting." He lifted one of his thick black eyebrows and nodded approvingly. "Not many military news guys around, especially Air Force types."

He continued to puff on the pipe, and rings of smoke floated toward the ceiling.

"It would be refreshing to get that perspective as opposed to the garbage the mainstream civilian press has been feeding us regularly about how the war has been going. When were you there?"

"1967 through '68."

"Do any reporting on the Tet Offensive?"

"Yes, Sir, at the Battle of Tan Son Nhut."

"Outstanding."

Gordon sat up and knocked tobacco from his pipe into an ash tray, put the pipe aside and folded his big hairy hands on the desk.

"Would you be interested in helping us compile a history on the year you were there, in my estimation the most pivotal year in the war thus far."

"I'd love to Mr Gordon."

"Great." he smiled. "Call me David." He stood up. "Let me introduce you to a Vietnamese woman who you'd be working with on that."

"Okay."

"I'll be right back."

David left the room and soon returned with the woman; a pretty, young Vietnamese.

"Mick, Mae, Mae, Mick."

The introduction sounded funny and everyone chuckled.

"How do you do?" Mae said, smiling politely. She presented her petite hand and Mick shook it gently.

"How do you do?"

"Mick will be working with you on that post '45 history, Mae," David said. "He was a reporter in Vietnam, and he covered the Tet Offensive, so he'd be able to provide some important insights on that. We'll work out a schedule later."

"Okay, very good. Nice to meet you, Mick, see you," Mae said, and she left. David sat back down at his desk and filled Mick in on her background.

"Mae's parents were originally from Hanoi. Her father taught economics at a university there before WWII when it was thought that Capitalism was in Vietnam's future. When the north of Vietnam became Communist under Ho Chi Minh after the war, and those with Capitalistic leanings were being persecuted, he tried to flee to the south with his wife, as many did, but they were caught and accused of being traitors. They imprisoned him, but soon let Mae's mother go, and at her husband's insistence she continued on to Saigon, not knowing at the time she was pregnant. Seven months later Mae was born. Two days after that her mother got word that her father had been shot trying escape the Communist prison he was in.

"While growing up in Saigon, Mae attended an elite school that prepared its student to qualify for scholarships at select American universities. She wound up at UCLA where she majored in political science. No doubt you will find her a pleasure to work with. Can you come in Monday afternoon at four o'clock."

"Yeah, that's when my last class gets out."

"Very good. See you then." Both stood and shook hands again.

While working with Mae Mick learned much about the history of Vietnam, particularly post 1945 when Ho Chi Minh and his Communist army, the Viet Minh, emerged on the international scene as a fledgling power to be reckoned with. They came into prominence as a resistance force against Japanese occupation during WWII. Then when the French, Vietnam's long-time colonial masters returned, having left to defend the homeland against Hitler, Ho boldly declared independence for his people, resulting in the famous August Revolution and the Indochina War which culminated at Dien Binh Phu with the stunning defeat of the French in 1954. After that war the Geneva Conference was convened in order to work out a post war accord. It divided Vietnam along the 17th parallel, formed the nation's of Laos and Cambodia out of the former Indochina. It also set up an interim government to reign over the South while Ho and his Communists were to govern the north with the stipulation he'd keep his hands off the South until national elections could be held within two years through which the people of both the North and the South would decide whether to reunify or remain divided.

Meanwhile Nguyen Diem rose to power in the South and the Geneva-mandated elections were forestalled. This aroused the ire of Ho Chi Minh and he began waging a guerrilla war against Diem and his South Vietnamese government troops. He was joined in the fight by southern Communist insurgents known as the Viet Cong.

With the French now gone, the U.S. became involved fearing that South Vietnam, as well as Laos and Cambodia, would fall to the Communists. So President Kennedy sent advisors and military and economic aid to help keep Diem propped up, but he was eventually toppled by a coup while we looked the other way, not being particularly pleased with him as he was corrupt, unpopular and ineffective in countering the Communists.

After a couple more coups Nguyen Van Thieu settled in as South Vietnam's president. After the Gulf of Tonkin incident, which may or may not have actually happened, we became even more involved militarily, sending troops, more military aid in the form of equipment and dollars, and we bombed the North in retaliation for the supposed attack on our destroyers in the Gulf of Tonkin. The war then escalated rapidly through '66, '67 and '68 as the North Vietnamese sent more and more men and weapons down the Ho Chi Minh Trail through Laos and Cambodia in support of their southern comrades, the VC, all of which was in blatant violation of the Geneva Accords of '54.

With the decimation of the VC in the Tet Offensive of 1968, the NVA stepped up their involvement in the South even more, and they established sanctuaries in Laos and Cambodia and the DMZ, where the US refused to pursue them for fear of being accused by the world and dissidents in the US of widening the war, although the NVA had done so without reservations. Geneva apparently meant nothing to them, although the South, under Thieu, had a hand in forestalling the mandated elections for fear the popular Ho Chi Minh might win and become the Communist president of both north and south, a prospect the US was certainly not in favor of as we were concerned about all of Southeast Asia falling to the Communist; thus the infamous Domino Theory.

Mick did enjoy working with Mae. He had always liked Vietnamese, especially the young women; so petite and pretty with their long, silky black hair, round brown faces and shiny hematite eyes. He remembered how they looked in Vietnam; like dolls in their *ao dais*; the colorful, high-collared, silk dress that was split up the sides to the waist, and worn with silk pantaloons. Riding on the backs of motorbikes with their boyfriends, husbands, brothers on the streets of Saigon, they looked like beautiful kites blowing in the wind. Today Mae dressed like an American girl, but he tried to picture how she'd look in an *ao dai*.

"Mick. Mick!"

"Huh? Oh, sorry, Mae, my mind was drifting off, to Vietnam. Do you miss Vietnam, Mae?"

"Oh yes, of course."

What do you miss most about it?"

"My house." She gazed out the window with a far off look in her eyes as though she could actually see what she talked about. "We lived in a big French house with a high garden wall. A villa that one of my teachers owned. On the grounds there were banana palms, and bamboo, and red flaming flower trees, and lotus and lilies on a pond, with golden fish in it."

"Plan to go back someday?"

"Yes, yes I do," her eyes returned to the room and she looked at Mick, "to become involved in politics, but right now I think it is important to teach American students about Vietnam to counter the misinformation they've been fed by the press and through Communist *dich van*."

"Dick van? Like in Dick Van Dyke?" Mick joked.

Mae laughed. "I see him on TV. Very funny man, like a clown in a business suit. No, Mick, I mean the propaganda coming out of Hanoi. Spelled different: d-i-c-h v-a-n. It is one of Ho Ch Minh's strategies to win the hearts and minds, not of Vietnamese, but of the American people to turn them against the war, so you will pull out and leave South Vietnam for the North to conquer. Its primary purpose is to encourage dissent, disloyalty and confusion among the American people. Hanoi believes that the war can be won in the US through the mass media, academia and the antiwar movement and in Congress; the mass media being the catalyst that it was following the Tet Offensive of '68. Despite the fact that the Offensive resulted in a crushing military defeat for the Viet Cong, as I'm sure you know, the press characterized it as a psychological defeat for the Allies because, they contend, it showed that the Communist forces were capable of launching a coordinated nationwide attack at any given time regardless of how many troops and how much money the US poured into the war. Such a characterization has discouraged the American people and given impetus to the antiwar movement which has impacted decisions by Congress regarding the war, namely the mandated withdrawal of all American combat troops. And when it comes to capitalizing on disloyalty, they found a valuable ally in Jane Fonda who has openly denounced the war before Congress, and when she visited Hanoi and posed for photographs on an antiaircraft gun she played perfectly into the hands of *dich van*. By acting out her opposition to the war on the front pages of the world's newspapers, she popularized the Communist cause.

"Speaking of the Tet Offensive, Mick, could you write up something on your perception of it from the viewpoint of a military reporter for this history I am putting together?"

"Yeah, sure, I'd be glad to."

"Good. I'm very tired. Time to go home. See you next time, Mick."

"Okay. Good night, Mae."

Chapter 10

Mick hadn't seen much of Jan lately, since he had become involved at the Center. Usually when he got home, relatively late after being at the Center or the Club, Jan had crashed in his room with the door closed. Even when Jazzpur scratched at the door and meowed wanting to get in, it remained that way most of the time. Jan had become a recluse. He hardly ate or fed the cat, which Mick had taken to doing. Jan's pot crop, the one he grew in the basement in winter, had been neglected too. And Mick suspected Jan had dropped out of school. He did leave the house on occasion, but never with books or his drawing paraphernalia, just the little carpet bag pouch, which he clutched in his hand as if it contained something life sustaining. One day Mick stopped him before he went into his room.

"You okay, Jan? You don't look too good."

His face was pale and drawn, his eyes looked hollow, and his beard and hair were scraggly.

"Leave me alone, Man," and he shut the door in Mick's face.

This wasn't the same Jan he had known since their reunion at Tommy Seno's Tap in Springfield, nor was he the same Jan that Mick had known before at junior college. While he had always been somewhat of a loner and quiet, he hadn't been a grouchy recluse. On occasion he seemed almost normal, even happy, but he always fell back into a funk. Had he gone schizophrenic? Had the war made him that way? Nothing to worry about, Mick thought, "I'll ask him to go out for a beer." He knocked on Jan's bedroom door. No answer. Had he gone out without Mick knowing it? No, Mick had been sitting in the kitchen for quite awhile with a view of the front and back doors. He knocked again lightly; still no answer.

"Maybe he's asleep. So let him rest in peace."

Mick went out for a beer by himself. Coincidently at The Club, he got a clue as to what could be wrong with his roomy. He made the acquaintance of a guy who had recently returned from Vietnam—a combat veteran. He talked about how the morale of American troops was suffering, even though they had been victorious on the battlefield. But because of the powerful influence the antiwar movement was having on American politics, LBJ, for fear of being accused of widening the war, prohibited U.S. forces from going after the Communist forces in their sanctuaries in Laos and Cambodia. As a result GIs had become frustrated and disgruntled, and many had turned against the war.

This fit Jan to a tee. He had expressed his frustration at being a sitting duck at Con Thien while the NVA pounded away at them with artillery being fired from Laos and the DMZ, but they couldn't do anything about it not being allowed to carry out search and destroy campaigns outside of the South.

"Hearing about all of this antiwar shit going on back home really got my dapper down," the guy said. "Made me feel like I was the fucking enemy, not Charlie. After awhile alls I wanted to do was kick back at base camp and get high on weed, but some guys took it a little too far."

"Whataya mean too far?"

"Smack, Man, junk, heroin. You could get it real easy in the village; easy as pot, an endless supply of it. Rumors had it that it was coming in from China compliments of Ho Chi Minh so as to fuck us up. It worked to a certain extent. Some guys got addicted."

A light went on in Mick's head. That's it, Jan could very well be a junkie, he thought. He got addicted over there, kicked it for awhile, now he's relapsed.

There was plenty of heroin around Carbondale, Mick knew. It was coming in from Chicago and St. Louis. "Shit, every kind of drug there is can be found in Carbondale."

Mick rushed home and knocked on Jan's bedroom door again, and again—no answer. He knocked louder, then pounded. Still no answer.

"Jan? Jan?" He opened the door slowly and saw him lying on the bed, a piece of rubber tubing tied around one of his bare arms; syringe resting between the fingers of his other hand. His eyes were fixed on the ceiling and there was a slight smile on his gray, almost blue face. Mick froze at the sight of the corpse. Nam had finally killed Jan.

Mick had never met Jan's parents. At the funeral in Springfield he introduced himself. He stood back away from the grave site at Butler National Cemetery as they lowered the casket down after "Taps," a three gun salute and the handing of the colors to his mom. It was one of the deepest, saddest feelings Mick had ever had.

Mick continued to rent the house in Carbondale. He inherited Jan's cat and the pot plants in the basement, which he knew nothing about growing. He'd harvest what was there for a stash then leave it at that.

And he continued working with Mae on a history of Vietnam at the Center. Since its opening there hadn't been any more demonstrations directly against it, although rambling articles and editorials appeared in a new, radical underground newspaper called the *Big Muddy Gazette* accusing the Center of being part of a national propaganda network for the CIA to counter the antiwar movement by justifying our continued "imperialistic" involvement in Southeast Asian affairs.

There also hadn't been any antiwar demonstrations in Carbondale, or nationally to speak of of late, as there had been a general lull in the fighting in Vietnam since the failed Communist offensive in late February and March, and the subsequent bombing of their sanctuaries in Cambodia.

After the February offensive had begun, more than a thousand VC had surrendered and defected to the Allies, and they continued to do so in droves in the weeks following, David Gordon told Mick one day at the Center.

"Another failed offensive by the VC has sent their morale plummeting, Mick," he said, smiling with smug satisfaction, "and Nixon's willingness to bomb in Cambodia when his predecessor wouldn't has Hanoi worried. That's why they've shown some behind-the-scenes interest in negotiating in earnest of late."

David looked at his watch. "It's officially after hours now, Mick, want a beer. I keep a little in the fridge in my office."

"Sounds great."

"Bud okay?"

"Sure."

David went to the fridge in a kitchenette adjacent to his office, popped the beers open, came back and handed Mick one. He sat in the chair in front of David's desk. David rocked back in his chair with beer in hand.

"I've gotten word that the Politburo, which is ultimately in charge of both the VC and NVA, has decided to pull back from large-scale campaigns in order to give their forces, particularly the VC, time to regroup."

"Then what?" Mick asked.

"They'll probably return to small-scale guerrilla-type warfare."

"Why's that?"

David took a drink of his beer. "To hold down casualties and bolster morale, and it'll protract the war, which works against us. The American people are growing increasingly impatient with how long it's dragged on already. And it will also serve to frustrate our troops, as their strongest suit is large-scale, conventional-type battles like at Loc Ninh."

"Where the enemy attacked in human waves, out in the open, only to be slaughtered by artillery and air," Mick interjected sharing his first hand knowledge of what had occurred at Loc Ninh in 1967.

"Yes," David said, "in contrast to small-scale, hit and run, hide and seek attacks in the boondocks where so many of our casualties are caused by the enemy's booby traps and land mines."

David took another swig of his beer, and continued. Mick took a drink which consumed about half a can.

"It is this kind of warfare that best suits Charlie, Mick, and buys him some time. Time is Hanoi's ally, and our enemy. That's why they're taking their sweet-ass time with negotiations. The longer they can drag them out, the more inclined they think the U.S. will be willing to make concessions just to get it all over with, and the sooner they can have at the South Vietnamese with us out of the way."

David put his can of beer down on the desk, picked up his pipe, loaded it, lit it up, puffed and rocked back again in his chair, apparently content with having just one beer. Mick wanted another, naturally, one was never enough, but he was too timid to ask.

"The Commies, both VC and NVA, have proven no match for GI Joe and his air power, but the South Vietnamese Army? Now that's an entirely different question. Only time will tell."

"So what is the status of negotiations?" Mick asked.

David smiled and shook his head.

"They're moving along at a snail's pace. Hell, they just recently reached an agreement on what size and shape the god damn table should be that they'd be sitting at in Paris."

"They're trivializing over shit like that while people are dying?"

"Yep, I'm afraid so, but while it may seem trivial on the surface, I must admit there is some underlying significance to seating arrangements in the world of detente, particularly in regards to negotiating the end of a war that involves multiple allies. A square table, for example, with allies like the VC and NVA, and the US and South Vietnam sitting at right angles to each other hints perhaps at division, while a round table brings them together, symbolic of cohesiveness and inclusion. Symbolism over substance perhaps, but that's politics. And politics is what this war is all about. Not religion like in Ireland or the Middle East. Communism versus democracy and Capitalism; that's what it all boils down to."

"So what are we going with, round or square?" Mick asked.

"Round," David said. "And we're going round and round over the issue of mutual troop withdrawals from the South; both North Vietnamese and ours, which is what we propose, while the unconditional unilateral withdrawal of our troops is what Hanoi wants. Through it all the North Vietnamese refuse to admit they have any troops in the South. Which of course is absolutely absurd."

"Hell yes," Mick said with a laugh. "I saw dozens of dead NVA in A-Shau Valley in '68. They wear very distinct military uniforms."

"Yes, and they insist, Mick, that all foreign troops must leave the South before any meaningful negotiations can continue in earnest. Since North Vietnamese technically are not foreign of course, this stipulation does not apply to them."

"What's our response to that bullshit?" Mick asked.

"Nixon has offered to remove major portions of U.S. and other allied forces over twelve months if the North Vietnamese would follow suit, with compliance monitored by an international supervisory body which would also supervise post-war elections in South Vietnam. But the Communists see no advantage in weakening their position through troop withdrawals, especially since we're under tremendous pressure here at home to de-escalate anyway. Then, to add insult to insolence, the Viet Cong insist that the Thieu government has to go before any further talks can proceed, which is totally unacceptable to us. We're committed to standing by Thieu. So now we're hopelessly deadlocked again. So much for round table discussions. But we'll probably start withdrawing troops regardless, because Nixon wants out of this thing. There's another election coming up in '72. Again, Mick it all boils down to politics."

David dislodged what tobacco was left in his pipe into the ash tray, and finished his beer.

"Well, Mick, I hope I didn't confuse you, but this war is so damn complicated, that's one of the reasons we've established these Vietnamese Studies Centers, to clarify as much of it as we can for students whose only source of information is the misinforming press, and left-wing professors."

"No. Thanks, it's been quite enlightening. I guess I better go. Thanks for the beer."

"No problem, anytime."

And sure enough, as David had speculated, in May of 1969, Nixon announced he was abandoning the old demand that NVA troops leave the South six months prior to US withdrawals. Instead he said he'd unilaterally withdraw our troops; the timetable of which would be contingent on the perceived ability of South Vietnamese troops to defend themselves without U.S. ground combat support, and air power. The Vietnamization of the war was now the plan for US disengagement, while we continued to negotiate some kind of final peace agreement.

Then, in June while meeting with Thieu on Midway Island, Nixon made it official by announcing that 25,000 American troops would be withdrawn from South Vietnam, the first step in the Vietnamization of the war. Nixon said we would also strengthen the South Vietnamese armed forces, as they would gradually assume sole responsibility in fending off the North Vietnamese and VC as we disengage. Pacification was to be part of the plan too, in order to win the hearts and minds of the people over to the Thieu government's side, while negotiations got back on track.

Out of the announcement at Midway came the Nixon Doctrine stating that in the future the United States would furnish to other nations fighting aggression, military equipment and economic assistance, but would not provide American troops.

Nixon's peace plan, or at least his plan to get us out of the war, did little to placate the peaceniks. Despite the announced withdrawal of US troops, nothing short of a complete and immediate pullout would satisfy them, and of course the end of the draft.

Chapter 11

One night after leaving the Center, as he walked through Thompson Woods on campus, Mick thought perhaps he was being followed. The person behind him, whom he caught a vague glimpse of out of the corner of his eye, kept the same distance regardless of Mick's pace.

To test his hunch further he turned off the asphalt path and started up through the trees pretending to be interested in a large mushroom glowing bright orange on a tree.

The person behind him slowed on the path as Mick looked the mushroom over.

Steeling a glance at the man again out of the corner of his eye, Mick finally recognized him as David. He lit his pipe while waiting for Mick to return to the path.

"Hope I didn't freak you out, Mick," David said apologetically.

"A little."

"Sorry. Can we talk while we walk?"

"Sure."

"Let's go this way," David said, veering off onto a secondary path that went deeper into the woods.

"I wanted to talk with you away from the Center," David said. "I think we have a security problem there."

"Security problem?"

"Yes, I believe we've been infiltrated by the local SDS. Inside information about our funding sources and personal stuff about me that will only serve to antagonize our adversaries, namely the peaceniks, is being leaked to the press one little juicy drop at a time. A Chicago newspaper reporter called me today for a response to certain accusations."

"Like what?"

"Like …," David looked around over both shoulders. He lit his pipe again, holding the match to it as he puffed and puffed. His face looked eerie in the red, smokey light as his eyes shifted following someone who came walking by. He paused until they passed.

"Like that I'm with the CIA and that we, the Center, are part of a nationwide network set up to disseminate misinformation about the war to American students to directly counter the antiwar movement. But in reality, as I'm sure you have discerned, the misinformation that's being disseminated about the war is coming from a network called the U.S. press who have unwittingly, I'll give them the benefit of the doubt, have unwittingly become conduits of Hanoi's *dich van* strategy."

"Oh yes, *dich van*, Mae told me all about it," Mick said.

"But, I'm convinced the SDS is not so unwitting a conduit when it comes to disseminating misinformation about the war, as some of their leaders, particularly in the Weather Underground faction, are known to have Marxist leanings and they are bent on undermining, not just the war, but the United States itself. I believe the leader of the SDS here has such leanings, and may be inclined to carry out the Weathermen's agenda which entails the bombing and burning of university and government facilities. And I'm convinced he is directly involved in the infiltration of the Center.

"Turn about's fair play, Mick," David looked around again. "We need someone to infiltrate them to find out just how pro-Marxist and anti-American they are, and if they are directly, or indirectly connected to Hanoi through *dich van*? If so, can we nail them for treason, or maybe conspiracy to commit armed violence against the U.S.? Something, anything, to shut them down."

This time Mick looked around over both shoulders.

"Are you asking me to-"

"Can you grow a beard?"

"Yeah, I suppose so, but-"

"Do you smoke pot?"

"Sometimes. Wait a minute David, damn, not so fast."

"It's your patriotism I'm appealing to most here, Mick."

"I don't know. I'm afraid this would be a little out of my league."

"Have you ever done any acting?"

"Nah." Mick laughed. "Well, come to think of it, a little, in junior college theater. I was an undercover cop in a play about heroin smuggling."

"Same basic principle, Mick, except your script would be the *Communist Manifesto*, which would give you some insight into these people's mind set. They're known to hang out at Mr. Natural's Health Food Store on Saturday nights where they read poetry, like that Commie Ginsberg's shit, and listen to protests songs like Joan Baez's. In fact, the leader, a guy named Stuart Bolshinsky, resembles Ginsberg, with the hair and beard and glasses and all. Think you could drag yourself away from The Club long enough to check out that scene?"

Mick didn't know that David knew he went to The Club, and he wondered how much more David knew about him.

"I don't know, David, I'd be like a duck out of water in that crowd."

"Not if you dressed right, grew the beard, wore some plaid flannel and bib overalls, maybe a little tie dye. Got to fit in. These people don't take too kindly to those who don't look like them."

"Would this entail taking part in demonstrations?"

"Fraid so, Mick, you'd have to play the role to the hilt."

"I jus-"

"Would it be worth ten grand on the barrel head to you?"

This really got Mick's attention. He had long dreamt of buying property somewhere in the woods on a lake where he could build a cabin; a place where he could write that book—a place he had thought a lot about while in Nam. Ten thousand dollars would do it.

And as far as patriotism goes—Mick still fumed over seeing demonstrators waving the VC flag around while they burned the US's, without being able to do anything about it because they were exercising their constitutional rights. Infiltrating them would provide him with an opportunity to make them pay for shitting in the face of every GI who had ever shed blood for what the Stars and Stripes stood for, as opposed to what the Viet Cong's represented—tyranny.

"When would I start?" Mick asked intently.

David looked delighted. "Saturday night. Mosey on down to Mr. Natural's; be laid back, pretend to be grooving on the poetry and music. Drop by on a week night too, get acquainted with the regulars, but not too hastily, don't want to scare anybody off. Find out who Stuart is and cozy up to him gradually. Observe mostly at first; discretely. Listen to the language, learn to speak it. Be seen reading radical literature like the *Manifesto*. And see if you can get your hands on Mao's *Little Red Book*. Read what they read.

"Did you happen to notice the VC flag being waved around at that demonstration against the Center?" David inquired.

"Boy, did I."

"Try to find out where those god damn things are coming from, along with Mao's book, if you find one. That could lead us directly to the Hanoi connection, and the one who's infiltrated the Center. They are probably one-and-the-same."

"If I do, this'll end my work at the Center no doubt."

"Yes, you most definitely can't be seen there anymore. But you and I will continue to communicate, of course, as you'll need to keep me informed about what you're finding out, on a weekly basis at least, unless something extremely significant should arise. Call me on this, let's say every Wednesday night at eleven o'clock."

They had gradually walked to the edge of Thompson Woods to under a light. David showed Mick a small, black contraption that resembled a transistor radio, except it was thinner, like a cigarette case.

"It's a phone basically, but it also serves as a tape recorder, right here in the back."

He flicked a switch. A lid opened and a tiny cassette popped out.

"Anything you record on this can be transmitted to me via the phone by pressing this green button. To record, press the red one. It'll pick up voices ten or so feet away through thick cloth." David smiled slyly. "Like flannel shirts and bib overalls. To call me press the white button here, then the one and two twice. Speak closely through this grid, and listen through the other one here at the top."

David plopped the contraption in Mick's hand. "So whataya say, think you can handle it?" he asked.

Mick thought about the ten grand and what it could buy for him on a lake, just a couple acres where he could write that book. But he also liked the idea of having a hand in exposing the SDS for what they were, the Weather Underground faction anyway: violent, anti-American rebel rousers who were undermining the war effort. And this was a war Mick believed could still be won; a war whose cause Mick still believed was noble; a war that was being fought for the freedom of the South Vietnamese people and others in the region who were being threatened by the oppression of Communism.

"Go to the library first thing, Mick." David became excited and talked faster, "Dive into the *Communist Manifesto*; try to grasp what Marx and Engel were saying, then make the scene at Mr. Natural's Saturday night. Remember, be laid back. Get a feel for the way they act. You know—smug and swaggering and judgmental about anyone who isn't like them; who doesn't dress like them, who doesn't eat the same kinds of food, dig the same music and literature. Just listen at first and learn the language, and never, ever, under any circumstances say anything positive about the United States. In fact, blast it at every opportunity, once you get acquainted. And try to befriend this Stuart Bolshinsky. He's the most fanatical. But be careful, Mick, these so-called peaceniks are known to play rough. And remember the tape recorder—keep it loaded and running and well concealed. Here's a good supply of tapes. Run the recorder on slow speed, to get as much as you can on each tape. Give me a call next Wednesday night at eleven to let me know how you're doing. But if you catch wind of anything like a bombing being planned call me anytime. I'll get your payment approved by the powers-that-be ASAP. Hope to hear from ya soon," and David walked away quickly.

Mick went to the Salvation Army thrift store the next morning and bought an ensemble to fit the role he would be playing—an old pair of bib overalls, hip-hugging, bell-bottom jeans, three faded tai dai t-shirts, he'd buy flannel shirts in the fall, a rather worn pair of leather sandals, and two pin-striped suit vests which he thought would be interpreted by the hipsters as a subtle anti-establishment statement when worn over a t-shirt with the jeans. At a head shop he bought a peace medallion on a strand of rawhide, and a little bottle of patchouli oil, the uni-sex cologne of the counter-culture.

There was one thing he hadn't thought of though. How would his sudden transformation be viewed by Reggie and John, especially the peace medallion. They weren't necessarily adverse to peace, just peaceniks, especially since the flag-burning incident. Then Mick came to the painful realization that the Club, like the Center, would be off limits now too, while he went undercover. If he were seen by the people he'd be consorting with, going into The Club, a known Vietnam vet hangout, he'd blow his cover. No, he'd have to change playgrounds and playmates for awhile.

Mick couldn't help but wonder though, where the $10,000 was coming from; surely not the Center itself, it generated no income. The CIA? Was the Center being backed by the CIA after all? Did David work for the CIA? Did Mick now work for them?

Saturday night Mick resisted an innate urge to go to The Club, and he headed for Mr. Naturals, but not without some trepidation. He would indeed be like a duck out of water there, not in appearance, as he had donned his disguise, but philosophically, which might be difficult to hide if they started up with their Marxist, anti-American shit.

"Like a duck in water let it roll off of your feathers," Mick advised himself. And despite himself, he'd have to act as if he liked their poetry. Mick liked some poetry, such as Li Po's, the Chinese poet of antiquity who drank wine by the vat full while communing with nature in the wild. That was what he planned to do someday in the cabin on his land in the woods by the lake which he'd buy with the money he'd get for infiltrating the SDS. With that in mind he pressed on.

When he got to Mr. Natural's he peaked through the window before going in. There were about ten people in the place sitting at tables, and a man was sitting on a stool before them reading from a book. Mick walked in nonchalantly, and went straight to the counter and ordered a tea.

"What kind would you like?" the woman asked.

The only kind he could think of was Lipton's instant, but instinctively he thought that wouldn't be the kind they'd be serving there. He hemmed and hawed a little.

"Red Zinger is good," she said, bailing him out.

"Okay, I'll have that."

Mick glanced around the store while she poured it. The place reminded him a little of an old fashioned neighborhood grocery store with its creaky wooden floors, and one of those big white and black, glass-enclosed porcelain meat counters, except theirs contained no meat; just cheeses, and organically-grown veggies and fruits, the sign said. And there were wooden bins containing grains and beans in bulk, and bags of different kinds of herbs and spices. The place smelled good.

"That'll be fifty cents," the woman said.

Mick paid and took his tea to a table and sat down. He felt strange being in such a quiet place on a Saturday night, sober. Normally he'd be in some noisy bar, probably The Club, getting drunk and telling war stories with ex-GIs.

The people at the other tables appeared to be drinking tea, maybe coffee. They had smiles (or were they smirks?) on their faces as they listened to the man reading poetry. Mick recognized it as Allen Ginsberg's. He had been exposed to it in a literature class. And then Mick noticed how much this guy actually resembled Ginsberg, with the dark, long hair and beard and glasses. David had said the leader of Carbondale's SDS looked very much like Ginsberg. What did he say his name was? Stuart something. "Oh, hey," Mick said to himself, "that's that baboon that was behind the bullhorn at the demonstration."

Mick listened intently to the anti-American establishment, socialistic, bordering on Communistic ranting called poetry. The last words to the last poem he read were, *"I hope we lose this war."*

The audience was fervent in their response to it, reveling in confirmation of what they were hearing. Apparently they too hoped we'd lose the war.

When the poetry reading was over the Ginsberg look-alike joined three people at a table and Mick heard them call him Stuart, confirming what he had presumed. One was a black man dressed all in black, and the other two were nondescript young white men, who didn't look radical or hippie, just typically student, in fact, making Mick feel as if he had over dressed for the occasion. Ironically, he was the only one in the place with a peace medallion on.

While sipping his tea Mick tried to eavesdrop on what this Stuart guy and the others were saying, but they spoke in such low voices he couldn't hear, except when the black man growled, "Burn, Baby, burn," then they all chuckled sadistically and got up and left.

Mick finished the bitter sweet tasting Red Zinger tea and for the first time in years he went home sober on a Saturday night. He slept well, until in the middle of the night he was awaken by sirens—many of them—nearby. He got up and looked out the window. The sky above campus was smokey red. There was a fire; a big one. Mick got dressed, went downstairs, got in his car and drove toward campus, but the streets surrounding it were blocked off by police, so he parked and walked, joining others who had come in droves to see what was burning—Old Main, SIU's beloved landmark building, he quickly discovered, was engulfed in flames. And although he was at least one hundred yards away, the heat forced Mick to move back even farther and watch it burn to the ground along with everyone else, including the firemen who were forced to retreat.

It had become a lost cause as the bricks and stones of Old Main, an enduring symbol of tradition, became ashes. And all the while Mick watched it burn he thought about what he had heard someone say at Mr. Natural's earlier that night at the table where this guy Stuart, the leader of Carbondale's SDS sat, "... Burn, baby, burn."

In the morning Mick relayed what he had on tape to David via the little phone, assuming by then he would have known about the fire.

"Hear-say evidence at best," David said curtly. "That's a general term used by radicals, mostly the blacks in reference to urban rioting. "Keep vigilant though, they may incriminate themselves yet."

The arson squad ruled the cause of the fire unknown, but Mick thought he knew, and he was determined to find out for sure.

Chapter 12

▼

Just before the spring term ended in June, a rock concert sponsored by the Southern Illinois Peace Committee (SIPC) took place at Giant City State Park south of Carbondale. The park was a popular place for students and others to go to on weekends. The headline band, Head East, which featured a girl singer/keyboard player who sang like Janis Joplin, set up on a knoll near a picnic shelter in a meadow surrounded on three sides by forty-foot cliffs—a venue with acoustics aunaturel.

The hard-rocking music amplified by the canyon walls, oscillated across the meadow to where Mick stood on an incline at the base of a cliff soaking up the sun and the wine he brought, which was still cool, not being that far removed from the liquor store.

The meadow had become crowded, but not so crowded that concert goers, and even their dogs didn't have room enough to run and leap after frisbees being tossed from atop the cliffs. In turn the frisbees were thrown back up creating an endless cycle of colorful discs swirling through the bright blue sky like little flying saucers.

A slightly discernable thin haze of marijuana smoke drifted ever-so-slowly overhead like incense dispersed by the breeze, as a long line of dancers, led by a tambourine playing woman formed, and began weaving through the crowd like a colorful snake in motion to the music. A Grateful Dead song, and the counter culture in all of its Bohemian array was on parade. Mick lit a joint, some of Jan's stuff, and he happily smoked while grooving on the scene, and even though he liked the way it looked, the way it sounded, even the way it felt, being high on wine and weed, he really didn't consider himself as one of them, even though he was starting to look the part. He rubbed his chin. He now had a bonafide beard. He looked at his feet, clad in leather loop-toe sandals protruding from scruffy-cuffed bell bottom jeans, all a part of his disguise. Smoking pot though, was something he had picked up in Nam. He took a toke and through the smoke he was surprised to see Stuart Bolshinsky not far away, standing alone. Yes, it was him alright. This would be a good time, Mick thought, to make his acquaintance. He approached.

"Excuse me, aren't you the guy who was reading Ginsberg's poetry Saturday night at Mr. Natural's?

"Yeah."

"Far out stuff," Mick said, not really meaning it.

Stuart nodded and grinned and blushed, as if he were the poet. "Thanks, Man."

Mick offered him the joint. Stuart took a hit and handed it back.

"You a student here?" Mick asked.

"Graduate student," he said setting the record straight.

"Oh yeah, in what?"

"Political science. You?"

"Undergrad in television journalism," then remembering he had a role to play he added, "but I'm thinking about switching to political science. TV's too bourgeois."

Stuart nodded in agreement. The joint went back and forth as they talked.

"I loved what Ginsberg had to say about this fucked up war. I was in the damn thing," Mick said.

"You were in Nam, Man?"

"Fraid so."

"Boy, that sucks," Stuart said. "Have you been actively involved in protesting it?"

"No, but I'd like to be. We've got no business over there. The Vietnamese people chose Ho Chi Minh as their leader a long time ago, but we can't accept it because he's Communist. What's so bad about Communism if it feeds your people, under Capitalism half of the Vietnamese would starve while that puppet Thieu and his crowd get fat on all the money we're pouring into there to keep him propped up. The money we're spending on that war could be used to feed some of the people who are starving in this country."

Stuart grinned. "I like the way you think. We, the coalition that is, will be meeting at Mr. Natural's at eight Wednesday night. You should come."

"Coalition?"

"The Southern Illinois Peace Committee, Students for a Democratic Society, the Women's Liberation Movement and the Black Panthers. We're forming a coalition."

"The Black Panthers? They're here in Carbondale?"

"Alive and well," Stuart said.

"Where? I mean I don't think I've ever seen one around here."

"Their headquarters is in a house over on the northeast side, not far from Mr. Natural's."

"So what's the purpose of this meeting?" Mick asked.

"To coordinate the movement. There's been too much fragmentation. We've got to bring all the factions together for a big demonstration we're planning in the fall, in September, when all the students get back from summer break. We'll burn the whole damn campus down to get our message across, if that's what it takes. Remember Old Main?"

"Yeah, I saw it burn," Mick said.

"Well that was just the beginning." There was fire in Stuart's eyes. "The Vietnamese Studies Center is next. It's nothing more than a front ya know, for the CIA to spread their anti-Communist propaganda."

Mick hadn't expected to come into contact with anyone from the antiwar movement this day, so he didn't have the tape recorder with him, and what Stuart said about Old Main and the Vietnamese Studies Center would only be hearsay, but he had plenty to tell David, hearsay or not.

"Peace," Stuart said, and he gave Mick the sign as he walked away. "Don't forget about that meeting Wednesday night."

"Yeah, peace."

"Peace, my ass," Mick muttered to himself. "This cat is bent on violence."

Mick's attention returned to the concert after Stuart left. He delighted in it, watching some of the women dancing, especially the ones who had gone topless, their lovely femininity exposed while appearing not to be the least bit self-conscious about it, reveling in the uninhibited sexuality of the times, free from the constraints of traditional society's bounds.

Mick put the bottle to his lips and sipped the sweet wine, and he danced in the meadow to the rousing rock 'n roll, with everyone else in the meadow until the sun went down. And for the first time since coming home from Nam he felt comfortable rubbing elbows with the counter culture. But then again he was drunk.

In the morning, suffering from a hangover, Mick didn't feel quite so sociable, in fact he felt embarrassed looking back at himself dancing around drunk and half-naked with that peace medallion dangling from his neck, which now lay on the night stand by his bed. He looked down at his sunburned chest. Having blocked the sun the medallion had left a white impression surrounded by red, a symbol of hypocrisy for some, concealing what was really in their hate-filled, militant hearts, like the devil wearing a crucifix. Mick would use it too, to make them think he was one of them. Perhaps he was, in a sense, devilish too, in that he was practicing deceit.

Chapter 13

Wednesday night Mick went to Mr. Natural's as he had been invited by Stuart Bolshinsky to meet with him and members of a newly-formed coalition that was planning a big antiwar demonstration for the fall. He activated the tape recorder, which was in his t-shirt pocket covered by a vest, before going in.

Bolshinsky was there as expected, and he motioned for Mick to join him at the table with the others at the very back of the store. He sat down and Stuart extended a partition blocking them off from the rest of the place where only two customers sat reading and drinking tea, paying no attention to them.

There were three others at the table; the scowling black man Mick had seen at the poetry reading last week, who Stuart introduced as Marcus, leader of the local Black Panthers, Paul, a skinny, pale-faced guy with floppy Beatle-like hair who was a member of the SIPC, and a stern-looking woman named Michelle who represented the SIU's Women's Liberation Front. No one shook hands, or even smiled for that matter.

"Mick's a Vietnam vet who's against the war," Stuart said, having adopted that presumption, which Mick gladly allowed. "We need more of them in the movement. Plus he's a television journalism major. Perhaps he'll be able to assist us in using the media to our advantage; our Minister of Information if you will.

"We'll talk more about that later. The first order of business tonight is to get organized. The pigs are tense around here," Stuart said. "They know if we get organized they won't be able to handle us without assistance from the Illinois National Guard, especially if the Panthers participate, which would embolden SIU's black students to become more involved, right Marcus?"

"Right on. They're against this war too. The draft has claimed a disproportionate number of the brothers, and a disproportionate number of them are dying while being asked to kill Cong. And they're down-trodden people of color too, oppressed by the West and it's imperialistic ways. Like Mohammed Ali said when he refused to register for the draft, Man, '... ain't got no quarrel against them Cong.' Speaking for the Black Panthers, I'll say this, Uncle Sam can stick that motherfuckin' finger up his hairy white ass," Marcus said in reference to the selective service posters seen in post offices depicting Uncle Sam pointing and saying, "I want you."

"Right on," Stuart said in kind. "If we can mobilize the black student population, then the pigs will really have their hands full."

"And the Women's Liberation Front?" Stuart inquired of Michelle.

"No problem there," she said. "We are totally united against the war."

"And what about you guys, Paul?"

"We're waiting for our marching orders. Just tell us when."

"September 19, the day classes begin again. The pigs won't be expecting it then. It'll give us the element of surprise like in guerrilla warfare. Which reminds me, we need to get our hands on a couple more of those VC flags. They really grab the attention of the press. Get's those camera's clickin'. I'll write to my supplier in San Francisco.

"Speaking of the press, people, we need to peak their interest in what is going on behind the scenes at the Vietnamese Studies Center, Mick," Stuart said, "since you're experienced in that area maybe you could help us there."

"Behind the scenes?"

"You know, hell, everyone knows, that the Center is a front for the CIA."

"Oh, yeah, so I've heard. Got any documentation to prove it? The press will want proof," Mick said.

"Our operative is in the process of trying to acquire some now; financial records primarily, that would reveal a direct link between the CIA, universities and Centers all over the country. The proof is in the dollar signs. Plus we know, and the documentation will show that David Gordon, the director of the Center here, worked for the CIA in training an elite little group of South Vietnamese commandos to go to Hanoi and assassinate Ho Chi Minh. Leak that to the press and they'll be demanding to see the documentation through the Freedom of Information Act, because the Center, at least up front, is supported by public funds, if we can't provide it to them by our operative rifling their secret files.

"Meanwhile, Mick, I'd like for you to send a letter-to-the editor of SIU's student paper, *The Daily Egyptian*, and the *Southern Illinoisan* newspaper voicing your opposition to the war on behalf of SIU's Vietnam veterans who are against it."

Mick knew of some at The Club who were against the war, but mostly because of the way it was being fought—half-assed, and apparently without any intention of winning it. A sentiment they expressed often among themselves, but they wouldn't be caught dead protesting it openly, arm-in-arm with the likes of the people Mick was now consorting with—draft-dodging, anti-American VC sympathizers. He had heard of a relatively large group that had formed on the east coast called the Vietnam Veteran's Against the War who were opposed to it for various reasons, but no organized group like that existed around Carbondale that Mick knew of. At least not yet.

"There are some," Stuart said, "who just need to be encouraged to come out and demonstrate. Maybe when they read what you write they'll be emboldened to follow your lead."

The last order of business at the meeting was to pass around a joint; like a peace pipe at a pow wow as it were. But Mick felt no peace coming from Marcus, who had been glancing at him periodically with looks of animosity and mistrust. At least that's how Mick perceived it.

The marijuana made him feel even more paranoid about it. Did Marcus have him pegged already? He could feel his heart pounding beneath the recorder that was still running at slow speed.

"We'll meet again in August, right here, on the tenth at eight," Stuart said. "I'll be out of town till then. I'm going to Austin for a Weather Underground War Council." He smiled broadly, but his smile quickly disappeared as he became deadly serious.

"Has anyone heard how the investigation of Gretchen's murder is going?"

"What investigation?" Marcus asked. "You think those honky-ass pigs in Cairo will lift a finger to find out who killed her. If they did they'd be pointing it at one of their cross-burning neighbors."

"There's one in particular who they should be pointing a finger at," Paul said. "Did you see that one red neck who got up in Gretchen's face at the demonstration. He just looked like he wanted to kill her."

"Yeah, I saw him, and she got right back in his face too," Marcus said. "She was tenacious when it came to standing up for the rights of others."

"And for her own rights too," Michelle added. "The Women's Liberation Front will certainly miss her tenacity in the way she stood up against the rampant sexism of this society."

Joint smoked and meeting adjourned, Stuart pulled back the partition. The people who had been there were gone, and the woman who worked there was in the process of closing up. The others left through the back door and Mick went out the front.

Walking home, about a block from Mr. Natural's, as he stopped and looked sideways before crossing a street, Mick thought he saw someone behind him. He quickly turned to look and saw nothing, but he heard a pebble being kicked in the alley he had just passed. He began to walk faster up the street feeling like he was being followed, but by whom. A mugger? No, not in Carbondale.

When Mick got to the next street, at the end of a building on the corner, he glanced back again just before turning and he saw someone step into the shadow of a tree, and then stand behind it. Now around the corner, Mick sprinted to the next alley and crouched behind a dumpster about twenty-feet in. He waited and watched for someone to come by, and someone did; a dark figure walking fast, past the mouth of the alley. Mick exited the other way and went back around the block to the corner again. He saw the man down the street looking lost, then he disappeared to the east back toward Mr. Natural's. Mick not only had given him the slip, but he wound up following the man at a good distance. Not for long though. Mick darted across the street into the shadows of trees and headed back west toward home.

Feeling very paranoid now, he kept the lights in the house off, and he pulled down the shades and sat in the dark in the kitchen and drank a cold beer to quench his thirst and steady his nerves. Jazzpur meowed and rubbed against his leg under the table.

"Who was it? Must have been Marcus," Mick answered to himself. It had been obvious at the meeting that he didn't trust Mick.

It made Mick shudder to think he had been found out already. But how could he know?

Mick went to the fridge for another beer. Jazzpur followed, looking for milk. He poured some in a bowl and sat it on the floor, and the purring black cat slurped it up.

This was one black cat who trusted him. Somehow he'd have to get Marcus to do the same.

Mick sat back down and pulled the tape recorder from his pocket, rewound it and played it back. Loud and clear, it had picked up all of the conversation at the meeting. David would need to hear this. Mick looked at the clock on the wall—a little past eleven, on a Wednesday night, coincidentally around the time he was to report to David anyway. He called him and fed him what he had on tape.

"Excellent, Mick. Just as I had suspected, they've got a mole in the Center."

"Any idea who it might be?"

"No, not yet. We'll just have to provide some bait in the form of some kind of phony declassified documents in a locked cabinet labeled Top Secret. Let's see, uh. Some cockamamie about a planned invasion by the U.S. of North Vietnam. That's it, under the guise of our troop withdrawals. They're being withdrawn only as far as Guam, where they'll be reconstituted for an invasion by sea and air. Not so farfetched really; an invasion has been contemplated I'm told. Hell, Mick, North Vietnam has slowly but surely been invading South Vietnam since the mid '50s. I'll divulge this to everyone at our meeting at the Center tomorrow, which will be attended only by those who have a top secret clearance, including my wife who takes minutes for me at these meeting, like she did in her capacity as a secretary at our office in Saigon. And I'll say where the key can be found, in one of my desk drawers, and I'll mark its placement with faint pencil marks so I'll know if it's been used. If it's used we can lift finger prints from it. We've printed everyone who works there. Yes, you too, Mick."

"But I've never-

"Touched anything at the Center, like a beer can?"

"Oh, yes, of course. So, David, what would you suggest about what Stuart wants me to do in regards to publicizing the antiwar movement, and recruiting vets for demonstrations?"

"Write those letters to the editors to begin with, and send one to that local radical rag too; what's it called?"

"The *Big Muddy Gazette*."

"Yeah, that's it. Good name for it. Everything they print is clear as mud. Lay it on thick, Mick; your opposition to the war, on behalf of other Vietnam vets who are against it. That should win them over for the time being."

"What about me leaking innuendos to the press about Vietnamese Studies Centers being linked to the CIA, and you training South Vietnamese to assassinate Ho Chi Minh." Mick asked.

"That can't be proven unless they can read confetti. Besides, why bother anymore, the old boy's in ill-health and he'll probably die without any help soon enough. Say, by the way, what's with all of this heavy breathing and scuffling sounds in the background at the end of the tape, Mick, rough sex?"

Mick laughed, but not for long. "I was being followed after the meeting by Marcus, the Black Panther. But I gave him the slip and wound up following him for a bit."

"Obviously he suspects something then. Make a special effort to win this guy over. In your letter to the papers be sure to give credit to the blacks in opposing the war. Meanwhile just keep doing what you're doing. Sounds like your making some inroads, but we need to find out who the mole is."

Chapter 14

Mick wasted little time in writing the letters-to-the editors.

On behalf of Vietnam veterans who oppose the war, I'd like to say, enough of the dying and killing, no matter what the supposed cause. This war has gone on long enough. Nothing's been resolved. We are destroying South Vietnam while pretending to save it. Save it from what? Themselves? Ho Chi Minh? He's Vietnamese. His army, the Viet Minh, lead by General Giap, defeated the French in a war of independence in 1954, freeing Vietnam of Western imperialism. But the West, namely the U.S., continued to interfere in the country's affairs by participating in the Geneva Conference which divided Vietnam into North and South. Ho Chi Minh was considered the president of the North and eventually Diem became president of the South, but according to Geneva, a national election was to be held within two years to determine who a unified Vietnam's president should be. Ho Chi Minh was expected to win it in a landslide, but the West could not accept a Communist as head of Vietnam. After all we had the Domino Theory to worry about, so the election was scuttled, Vietnam remained divided and a civil war erupted in the South with the Communist Viet Cong on one side and the South Vietnamese government and the U.S. on the other. Now we've gotten ourselves into one hell of a smelly mess because we, as the self-appointed policemen of the world stuck our noses into Vietnam's affairs and it's about to get chopped off.

Save face, Uncle Sam. Get out now and let the people of Vietnam determine their own future be it Communist or Democratic, or a combination thereof, but let them decide. Either way, this little country is no threat to us, 10,000 miles away across the Pacific. Enough American men have died in a war that we have no business in."

Finally, Mick added, in an attempt to placate Marcus, should he read the letter.

> *I urge Vietnam veterans to take a public stand against this war, especially black vets who have been fighting and dying in disproportionate numbers for a country that treats them like second class citizens at home.*

Chapter 15

▼

Like Marcus and Stuart, Paul and Michelle, most everyone was convinced that Gretchen Witherspoon had been killed by one or more of Cairo's white supremacists because of her tenacity in protesting against them; the way she had gotten in their faces, nose-to-nose, toe-to-toe; she a smart-mouth hippie, rebel-rousing outsider, and a white woman no less who marched arm and arm with blacks against her own race.

"Nigger lover," Will Simmons snarled at her through gritted teeth. He hated her; he hated the others too, the other whites who were siding with the blacks. They had turned on their own kind. He thought of them as traitors.

"Nigger lover," he sneered, and he spat tobacco on one of Gretchen's sandaled feet.

She kicked the wad off of her foot and onto his pants, and she smiled in his face and continued singing ever-louder along with the others, "we shall overcome."

This infuriated Simmons even more. He vowed to his friend Herbie Long, who stood next to him, that he'd make her pay "for sidin' with the niggers against her own race."

Simmons had a history of mixed race relations. His sister had a child with a black man and he hated her for it, and he hated the child. He believed that whites should stay with whites and blacks with blacks; mixing only led to trouble like in Cairo where blacks were horning in on white society by trying to integrate the city swimming pool, the little league, the fire and police departments, the schools, housing, the neighborhoods.

"They've got their place, we've got ours. That's all I'm sayin'," he told Cairo police when they brought him in for questioning because he had appeared to be the most confrontational among the counter demonstrators.

"You stood out like a sore thumb there, Will. You had blood in your eyes, Boy. Looked like you had it in for that Gretchen Witherspoon gal," one of the cops, a short, skinny man with a rodent-like face, said.

"She the one who got murdered?" Will asked.

"That's right. Know anything about that, Will?"

"No, why should I?"

"Because we hear tell you threatened her. Somethin' about makin' her pay for sidin' with niggers."

"No, I didn't say nothin' like that. I called her a nigger lover that's all, and that's what she is alright. Ain't no law against speakin' the truth, is there?"

"No, but the law don't take too kindly to lie'n, Will," one of the other cops said.

"Tell us where you were that night of the demonstration, after it was over."

"Sandbar Tavern for awhile, then I went home. My wife'll vouch for that."

"She at the tavern with you?"

"No, hell no, but anybody'll tell ya I was there. I'm there every night but Sundays when it's closed."

"We'll check it out, Will."

"So whataya sayin', I'm a suspect in this here killin'?"

"No, not yet, we're just checkin' things out. But stay around town for awhile."

The police checked out Will Simmons alibi. His wife said he had come home after being at the Sandbar Tavern, where the bartender/owner said Will had been the night in question. That was good enough for the Cairo police. They were satisfied that Will Simmons hadn't done it, and they had no other suspects for the time being.

But Sam Taylor, an investigative reporter with the *St. Louis Daily Record*, who had been sent to Cairo to do a story on the murder, had a few questions of his own to ask, namely, why was Gretchen's car found in Cairo while her body was found a few miles away in Horseshoe Lake? Had she been killed in town or at the lake? Had she been driven, dead or alive, to the lake by the killer in his car? Or had they driven there in her car with her being dead or alive? If this were the case then the killer would have driven her car back to Cairo. Were there any fingerprints on the steering wheel other than hers? Yes, the police told Sam; a Marcus Jackson's, but he had driven the two of them from Carbondale to Cairo for the demonstration because she wanted to read up on the ongoing situation there in that day's newspaper, the *Southern Illinoisan* which was reporting on it daily.

Now, if she had gone to the lake in the killer's car, had she been accosted, or did she go willingly? If willingly she knew the killer. Either way, with no evidence, a witness was needed, but unless there had been a struggle there wouldn't have been anything out of the ordinary to witness, aside from a woman getting into the man's car. Nothing particularly noteworthy about that, Sam thought, unless, unless the man was black and the woman was white, which would get the attention of local whites; surely some red neck would have noticed that. Would have noticed that they had come to the demonstration together. After the demonstration had they ridden together to somewhere else like the lake? Sam went to Carbondale to get some answers.

Learning that Marcus Jackson was the leader of the Black Panthers there he went to their headquarters on Washington Street. This was area of town Sam had never been to before. It was the black part of town. When he was a journalism student at SIU a few years before, he, like other white students, thought of it as a separate town, that's how segregated Carbondale and most southern Illinois towns were. Actually though, Sam wasn't all white; his mother was one quarter Cherokee. He looked that one quarter; dark eyes, dark skin, high cheek bones, nose like the beak of a hawk, and it was this one quarter that caused him to tread lightly, like a Cherokee scout, when embarking on unfamiliar territory.

Despite its innocuous appearance Sam felt apprehensive in approaching the two-story, white-framed house. Looking up at the second story porch he noticed a black man watching him. He was being watched too, through parted blinds in one of the first floor front windows. He walked slowly up to the front door beneath the upper story porch and knocked. No answer. He knocked again. This time someone opened the door; a crack and peeked out. He too was black, and he didn't look friendly.

"Whataya want?"

"I'm Sam Taylor, I'm a reporter for the *St. Louis Daily Record*. Is Marcus Jackson here?"

"Whataya want him for?"

"To ask him some questions about Gretchen Witherspoon."

"Let him in," a voice behind the man in the door said.

The door opened wider. Sam could see the dark figure of a man inside the dark house. He stepped in.

"I'm Marcus Jackson. What about Gretchen?"

Having been outside in the bright sun it took a moment or two for Sam's eyes to adjust to the darkness of the room.

"I just wanted to ask you some questions about the night of her disappearance for a story I'm writing about her murder."

"Have a seat." Marcus nodded toward a chair. Sam sat down. Marcus sat in a chair across from him. The man who had let Sam in left the room.

"I understand Gretchen disappeared in Cairo the night of your first demonstration down there, a couple of days before her body turned up in Horseshoe Lake."

"Yeah, that's right. She was supposed to be staying all night at my cousin Rita's house after the demonstration, but she never showed up. I waited around for my cousin to come home from work then I went to the Catholic Church rectory where some of the others were staying to ask them if they had seen Gretchen. They hadn't. We wanted to drive around and look for her, but Stuart Bolshinsky, one of the other demonstrators, had left with his van to gas up. He was gone a long time. The folks who came in the other van had already gone back to Carbondale because a couple of them had classes the next morning. The ones who stayed figured that was the case with Gretchen, but I wondered why she would have just up and gone back without telling me since I rode there with her. Knowing Gretchen she wouldn't have, so I knew something was wrong. Now we know what. One of those honky red necks down there isolated her and killed her and dumped her in that lake that night."

"So it would seem," Sam said.

"Ain't no seem about it, Man."

"Where can I find this Stuart Bolshinsky?"

"At Mr. Natural's Health Food Store uptown. He's there about every night."

Sam nodded, thanked Marcus for his time and left.

Not knowing what Stuart Bolshinsky looked like Sam asked the woman behind the counter at Mr. Natural's if he was there. She pointed him out reading at a table by himself. Sam walked over and introduced himself, saying he wanted to ask a few questions about Gretchen Witherspoon for a story he was writing for the *Daily Record*.

Bolshinsky gave Sam the once-over then he asked him what he needed to know.

"Mind if I sit down?" Sam asked.

"Suit yourself."

"Thanks. I understand you participated in a demonstration with Gretchen in Cairo."

"That's right. The last one before she was murdered."

"It's also my understanding that there was a rather significant confrontation between her and one of the counter demonstrators."

"Uh, oh yeah, she got into it with some little sawed-off dude. He acted like he was going to kill her. Maybe he did."

"When was the last time you saw her alive?" Sam asked.

"When we split up after the demonstration, around sundown."

"You guys hadn't gone to Cairo together?"

"No, I drove my van. She had a class that day that she couldn't miss so she left Carbondale later than the rest of us. She drove herself, but not by herself. Marcus Jackson rode along. They planned to stay all night in Cairo with Marcus's cousin Rita who's a member of the United Front. She was a friend of Gretchen's. They knew each other from SIU when Rita was a student there. But after the demonstration Marcus said he lost track of Gretchen. He went to his cousin's house thinking she'd show up there but she never did. The rest of us crashed at the Catholic Church rectory. The priest participated in the demonstration along with other clergy from as far away as Georgia. We demonstrated the next day too, but without Gretchen. No one knew where she was. We figured she went back to Carbondale for some reason. Marcus rode back with us. Two days later I heard on the radio that a body identified as Gretchen's was found in Horseshoe Lake."

"Did Marcus come to the rectory to inform you that Gretchen had disappeared?"

"Yeah, but I was out gassing up the van, then I drove around for awhile. Interesting town, Cairo, very southern-like."

"Maybe a little too southern-like," Sam said, thinking about the other unsolved murders of civil rights activists in the south. "Well, that's all I wanted to ask you about, Stuart. Thanks for your time."

Stuart said nothing.

Walking to his car, one particular thought struck Sam like a lightning bolt. During a certain period of time after the demonstration on the night in question, the night it was determined Gretchen Witherspoon had been murdered, she, Marcus Jackson and Stuart Bolshinsky were all unaccounted for simultaneously. She had vanished, Marcus was supposedly at his cousin Rita's house, alone; his cousin was at work, and Stuart had gone out to gas up his van then he drove around Cairo for awhile, he said. Should he make the police aware of this? Was it his job as an investigative reporter to lead the police? Or should he instead be following their leads; of which there were none that he knew of. The case had gone cold as far as they were concerned, apparently, since Will Simmons had a alibi. But there was something in Sam's journalistic makeup that had given him the characteristics of a sleuth, and he continued to snoop like a bloodhound. He wanted to find out the exact nature of Gretchen's relationship with Marcus and Stuart. He asked around and was told that a woman named Michelle of the Women's liberation Front would probably know since she was relatively close to Gretchen.

The Women's Liberation Front operated out of a house near campus. Sam went there and immediately made the acquaintance of Michelle. At first she was reluctant to share what she knew.

"Surely Marcus and Stuart aren't suspects."

"No, not at all. I'm simply looking for some insights into the dynamics of the relationships between members of the coalition to enhance the human interest aspect of the story."

"As if the murder in-and-of-itself isn't humanly interesting enough. Very well, I'll provide you with some insights, but only if I remain anonymous."

"Fair enough."

And Michelle opened up.

Stuart Bolshinsky felt closer to Gretchen than a lot of people realized. They first met through her father, Professor Harold Witherspoon, when Stuart, a graduate student in political science served as the professor's assistant. He had been invited to the Witherspoon's house for wine and cheese on a couple of occasions where the conversation usually centered on the Vietnam War, women's liberation and civil rights. As leader of SIU's Students for a Democratic Society, Stuart was active in protesting the war, while Gretchen was an active member of the Women's Liberation Front. They had joined forces in protesting the shoddy treatment of blacks in racially divided Cairo, and in turn the Women's Liberation Front participated in demonstrations on campus against the war. Out of this developed a friendship between the two which Stuart seemed to take a little more seriously than Gretchen. She was only interested in keeping it confined to the parameters of the coalition that was forming between the various activist factions on and around campus, which now included, in addition to the SDS, the SIPC and the Women's Liberation Front and the local Black Panthers, of whom Marcus Jackson was the leader.

A friendship had also developed between Marcus and Gretchen, the nature of which seemed a little more dynamic at times than her relationship with Stuart. There was a little flirting going on; some teasing, light touching and blushing, and Stuart didn't like it. He was jealous, Michelle said she had observed, based on how tense he'd get when he was around when they were together.

"His face would get real red. He couldn't hide it."

Chapter 16

With Jan gone Mick would have to stay in Carbondale for the summer in order to hang on to the house. The landlord told him if he left for longer than a month he'd have to rent it out to someone else. He didn't like absentee tenants. Another place as good as this one would be hard to find in Carbondale, as SIU's enrollment had increased substantially because of the war. People were trying to avoid the draft by being in school.

And with Stuart out of town until August, Mick would be able to take a break from his undercover role and go back to being himself for awhile—drinking beer with Reggie and the guys at The Club. Maybe he would even sneak back to the Center some night to visit Mae, although he was concerned about being seen there by others in the coalition. If they saw him going into The Club though, he could say he had gone there to recruit vets for the demonstration. Just to be on the safe side he'd slip in through the back door.

Reggie was there of course, throwing darts. He roared when he saw Mick.

"Where in the fuck have you been? What's with the beard?" Reggie tugged at it, "and that peace medallion? You ain't goin' hippie on us are ya, Man. How long has it been, Mick, two months?"

"About that, Reggie. What's been happening?"

"I'm engaged," he said proudly. "Trudy and me are gettin' hitched."

"Yeah," John chimed in as he brought Mick a beer. "Her old man totes a mean shotgun."

"Yes, this is true," Reggie said. "It's a 'have to,' Mick, but I would have married her anyway."

Mick knew then that Reggie could.

"I want you to be the best man, Mick, and John the bridesmaid. You'd look so sexy in silk and chiffon, John, hairy legs in nylons, damn, I think I'm gettin' a boner."

"Nothing's changed, Reggie, you're still a son of a bitch," John retorted, and he winked at Mick.

"When's the wedding?" Mick asked.

"Two weeks from Saturday night, at Giant City."

"At night?"

"Yeah, Man, Trudy wants to have it outside under the stars, when the sun is in Taurus, and Jupiter is aligned with Mars, and Uranus is in retrograde or some shit like that. Alls I care about though is when Leo is aligned with Aquarius," he said, referring to each of their signs, "Later that night, on our honeymoon at the lodge. Trudy'll have to carry me across the threshold. It's not handicap accessible."

Same old Reggie, still making light of being in a wheelchair.

"Got any champagne back there, John?" Mick asked.

"Some of that cheap, plastic cork stuff."

"That'll do. Pop one open."

John took a bottle from the cooler and dislodged the stopper with his thumb. It popped loudly and ricocheted off the ceiling and the back bar. Foam spewed from the bottle and John quickly poured the bubbly into three wine glasses. They toasted to Reggie and Trudy, who had just come in, which called for opening another bottle. She declined to drink though, being pregnant; something to do with fetal alcohol syndrome she said, but the boys drank plenty, returning to beers after the champagne and the impromptu wedding party was on. They had the place to themselves pretty much, being a Tuesday night in the middle of the summer when most of the students were away. At one o'clock John locked the front door and they continued drinking until three, at which time Mick, loaded to the gills, headed for the back door.

"See you two weeks from Saturday night," Trudy said. "Don't forget; nine o'clock, Giant City State Park, meet us at the entrance."

Chapter 17

▼

On a sweltering mid-July night in Carbondale (what night wasn't sweltering in Carbondale in July?) Mick looked up at the moon. It seemed closer than ever before, perhaps because man had just landed on it in a lunar module called the Eagle. Mick had watched it happening inside on TV, as astronaut Neil Armstrong stepped off a ladder and onto the surface, which looked dusty and gray not yellow.

"That's one small step for a man, one giant leap for mankind," he proclaimed.

The Eagle had come down 50,000 feet from the orbiting Apollo 11 space capsule that had been sent 230,000 miles to the moon by the gigantic 36-story high, 7.5 million-pound-thrust Saturn V rocket launched four days before on July 16, from Cape Kennedy, Florida, USA.

Mick, gazing skyward, tried to comprehend the magnitude of this achievement. Man had harnessed fire and used it to fly free of the bounds of Earth, beyond the threshold of outer space where the secrets to the beginning of the universe awaited discovery. If indeed there ever was a beginning, and conversely would ever be an end. For perhaps everything always has been and always will be he thought.

Mick's imagination had reached its outer limits, for the time being anyway, and he had gotten quite a crook in his neck, so he went inside and drank a beer and ate some cheese and went to bed knowing one thing for sure—the man in the moon was real.

Chapter 18

On July 24th Trudy and Reggie got married in Giant City State Park under a full moon that now had man's footprints on it. John, Mick and Trudy's sister, Suzie, were in attendance. No parents attended, as Reggie's remained in Chicago for some reason, and her's didn't come because they were hard core Southern Baptists who didn't approve of pregnancy before marriage, especially their daughter's.

A fat woman who was some kind of priestess from the new wave church Trudy belonged to, stood before the bride and groom. In the moonlight, with her pretty face veiled in white lace, Trudy, pregnant or not, looked angelic. Reggie, sitting in his wheel chair beside her, wore black pants, a white shirt, no tie and a white dinner jacket with a pink carnation. Before the priestess began the vows Reggie asked Mick and John to help him stand up. Without question they obliged.

He felt very heavy and wobbly at first, then suddenly lighter as he stiffened his back, grimacing some from the strain. Mick was surprised to see how tall he actually was, as tall as John who he guessed to be about six-foot-two; four inches taller than Mick.

"Okay, Fellas, you can let go."

"But...." Mick didn't want to.

"Let go," Reggie demanded.

So they did, but slowly, and Reggie remained erect, but still a little wobbly. Trudy gasped and started for him.

"No, wait, I'll come to you," and he took a small, shuffling step, first with his left foot, then his right, left then right, then he opened his arms and Trudy came to him, they embraced and she cried and Reggie laughed.

"I've been keeping it a secret for awhile. I took my first steps a month ago, but I didn't want ya to know until tonight," he told Trudy.

"You won't be carrying me across the threshold, Sweetheart, I'll be carrying you. So, let's get on with the vows."

They had written something to say to each other; poetic and gushing of course, and the priestess blessed them and they kissed.

"Okay, Mick, John, push that thing up behind me. I've got to save my strength for later."

He sat back down and took a deep breath.

"Reggie, when, what, I mean, how....," Trudy was absolutely stunned, as was everyone else.

"I started getting a tingling sensation in my toes several weeks ago. I just sat there and stared at them for an hour, willing them to move. It was like tryin' to force a bowel movement. I sweat and grunted and God did I pray, then it happened, they moved and I hooped and hollered and laughed and cried, then I called my physical therapist. She came over right away and took me to the hospital for x-rays. They revealed that the bullet, which had been lodged in a crevice in my spine compressing a nerve, had moved just a fraction of an inch to where they could get it out. It had been in a place that if they had tried to before there was a risk of becoming paralyzed from the neck down, so we had always settled for the waist down. But now that the bullet's out I'll be able to walk again, after some intense therapy of course. The muscles in my legs have suffered severe atrophy over the years. I'll never be a sprinter, that's for sure, but to be able to stand up on my wedding night and hold you in my arms this way," he said to Trudy, "well that's all that I could ever ask for."

"Me too, Reggie," Trudy said softly, tears streaming down her cheeks.

And he wasn't kidding about carrying her across the threshold. When they got up to the lodge he directed Mick to wheel him to the door to their cabin. Reggie positioned Trudy in front of him there.

"I've been practicing this with my physical therapist. Somebody open the door. Okay, Fellas, help me up again. Trudy, stand sideways and put your arms around my neck."

Reggie put one of his arms around her waist.

"Now lift your left leg, Honey," and he cradled it in his other arm. "Okay, hop up. Go ahead, hop up," and she did and Reggie was holding her in his arms, standing tall, strong and erect, and again he took one, slow, shuffling step at a time until they were across the threshold.

Glancing back at the wedding party over Reggie's shoulder, Trudy smiled and kicked the door closed in their faces.

That would be the last Mick would see of them for awhile. Stuart was due back in town soon and he'd have to go undercover again, but before he did he'd sneak in a visit to the Center for old times sake. He missed the place, especially Mae, whom he had learned a lot about the history of Vietnam from.

He waited until dark, not wanting to be seen. She usually worked late on week nights, at least until 10. It was now only nine.

From the walk he could see the light on in David's office on the third floor. Arriving at the top of the stairs he saw that the door to the office was open just a crack, casting a sliver of light across the hall. Normally David kept the door shut, being very private and Mick would knock before entering, but since it was ajar, he opened it a little farther and stuck his head in, and to his surprise he saw Mae standing at one of the file cabinets. Mick's presence gave her quite a start.

"Mick, surprise to see you. Where have you been for so long. Thought maybe you dropped off face of the planet."

"Yeah, well, sometimes I feel like I have."

Her question gave Mick the impression she didn't know what he had been up to. Apparently David hadn't told her. So what excuse could he give her for not being at the Center of late? Mick was quick off the cuff.

"I had to go back to Springfield for awhile. My aunt, who's like a mother to me, is very sick."

"Oh, sorry to hear," Mae said.

"Will you be working much longer tonight?" Mick asked.

"No, finished now. Why do you ask?"

"Thought you might want to go get a bite to eat."

"Yes, I'm hungry. Where to?" Mae asked.

"Do you like Italian?"

"Spaghetti, pizza?"

"Lasagna, rigatoni, manicotti, sausage sandwich, whatever you'd like, Mae. The Italian Village has it all."

"Okay, let's go."

Mae locked up and they headed out.

"We can take my car," Mick said.

"Yes, I walked to the Center today," Mae said.

When they got to the car Mick opened the door for her; something he hadn't done for a woman for awhile. In fact he hadn't been on a date for awhile, although this one wasn't planned; not since he had taken his Vietnamese girlfriend, Tron, to the Saigon Zoo way back in '68.

As they drove off Mick thought about those days. Not all the dates he had in Vietnam were with bar girls. Tron was a nice, ordinary girl, the daughter of the baker man whom he had met, where else, at the corner bakery in the neighborhood where he lived in Saigon. Since coming home though, he had had only one night stands because that was the trend in the USA these days; one night stands—sex, with no strings attached.

The restaurant was done up in typical Italian motif; ornate, black ironwork, red checkered table clothes on tables lighted by candles, and sconces on the walls which were decorated with pictures of Rome, with Italian music playing on the stereo.

Mae looked very pretty in the soft, yellow glow of the candlelight. She reminded Mick of the way Tron's face had looked in the moonlight the night they had made love in the garden of the villa where he lived in Saigon. An image that came back to Mick now and then, late at night when he was lying in bed unable to sleep.

"Tron, er uh, Mae, would you like some wine before we order food?"

She didn't notice that Mick had called her by the wrong name. She was thinking about how nice it was to be out with a man. It had been awhile. Oh, she had been to dinner at the Emperor's Palace with Nguyen Lu, who also worked at the Center, but he wasn't interested in her as a woman in a romantic sense, only as someone to engage in girlish gossip with.

Mae liked the feeling she had in thinking that Mick was interested in her as a woman romantically. That was the impression she got from the way he looked into her eyes and smiled: face slightly flushed. She was right. Mick saw her in that light.

"Mae? Wine?" Mick asked again.

"Oh, yes, please," she said, finally hearing him.

Mick wasn't so sophisticated in that department so he had the waiter suggest one.

"Matuese is a good one."

"That'll be fine," Mick said.

The wine came and they looked over the menus. Mae ordered lasagna and Mick manicotti, and the waiter brought a basket of bread and two tossed salads.

Neither ate much of their food, but the wine flowed a plenty along with conversation which soon centered on what else—the Vietnam War and Nixon's plan for Vietnamization. Mick asked Mae what she thought about it.

"Not so good for the South, very good for the North."

"Why do you say that?" Mick inquired.

"The South Vietnam Army will be at a great disadvantage with Americans gone. The North Vietnamese Army is very motivated to win for Ho Chi Minh. He is their leader of destiny they think. They feel Vietnam is destined to be Communist, both North and South, as an independent nation, not dependent on the West for validity."

"Yeah," Mick said, "I'm concerned too, about how well they'll do without us. Based on their track record they just don't seem ready to shoulder the brunt of combat, especially without American air power. If they aren't ready now, I wonder if they ever will be. If only Westmoreland had been given the troops he requested right after the Tet Offensive in order to go after the NVA and VC in their sanctuaries in Laos and Cambodia, the war might have been won by now."

"Yes," Mae concurred, "I'm afraid that opportunity has passed. It is just a matter of time now, I believe, before the Communists win," Mae said candidly, so candidly in fact, Mick was taken aback by it.

"I trust that this opinion will stay between me and you, Mick," she said nearly whispering.

"Yes of course. Well, I believe I'll call for the check."

Mick drove Mae home as it was now quite late, and he walked her to the door, something else he hadn't done for awhile. He was tempted to give her a kiss, but then suddenly she gave him one, on the cheek and she laughed.

"I've never felt my lips on so much hair before. It tickles very much."

Which tickled Mick as he remembered how fascinated the women in Vietnam were by GI facial hair, as most of their men didn't have much, or at least they didn't let it grow, although the flamboyant vice president Nguyen Cao Ky had a fine black mustache.

"Goodnight, Mae."

"Goodnight, Mick. I owe you a dinner now. Maybe you could come to my house sometime for traditional Vietnamese.

"I'd like that, as long as you don't serve *nuouc mam* with it," he said, referring to the repugnant smelling, fermented fish oil Vietnamese used as a sauce to flavor their food.

Mae laughed. "Okay then, see you."

Chapter 19

▼

August 12, 1969, after a lull in the fighting throughout June and July, as negotiations remained stalemated, Communist forces attacked more than one hundred towns and cities in South Vietnam. It was rumored that Nixon considered retaliating by mining North Vietnam's Haiphong Harbor, bombing Hanoi again, and possibly bombing the dikes on the Red River (which would flood vast areas of the North). There was also some thought of introducing nukes into the fray, but the President, concerned about the American public's reaction, particularly the ever-growing power block of antiwar dissidents, reconsidered and opted to do nothing, which sent a signal of weakness to Ho Chi Minh and only served to embolden the Communists further, in their aggression against the South.

The decision not to respond to the Communist attacks for fear of how the dissidents would react only gave impetus to them knowing that they held sway over the administration's war policies now, and were in a position to dictate it even further. The antiwar movement was on the verge of winning it for Ho Chi Minh.

A movement of another kind, not necessarily related to the antiwar movement, had gained momentum in the United States—the counter culture movement, whose heyday had come to a farm in mid-August in the Catskill Mountains of upstate New York, near Bethel, and they called it Woodstock—a three-day outdoor rock concert. Four-hundred thousand of America's youth went there to be entertained by the likes of Crosby, Stills, Nash and Young, Richie Havens, the Who, Janis Joplin, Jimi Hendrix, the Band and Jefferson Airplane, and to entertain themselves, dancing naked in the rain (which it did most of the time), smoking grass and tripping on hallucinates; images of a hip generation in all of its swirling paisley and tie dye array. This the anti-establishment generation whose symbolic birth had been on display in the summer of '67 in Monterey. Now the movement had gone coast to coast sweeping through places like Carbondale as Mick had witnessed at the concert at Giant City not along ago, where he too had been swept up in it, being high on wine and weed, and dancing with topless women in the sun.

Chapter 20

Toward the end of August, on a Saturday night, Mick went back to Mr. Natural's to see if Stuart had returned from Austin. Before going in he peaked in the window and sure enough there he was holding court at a table with Marcus, Paul and Michelle. Time to go undergcover again.

Approaching the table Mick felt about as apprehensive as the first time he had gone to Mr. Natural's. He was worried that perhaps in Stuart's absence he had been seen going into the Center (the night he and Mae went to the Italian Village) or The Club. He always looked around to see if he was being followed before ducking into The Club through the back door in the dark alley. Mick was sure that it was Marcus who had followed him the last time the coalition met at Mr. Natural's in early summer, but he had managed to give him the slip.

His paranoia was quickly allayed when Stuart greeted him with enthusiasm.

"Read your letter to the editor," he said smiling. "Great!"

Even Marcus managed a slight smile, and he nodded his approval. Perhaps the letter had won him over as Mick had intended. It certainly seemed to please Stuart, which had also been his intention. Stoical Paul and Michelle looked at him with indifference as usual.

Mick took a chair from the empty table next to them and sat down. The place wasn't as crowded as it would be when the fall semester began in a little more than two weeks. A few people were sitting at the other half-dozen or so tables sipping tea and carrying on low key conversations.

"Well, since we've got everyone here again, why don't we talk a little business," Stuart said.

He looked around and began speaking a little more quietly. "While in Austin this summer I met with representatives of SDS chapters from all over the country, including the Weather Underground, to discuss the direction of the movement. Some advocate a more passive approach in the spirit of the Reverend Martin Luther King, Jr., while others maintain, particularly the Weathermen, that militancy is the way," an inclination Stuart apparently had judging from the look of madness in his eyes and the hostile inflection in his voice when he said, "…. militancy is the way."

"They say that's what got the Man's attention in Chicago last August; going toe-to-toe with the pigs. Soon the nation's attention will be focused on Chicago again when eight of our brothers go on trial for conspiracy to incite a riot at the Convention."

"It was the pigs who rioted, Man," Marcus interjected angrily.

"Yeah, well, I guess that's why seven of them are going on trial too, for assault," Stuart said, "if the charges aren't dropped. But the Chicago Eight will be convicted for sure as examples for the rest of us, but the Weathermen have decided not to go down without a fight. They're planning to protest the trial violently as soon as it gets underway. And they want us, that is the rest of the SDS, to join them in protests nationwide, which could coincide with the demonstration we had planned for September when classes resume. The question is, do we, of the new Coalition, go the way of the Weather Underground and become more militant?"

"Militant?" Paul asked. "In what way?"

Stuart smiled, a wry smile. "We had a nice little workshop in Austin on how to turn pipes into bombs."

"I represent the Southern Illinois Peace Committee," Paul said, with an emphasis on peace. "The focus of our protests have been against the use of bombs. We, and I'm in a position to speak for the others of the Committee, can hardly condone the use of bombs against our own people. Remember, Stuart, the SDS has its roots in Quakerism."

"They wouldn't be used against people, Paul, but against buildings in the middle of the night when no one is around."

"What buildings?" Paul asked.

"Vietnamese Studies Centers and research facilities, like the US Army's Math Research Center at Wisconsin, which teaches the science and technology of advanced weapons of mass destruction, and Dow Chemical, which manufactures Agent Orange and napalm. You were in Nam, Mick, you saw what this shit can do."

Mick nodded. Yes, admittedly he had seen the hundreds, thousands of square miles of defoliated forest from the air, once fertile land and waters laid to waste for years to come. The people who had been exposed to it, including GIs, would perhaps even die from it later on.

"I think we've come to a crossroads, people," Stuart continued, "as the war lingers on with Nixon taking his sweet-ass time to withdraw US troops. Should we be passive and go along with his timetable which could take another three, four, maybe five years before we wash our hands of this mess, or shall we be more aggressive and demand on no uncertain terms that we get the fuck out now, or buildings will burn. Old Main went down and the Vietnamese Studies Center is next," Stuart snarled, becoming more and more bellicose with each inflammatory word, as he pounded his fist on the table causing everyone to jump, including tea out of Mick's cup. That got the attention of others in the place, but they looked away when Stuart nodded and smiled at them as if to say everything's okay.

"But it's not just about the war, remember," Marcus said, keeping his voice down. "It's about the System—a class system that exploits the down-trodden for the benefit of the Man. The Man, Uncle Sam, in other words, the motherfucking honkies in Washington who send poor people, mostly blacks, off to fight this imperialistic war. In Chicago it'll be the System that goes on trial. And wait and see, they'll tar and feather Bobby Seale because he's head of the Black Panthers and an 'uppity-ass nigger' who's against the brothers killing and dying for the racist Man! Militancy, Stuart, that's where the Black Panthers are at," Marcus said through gritted teeth, leaving no doubt about what his stance was.

"And you, Michelle?" Stuart asked. "Where do you stand."

"The Women's Liberation Front, it should go without saying, is against this war unequivocally, but we oppose violence as a means of protesting it. Violence is the way of men, who like temperamental little boys, resort to it instead of diplomacy when conflicts arise. We will continue to oppose this war vociferously, but only through peaceful means."

Ironic, Mick thought, such animosity towards men and the military coming from a woman who dressed like a man, and who had a military-style haircut.

"Well then, Mick, between me and Marcus and Paul and Michelle, where are you?"

With Stuart, leader of SIU's SDS now leaning toward the Weather Underground's more violent philosophy, Mick would have to appear to be leaning that way too. He had been recruited in part to cozy up to him to find out how much of an influence the militant faction was having on the mainstream antiwar movement.

"I'm with you," Mick said.

Paul and Michelle started to leave.

"Wait," Stuart said. "There's something I'd like to share with all of you. While in Austin, by the way we met at a Holiday Inn convention center." He chuckled. "Holiday Inn, an icon of America's bourgeoises, can you imagine? Marxists with mints on their pillows?"

Even stone-faced Michelle laughed at that.

"Anyway, at the meeting in Austin we received this little telegram from Pham Van Dong, North Vietnam's Premier, congratulating us on the effectiveness of the antiwar movement in swaying public opinion and influencing political and military decisions relative to the war. He encouraged us to continue with it until Nixon gets the message to withdraw all American troops immediately without condition. Here, I made copies of it for everyone."

Stuart handed them out. Mick was hesitant to even touch it, much less read it—a congratulatory telegram from a leader of the enemy who at this very moment were killing GIs, but it served as proof positive that there was indeed a definite connection between Hanoi and the antiwar movement in the U.S.—the *dich van* conduit that David and Mae had spoken of.

So what would be expected of Mick now—now that he had allied himself with Stuart who now was apparently in the militant Weather Underground camp. He found out fast.

"I'll be going to Chicago to join the Weathermen in their protest of the Conspiracy Eight trial which begins September 24. I've got room for six or seven. Who's in? Marcus?"

"No, I've got to stay here. I'll be involved in planning a little something of our own in protest of the way the Man is treating Brother Bobby Seale in that Kangaroo Court up there."

Paul and Michelle opted out, citing the level of violence they expected.

"It'll only lead to more trials," Paul said.

"Mick, you coming?"

What excuse did he have not to.

"Sure, when do we leave?"

"Wednesday morning at six o'clock from here. Bring a sleeping bag and non-perishable food. We'll be gone for three days. Oh, and enough cash to bail yourself out of jail with. Meeting adjourned. See you Wednesday, Mick."

"Right on."

Everyone went their merry way. Alone in his car driving home, Mick called David and relayed what he had on tape. Stuart had made it quite clear that he was now in the Weather Underground camp, and he had talked of their tentative plans to bomb certain facilities, such as the US Army's research building at the University of Wisconsin, and Vietnamese Studies Centers nationwide, including the one at SIU.

"I'll send a heads up to the Madison office of the FBI, and we'll tighten security here at the Center, especially after hours. That's when they're most likely to strike in order to avoid casualties. I doubt they'll want to incur any murder raps."

"But you're always working there late, David."

"Yes, and I'm sure they know that, which will serve as a deterrent, hopefully. But I'll hire a night watchman and have campus police patrol here regularly all night."

"So I guess we've got proof now with this telegram from Pham Dong, David, that *dich van* is more than just theory."

"Yes, and Tom Hayden, one of the Chicago Eight boys helped lay the groundwork for it when he and Rennie Davis payed Uncle Ho and Dong a little visit in Hanoi back in '65. Mail your copy of that telegram to me right away. It's evidence that they are consorting directly with the enemy. So, you're going to Chicago, eh, Mick?"

"Do I have a choice?"

"I suppose not. But be careful, it's probably going to get rough up there. The cops are expecting trouble surrounding the trial. We know damn well the Weathermen will be confrontational. They sure as hell won't be extending flowers. Hang with these guys for as long as you can as they prepare for battle. They'll be running off the mouth as usual, incriminating themselves. Get it on tape for the next big conspiracy trial. When the shit hits the fan duck out of there though. I'd hate to see you get hurt or thrown in jail for rioting again."

Chapter 21

Wednesday morning at six o'clock, along with his sleeping bag and backpack containing clothes and food (apples and oranges and peanut butter sandwiches), Mick squeezed into the back of Stuart's van with six others; members he assumed of the SDS whom he hadn't met yet. He thought he recognized a couple of them from Mr. Natural's, but they hadn't attended the so-called New Coalition meetings for some reason. Perhaps they weren't considered a part of the inner circle, of which apparently Mick was, probably because he represented, albeit unofficially, the New Coalition's token Vietnam vet against the war, presumably.

All exchanged names but no one shook hands as apparently that just wasn't cool among the hip, nor apparently was wearing deodorant. It got real close real fast in that little van.

For the six-plus hours it took to drive up to Chicago from Carbondale on I-57 through the golden corn and soybean-covered plains of eastern Illinois—a certain percentage of which when harvested would be shipped off to hungry Communist nations—Mick was subjected to an endless diatribe on the merits of Communism and the failings of Capitalism, especially in third world places like Vietnam.

"Where the people have been oppressed for centuries by French colonialists ...," Stuart proclaimed, looking back at his riders as he veered off onto the shoulder of the road. "And so now Uncle Sam has plans to suppress the voices of the masses, who would gladly, given the opportunity in a national election involving both the North and the South, choose Ho Chi Minh and the Communist Party in a landslide over the U.S. backed South Vietnamese puppet regime of Thieu's to govern a unified Vietnam," and he went on and on, pausing only momentarily when the joint that was going around came to him.

"Under Communism, the Vietnamese people would be free of the imperialistic property-hoarding, money-hungry upper class aristocrats of Capitalism. They'd be free of the almighty dollar. They'd be free of class envy in a society where the working class rules. Power to the people!" Stuart exclaimed loudly.

"Power to the workers of the world!" the man next to Mick shouted.

Finally the conversation shifted to the trial as Stuart had turned the van radio on near Chicago and a report on it came over the news.

Presided over by Judge Julius Hoffman, the trial had become a circus, according to the report, as the defiant defendants David Dellinger, a long-time pacifist, the two yippies (Youth International Party)—Abbie Hoffman and Jerry Rubin, the two founders of the SDS and pals of Ho Chi Minh—Tom Hayden and Rennie Davis. The two college faculty radicals—Lee Weiner and John Froines, plus Bobby Seale, the Black Panther read comic books, passed around jelly beans, threw kisses to the jurors, and staged an impromptu antiwar demonstration, complete with a VC flag.

As the Chicago skyline came into view, Stuart laid out the battle plan.

"Our staging area is an old garage in a warehouse district near downtown. We'll park inside on the lover level and crash upstairs. We'll be well-equipped to battle the pigs. There's a stockpile of billy clubs and helmets waiting for us. There are other staging areas too, scattered about on the fringes of the Loop. It's my understanding we'll be moving out for the court house around four or five this afternoon. I've been told there will be at least six hundred of us. On camera it'll look like thousands. The whole world will be watching, only this time we'll be wielding clubs too, unlike at the convention when the pigs had them all. The plan calls for three days of protests. By the third day our numbers will have dwindled considerably through attrition, as many of us will no doubt be jailed or hospitalized. Hopefully though, as news of the protests spread we'll get reinforcements."

After crossing the Chicago River and turning off the busy street they had come in on, Stuart drove into a warehouse district. Suddenly he stopped in front of large wooden double doors which parted when he honked. The van was waved in by a man who directed them to a place to park, and the doors were quickly closed behind them.

Several vehicles had already arrived and were parked in a row on one side of the cavernous garage. They bore the plates of various states. People were milling about an iron staircase at the rear of the building and Mick's group joined them. The conversation, naturally, centered on the trial. There was laughing about the antics of the defendants, which they too must have heard about on the news.

Mick smiled as if he were amused by it all, but he really wasn't. While the others conversed—Stuart was in the middle of it all of course—Mick looked around.

The walls were brick with no windows, the only light coming from two solitary yellow light bulbs hanging from the ceiling which was supported by half a dozen iron posts. The place felt chilly and damp like a cave. It smelled musty, yet dusty, mixed with the nauseating scent of old oil and gasoline the concrete floor was stained with. Piled along the rear wall were the helmets and clubs they'd be doing battle with later. "They," Mick emphasized to himself, as he planned not to be on the front lines when the melee began. In fact he'd be well to the rear.

Before long, as vehicles gradually came in one after another, the garage filled up and new arrivals were directed to other staging areas. Mick thought Leo, the man who had been minding the door, resembled Tommy Smothers because of his baby-like head and face and silly grin.

Then the door was barred from inside and Leo asked for everyone's attention.

"Around four o'clock," he looked at his watch, "that's three hours from now, we'll be heading out for the court house. The pigs will be waiting."

Leo's silly grin quickly became a smirk. "They're expecting us. There is no doubt they've infiltrated our ranks. For anyone of you who is among us now, I say fuck you." The man standing next to Mick looked at him and laughed.

"The trial has already become a farce," Leo said. "There will be no justice for our comrades with the fascist pig Hoffman and his prosecutors running the show. Remember, it's not the antiwar movement that's on trial here as much as the American justice system itself. It is our constitutional right to protest the prosecution of this illegal, undeclared war being waged against the revolutionary army of Ho Chi Minh. And when we go to the Cook County jail today for exercising our First Amendment rights in protesting the travesty of this war and the trial, then it will be as political prisoners. Some of us might even wind up in the Cook County Hospital, but so will some pigs.

There was an uproarious response to Leo's angry words, like what might be heard from a coach sending his team out to play the big game. When the noise subsided Leo suggested that everyone go upstairs and kick back for awhile.

"That's where you'll be sleeping for the next two or three nights," he said. "There's a freight elevator over there, or you can take the stairs. The floor is a little hard but this ain't the Hilton."

"The mob used this place years ago as a chop shop," Mick heard Leo say from behind as they walked up the stairs. "And rumor has it that Capone had a big still here in the '20s."

"Mmmm, a beer, what I wouldn't give for a beer," Mick mumbled to himself."

It took awhile for the hundred or so people to get upstairs and settle down on their sleeping bags, pads and air mattresses around the perimeter of the upper level, which looked just like the lower level.

Some began to eat what they had brought, as did Mick—a peanut butter sandwich and an apple. Soon a joint came around. Impulsively, Mick took a hit and passed it on. He enjoyed getting high, but he was in the habit of getting high with friends, like Jan and some of the guys he had met at The Club in Carbondale, and a few women too, mainly Trudy.

It felt different getting high with these guys though; people Mick considered to be the enemy. Hell, he might as well be toking up with Cong. He began to feel very uneasy, and the next time the joint came around he passed it on without taking a hit. He didn't like the way these people smelled, or talked, or even walked—with a swaggering air, looking down their noses at others who weren't like them. They were smug, pseudo intellectual snobs who hated Uncle Sam and loved Uncle Ho. Yes, they were the enemy.

The feeling Mick had wasn't paranoia though; it was fear based on delusions and irrational suspicions. He had good reason to fear these people who he knew to be violent revolutionaries bent on the overthrow of the U.S. government. And if they found out about him? He wanted to leave, briefly, just to get some fresh air and regroup. Mick got up and discretely asked Leo to let him outside, explaining that he felt sick.

"Over there through that door, it leads to the alley."

On the way out Mick passed where Stuart was sitting and told him he'd be back shortly.

In the narrow, dead-end alley Mick felt claustrophobic so he walked out to the street just as a Chicago Police cruiser drove slowly by. Not wanting to appear as a loiterer he continued walking down the street and around the corner. He kept walking around the block, so he thought. But instead of coming back to the deserted street he had started off on, he somehow wound up on a very busy street outside of the warehouse district. The sign said N. State Street. He back tracked only to come out on State Street again, this time less than a block from the Chicago River. Hadn't they crossed that coming in just before they turned off into the warehouse district? But off of what street and from which way? Mick was totally confused and thoroughly lost. He attempted to retrace the route he thought they might have taken in. He continued down State Street past the Chicago Theater and into the Loop with its commuter trains passing on the elevated tracks above. He knew now for sure that he was going in the wrong direction, as he certainly hadn't seen these while coming in to Chicago.

They had to have come in on a different street. He headed east and when he came to Michigan Avenue something familiar came into view—Grant Park, scene of the 1968 Democratic National Convention battle. That led to the Conspiracy Eight trial he had come to Chicago to protest under the guise of being a member of the SDS's Weather Underground faction—a protest he would probably now miss. What a shame, Mick thought sarcastically. But how would he explain his absence to Stuart? Got lost? That would be the truth. How juvenile and embarrassing.

Not having worn a watch Mick looked to the sun to help him gauge what time it might be, but it had gone down behind the tall buildings on Michigan Avenue. Yet it was sill high enough in the sky to beam light farther out on the lake whose beautiful turquoise water Mick could barely see on the eastern horizon. He guessed it to be about five, maybe six o'clock. Yes, of course, the heavy vehicular and pedestrian traffic downtown meant rush hour.

It was too late now to become involved in the protest even if he found the warehouse soon. Leo had said they would be departing for the court house around four.

Hungry, tired of walking, and thirsty, Mick looked for a place to get something to eat and drink; not water, but a relaxing beer. He went north on Michigan Avenue, and just across the river he spotted an Old Style Beer sign glowing brightly in the early evening shadow of the Wrigley Building, one of Chicago's most recognizable landmarks. Energized by the thought of a cold one, Mick stepped sprightly over the bridge expecting a bar to be there, but surprisingly there was just the sign mounted on the iron railing of a staircase leading down below the street. How peculiar. Curiosity aroused, he descended the stairs and found himself at the edge of a dark, dingy, subterranean street which carried a fair amount of traffic. Then he saw another beer sign, advertising Schlitz, above the entrance to a place called Billy Goat's Tavern. He opened the door and there were a few more steps to go down.

He smelled food frying and he heard the low murmur of voices punctuated by laughter, and glasses clinking, and a TV, and he heard someone shout "Cheeseborger, cheeseborger!" as he walked down the stairs and in. Sure enough it was a tavern looking very much like some of the old neighborhood ones back in Springfield. Unusual for North Michigan Avenue, Mick thought; the famous Magnificent Mile. But at first it didn't feel too friendly there, the way some of the other customers looked at him; probably because of the way he was dressed—like a hippie.

He went to the bar and sat down on a stool directly beneath one of those lighted-from-within, Schlitz beer globes that was spinning around. Mick could hear it squeaking faintly.

The bartender was friendly enough, and smooth. He whistled a little while wiping off the bar in front of Mick.

"Whataya have?" he asked.

"Whatever's on tap."

"That would be Schlitz."

"Okay."

He brought the beer and placed it on a coaster.

"Cheeseborger," Mick heard again. "Cheeseborger."

Glancing over his shoulder he saw an aproned older man behind a counter at a grill. A cheeseburger sounded very good, but at the moment he was well satisfied with the taste of the cold beer. He gulped it down and ordered another.

The place gradually became very busy as the after-work crowd came in. A man sat down on the stool between Mick and another man who was standing around the corner of the bar watching TV. They were both middle-aged, balding men. The man who stood was dressed casually, and the man who sat next to Mick wore a suit and glasses that rested on a rather large nose.

"Mike," the man standing addressed the man who had just sat down next to Mick.

"Slats," the man sitting said in return.

That was all they said at first, until Slats nodded toward the TV, "Looks like all hell's breaking loose at the court house."

"Yeah, so I've heard," the man named Mike said.

And there it was in living color, the battle Mick was supposed to have been in at the trial of the Chicago Eight, and it looked like the demonstrators were taking it to the pigs pretty good, as they had planned. On camera, as Stuart had said it would, it appeared as though there were thousands.

Most everyone's attention became riveted on the tube as Mike and Slats continued with their conversation.

"So what's this supposed to be all about, Mike, the war? Isn't that what they're shouting, 'No more war,' or that trial?"

"Both. Their buddies are on trial for rioting in protest of the war at the Democratic National Convention last year."

"Well, then why all the violence? I thought they were supposed to be peaceniks. You know, flower power, make love not war, and all that stuff."

"Yeah, well, I guess they've decided that petunias are no match for billy clubs," Mike said. "Looks like they've brought a few of their own, and they know how to use 'em."

"In my neighborhood it's against the law to whack a cop," Slats said.

"That's why they brought the paddy wagons, and ambulances too. Looks like it's getting pretty bloody out there."

"Jail, Mike, that's where they all belong. Sure, they've got a right to demonstrate against the war, but...."

"This isn't really about the war, Slats. If it were they'd be celebrating, not rioting, because Nixon is getting us out of it. It's about politics and philosophy; political philosophy."

"Republican versus Democrats, right?"

"Nope, more like Socialists, and in some cases Communists against Capitalists. It's not the war that they've been opposed to, it's who we're fighting—Ho Chi Minh, a Marxist Communist, the kind of revolutionary they admire, like Che and Castro. A lot of those guys you see up there are Marxists."

Mick knew that that's what most of them were. Their bible was Marx and Engels' *The Communist Manifesto*. He had read it, and it called for the abolishment of Capitalism, aristocracies and the bourgeoises through violent social upheaval like Russia's Bolshevik Revolution of 1917, and Mao Zedong's Cultural Revolution in China in the '40s.

"You know, if they tried to demonstrate like that over there in Russia," Slats said, "they'd all be shipped off to Siberia without any trial at all."

Mick got the impression the remark was made indirectly at him for his benefit, in an off hand way as this guy Slats glanced at him askance when he said it. Then Mick remembered what he looked like; like one of the rioters on TV. To ease the tension, in a friendly way Mick asked them what they thought of the war. At first the two acted like Mick's question was an intrusion, but after a brief moment Mike answered with a question of his own.

"You look to be about draft age. Were you in it?"

"The war? Yes, yes I was, but I wasn't drafted."

"Volunteer?"

"No. I joined the Air Force to avoid it, to be honest, but I was sent there anyway."

"In what capacity?" Mike asked.

"As a combat reporter."

"Like Ernie Pyle?" Slats asked. "He was a reporter in my war, ya know."

"Yeah, I know," Mick said, "only I used a tape recorder instead of a typewriter." Mick was reminded that he had a tape recorder in the breast pocket of his flannel shirt. It had stopped running long ago, but hopefully not before Leo's diatribe at the warehouse. "Not that I was in his class anyway. So you don't consider the Vietnam War yours, huh?" he asked Slats.

"Nope. Mine was WWII," he said with a certain amount of pride, as he stood a little taller and took a drink of beer. "And Mike's here was Korea."

"Every generation has to have one to identify with, it keeps the tradition going," Mike said with a tone of sarcasm. "What would have happened if WWI really had been the war to end all wars? We never would have come up with the B-52, or the A-bomb, or nuclear subs and Cold War arms races, and belligerent, excrement-slinging, potty-mouthed peaceniks getting their heads bashed in, or the election of Nixon who nobody would have ever heard of because Ike wouldn't have been a war hero-turned-President with Tricky Dick as his V.P.," and he added after finishing his drink and standing up. "There'd be no more awarding of Purple Hearts, or the need to expand national cemeteries. Hey, Freddie," he called to the bartender, "another round here for Slats and this young man too."

"How about you?" Freddie asked Mike.

"No, gotta go."

He left, and soon after, Slats followed, leaving Mick to watch the riot on TV while drinking yet another and another beer, until the after work crowd had dissipated. Mick looked at the clock on the wall; it had gotten fairly late—past nine now, and he had gotten fairly drunk. Where would he go? To a hotel? He had brought plenty of cash to bail himself out of jail if need be. He could get a room. But how expensive would that be in downtown Chicago? Better yet he could get on a train if one would be going down through Carbondale so late; a train-tel as it were.

Mick ordered a cheeseburger to go and asked Fred to call him a cab to take to the station. When he got there he found out that the train to Carbondale wasn't due to leave until six a.m. The big clock in the palatial old train station's main waiting room said ten till twelve—six hours to kill, with sleep if he could, on one of those inviting wooden benches.

First he sat snuggled in the crevice where the arm rest met the bench's back, but his shoulder got cramped, and the hardness of the wood hurt his head and hip. He sat up and tried to sleep that way. He managed to doze a little, but his head kept bobbing hurting his neck, so he stretched out lying on his back with an arm tucked under his head for a pillow using a discarded newspaper to shield his eyes from the bright overhead lights. That was fine for awhile until he got chilly, so he curled up in a fetus position for warmth, still using an arm for a pillow, which went to sleep leaving a terribly uncomfortable tingling feeling from his shoulder to the tips of his fingers. He sat back up, resigned to staying awake all night, fully conscious of the hangover that finally hit him with Billy Goat's greasy cheeseburger bubbling in a belly full of Schlitz. Mick got to the bathroom just in time to throw it all up in a toilet. That seemed to sober him up a bit after washing his face and gargling with cold water, and a swig of lukewarm, gritty, muddy-tasting coffee from a vending machine.

He went back to the bench with the coffee and sat there reflecting on the day. It seemed like a week ago that he had left Carbondale with the merry band of dissidents bound for Chicago. And it seemed like a bad dream being in that garage with many more, listening to their pro-Communist anti-American ranting as they prepared to do battle with the police over the Vietnam War, and the trial of the Conspiracy Eight.

Mick patted the shirt pocket containing the recorder. He had gotten it all on tape, further evidence of Stuart conspiring to riot that could be used against him in court. That had been the purpose of Mick going along on the trip, not participating in a riot. Mission accomplished, he kicked back and relaxed and read the discarded paper as much as his tired eyes could handle while waiting for his train to depart at six. The front page screamed: **STREET BATTLES RAGE AROUND CONSPIRACY 8 TRIAL—Several Police Badly Beaten by Weathermen. Hundreds Jailed, Hospitalized.**

Mick read the articles about the bloody battle which spilled into the back pages where he discovered a short piece on the murder of Gretchen Witherspoon, furnished by the Associated Press.

> CAIRO, Illinois—The investigation into the murder of Carbondale civil rights activist Gretchen Witherspoon continues. Her body was found by fishermen in Horseshoe Lake near Cairo last month. She had been strangled.
>
> Other civil rights activists from Carbondale claim police are dragging their feet in making an arrest because the number one suspect is a white supremacists who they are trying to protect in this southern Illinois community that is deeply divided along racial lines. However, Cairo police insist this is not an open and shut case. There are numerous suspects they say.
>
> A number of murders of civil rights activists in the South have gone unsolved.

At a quarter till six an announcement came over the PA that the train to Carbondale would now be boarding on track number nine."

Quite a few people had arrived at the station by this time, and Mick had to stand in line for his ticket. He got it, bought a hot-off-the-press newspaper and boarded. A cushioned seat had never felt so good. He looked at the paper, a *Chicago Sun Times*. The entire front page was devoted to the riot, along with photos of demonstrators and cops colliding. News of it spilled over into the following pages which Mick struggled to read being so tired. Soon the train pulled out of the station gradually gaining speed as it left downtown, swaying like a cradle and Mick fell asleep and he stayed that way until the conductor came through his coach announcing next stop Carbondale several hours later.

Back at the house Mick listened once again to what he had gotten on tape in Stuart's van en route to Chicago, and while at the staging area in the warehouse district before he went out to get some fresh air and got lost.

He had run a 120 minute tape on ultra slow speed which allowed him to record what had been said for about six hours without reloading. Most of what had been said, particularly in the van, consisted of your typical anti-establishment jive. Nothing really, that could be used against anyone in a court of law. But at the garage/staging area, when Leo, leader of the Weather Underground's Chicago chapter incited those who had gathered there to commit acts of violence against the police while providing them with clubs and helmets to carry it out with, Mick had concrete evidence of a conspiracy to riot, the charge which had been leveled against the Chicago Eight. He had too much on tape to feed David over the phone so they met at the Center that night and went over all of it there. David smiled with delight as they listened.

"The evidence against these guys is mounting, Mick. Keep up the good work."

When Mick finally saw Stuart again, three days later at Mr. Natural's he fully expected to be chastised for missing out on the riot, but when he explained rather sheepishly what had happened to him Stuart was sympathetic for, "… missing out on a hell of a lot of fun. Except jail was kind of a bummer. The bastard pigs made us sleep naked on steel slabs, and every time one of them walked by our cell he ran a metal cup along the bars. We got no sleep, not that we could have anyway. They kept us there for two nights and two days even though most of us had enough bread to make bail. We were political prisoners for sure. The ACLU's gonna hear about this."

Chapter 22

Professor Witherspoon had always been a patient man, but his patience with the investigation of his daughter's murder was wearing thin, so he paid a visit to the Cairo police to pressure them to move it along.

"Don't you have any suspects yet?" he asked one of the cops who rocked smugly in his swivel desk chair.

"We had one, but he's been eliminated because of his alibi."

"Do you mean to tell me that out of all of those people who viciously counter-demonstrated against my daughter and her friends, only one qualified as a suspect?"

"Fraid so, Sir. Out of those people there was only one," the cop said with an emphasis on those people.

"Do I take that to mean there's another pool of suspects?" the professor asked.

"Could be. Could have been an inside job so-to-speak, Professor."

"Inside job? One of Gretchen's friends? Impossible, she was too loved."

"Yes, that may have been the problem. Her murder had all the markings of a crime of passion; the way she was strangled by hand. A spontaneous killing resulting from an instantaneous fit of rage."

"So then, who do you suspect?"

"We have some people in mind, Sir. That's all I can say at the moment. Sorry, Professor, but we don't want to compromise the investigation."

"Very well then, I'll leave it up to you guys as long as it is progressing."

The Cairo police thought perhaps that Gretchen Witherspoon's murder was an inside job committed by one of the men of the coalition whose advancement she had spurned the night of the demonstration she was last seen at alive.

There were five men from the Carbondale coalition who had participated in that particular demonstration—Paul Darling, Marcus Jackson, Bobby Fredrichs, Stuart Bolshinsky and Albert Reynolds. Out of them only two, it was determined after questioning, had no alibis for a period of time on the night in question: Jackson and Bolshinsky. The others had been together at the Catholic church rectory while Bolshinsky had left for a good while to gas up his van and to go for a ride. Jackson had said that he spent most of the evening at his cousin's house alone waiting for Gretchen to show as she was supposed to be staying all night there.

Which one, if either or perhaps both, was interested in Gretchen romantically? This was something the police could not determine through questioning. Both claimed their relationships with her were strictly platonic. However, when questioned, Bolshinsky said he thought there was something more going on between her and Jackson.

"What makes you think that?" the police asked.

Bolshinsky's face turned red.

"Sexual tension," he said with a tone of resentment. "You could practically smell it," he sneered.

Jackson didn't like being visited by the police at the house that served as the headquarters of his Black Panthers. Pigs, especially Cairo pigs, weren't welcome there.

At first he wasn't going to answer the door thinking they might have a warrant for his arrest for rioting in their red neck town, as the demonstrations had been characterized in the Cairo paper. The police saw him peeking through the blinds, so to allay his paranoia they announced loudly through the door that they just wanted to ask him a couple of questions about Gretchen Witherspoon.

Jackson stepped out onto the porch.

"What about Gretchen?"

"I'm going to be blunt about this Mr. Jackson," one of the cops said, were you romantically involved with Gretchen?"

"Romantically?" Jackson snickered. "You mean did we get it on?"

"Yeah, that's what I mean."

"None of your business, Man."

"In a way it is, Marcus, we think it might have some bearing on the case."

"What? Like I killed her having rough sex, or I found out she was gettin' it on with somebody else and I killed her in a jealous rage?"

"Did you?"

"Look, Man, unless you're serving me with a subpoena to testify before a grand jury or at some trial, I ain't answer'n no more questions."

"Well, okay then, but don't be surprised if your are subpoenaed, maybe to testify on behalf of yourself."

"Are you saying that I'm a suspect?"

"Your whereabouts the night we think she was murdered is in question."

"The others can verify that I was at the Catholic Church rectory looking for her there."

"A good while after she vanished."

"I was at my cousin's house the rest of the time. I went there immediately after the demonstration."

"But your cousin wasn't there, right? She was at work."

"That's right."

"So then, there was no one there to verify that you were there."

"God, Man, God is my witness. Cross examine his ass. Now get off of my property unless you've got a warrant for my arrest."

"We don't yet, Mr. Jackson. So long."

The police had no evidence—zilch, notta, zero—that would in any way implicate either of their three suspects, even though two of them, Bolshinsky and Jackson, had no alibi the night Gretchen Witherspoon was murdered. The third one, Will Simmons did, but it was flimsy at best because it was based on what his wife and the bartender of his second home said. Two people who would likely lie for him if necessary.

They contemplated hooking everyone up to a lie detector, but the Alexander County state's attorney advised them that many judges, including the one who would hear this particular case considered such tests, when administered by the prosecution, to be inconclusive because some of the questions could be construed as leading. Without evidence, alibis or not, Gretchen Witherspoon's murder investigation reached a dead end. But her father wouldn't let it die. He contacted Sam Taylor and asked him to keep the case alive by continuing to write about it. Sam had planned to, and for his next story he consulted the professor to get some biographical insights into his daughter—an expanded eulogy of sorts.

Professor Witherspoon happily expounded on some of the highlights of her life, all the way back to when she was a little girl. He showed Sam a family photograph of himself, Mrs. Weatherspoon and Gretchen when she was small. The professor hadn't changed that much really, except he had grown some around the waist and his beard had grown gray. He still stood tall with shoulders back and his chin held high, although when he spoke of his deceased daughter he slumped some.

"Her mother died of cancer when Gretchen was only four," the Professor said. "Gretchen was a very independent child. I used to worry that she didn't have many friends, but she seemed content enough anyway. She was content with herself, but not in a smug way. She had a lot of compassion for the down-trodden. In high school in Chicago she worked as a volunteer at a Catholic Charities' breadline dishing out soup."

"Did she date?" Sam asked.

"Rarely, although in college at Northwestern she had a regular boyfriend. They lived together for awhile, until he proved to be physically abusive. He didn't like independent women. As a result she became active with women's liberation groups, which eventually led to becoming active with the Southern Illinois Peace Committee when she transferred to SIU to be closer to me."

"Did she have any political aspirations?"

"Beyond the grass roots level, no, I don't believe so. She felt that making societal changes at the grass roots level was the most effective way of changing society as a whole. That's why she was so interested in demonstrating against racism in little Cairo. She saw it, the racial problems there, as a microcosm of what was happening throughout much of the South despite the civil rights legislation of the '60's. Same thing with the antiwar movement. She felt that despite its relative obscurity geographically, it was just as important to make a stand against the war in Carbondale at SIU as say at Berkeley on the west coast, or at Columbia University in New York City, because there were many men from this region who were losing their lives in Vietnam too. She genuinely cared about the young men who were dying. She didn't protest just because it was the hip thing to do. She cared about the general population of the Vietnams too, who she saw as victims caught up in the crossfire between war mongers.

"I'm going to set up a scholarship in her name, Sam, with the political science department—the Gretchen Witherspoon Peace Award. Ironic isn't it, considering how violently she died."

"All the more poignant I would say, Sir," Sam said, "to establish it in the name of peace."

The article Sam wrote, based on Gretchen Witherspoon's altogether too brief of a biography, grabbed Mick Scott's attention. He had heard a lot about her while working undercover. She was practically idolized by those in the coalition. Michelle spoke of her as if she were some kind of goddess. Looking at the photograph of her that accompanied the article, Mick thought she resembled one. Gretchen was beautiful.

But what really caught Mick's eye was Stuart Bolshinsky's demeanor while he read the article at the table they sat at at Mr. Natural's; the way he pushed the paper aside with an air of disdain when he was finished. It belied grief.

Chapter 23

Janice Davis went to Horseshoe Lake often, usually around sundown, which to her was the most peaceful time of day. She liked to hike on the trails along its shores. There were benches here and there that she'd sit on to read whatever book she had going at the time. Her favorite bench sat on a secluded cove. It offered a view of the opposite shore where a grove of white pines stood. When a breeze blew across the cove from it she smelled the pine's scent; a clean and refreshing fragrance, and she'd close her eyes and inhale, while listening to the water lap at the shore. It put her in a meditative state. But the serenity was suddenly disturbed one early evening by the sound of a vehicle. She opened her eyes and saw a van parked in the pines. She thought nothing of it at first, but then she heard what sounded like a muffled cry or scream coming from the van.

"A baby," she thought.

But occasionally in dreams over the next couple of weeks, the sight of the van, the sound of the cry, came back to her. It haunted her, like the news of the body of Gretchen Witherspoon being found in the lake, not far from that cove, and it finally came to her that there could be some connection, so she went to the police.

"Were you able to make out anyone who was in the van?" they asked.
"No."
"What kind of van was it."
"I think it was one of those VW vans—beige and orange."
"How long did it remain parked in the pines?"
"About half an hour."

"Did you see where it went after that?"

"No."

Janice hadn't witnessed enough of anything unusual, really. The muffled cry could very well have been a baby. But then she remembered seeing something distinguishing about the van when it drove away; a peace sign decal in the rear window.

Not so unusual, the police noted—a VW van with a peace sign went hand-in-hand these days, but around Cairo? It must have belonged, they concluded, to one of the Carbondale crowd who had come to Cairo to demonstrate. Again though, so what? The sound of a muffled cry that she had heard coming from the van peaked their interest however.

Knowing that one of their suspects drove a VW van, they needed to find out if it had a peace sign decal in the rear window. Even if it did, the suspect, Stuart Bolshinsky, had said that after the demonstration the night it was determined that Gretchen Witherspoon had been murdered, around sundown, he had driven around the Cairo area, but by himself. So, if it were he who had been seen parked in the pines, who, what, had been the source of the muffled cry.

The police went to Carbondale to the address Stuart Bolshinsky had given them, and in the driveway they saw his beige and orange VW van with the peace sign decal in the back window. They knocked on the front door. After a moment or two Stuart answered. He didn't invite them in, instead he stepped out onto the stoop.

"Gotta a couple questions for ya, Stuart. You took a ride around Cairo the night Gretchen Witherspoon vanished, right?"

"That's right."

"Go to Horseshoe Lake?"

"Uh, yeah, I did. How'd you know that."

"We've got a witness who saw your van there. The witness also says she heard a muffled cry, or a scream coming from the van."

Stuart thought for a moment, then he began to laugh hysterically.

"I had a loose van belt. That must have been what she heard. It made a squealing sound. Muffled? Yeah, with the door of the engine compartment closed it would be."

"Pardon the pun, Stuart, but isn't that a bit of a stretch? A loose fan belt?"

"That's the only thing it could have been."

About this the police took his word, for the moment, but they felt they were one step further along in the investigation in that his van had been placed at the lake around the time of the murder. The next step was to get a search warrant to look inside the van for evidence—like hair, which they did and it came up clean. Nevertheless, the police were ever-closer to making an arrest based on circumstantial evidence; the circumstances that lead to Stuart Bolshinsky's van being at Horseshoe Lake the night Gretchen Witherspoon was murdered there.

Chapter 24

The violent riots surrounding the Chicago Eight Trial came to be known as the Days of Rage, and it did little to disrupt the trial. That was done quite adequately by the defendants themselves inside the courtroom. Meanwhile, more peaceful demonstrations prevailed when less militant war protesters who wanted the U.S. out of Vietnam faster than the President planned, organized moratorium days beginning October 15.

In one of the most massive protest demonstrations in American history, an estimated one million persons across the nation marched simultaneously in condemnation of the war.

The biggest single "Moratorium day" observance took place in Boston, where an estimated 100,000 gathered on the Common, in Washington, where Mrs. Martin Luther King, Jr. led 45,000 on a candle-light walk from the Washington Monument to the White House, and in New York City, where 40,000 rallied in Bryant Park. This was followed by an even larger demonstration a month later as 250,000 marched in Washington D.C., the largest such gathering in the Capital's history.

While President Nixon took to TV, and in a nationally broadcast speech urged Americans to be patient while he followed through with his timetable for bringing U.S. troops home from the war, and gradually Vietnamizing the conflict, thousands of Americans chose Veteran's Day on November 11 to stage marches and rallies in Washington D.C., New York City and other cities in support of the President's Vietnam policy, and in direct opposition to the moratoriums. And VP Spiro Agnew weighed in on the participants of the moratoriums calling them "an effete corps of impudent snobs," and he accused the three national TV networks of bias in political reporting. He said that a "small and unelected elite," a dozen or so commentators, producers and anchormen, decided "what 40 to 50 million Americans will learn of the day's events."

But biased or not, they had no choice in dutifully reporting that after four months of investigating the circumstances surrounding the assault on the Vietnamese village of My Lai, the U.S. Army announced that it had charged First Lieutenant William L. Calley, Jr. with being responsible for the massacre of up to 500 civilians in March of '68.

Once the gun smoke had settled, at least temporarily over My Lai, the nation's attention became focused once again on the trial in Chicago. Black Panther leader Bobby Seale, one of the Conspiracy Eight, was gagged and shackled to his seat by order of Judge Hoffman for his disruptive courtroom behavior. Seale yelled at the judge that he was a "fascist, racist pig," after Hoffman had refused to grant him permission to conduct his own defense since his lawyer became ill and was being hospitalized in San Francisco.

In the courtroom Seale remained shackled to his chair for three days. When freed he jumped up and proclaimed the trial "a complete, overt, fascist operation," for which Hoffman promptly found him in contempt of court and sentenced him to four years in prison, the longest sentence ever handed down for that charge.

This infuriated Black Panthers nationwide, resulting in numerous confrontations between them and police in various cities. In Chicago there was a deadly shootout that claimed the lives of Illinois Black Panther chief Fred Hampton and one of his lieutenants.

The outrage over Seale's swift conviction and sentencing was not confined to big city Black Panthers alone, however. In Carbondale Mick again encountered local Black Panther leader Marcus Jackson one night at Mr. Natural's. He looked angry and ready to go to war, dressed all in black—the uniform of the Panthers; pant legs tucked into spit-shined combat boots: black beret. His eyes flashed with rage as he spoke with Stuart at one of the tables at the rear. As Mick approached Marcus shot him a glare making him think he wasn't welcome at the table, but Stuart nodded for Mick to sit down, and the conversation between the two continued.

"The motherfuckers has tarred and feathered Bobby Seale," Marcus said to Stuart in a low, growling tone. "The pigs are going to pay. I need your van to transport some guns and ammunition from a house we've got 'em stashed in near campus to our headquarters over on Washington Street. We haven't been keeping them there in case the pigs decided to raid us, but the time has come to make a stand on our turf."

"Sure, Man," Stuart said without hesitation, "when do you need it?"

"Right now."

"Under one stipulation, Marcus. If you're caught the van was stolen."

"Okay, let's roll."

"You didn't hear this conversation, Mick," Stuart said. Marcus glared at Mick and then the two left.

Not only did Mick hear it, but the recorder did too.

In the middle of the night Mick heard the shooting and the sirens, and in the evening paper the following day he read about what had happened. The battle began about two a.m. when SIU security police stopped a suspicious van near campus. A man in the van fired at the police, wounding one in the leg, and then he fled on foot toward the east side into an area called the levee where the SIU police, joined now by Carbondale's, gave chase. They were ambushed near the Black Panther Community Center on North Washington Street and another cop was wounded. An intense gun battle ensued between occupants of the Community Center and police who surrounded the house and peppered it with bullets and tear gas as several Black Panthers returned fire.

While police searched the van that had been abandoned near campus, a car pulled up and a man jumped out and fired a shotgun wounding two more officers in the legs. This assailant then fled on foot too.

The shooting at the Black Panther's headquarters continued until local civil rights activist Elbert Simon got permission from police to enter the house and attempt to negotiate a surrender. Under a cease fire, for half-an-hour Simon talked with one wounded Panther inside, while two of them on a second floor porch led a growing crowd of onlookers in Black Panther Party cheers.

Finally though, all three men surrendered and were taken to jail. The van, which was discovered to be transporting numerous weapons and ammunition, was impounded as evidence.

In a follow-up article in the paper the next day, Marcus, Marcus Jackson was named as one of the participants in the shootout of course, being the leader of Carbondale's Black Panthers. He was arrested and charged, along with four others, with attempted murder. And, the article said, ownership of the van carrying weapons and ammo had been traced to an unidentified white man who was not at the scene. In fact, the article said, when questioned by police at his home, the owner of the van claimed it had been stolen. Charges against him were pending further investigation.

Mick knew the man was Stuart Bolshinsky. He had been privy to the conversation in which Marcus had solicited use of the van to transport some guns and ammunition, to which Stuart readily agreed under the stipulation that if the van should be stopped he'd claim it had been stolen regardless of what kind of legal jeopardy that might put Marcus in, which would pale to the attempted murder charges he now faced.

Mick contacted David by phone to tell him what he knew of Stuart's involvement in the episode, and that he had it on tape."

"Great," David said. "We're slowly but surely building up a case against this guy that'll give him a stretch so long he'll never see the end of it. In fact we've probably got enough to go to the locals with now regarding his Black Panther involvement, but a good lawyer could probably get him off."

"Yeah, I've heard some judges don't take too kindly to secret recordings; they consider it an invasion of privacy," Mick said.

"Perhaps, but if Stuart remains free and in the proximity of that little tape recorder, he may wind up divulging who their mole is here at the Center, I'm just as interested in nailing whoever that might be as I am in nailing Stuart. Well, almost anyway. He and his ilk are nothing more than god damn traitors bent on overthrowing the government, while the mole is just a spy trying to undermine the U.S. war effort, which they've managed to do quite effectively through Hanoi's *dich van* plan," David said.

"In my book there's a big difference between a traitor and a spy. A spy does what he has to do to help his country out, like you, Mick. Whereas on the other hand, a traitor like Stuart forsakes his country in time of peril, like a turncoat who sides with the enemy in the middle of a battle on his home turf."

"Any idea at all who you think the mole might be, David?"

"No. Hopefully you'll be able find that out from Stuart sometime soon. Question is, with the heat on over his van being used to transport weapons for the Black Panthers, will he be accessible now, or will he be lying low?

"Oh, by the way, Mick, Mae's been asking about you. She said the two of you had a very nice time at the Italian Village back in July. She seemed disappointed that she hadn't heard from you since and she wanted to know if I knew how to reach you so she could invite you over to her place for dinner or something. I gave her your phone number. I didn't think you'd mind."

"No, not at all."

Chapter 25

▼

With the war and the antiwar movement in dormancy, and with Stuart, as David had guessed he would be, keeping a low profile since the Black Panther shootout—he hadn't been seen in Mr. Natural's for awhile—Mick took a holiday break. But he didn't go back to Springfield for Christmas this year. Instead he stayed in Carbondale hoping to see Reggie and Trudy whom he hadn't seen since their wedding in July. By now they would have had their baby as Trudy had been pregnant back then. Would they still be going to The Club? He knew where they lived but he didn't like dropping in on people unexpectedly, especially married couples, so he went to The Club hoping to run into them there, on this Saturday night, couples night out.

They weren't there, but John was, as usual, tending bar. He poured Mick a beer from the tap as soon as he saw him come in.

"Good see'n ya again. Put your money away, Man, it's on me. How ya been?" John asked.

"Okay. You?"

"Same, same."

Mick took a drink and looked around. There were only five or six other people in the place; a couple in a booth and some guys in the game room throwing darts.

"Yeah. Everybody's gone home for the holidays, except us townies," John said, twisting one of the curls of his handle bar mustache, and then the other to keep it well balanced, a habit he indulged in often.

"Speakin' of which, seen Trudy and Reggie lately?" Mick asked. "I guess he qualifies as a townie now, having married one."

"They went to Chicago to show his parents the baby."

"Did they know Reggie could walk again?" Mick asked.

"No, he's going to surprise them.

"By the way, John, I've come into a little money, enough to buy some land to build a cabin on once I've graduated, which will be in a couple of years yet. Maybe longer if I don't hit the books more. Anyway, I've got my eye on about five acres down at Lake Wells. I checked with a realtor and she said some old guy she knows might be willing to sell it if he gets the right price. If you're still around, John, I could use some help building the cabin. As a former Sea Bee I imagine you'd be pretty good at slapping a few logs together. I could provide all the beer you can drink."

John chuckled. "No you couldn't, Mick."

But John gladly provided Mick with all the beer he could drink this night, for a small price of course, and not having drunk so much for awhile, not since that night at Billy Goat's Tavern in Chicago, he got tipsy fast and went home feeling no pain. In the morning though he felt plenty waking up to a rip-roaring hangover and he swore off drinking again. And while many reached for an Alka-Seltzer for relief, Mick had discovered that smoking marijuana the morning after, alleviated, in fact, eliminated the sick stomach, the heavy, fuzzy head, rattled nerves, and in his case, depression. In other words it took the edge off and replaced it all with a comfortable feeling of euphoria; a toastiness as it were, especially on snowy winter days as this one had become. He watched the white stuff falling with a purring Jazzpur who sat on the desk under the window looking out at it with Mick. On the ground an inch or so had accumulated.

"Perfect, Jazzpurr, perfect for a winter's hike in the woods, and on Christmas Eve day no less."

Mick loved the woods in the winter when it snowed.

He ate a quick breakfast of instant oat meal and raison bread toast, fed Jazzpur, rolled another joint, bundled up and drove off to his spot at Lake Wells.

The snow continued to fall, and by the time he got to the lake there was from three to four inches on the ground. The roads were passable though. The main county road had been plowed at least as far as Mick intended to go before hiking, although he was a little worried that if enough snow fell going back it might be a different story.

When he came to the turnoff he normally took to Lake Wells, recognizable because of the unusually large, old red cedar tree at the intersection, he parked beneath it where not very much snow had reached the ground and he began to walk. Soon the snow stopped and faint patches of blue appeared in the soft gray sky allowing enough sunlight through to cause the snow on the ground and in the trees to sparkle some, especially when the wind blew it. It sprayed Mick's face as he breathed the cold, refreshing air while hiking toward the lake which he knew to be about a half-a-mile away. His legs felt strong and he felt lucky to be alive.

In the winter, without leaves, trees have a different kind of beauty. Their bare, dark limbs, branches and stems form an intricately-patterned global shape against the sky so complex even the best of artists with the keenest of eyes would find it difficult to duplicate. Held fast against the wind by trunk and roots, the trees of winter embody nature's raw beauty and strength.

A giant gray-colored oak stood out among them—a tree so old Mick reckoned, judging from the circumference of the trunk and its huge limbs, it had outlived a few generations of man and beast. In deference to its longevity, Mick gave the majestic old tree wide berth as if it were a sage standing on hallowed ground. But then again he considered all woods to be hallowed ground—godly places like Eden had been before man. Perhaps this was why Mick always felt like an intruder when he came to them.

He walked as softly as he could through the snow. Occasionally he'd stop and stand very still and listen to the sounds. In the winter there aren't as many as in spring. Usually it is just the wind, or maybe a Cardinal chirping. Mick saw one flitting about in a snow-dusted cedar giving a brush of bright color and action to the generally black, gray, brown and white, still life-like scene. Then in the distance he heard the sound of geese honking, which gradually grew louder. He looked up and saw them flying in a loose V-formation so low he could hear their powerful wings swishing through the air. The lead goose veered off, and the others, there must have been fifty, followed him toward the lake where they'd land, as the water hadn't frozen over. Mick heard them splash down. The lake was near; he smelled it in the wind, and soon he reached the shore where a blast of cold air, coming off the choppy gray-green water, greeted him. Invigorated by it, but feeling chilled, Mick looked around for any dry wood that might have remained above the snow. He found some, including a dead oak branch with its crisp, brown leaves intact.

He swept an opening in the snow with gloved hands, down to the bare ground, put the wood on top of the leaves there, and lit them, and soon he had a crackling fire. He rolled a nearby log up next to it and sat down, his rump protected from the wetness by his long coat.

This was what Mick enjoyed most about going to the snowy woods in winter—the fire warming his body as he gazed into the heart of it, entranced by the dancing flames and the ever-changing configurations of burning wood fed by the wind and a fertile imagination.

He saw in it many things. He saw dragons, and the devil, and a pot-bellied "Happy Buddha" smiling, like the ones that were on the tables at Henry Chin's Emperor's Palace Restaurant in Carbondale, with candles burning inside of them. "Happy Buddha's," Mick had learned from his girlfriend Tron in Vietnam, represented the light-heartedness of life, and he felt that way now.

He lit the joint he brought with a stick from the fire and his attention shifted to the surrounding woods, and a disturbing thought came over him. If he were to build a cabin here, a number of these trees would have to come down for logs and for space. To live in the woods he'd have to destroy some of it. What choice did he have though; not to build, and just leave this place as it was? Perhaps, he thought, for after all, hadn't man intruded on nature enough?

Mick harkened back to the week he came back from Nam, when he went to revisit his favorite little spot where he often had gone as an adolescent to escape his unhappy home life—the drunkenness of his parents, before they were killed in that car wreck. He had anticipated with joy seeing it again; a cool, ferny glen with a small lagoon tucked away in pines just a mile or so beyond the city limits of Springfield, where he'd sit very still on a rock near it like a big frog and watch deer come there to drink.

The first thing he noticed were the traffic lights at a new intersection, and the traffic on the new, wide road going through it, which had replaced a gravel road.

He followed the traffic, and his heart sank when he came to where he used to hide his bike in the tall weeds before hiking into the pines. Sprawled out before him was the parking lot of a new K-Mart that stood exactly where the pines and the glen and the lagoon used to be. Yes, man had intruded on nature enough. There was just no way Mick could resort to cutting down any of these trees for a cabin. His dream of living here suddenly no longer seemed feasible. Oh he could still buy the land, if the owner would be willing to sell, as the realtor thought he would be, and come to it periodically to hike and camp and fish, but not to live if it meant destroying some of the woods.

He solemnly glanced at Lake Wells lapping at the stony shore.

"Stone, that's it, this land is full of them. I could build a stone house, maybe a round one. No trees would have to be cut down." The prospect excited him. Of course he'd have to use some wood for the roof, doors, window frames and floor, but not that much really. He'd probably be able to buy all that he'd need at a lumber yard.

A stone house would be cool in southern Illinois' oppressive summers. In the winter he would be kept warm by a fireplace in the center, with the hearth opening on opposite sides, and hopefully by a woman someday. Although he was somewhat of a loner, Mick had no intention of becoming a hermit. He fully intended to share his life with someone.

"Living alone out here could get awfully lonely pretty fast," he said to himself.

He looked back at the fire before him, which had dwindled into a glowing pile of embers. The sky had become a darker gray, and the wind had picked up considerably. The time had come for him to leave while it was still light enough to find his way back to the car through the woods.

Driving back to Carbondale Mick caught himself humming a tune (the car radio was on the blink) that always seemed to be in the back of his mind these days; *Woodstock,* the counter culture's anthem, written by Joni Mitchel and made more famous by Crosby, Stills, Nash & Young.

Perhaps as John had suggested, the counter culture was beginning to rub off on him—not politically though; he certainly couldn't identify with radicals like Stuart and the Weather Underground; no way, but more in respect perhaps with the back-to-nature movement.

"We are stardust, we are golden, and we got to get ourselves back to the garden," Mick sang.

Getting back to the garden was something he had planned on since getting out of the service, but being a loner he hadn't planned on becoming a part of any movement in doing so. Movements ultimately become encumbered by mass and unbending ideologies, like Mao's revolution became, at the expense of individualism. He preferred to do it individually like Henry David Thoreau had done at Walden Pond in 1845 near Concord, Massachusetts.

And while the famous naturalist also advocated civil disobedience as a means to protest slavery and the controversial Mexican War, and what he perceived to be government interference with individual liberties, Mick had no particular gripe against the U.S. government presently, except for the way it was handling the Vietnam War. They had started it but were not willing to finish it honorably after so many GIs had died over there.

Died for what, was the question Mick had been asking of late. For the South Vietnamese to lose the damn thing, as Mick privately thought they would without continued US assistance.

"Damnit," Mick admonished himself, "don't spoil the party by getting bummed out over the war."

He sang holiday songs the rest of the way home.

It felt good to be back in a warm house after spending a winter's day outside. Jazzpur sniffed and sniffed at Mick's clothing. He had brought home with him the pungent smell of wood smoke which went well with the smell of the whiskey he poured in celebration of a snowy Christmas Eve. Mick slept well that night.

In the morning he was awakened by the telephone ringing.

"Merry Christmas."

"Who's this?" Mick asked.

"Mae. Remember me?" she asked sarcastically.

"Yes, of course, Mae. Merry Christmas to you," Mick said, knowing her to be a Catholic Vietnamese, not Buddhist.

"Thank you, Mick. Santa Clause come to see you?"

"He just did. I'm glad to hear from you. I've intended to call you but...."

"That's okay." Mae cut him off, saving him from having to come up with some lame excuse. "Do you have any plans for New Year's Eve?"

"No, not yet," Mick said.

"Good. Would you like to come to my house for dinner and drinks? I owe you for Italian Village. No lasagna though, we'll have traditional Vietnamese. Okay with you?"

"Sounds great. What time?"

"Bout eight o'clock."

"See you then."

Mick spent the week between Christmas and New Year's Eve reading up on building stone houses at the city library. And he went to The Club a couple of nights to visit with John and to watch some of the college holiday bowl games on TV, something he hadn't done for awhile—watch sports, or any television for that matter, except for Johnny Carson, Laugh In and the Smothers Brothers occasionally. He had stopped watching the nightly news because of the biased anti-US reporting on the war. Even Laugh In and the Smothers Brothers had begun to do the same. In fact, Mick was surprised that CBS, the network of television news anchorman Walter Cronkite, one of the most outspoken critics of the Vietnam War, canceled the Smothers Brothers because of their consistent anti-establishment, antiwar, pro-protester tone, often presented by controversial musical guests like Pete Seger and Joan Baez who sang scathingly about the war.

Chapter 26

Mick looked forward to seeing Mae again. While he hadn't really thought of her as a girlfriend yet, he enjoyed her company and found her to be stimulating intellectually. She was certainly more outgoing than the other Vietnamese women he knew who worked at the Center—Su Vinh and Tran Le. They were so reserved they hardly ever spoke. The Vietnamese man who worked there however, Nguyen Lu was a little too outgoing with Mick. While Mick had discovered quite shockingly in Vietnam that it was customary for men to hold hands while walking, it wasn't so customary in the U.S. except in San Francisco, and Mick didn't like Lu trying to hold his hand one night while they were walking from the Center to the library through Thompson's Woods.

On the way to Mae's, Mick stopped at a liquor store and bought the customary New Year's Eve bottle of champagne; the kind those living on the GI Bill buy—cheap, bottled yesterday and with a plastic cork.

When he arrived he was stunned to see her wearing an *ao dai*. It was red, and the pantaloons were black, and she wore her hair down; long, silky black hair that fell beautifully over her shoulders. Her pretty, golden brown face and dark eyes needed no makeup, but it appeared she had applied some lipstick, which went fabulously well with the red of her dress. And she was barefooted, and Mick was surprised to see she painted her toes—an American touch. He hadn't seen that in Vietnam.

"Well come in, Mick. Don't just stand there and stare."

"Sorry. It's just that I haven't seen anyone wearing an *ao dai* since I left Saigon. I've missed seeing them."

"Yes, and I've missed wearing them. Thought New Year's Eve would be a good time. Very cold tonight, would you like a nice warm glass of rice wine?"

"Sounds good."

"What's that you brought?" Mae asked.

"Champagne."

"I'll put it on ice for later. Please sit down anywhere you'd like."

"Thanks."

Mick chose the couch where he waited for Mae to return from the kitchen.

He glanced about the room. Everything looked neat and clean. The wood floor shone, reflecting the soft lighting a yellow shaded lamp on one of the glass end tables provided. The coffee table was glass too, making the Oriental throw rug beneath it visible. Aside from the couch, the coffee and end tables and a high back Rattan chair, the room was sparsely furnished, but house plants were plentiful, giving it a delightful tropical look. She did have a TV, and a stereo that played soft jazz. A large Oriental-looking watercolor of a misty mountain scene hung on the wall facing Mick. Along with the music it had a calming effect on him, for he had been a little tense in anticipation of such a formal date.

They had been out on a date before—a casual, spontaneous one. But tonight, with Mae being so dressed up, it was as if he were seeing her for the very first time.

It wasn't exactly a mismatch though. Mick had worn a nice pair of gray, corduroy jeans, a blue crew neck sweater and a blue-brown-gray Harris tweed jacket, and new, hand made, brown leather high top shoes. With his long, curly, sandy-colored hair and beard, he resembled one of those young English professors who fancied the Oxford look. A far cry from the hippie ensemble he wore undercover; outfits that he had grown accustomed to wearing actually, even when he was off duty so-to-speak. He felt a little stuffy in the jacket, so he took it off.

Mae returned from the kitchen with a bamboo tray containing two glasses of the rice wine. The glass felt warm, almost hot in his hand. She sat the tray down on the coffee table, took her drink and sat next to Mick on the couch, but not too close.

"Very good for stimulating the appetite," she said smiling. "Have you had rice wine before?"

"Oh yes, in Vietnam."

Mick remembered how high he had gotten on it, to be more exact, drunk.

"Have you eaten Vietnamese food before?"

"Some."

"I'll spare you the *nouc-mam*," she said.

"Thank you. Something smells very good, Mae. What is it?"

"Roast duck. I must go check on it. Finished with wine?"

Mick hadn't quite, but she had, so to keep up he downed what was left, and she took the tray with empty glasses back to the kitchen. She returned shortly with refills.

"Dinner will be ready soon."

Good thing, Mick thought, as he wasn't sure how many more rice wines he could drink on an empty stomach. Just the one had given him quite a buzz. Thankfully, before they finished the second one a bell rang in the kitchen.

Mae jumped up. "Duck done!"

It sounded funny. Mick laughed and so did Mae.

"Please come in and sit at the table in the dining room, Mick."

The dining room was furnished sparsely too, with only the table and two chairs and a buffet. There were photos of what Mick assumed to be family and friends on the walls. The table was set with the basic dinnerware, including bowls at each place. Mae appeared with a crock containing soup, ladled it into the bowls, and sat down at the opposite end of the table from Mick. It tasted quite hot spice-wise, and Mick utilized his glass of water.

"Too hot?" Mae asked smiling.

"Not too, but close. It tastes very good though."

"Pepper egg-drop soup," she said.

Mae finished hers first and went to the kitchen again. She returned shortly with a platter of dark meat smothered with vegetables, and a large bowl of rice.

"Duck done!"

They dined while engaging in small talk about the Center, and school, and the winter weather which Mae said she still hadn't gotten used to having lived most of her life in Saigon and Los Angeles.

"Only I do like the summers," she said. "They are very much like southern Vietnam's, except we get occasional rains from the sea to cool things off, for maybe five minutes, then it's hot like hell again."

"Yes, I remember, like Carbondale in July, without sea-spawned rains," Mick said.

"Will you be staying here after graduating, Mick?"

"I think so." And Mick told her of his plans to buy land and build on it, and to write a book there about his Vietnam experiences. She seemed intrigued and offered to assist him in any way that she could with the book, and she offered Mick more rice wine.

"Very good for digestion you know."

She poured two glasses of it from a porcelain pitcher that had been kept warm by a candle in a rack holding it, then they retired with their drinks to the living room where again they sat next to each other on the couch, but a little closer this time, and suddenly the conversation became more personal. Out of the blue Mae asked Mick if he had had a girlfriend in Vietnam.

The only woman of the few he had known there whom he considered a girlfriend was Tron. Mick told Mae about her—about how they had dated in the traditional sense (not like GIs and bar girls), going out to dinner, to the movies now and then, and to the Saigon Zoo on Sundays.

"Did you love this girl, Tron, Mick? Or just have relationship of, how should I say, convenience for lonely GI?"

Mick knew what she meant by convenience, and lonely, and as far as love went, well, it had taken them as far as they had wanted it to go one hot night in the moon shadows of the garden of the villa where Mick lived. A night too hot to wear clothes, so they lay together on the cool grass without them and did what comes natural between a man and woman in that situation. Mick's longing smile gave him away.

"Hope you did not love her and leave her with child, Mick."

She looked serious. Mick's smile disappeared. This was something he didn't like thinking about, it was just too unsettling—the possibility that he may have fathered a child over there. He really didn't know because he left Vietnam soon after they had made love, without protection. Mick grimaced inside.

"GIs are leaving many babies behind you know, Mick. They will not be accepted by Vietnamese society. These children will only remain as reminders of the war long after it is over, especially if the South falls to Communism, and their mothers will be scorned too, for such unsavory behavior with the enemy."

"The enemy?"

"Oh, yes, I mean from the perspective of the Communists of course. So, Mick, do you miss coming to the Center?" Mae asked, changing the subject abruptly. "Thought since you've come back from Springfield you'd become involved with us again."

"I've been planning to, but with the new semester starting soon I'll have to hit the books extra hard to make up for lost time since I dropped out last semester to take care of Aunt Jenny (which of course was a lie). I'd like to graduate sometime this century."

"More wine?" Mae asked.

"Sure." Mick wasn't so concerned about getting drunk too fast since he had eaten.

She returned with the refills and sat even closer to Mick, and the fragrance of her perfume, which he had been smelling faintly, became as intoxicating as the wine, causing him to feel light headed and turned on. He looked into her eyes and she in his and they smiled. He was tempted to kiss her but there was a matter he had been wanting to discuss with her first before they went on to something else.

"Mae, as I've said, I'm planning to write a book about the war and I'd like to get a Vietnamese's perspective on what happened at My Lai."

She was in the process of taking a drink and she swallowed hard and there was silence for a moment—the moment of silence that naturally follows the mention of such an unspeakable thing. She then turned the tables on Mick.

"Maybe more importantly, what does an American think of it?"

Images of the photographs of the massacre Mick had seen in a magazine came to mind.

"Horrific," he said. "It's difficult to imagine American troops doing such a thing. I've tried to rationalize it somehow. Maybe the stress of combat caused it, or the frustration of trying to flush out an enemy who is given sanctuary in villages like My Lai who pretend to be friendly to GIs. Or maybe it was from the frustration of having to fight a seemingly endless, winless war, at least a war the U.S. no longer has any intention of winning apparently, as they turn it over to the South Vietnamese Army. Yet outfits like Lt. Calley's are expected to continue to fight and die for certain Vietnamese people who are sympathetic to the Communists. But that's no excuse to slaughter them, especially the children, my God!"

"The children," Mae said, "yes, this is the tragedy of war." She stared into her glass of wine. "They are always the victims caught in the crossfire of armed conflict."

"Generally speaking though, Mae, aren't you in support of the war as a Vietnamese who is opposed to a Communist take over of the South?"

"Yes, of course, but to be perfectly honest with you, Mick, I would have preferred the national elections being held as mandated by the Geneva Convention of 1954 following the French-Indochina War, instead of yet another war being waged to determine who would govern a re-united Vietnam."

"Even if Ho Chi Minh would have been elected as president of both North and South Vietnam?"

"Yes, even if, because it would have been determined by choice of the people through the democratic process. But a coalition government including the Viet Cong and Thieu would probably be the most realistic at the present time. If this is what it would take to bring peace to my country before it, the North and the South are destroyed, then so be it," Mae said.

Mick was surprised by her apparent willingness to have Communists take part in a South Vietnamese government when the original reason for the war had been to keep them out and confined to the North.

It was especially puzzling because of what had happened to Mae's parents for advocating Capitalism for Vietnam's future. But who was Mick to argue with her about what she, a Vietnamese, thought was best for her country. Although it could be argued that Americans who served in Vietnam, those who had risked life and limb to keep the South free of Communism, had some say so in the matter too. At the moment though, Mick chose to keep it to himself.

"I know my willingness to accept a coalition government for South Vietnam simply for the sake of peace would not set well with David, as the Center is decidedly anti-Communist, so please, for the time being, Mick, may we keep this between us?" Mae placed a hand on Mick's leg and looked into his eyes.

"Sure, Mae."

Mick glanced at his watch. "Hey, where's the time gone, it's almost twelve o'clock. Let's have some champagne."

"Come with me to the kitchen and open it," Mae said.

Mick followed her. Even from behind she looked beautiful walking, with her long, gleaming black hair cut in a straight line across the top of her hips clad tightly in the silky red *ao dai*; her bare, petite feet showing beneath the black pantaloons. She took the bottle from the refrigerator and handed it to Mick. He tore away the foil and unwound the wire that held the plastic cork in place.

"Aim it outside, don't want to break anything," Mae said.

She opened the kitchen door and Mick pushed the cork out with his thumbs, and it flew into the night with a loud pop causing dogs to bark, and he quickly poured the bubbly into two chilled glasses Mae held out. They counted down to midnight and drank. And when the radio played Guy Lombardo's *Auld Lang Syne* they danced, and Mae laughed at the strange sound of the song, with its oscillating muted horns. The old holiday standard was followed by modern jazz, and the laughing stopped and they kissed for the first time, softly at first, then more passionately, and they whirled around to the couch and laid down still kissing and caressing until Mae suggested they go where it would be more comfortable—her bed, where they stood beside it and undressed; she gracefully, while smiling with poise.

Mick nearly fell over hurrying so. Perhaps that was why she smiled, watching him clumsily undress, but he was not so clumsy in the way his hand moved smoothly over her breasts. He brought them up to his lips. She crossed her arms around his neck, raised up on her toes and lifted herself while wrapping her legs around him.

"Wait, Mae, wait, I didn't bring a-

"That's okay, I'm a modern Vietnam girl. I take the pill."

They rolled onto the bed; a water bed, in the position they had been standing in. With he on top of her, hips firmly between her legs they moved with the motion of the waves created by the motion of their love making. She groaned and whimpered with pleasure and Mick sweat trying to hold off long enough to please her, and their eyes locked onto each others as the passion welled up from deep inside until they climaxed simultaneously—the ultimate consummation of sexual desire. Spent by its intensity they lay in silence side-by-side and drifted off to sleep.

At dawn Mick was awakened by a multitude of finches chirping furiously in a tree outside the window. He glanced at Mae who was still sleeping. He slipped out of bed, got dressed and left.

Mick had never felt comfortable waking up sober next to a woman he'd had alcohol-induced sex with, especially one who he had heretofore considered more of a friend than a lover. It was hard to be both, and once you've crossed that line from friend to lover it's difficult to go back. Had Mick crossed that line with Mae, even though they were drunk? What would he say the next time he saw her? What would he do? Act as if it had never happened, or arrange for it to happen again? Or try, as difficult as it might be, to resume their plutonic relationship?

At the moment Mick didn't have the answer. He was suffering mightily from a horrendous, cheap champagne/rice wine hangover, perhaps the worst he had ever had. He made a New Year's resolution not to drink again for at least another six months. He had sworn off alcohol in the throws of a hangover before, just last week in fact, but the longest he had ever been on the wagon for the last three or four years was maybe a month at best.

Mick had heard that alcoholism runs in the family because of environmental influences and genetics. His Aunt Jenny, the drunk, and her sister, his mother, and his father, both of whom had been killed in a car wreck on their way home from a roadhouse on the outskirts of Springfield, had an influence on Mick. He had developed a pattern of behavior of late, getting drunk on a fairly regular basis, mostly just on weekends though, and maybe one night in between, oh, and on holidays of course. But Mick didn't think of himself as an alcoholic or anything like that; or even a "juicer" for that matter, as he also smoked grass.

No, he wasn't an alcoholic—just a typical '60s "College Joe," although a little older one having spent four years in the service.

It took years and years of drinking hard liquor day in and day out to be an alcoholic, like Aunt Jenny, he told himself. Mick was too young, and he usually only drank beer. Besides, he could quit if necessary. When he worked undercover he abstained, as Stuart and his crowd seldom drank anything but herbal tea and occasionally a sip of wine at Mr. Natural's when there was live music or poetry readings. Mick wasn't a sipper. He was more inclined to gulp like he had done at Mae's last night, so it was best not to even get started in the presence of that crowd. He might blow his cover if drunk.

Since the Black Panther affair Mick hadn't seen Stuart at Mr. Natural's the two or three times he stopped by there looking for him. Apparently he was still keeping a low profile since the police knew his van had been used to run guns the night of the shootout. And although he had reported it stolen, Mick had heard the police suspected him of being a co-conspirator.

With the heat on Mick wondered if Stuart continued to contemplate some sort of action against the Center. If so, he hoped he wouldn't find out too late to warn David.

CHAPTER 27

▼

Following the Days of Rage in October in Chicago, and the more peaceful Moratorium Days of October and November, notwithstanding the brief but violent eruptions over My Lai, in general, the intensity of the antiwar movement waned somewhat in early 1970. The Chicago 8, except for Seale, were stunningly acquitted and the fighting in Vietnam slowed. The fighting had subsided, according to an article in a *US News and World Report* that Mick read, because the North Vietnamese had changed strategies, and captured enemy documents revealed that the Viet Cong—or what was left of them after the Tet Offensive of '68—were tired, hungry and demoralized. Insurgent operations by them had practically ceased. The article also said the war was being carried out almost entirely by the North Vietnamese Army whose new strategy basically was to disengage, and wait out Nixon's plans for Vietnamization, confident that this would be to their advantage. They believed the South Vietnamese Army, without the Americans, would be no match for them in the long run through a protracted war, which they had plenty of patience for.

Yet while there had been a lull in the fighting in South Vietnam, the Communists were quite active in neighboring Cambodia where Prince Norodum Sihanouk, in trying to straddle the fence between Red China and North Vietnam on one side and the United States on the other, allowed them to establish large base areas in his country. He also granted them the unfettered use of the important port city of Sihanoukville to supply their forces in the southern regions of South Vietnam.

Simultaneously, the double-dealing prince urged the U.S. to bomb the NVA bases with the understanding that such attacks be kept secret. But because of Sihanouk's cozy relationship with Hanoi, the United States cut off aid to Cambodia, causing the national economy to falter badly. This, coupled with the ever-increasing intrusion of Vietnamese Communist forces into their country, caused the Cambodian people to turn against the prince. When he took an untimely vacation to France, coups and counter coups quickly erupted and in March the Cambodian National Assembly, led by the pro-Western Prime Minister Lon Nol, voted unanimously to oust Sihanouk.

Lon Nol wasted little time in closing Sihanoukville to the Communists and announcing that he wanted them out of their base areas, most of which had been established in the east along the border with South Vietnam.

In defiance, the NVA and elements of the VC, some 40,000 to 60,000 strong, drove west instead and threatened Cambodia's capital of Phnom Penh. If it fell, along with Lon Nol and his government, and it surely would without assistance from elsewhere, then the port at Sihanoukville would be reopened to the Communists and all of Cambodia would become their base area, outflanking Allied forces in South Vietnam. It could very well be said the first domino in Southeast Asia was about to fall.

By mid-April the situation worsened, and it became crucial for the U.S. to intervene. At the end of April the National Security Council met and decided that the South Vietnamese Army, with American air support would attack enemy sanctuaries in the infamous Parrot's Beak, a renowned geographical feature along Cambodia's eastern border with South Vietnam, while U.S. ground forces attacked the other principle Communist base area known as the Fish Hook. The raids it was thought, would send a message to Hanoi that Nixon wasn't playing by the same old rules of the previous administration, by not going after the enemy in their out-of-country sanctuaries.

In addition it was hoped that a successful Cambodian campaign, particularly on the part of the South Vietnamese Army, would buy some time for Nixon's Vietnamization.

In the Fish Hook the attacking forces, which included American armor, elements of the U.S. 1st Cavalry Division and South Vietnam's 3rd Airborne Brigade, consisted of about 15,000 men.

On May 1st, following B-52 and artillery bombardments to soften enemy positions, the tanks and troops moved west and south into the Communist base areas expecting much resistance, but there was none because the enemy had hurriedly fled west leaving vast quantities of supplies to the Allies.

Practically the same thing occurred in the Parrot's Beak where the South Vietnamese Army captured and destroyed the fleeing enemy's equipment, arsenals of weapons and ammo, supplies, food stores, bunkers, hospitals and barracks. However, not all the enemy had gotten away. The two raids cost them an estimated 11,000 killed and 2,500 captured. Conversely, less than 1,000 Allied troops died in the fighting. And at last, after years of being attacked by the North Vietnamese Army from Cambodia in violation of the Geneva Convention of 1954, Allied forces under orders from Nixon, had in fact sent that message to Hanoi that their sanctuaries would no longer remain untouchable.

The raids also bought time for Lon Nol to build up his forces in order to resist further Communist incursions into Cambodia's interior, while testing the South Vietnamese Army against Communist forces in preparation for Vietnamization.

But the American public, particularly those of the antiwar movement, were decidedly less impressed, in fact they were downright incensed over the Cambodian raids, or invasion as they characterized it. Antiwar dissidents viewed the raids as an expansion of the war, and violent demonstrations in protest of them took place on many campuses. But not all occurred at the traditional hotbeds of student radicalism. On May 2, at Kent State University in Ohio, after students and other protesters looted stores in downtown Kent, and the university's ROTC building had been burned down, the state's national guardsmen were called on to campus to quell the rioting.

The following night, when the rioting resumed, the guardsmen drove the demonstrating students off the streets and into their dorms, making 69 arrests. Then on the 4th of May about 2,000 protesters congregated again for a noon rally and the guardsmen attempted to break it up with tear gas. Some of the demonstrators dispersed, but a group of about 1,000 moved to a campus parking lot and began throwing pieces of pavement, rocks and other objects at the guardsmen, who initially responded by retreating, but then unexpectedly they turned and began firing their weapons into the crowd. Four students were killed and nine were wounded.

After six long years the war had shifted from the battlefields of Vietnam to a college campus in middle America.

The shootings at Kent State sparked even more violence on other US campuses, including SIU's in Carbondale. It erupted at the usual flash point, in front of the Vietnamese Studies Center. Mick, having left his last class of the day in the building next door, saw Stuart, his hiatus apparently now over, standing on the steps before a fast-growing, highly-agitated crowd shouting over a bullhorn his outrage over the Kent State killings, the "invasion" of Cambodia and the Vietnam War in general, all of which he blamed on Nixon. His wrath was then directed at the Center itself for being a mouthpiece for pro-war propaganda. He shouted, "Burn, Baby, burn!" and a VC flag appeared, waving in the faces of some of the staunchly anti-Communist Vietnamese who were peering in terror out the third floor windows of the Center.

The crowd, which Mick estimated to be several hundred now, followed Stuart's lead, chanting "Burn, Baby, burn!" as they pressed against the building's front doors, making it impossible for anyone to get out that way.

"Burn, Baby, burn!" the chanting continued louder and louder with Stuart shouting it over his bullhorn. Fearing that the Center would soon be torched, Mick hoped the occupants of the building, who were no longer visible through the windows, had evacuated out the back.

Then, in the distance, Mick heard the sirens and soon the campus, city and state police equipped with helmets, clubs and shields arrived to handle the riot. That's what it had become. They waded in and managed to isolate groups of the most vociferous and animated demonstrators who fought with them in return.

In the melee Mick lost sight of Stuart as his bullhorn had fallen silent. Many of the demonstrators were bing arrested and taken away in squad cars, while others dispersed and ran toward uptown. Had Stuart been arrested or had he gotten away? If he had gotten away, Mick speculated he probably would have sought refuge at Mr. Natural's. Mick hoped to find him there, blood still boiling from the heat of the battle. Perhaps he'd be able to get something on tape regarding what Stuart now intended for the Center.

He had made veiled threats against the Center before, in private, which Mick had captured on tape, and just now at the demonstration he had threatened it indirectly shouting "Burn, Baby, burn!" over the bullhorn in front of hundreds before he was silenced by police. But Stuart would not be silenced for long, Mick knew.

And there Stuart was as Mick had hoped, at Mr. Natural's, blood boiling and bubbling from a cut on his head that the woman who worked there tended to. He shouted when he saw Mick come in: "Those Gestapo pigs were way out of line, Man! They knocked the bullhorn right out of my hand. Ouch!"

Stuart flinched as the woman pressed on the cut with a wet wash cloth.

"That's tantamount to suppression of free speech. The fascist bastards! Nixon says he wants to end this war, yet he expands it by invading Cambodia. Like most American politicians he speaks from both sides of his mouth. They'll say anything to get elected and re-elected. At least under Communism you don't have that problem, the leaders are selected by the party, and there's no need for them to lie and make empty promises to a gullible constituency!"

"Yes, and under Communism, you stupid sonofabitch," Mick cursed at Stuart to himself, "The only bullhorn you'd ever come close to would be on the head of the water buffalo whose ass you'd be plodding behind on some god damn state-owned farm you'd been banished to for being a smart ass malcontent dissident."

"Someday soon, Mick, we're going to shut that South Vietnamese/CIA propaganda center down."

"When? How?" Mick asked, prodding Stuart for specifics.

"I can't say right now. They're watching me, us, the Weather Underground very closely. When the heat lets up, hopefully by the end of summer, early fall. But one way or another that Center's going down, along with Mr. David Gordon of the CIA."

"So what exactly do you mean by this David Gordon going down?" Mick asked.

"In flames with the Center when we bomb it with him in it."

This was the first time Stuart had threatened an individual connected to the Center by name. His animosity had suddenly become more personal than before. Before it had been directed at what the Center was established to promote; primarily a democratic South Vietnam totally free of Communism.

Immediately after leaving Stuart at Mr. Natural's Mick went home and relayed what he had on tape to David who was apparently now a marked man. David's reaction to this was surprisingly nonchalant. He seemed more concerned about the fate of the Center itself, and the effect its demise (and the handful of others nationwide) could have in countering left wing academia's influence on the U.S. government's conduct of the war, and its negotiations with Hanoi in trying to end it honorably.

"If left wing academia and the antiwar movement prevails, Mick, South Vietnam will be handed over to the Communists—the Viet Cong and the North Vietnamese—within two or three years, unless we, the Centers, continue to oppose them by promoting democracy and capitalism for the South regardless of whether we are fighting there or not," David said, sounding more anxious than Mick had ever heard him sound before.

"I'm not overstating the situation here, Mick. LBJ was so intimidated by the antiwar movement he chose not to run again for a second term, and it has persuaded Nixon to compromise our original commitment to the South Vietnamese by withdrawing U.S. troops." David took a breath and calmed down.

"The antiwar movement, which includes many in academia, has proven to be a powerful lobby in influencing war policy decisions," he said. "And I fear it'll carry over to the negotiating table. Many of its leaders who are Marxists, like Stuart, will demand no less than a coalition government for the South. You know, one that includes the Viet Cong as a stipulation to a peaceful settlement, which would be a foot in the door for the North Vietnamese Communists."

"Which of course is one of the goals of *dich van,* right?" Mick said. "By encouraging the antiwar movement, and hoping that it will influence negotiators to act in Hanoi's best interests, like with that telegram from Pham Dong congratulating the movement on their successes, and encouraging them to continue with it."

"Yep," David concurred, "and Hanoi must be elated about what happened at Kent State. The killings will certainly turn many more Americans against the war now. The war has come home, Mick. My battle now lies with Stuart Bolshinsky, so it seems, as he has personally threatened me, and he's apparently planning to destroy the Center soon. Try to find out just exactly when that might be."

"He's indicated it'll probably be around the end of summer or early fall," Mick said.

Chapter 28

SIU, like many other campuses racked with riots resulting from the Cambodian raids, and the ensuing killings at Kent State, closed its door prematurely before the spring semester of 1970 would officially end, postponing many students' scheduled graduations. So again repercussions from a war being fought 10,000 miles or so away continued to disrupt American life.

And having been overshadowed by the news of Cambodia and Kent State, news of peace negotiations, which had resumed in secrecy in a lower middle class apartment in a suburb of Paris in late February of '70, did not come to light until it was belatedly leaked to the world by the French press.

The talks had continued through April with Henry Kissinger, the U.S. chief negotiator and North Vietnam's Le Duc Tho wrangling over the issue of troop withdrawals. Washington, having already announced the planned withdrawal of American troops from South Vietnam, wanted the North Vietnamese to do the same. Not only did the Communists reject this out-of-hand, they boldly demanded the dismantlement of the Thieu government, and they wanted the Viet Cong to be included in a new coalition government which Kissinger rejected and this phase of negotiations collapsed.

Hanoi, knowing that the antiwar movement in the U.S. was having an impact on decision-making, namely the decision by Nixon to begin withdrawing troops regardless of whether they did so in-kind, saw no pressing need to negotiate in earnest. What they had demanded they believed would come to them in due time as the American general public's support for the war eroded. After six years with no apparent resolution in sight they were growing weary of it. Regardless the war continued, but without the 1st Infantry Division, the famous battle-hardened Big

Red One. They were withdrawn as part of Nixon's Vietnamization plan, followed by the 9th, 4th and 25th Divisions.

Mick had covered the 25th for Armed Forces Radio at the Battle of Loc Ninh on Halloween night in 1967. It had been a nightmarish battle, mostly for the Viet Cong who attacked the 25th in human waves from the surrounding rubber tree plantation, running headlong into American artillery firing fishhook-like ammo at point-blank range. Miraculously some of the enemy made it to the barbed wire and sandbag perimeter and engaged American infantry in close combat. From a makeshift foxhole that had been made by an enemy mortar round, Mick watched the fighting in the light of the artillery flashes and parachute flares being dropped from a circling airplane.

The ground beneath Mick shook with each thunderous clap of the big guns, and the electrifying crackle of small arms fire, and the screaming and shouting chilled the marrow in his bones. He was terrified that the enemy would get through, and a few did, only to be gunned down. One wound up dead in the foxhole with Mick, his face blown away from the bullet he had taken through the back of the head, an image that sometimes came back to Mick in a reoccurring dream. He would awaken from it with a scream. Afraid to go back to sleep again, lest the dream resume. Instead, he'd read, or write, maybe drink, or just think.

On this particular night he thought a lot about his undercover role and the danger it now posed since Stuart Bolshinsky had proclaimed his intent to bomb the Center. As his allie, how far would Mick be expected to go along with the plan? Mick did not like the thought of having to mess with explosives. They were just too damn volatile, especially in the hands of someone as volatile as Stuart, who Mick considered to be the personification of the proverbial "loose cannon." He was capable of causing people around him to get hurt, as many had who participated in his tirade-driven demonstrations turned riots.

Collateral damage seemed to be the least of his concerns, which worried Mick because if Stuart was serious about bombing the Center would it be done while people were in it—specifically its director David Gordon who Stuart had threatened to harm?

If Mick were involved in the planning then perhaps he'd be able to sabotage it. To do so he'd have to get even closer to Stuart, like a shadow following his every move. Mick did not want the bombing to come as a surprise without being able to warn David in time, even if it entailed helping the bastard build the damn bomb.

Not knowing where Stuart lived, Mick went to Mr. Natural's, where he could usually be found around 7 o'clock on any given night, but he wasn't there yet.

Mick let the recorder in his pocket roll anyway in the event he showed later, while Mick was still there.

Mick was hungry so he ordered something to eat while he waited—a bean sprout, avocado, tomato, cheese and red onion sandwich on whole wheat bread with mayo, and herbal ice tea, served by a woman Mick had not seen there before. She had long, curly red hair and green eyes, in a mid-length, white linen dress which was just short enough for Mick to see that she didn't shave her legs. He had heard young women complain about being expected by society to shave, especially to please men. Not many were independent enough not to, but apparently this woman was, and in a way Mick admired her for it.

As he finished his sandwich Stuart walked in and sat down at his table. After glancing about to see where the waitress had gone—a fair distance from them waiting on the only other customer—he leaned close to Mick.

"I need your help," he said in a low grave tone. The pupils of his large, brown eyes, magnified by the thick glasses he wore were dilated with intensity. He looked mad.

"How so?"

"To infiltrate the Vietnamese Studies Center ..."

Stuart looked around again. The waitress was busy behind the counter, and the customer paid no attention to them as he read while he ate.

"... and plant a bomb there."

Just as Mick feared. He squirmed and his stomach turned.

"They've heightened security at the Center since the last demonstration. I wouldn't be able to get within a stone's throw of the place now. The pigs know me too well," Stuart said, still leaning close to Mick and speaking low and deliberately, "but they don't know you. You'll need to cut your hair though, and shave, and dress a little more conservatively. You'll have to stop wearing that peace medallion for sure."

Stuart thumped it with his middle finger and smirked. "Passive resistance," he said with disgust. "King tried it and where did it get him—six feet under.

"Oh, and you'll need to start toting a backpack with books in it, and tell them that you're there to do some research on Vietnamese history for a paper. After a couple times the guard probably won't check the backpack anymore, which will eventually free it up for the bomb."

"Where's this thing coming from?"

"I'm making it at my house. Let's go I'll show you."

They rode together in Stuart's van. Mick didn't like being alone with the man in such close quarters. He smelled, not being one who bought any products made by Proctor & Gamble, a big corporation enemy of the people. And Mick considered Stuart as much of an enemy as any NVA or Viet Cong. He remembered well, how much delight the man had shown in reading Ginsberg's poem about the Vietnam War. *Let the Viet Cong win over the American Army!* the poem said.

It was surprising to see that Stuart lived in a ranch style house. It was so middle class. But inside, posters of Che, the neo-Marxists poster boy, Marx himself, and Lenin covered the walls. The licentious poster of Jane Fonda as *Barbarrella* looked totally incongruent juxtaposed with the one of Ho. The photo of her consorting with the enemy on the North Vietnamese anti-aircraft artillery gun would have been more appropriate, but it did serve to reveal Stuart's lecherous tendencies as opposed to taking women more seriously, like today's revolutionary was supposed to do.

The place was heavily cluttered with books, magazines and newspapers, mostly the *New York Times*. Stuart hailed from the Big Apple, Mick had learned, where he got his BS from Columbia. He had managed to leave enough open space for a desk with typewriter and lamp. In the kitchen, which they passed through, the sink was piled high with dirty pans and dishes, and from underneath the sink garbage tumbled out of a can onto the floor.

They went down some steps and into the basement, and spread out on a workbench under a bright light was what Mick presumed to be a partially assembled bomb. A wire connected a small, battery-powered clock radio to a large chunk of what looked like putty packed into a big tin container. Stuart waved his hand backwards over the workbench, proudly presenting his works in progress. He smiled broadly.

"When it's done all of these innocuous little parts will combine to blow that fucking Vietnamese Studies Center to bits. Don't worry, Man," Stuart said, seeing that Mick did indeed look very worried, "it won't be set to go off until you've had plenty of time to plant it and clear the building."

It was this statement that finally brought Mick to the stark realization that yes, he would be planting the bomb at the Center, and probably soon.

"So when's D-Day?" Mick asked.

"Late August, early September, before the fall semester begins. We wouldn't want any students to get hurt. It'll be set to go off when no staff are around. However …," Stuart smiled a very chilling smile, "… I've been told that the Center's director often works there alone late at night. Perhaps you could find out when one of those nights might be."

No doubt about it now, Stuart was bent on killing David in the process of destroying the Center, but by putting the bomb in Mick's hands, he'd be sabotaging the plan himself, as it would be quickly defused by police who'd be waiting for Mick to bring it in with Stuart's grubby fingerprints all over it.

And so, in a sense, Mick had become a double agent having been recruited by the Center's CIA-connected director to infiltrate SIU's SDS/Weather Underground faction, whose leader in turn assigned him to infiltrate the Center under the guise of doing research there, and to plant a bomb there to destroy it with the director in it.

But, of course, it wasn't necessary for Mick to infiltrate the Center as he was, unbeknownst to Stuart, quite well known there.

Mick went there immediately after Stuart dropped him back off at Mr. Natural's to inform David of the role he'd be playing in Stuart's plot, and to let him listen to what he had on tape.

"Carry it out to the last possible moment. I'll have people waiting to defuse the bomb. It'll have his finger prints all over it, and his voice prints all over the tapes we're accumulating."

As expected, at first the newly-hired security guard, Gus, checked Mick's backpack, and then as expected he stopped after a few visits and waved him in routinely.

He had returned, he told Mae and the others, to keep abreast with Vietnamization, because the Center would be privy to its progress unfiltered by the press through a teletype machine David had installed connecting them with the CIA office in San Francisco that received its information from the office in Saigon via satellite. This also served to confirm the suspected connection between the CIA and the Center.

"Thesis?" Mae questioned. "You're still an undergraduate aren't you?"

"Yes, but I want to keep up with Vietnamization from the very beginning," Mick explained. "By the time my thesis is actually due in two or three years when I'm working on a masters, the results of it will be known and I'll have a day-by-day chronicle of it ready-made to turn in. At least that's my plan."

"Oh," she said.

Despite it being a ploy, Mick went about researching Vietnamization in earnest. Spending so much time faking it would have been fruitless and a waste of time. If he did indeed decide to go on to graduate school, then he will have gotten a good head start on the thesis.

Vietnamization had officially begun June 8, 1969 when President Nixon announced 25,000 US troops would be withdrawn from South Vietnam, and it continued as more were periodically withdrawn throughout the rest of '69 and '70.

While withdrawing US troops was an important step toward turning the war over to the South Vietnamese Army, pacification, David informed Mick when they were working late one night at the Center, was important as well. It was necessary to win the people over to the U.S.-backed Thieu government. Its over-riding goal being basically to expand territory under government control, to retake hamlets previously lost to the VC, and to arm and train local militia and civil defense groups.

Having failed for the most part early on in the war when the Viet Cong's influence was strongest—David told Mick between puffs on his pipe—pacification began to show signs of success soon after the infamous Tet Offensive of '68 as a result of the VC being virtually wiped out.

David's occasional long-windedness came in concert with the smoking of his pipe, as if it were a part of his speech pattern. He'd often smugly puff smoke rings after saying something poignant, and rock back in his chair and admire them swirling toward the ceiling. At times David came across as a little smug. "The Viet Cong were unable to replenish their forces through the recruitment of young South Vietnamese," David said. "They've filled the missing ranks with NVA soldiers, who were in essence foreigners to their southern counterparts, particularly in the area of language, cultural background and ideology, which caused some divisiveness.

"President Thieu saw this as an opportunity for pacification to make some headway with the rural population. He's lent his personal support to it by actually appearing in the villages to encourage the inhabitants to take control of their local affairs through the democratic political process."

"Has it done any good?" Mick asked.

"Oh yes. It's resulted in the election of village councils and chiefs who have been given control over the defense groups. Some of whom have been integrated into the regular South Vietnamese Army. And surprisingly, Thieu has given the village councils control over the government's rural development funds which are being used to increase agricultural and livestock production."

"Mae mentioned something to me about a land reform program. What's that all about?"

"Every peasant gets up to a little more than eight acres of land to be used to produce rice and other crops," David said. "This year the village councils redistributed more than 600,000 acres.

"Tractors have been issued, and pumps and irrigation systems have been built too. As a result, rice yields have reached a new post-WWII high. And government troops supported by the newly-trained and armed local and regional security forces have opened roads and canals that the VC had sealed for years, allowing for the free movement of goods and ag products to the cities.

"Through pacification, the rural populace has experienced first-hand the advantages of democracy and free enterprise at the grass roots level. It has succeeded in neutralizing Communist influence in the countryside.

"In the long run, though, the outcome of the war will depend on how well the South Vietnamese government's military performs against the NVA without us. Right Mae?"

Mick looked up and saw her standing in the doorway, apparently interested in what David had been telling him about Vietnamization. She concurred with his final analysis, and then added,

"Much will depend also on the negotiating skills of the U.S. delegation in Paris if the peace talks should resume. How will they maneuver around the Communist's steadfast demand that the Thieu government be dismantled?"

"By bombing the hell out of Hanoi again," David said flatly. "But this time don't stop until they come back to the table with a white flag in their hand," and he got up and left Mick and Mae alone—the first time they had been alone since New Year's Eve. Mick hadn't called her. He had been trying to avoid situations that entailed the drinking of alcohol because of the New Year's resolution he had made not to drink for at least six months. Mae liked to drink rice wine.

Neither spoke at first, and there was tension in the silence until Mae broke the ice with an admonishment.

"Why haven't you called me?" she asked, putting her hand on Mick's arm. And why did you leave so early in the morning New Year's Day?"

"I uh, I wasn't used to sleeping on a waterbed after having so much to drink. I felt sea sick and I didn't want to embarrass myself. And as far as calling you goes, well, I...."

"Never mind, Mick, I'm sure you have your reasons," she said, mercifully letting him off the hook. "But I did enjoy our evening together very much. Would you like to do again sometime? I mean dinner of course." She smiled.

"Sure." Mick quickly calculated the six months were about up, give or take a week or two. "Anytime," he said gladly.

"Good, then give me a call," Mae said. "This time maybe we can cook out steaks and drink beer, American-style since it's summer."

Mick vowed to call her soon. And he did, and they ate steaks and drank beer—a brand Mae bought because she said it had a cute label of a deer on it—Buckhorn, a rot gut Kentucky brew that went for 89 cents a six pack. Mick got too drunk on it and rice wine to do what they had done New Year's Eve, and he passed out on Mae' waterbed. And this time it was she who left early for the Center, being a Monday morning, but not before Mick had crawled to the bathroom and puked his guts out.

Chapter 29

▼

Throughout the summer, as time approaching Stuart's planned bombing of the Center ticked away, Mick kept in touch with him almost daily to make sure nothing had changed. It was important to keep David apprised, for when the moment came, sometime in early fall, he'd be ready with the state police after Mick brought the bomb in in his backpack.

"The guard has stopped checking my backpack," he informed Stuart.

"I thought they would. Have you met the director yet?"

"Yes, he's assisted me some with the research I'm supposedly doing."

"What's the subject of your research?" Stuart asked.

"Vietnamization."

"Vietnamization?" And he launched into one of his breathless, raging diatribes. "Now isn't that big of Uncle Sam to allow the Vietnamese to fight their own civil war," Stuart said jeeringly. "How ironic. We're about to have another civil war here over theirs. This country hasn't been so divided since 1861. On the one hand you've got what Nixon calls the 'silent majority,' in other words, those who go along with whatever their government decides like a nation of sheep. And then there are those of us who, when they think the government is wrong, stand up and say so, as is our Constitutional right." His rage increased.

"We're standing up against a government who uses its gestapo police to gun us down, so we have no choice but to bare arms as is written in the Constitution, and in my book that includes bombs. That said, I think you'd be interested in knowing, since your supposedly researching the subject now, Vietnamization may not be what it seems. Through the Weather Underground intelligence network we recently learned that the troop withdrawal aspect of it may just be a smoke screen to cover a planned invasion of North Vietnam by the US."

"What?"

Mick acted shocked, in fact he was. He knew right then that the enemy—Stuart, the SDS, the Weather Underground, did indeed have a mole in the Center as David had suspected, and it, he, she, whatever, had taken the bait. That being the key to the file cabinet containing the phony documents about an invasion David had contrived to entrap.

"Under the smoke screen of troop withdrawals they are actually being repositioned at Guam from where the surprise invasion will be launched."

"Unbelievable," Mick said, looking more astonished than ever.

"Yeah, I know, that's why I've been hesitant to leak it to the press," Stuart said. "It's just too damn unbelievable. But if we can come up with something to substantiate it then Nixon's head will roll."

Mick knew though that nothing existed to substantiate it, so Stuart's threat to go to the press didn't concern him unless he decided to go to them with what he had at the present time. If that happened David's scheme to entrap the mole will have backfired, although it was doubtful the press would use something so outlandish without substantiation. But if nothing else, it had succeeded in verifying that a mole was operating at the Center. So who could it be? Mick suspected no one, but did David?

"I haven't a clue," he said when Mick told him that his cockamamie invasion thing had succeeded in confirming his suspicion that a spy was operating in his midst.

"I'll dust for fingerprints on the key, files and cabinet, but I doubt there'll be any but mine. No legitimate spy would be stupid enough to leave any. They'd use wax to cover their finger tips or simply wear tight-fitting gloves.

"Sit down, Mick. Beer?"

"Sure, okay, as long as it's not Buckhorn."

"No, it's Bud."

David brought the beers from the kitchenette, sat down and lit his pipe.

Mick took a drink of the cold beer. It tasted very good. That first sip always did, like when he was a kid and his folks gave him some, then it starts tasting like the damn can.

"Whoever it is though, knows somehow when you're in the office, David, and when you're not, unless they're so bold to pilfer the files right under your nose," Mick said.

"Well, I do have a tendency to doze a little when I'm working late. From now on it'll be with one eye open.

"What I'm most concerned about, Mick, are the authentic fiscal files linking the Center to that mysterious agency which intelligence is central of." David winked, and he popped off a couple of smoke rings.

"They also reveal that we are paying someone, a Vietnam vet, to infiltrate the SDS. You are not named. All of this is technically illegal of course, because the funding comes from under-the-table without Congressional approval, but the documents do contain the signature of a very high up government official which vouches for their authenticity."

"Boy, would the press love to get their hands on those documents," Mick said. "And if Stuart did, Christ, he could very well conclude that the Vietnam vet is me. He knows I'm one."

"Don't worry, Mick, it's all in very safe keeping. Regardless, we know now that the enemy is in our midst; a North Vietnamese, I'd venture to say, who is posing as one of the South Vietnamese who works here."

"How do you know they're Vietnamese?"

"Who else would it be? There are only three Americans here; you, me and Tracy, and she's married to a GI who's in Nam. Everyone else is Vietnamese. Problem is I trust each one implicitly. There is nothing in any of their backgrounds that would give me any reason not to, as far as I know. They are all fervently anti-Communists."

Fervently? Mick couldn't help but think about some of the things Mae had said to him recently. She had spoken almost endearingly of Ho Chi Minh and the August Revolution which had put him and his Communist party in power in Hanoi in 1945, and she seemed impressed by his victory over the French in Vietnam's war of independence from them in 1954. And she seemed to be leaning in favor of a coalition government for South Vietnam as a means to ending the war honorably for all sides concerned.

But Mick did not share this with David. He thought of Mae as a good enough friend, and now a lover, to give her the benefit of the doubt. Perhaps he was just reading too much into it. Besides, with her family history there was just no way she could be a Communist spy. Her father—a highly-regarded economist/educator—had been killed by them, basically for advocating Capitalism for Ho Chi Minh's Vietnam.

"Sooner or later, though," David said, "we'll find out who it is. I just hope it's sooner. Work on Stuart, Mick. Ask questions about his intelligence source. But be subtle, don't spook him. Questions like, in reference to the informant, 'Does he, she, know when the US invasion of North Vietnam is supposed to be. Perhaps he'll unwittingly divulge the gender. That would narrow it down some."

"Okay."

"In the meantime, I'll be asking a few subtle questions of my own around here. Eventually I may have to resort to intense interrogations, or a lie detector or truth serum as a last resort. And since you're around the Center a lot, Mick, see if you can detect anything in anyone's behavior that would indicate some sort of sentiment for the Communist cause. Although I can't imagine anyone here having any of that based on their backgrounds. They've all supposedly been affected negatively in one way or another by the Communists. But apparently one of them is lying about that."

Mick stayed later than usual at the Center one night, even later than David, who had given him permission to stay as long as he needed to work on his thesis, which had developed into a bonafide project, and not just an excuse to be there for the sake of helping Stuart carry out the bombing.

"We keep the lights on all night anyway for security reasons now," David said, "someone might as well put them to good use."

Mick had settled in to the library room where he sat at a table with his research materials spread out before him. He was surrounded by four walls of shelves containing volumes on Vietnamese history and culture dating back centuries, and there was more current information that had come over the teletype about what had occurred in Vietnam as recently as the day before.

Much of the most current information dealt with Vietnamization and pacification, and it had the affect of lulling Mick half to sleep as the antique clock in the hall tick-tocked away. But the sound of something else in the hall caused Mick to perk up—the creaking of the old wooden floor. Then he heard a key in a lock. Had David come back?

Mick got up and looked out into the hall just in time to see the door of David's office closing slowly, painstakingly so, as if he didn't want anyone to hear him going in. Why would he care, it being his office? And why wouldn't he have come to the library to see if Mick was still there, and to say hello?

Mick stood in the door of the library and listened. He heard the drawer of a file cabinet slowly rolling open, then he heard a few faint clicks followed by the sound of the file cabinet drawer being carefully closed. This would not be David trying to be so quiet in his own office.

After a moment or two Mick crept down the hallway for a closer listen when the door of David's office began to open. Not wanting to be seen by whoever it was, Mick scurried back into the library. By the time he turned and inched his head back out around the doorway far enough for one eye to barely see, the intruder had swiftly vanished into the stairwell.

And by the time Mick got down the four flights of steps the intruder had spirited past the sleeping security guard and out the door. The intruder was a woman. Mick smelled perfume as he dashed out the door in pursuit, but he saw nothing in the darkness but fireflies. He went back in. Gus, the guard, had awakened.

"Gettin' some fresh air there are ya, Mick?"

"No. Someone was in Mr. Gordon's office. They ran out before I could see who it was."

"I didn't see nobody," Gus said. "Maybe you've just been working too late, Mick. Get too tired and your mind starts ta playin' tricks on ya."

"Yeah, well, I've still got some work to do. I'm going back upstairs."

"Suit churself."

The smell of perfume lingered in the stairwell, and it smelled faintly familiar to Mick. Someone he knew wore it.

Ordinarily Mick would not call David at home so late, but what had just transpired certainly warranted it. He told him what he had seen and heard.

"Wait there if you would please, Mick. I'm on my way."

David arrived at the Center shortly. He unlocked his office door and went straight to a safe-like file cabinet with a built in combination lock on it. He quickly dialed the combination and pulled out one of the drawers. After going through the files in it he declared none were missing.

"Whatever they were looking for they probably photographed it. That was the clicking you heard. God damnit, how did they know the combination? But of course they wouldn't have to know it if they had the skills of a safe cracker, or the tools. They must have picked the lock to the office. I've got the only key. You say you think it was a woman, Mick?"

"I smelled perfume."

"Based on how quickly you say she came in and got out I'd say she knew exactly what she was looking for."

"So what do you think that would be, David, if you don't mind me asking?"

"My guess is that fiscal information I told you about, and as I said the press would be very interested in it. It could shut us down faster than any damn bomb. And since we know that our little spy is in cahoots with the SDS now—how else would Stuart know about that invasion malarkey I made up—then there is the danger they'll find out about you. We've got to flush her out fast. I'll try to get some fingerprints, but again, I'd be very surprised if they left any. The perfume, Mick, you say you think you've smelled it before?"

"Somewhere. It could have been in one of my classes, maybe in a bar. I don't know. If it's popular enough it could have been anywhere—passing someone on the street even."

"There are four women working here; the three Vietnamese and Tracy. I'd bet my life that it's not her. So it has to be one of the Vietnamese. It was an inside job."

"Why do you say that?"

"Because whoever it was knew that I wasn't here, and they went straight for the most damaging information to the Center that we've got here on file. And they must have known of Gus's habit of sleeping on the job. I should have fired his ass long ago. He sure as hell won't be here after tonight. Speaking of sleep, Mick, go home and get some, then be back here by mid-morning. All the women are scheduled to be in by then. See if you can detect the scent of that perfume on any of them while it's still fresh in your mind. When will you be seeing Stuart again?"

"Probably tomorrow."

"Be especially perceptive of any change in his attitude toward you. If it has changed in any way that may indicate he's been tipped off about you being on the payroll."

"So then, David, what will you do if you find out who the spy is?"

"Simple. Nail the bitch for espionage."

"Who do you think she's working for? The SDS?"

"No, Hanoi. But indirectly for the SDS. North Vietnam considers the SDS and the Weather Underground as a allies, ever since Hayden visited Hanoi. The telegram they received from Premier Pham Dong proves it."

"And if I do detect the smell of the perfume on one of the women?"

"I'll isolate her in my office and interrogate. Now go home and catch a wink, I'll see you around ten."

Mick went home and tried to get some sleep, but he couldn't for thinking about what would happen if the spy in question had found the payroll information pertaining to him. Would she have relayed it to Stuart right away if she was working in partnership with the SDS, and she probably was based on the fact that the contrived invasion thing had found its way from the Center to Stuart. And what would happen if Mick were exposed, besides having to come in from the cold?

Mick arrived back at the Center around ten. He immediately came across Mae and Su Vinh in the library, and in order to get close enough to smell their perfume, if they were wearing any, he pretended to be interested in what they were working on. He smelled nothing.

He then found Tran Le in the lecture hall arranging chairs for the one David would be giving that evening. He helped her, but again nothing there.

He reported his findings, or lack thereof, to David.

"Well then, I believe the time has come for a little interrogation. It has to be one of the three, maybe two, or who knows, maybe all of them. Let me ask you, Mick. Of the three who would you suspect the most?"

Mick was reluctant to finger a friend, but his life, if Stuart determined he was a spy, could be hanging in the balance.

"Mae."

"Hmm, tell me why."

"Because of some of the things she has said to me lately about the war."

"Like what for instance?"

"On occasion it has sounded as though she is sympathetic to the Communist cause. She speaks rather endearingly of Ho Chi Minh and disparagingly of the South Vietnamese government, and she seems to be in favor of a coalition government that would include the Cong. And she is of the opinion Vietnamization will fail. In other words she apparently believes the Communists will win the war."

"Unsettling," David said, "coming from someone whose father was killed by them. You'd think she'd have nothing positive to say about them at all. Now that you've mentioned it, Mick, in some of her lectures she often refers to the August Revolution as if it were some great moment in Vietnam's history, and of course it would be viewed that way if one were a Communist."

"I don't know though, David. Despite all of that, Mae seems much too bourgeois to be a Communist. She likes to watch TV—Dick Van Dyke, Laugh In and Get Smart, and would you believe Hullabalu, you know, that go-go thing. She digs rock'n roll and American movies, drives a pretty nice American car, normally dresses like an American girl and she loves Big Macs."

"You ought to see the way Soviet diplomats live in Washington and New York, Mick. When Commies are abroad, especially in the U.S., they gladly indulge in whatever Capitalism has to offer, while the folks back home stand in long lines for whatever they can get to put in a pot of some paltry soup. What about Su Vinh and Tran Le? Any thoughts about them?"

"I don't know. They're somewhat of an enigma to me. They keep to themselves so much, they hardly ever speak. I guess they're just shy."

"In my capacity as director here I've spoken with them at length about the politics of Vietnam. They are decidedly pro-democracy and they are not shy about expressing their disdain for Communism. But it has been my experience that sometimes those who are the most adamant about something, are able to hide what they really believe, sort of along the line of Shakespeare's expression, 'me thinks ye protest too much,' if I may paraphrase. Being the suspicious soul that I am, perhaps that applies here. We shall see, hopefully."

"I'll start with Mae. Tell her I'd like to see her, will you please, Mick? When I'm finished with her send Su Vinh in right away, before Mae has a chance to tell her about the interrogation. Same thing with Tran Le. Try to steer Mae and Su Vinh away from her before she's been interrogated. Occupy them with questions about your research, or something."

When Mae came out of David's office she looked upset; in fact angry and she immediately left the Center in a huff. Neither Su Vinh or Tran Le saw her leave; they were elsewhere in the Center.

Mick found Su Vinh in the library and he told her David wanted to see her, meanwhile he corralled Tran Le in the library and preoccupied her, as David had asked him to do, with questions regarding her opinion of Vietnamization, an interrogation of his own of sorts.

He had never asked Tran Le about it before, and he was curious if she thought it would be a success or failure. The answer might give a hint as to whose side she really sympathized with—the Thieu government or the Cong and North Vietnamese.

He was relieved to hear her say she thought it would be successful in contrast to Mae's less optimistic assessment, which had cast suspicion on her loyalty. Suddenly Su Vinh appeared in the doorway of the library, catching Mick by surprise. David had told him to keep her away from Tran Le until she had been interrogated too, but the relaxed look on her face gave Mick the impression she felt no urgency in telling her sister about being interrogated anyway.

"Mr. Gordon would like to see you now, Tran Le," she said with a smile.

Tran Le left and Su Vinh sat down at one of the tables in the library where she had been working before Mick told her David had wanted to see her. She seemed not the least bit upset about the interrogation. Mick left and went to the lecture hall with a book and read, killing a little time until Tran Le's session with David ended. About a half hour later she came down the hall past the lecture room toward the library. Mick read awhile longer before going to David's office to ask him how it all went. He frowned, shook his head slightly, sat down at his desk and sighed.

"The sisters have mutual alibis for last night," he said. "They live together and each vouches that the other remained home all night. It rained unexpectedly, as you may recall, and both were running all over the house closing windows. It's air tight. I asked them a few questions about their opinions of Vietnamization and what they thought would become of their country should the Communists win. None of their answers indicated to me that they might have Communist leanings."

"So what about Mae? She left here very upset ya know," Mick said.

David fidgeted with his unlit pipe. The frown on his face remained.

"Yes, I know. Her alibi can't be substantiated, and it, the one she provided is somewhat embarrassing to her. Plus, her answers to the other questions I asked cast a little doubt on her loyalty, although I must give her credit for being brutally candid about what she thinks of Vietnamization. She thinks it will fail. I can't say that means she is pro-Communist, although she does think a coalition government that includes the Viet Cong would be a reasonable alternative to the total dismantlement of Thieu's government."

"So just what was her alibi?" Mick asked.

David lifted an eyebrow and grinned.

"She said she was in bed with a lover …,"

Mick felt a tinge of jealousy; actually he felt more than a tinge.

"… an SIU professor who is married, so she won't reveal who it is, therefore her alibi cannot be checked out." David's grin disappeared.

"As it stands right now, Mick, she's our number one suspect, but we need hard evidence, like photographs of the fiscal files. I'm sure that's how she would have captured the information, unless she's got a photographic memory. Incidently, I dusted the lock and safe this morning and there are no fingerprints but mine. Listen, you two have dated, right?"

"A couple times," Mick said.

"You need to get together with her again, as soon as possible, at her house, ideally tonight. Call her and tell her you'd like to come over and talk with her about what made her so upset today. Didn't you once tell me that Mae is fond of libations?"

"Rice wine. She has an ample supply of it at home, imported from Nam."

"And she likes to entertain her guests with it, I believe you said."

"As soon as you walk in the door she's there waiting with two glasses of it."

"Spike her second or third drink with this if you can get her to leave it for a moment."

David presented Mick with a pencil-thin, glass vile containing a white powdery substance.

"She'll never know what hit her. In the morning she'll just think she drank too much. While she's out you can have a little look around for the photographs and whatever you can find that would link her to the North Vietnamese Communist Party and the SDS. If we can establish some connection then we could nail her for espionage since she's a US citizen now; aiding and abetting the enemy, etc. etc. And if she is connected to the SDS, i.e. Stuart Bolshinsky, then we can nail his ass too, as a co-conspirator, for the same damn things. Most importantly though, if she's the one who accessed the fiscal files and you can find some evidence of it tonight, while she's out, then hopefully we can head her off at the pass before she gets to Stuart with whatever she's got, if she hasn't already."

"And if she has?"

David finally lit his pipe and rocked back in his chair.

"Well then, as I've said before, the Center's ties to that mysterious agency of which intelligence is central will be exposed along with the role you're playing with us. They may ascertain that it's you through logical deduction since she knows that you are a Vietnam vet and that you have met with me here in private a couple of times. I've led them all to believe it was done for the purpose of discussing the possibility of having you do a short lecture series on your experiences as a reporter in Nam.

"Again, Mick, be aware, like with Stuart, of any change in her attitude toward you, which may indicate that she, that they know about you. But we won't let on that we know that they may know, if you follow me." He smiled. "Do I sound like an Abbot and Costello routine? Anyway, we still need you to assist Stuart in carrying out his bombing plan in order to get his prints on the device after it's been disarmed here. I doubt if he's building the thing wearing gloves—too cumbersome for the delicate wiring they require."

"You're right, I've seen him piddling with it. He doesn't wear gloves."

"By the same token he'll need your help getting the bomb into the Center, so even if he does learn of you he may act as if he doesn't so as not to scare you off. First things first though. Call Mae right away."

Mick did under the pretense of wanting to talk to her about what had made her so upset that day.

"Yes, please, Mick, come over."

He got there about seven, and as expected May was waiting with two warm glasses of rice wine.

"So you noticed I was upset when I left the Center?"

"Yes, why?"

"David called me on the carpet as they say."

"About what?" Mick asked playing dumb.

"He wanted to know where I was last night. I did not like him delving into my personal life."

"Why did he want to know that?"

"Someone had opened a top secret file in his office. Apparently he suspects me."

"I think he must suspect others too then, Mae. He also met with Su Vinh and Tran Le."

"Sit down, Mick. Here, on the couch with me."

They sat down close together and this time Mick caught a tell-tale whiff of the perfume in question; the perfume he had smelled in the stairwell of the Center the night before. It sickened him to think that Mae was the one. It angered him too, that she had deceived them, pretending to be an ally, when in fact, so it seemed, she was an enemy spy.

But of course the same could be said of himself. He was spying on the SDS while pretending to be one of them, and he had come to Mae's this night under the pretense to console her, only to drug her and snoop around her house looking for evidence that could help convict her of treason no less.

"I was particularly insulted by his insinuation that I have Communist leanings just because I have stated in private on occasion, but not in lectures, that the acceptance of a coalition government by the Allies may be the only way the North Vietnamese will negotiate a settlement that would end hostilities, honorably, for all concerned. I'll get some more wine."

She went to the kitchen and returned with an entire cannister of it. She filled their glasses and quickly drank most of what she had poured in hers, then filled it again. At the rate Mae was drinking Mick thought perhaps he wouldn't need to slip her that Micky Finn; she'd drink herself into a stupor without it. When she went to the bathroom, leaving half a glass of wine, he sprinkled the powder in and it quickly dissolved. Mae came back and drank it, and before she could get the next full sentence out of her mouth she passed out. Mick picked her up cradled in his arms, carried her in to her bed and laid her down. When she awoke Mick hoped, she'd think she had simply gotten drunk and gone to bed with her clothes on. He then began to have that little look around, starting first at a desk.

The middle drawer contained a couple of pencils, a note pad, paper clips, a roll of stamps and rubber bands, and an address book with telephone numbers. One of them was Mick's. Some were of people in Los Angeles and Saigon, mostly Vietnamese; Su Vinh's and Tran Le's in Carbondale and David's at the Center. There was a phone number without a name underlined in red. Mick wondered if that would be Mae's secret lover's.

There were personal papers in one of the other drawers; general stuff regarding the payment of bills, bank statements, a car insurance policy and—and a receipt indicating she had taken a roll of film to K-Mart that day to be developed. Allow three days it said. Could this particular roll contain photos of the fiscal files?

He went back to the bedroom, checked on Mae, and then he began to search through her dresser drawers. She had a delightful variety of underwear, some of it designed obviously to cover the bare minimum. Mick tried to picture her in it, although he had actually seen her completely without it.

On the floor of the closet were countless pairs of shoes. Yes, Mae had become an American girl all right. But of course females all over the world, regardless of nationality, were afflicted with the fetish, it being a congenital thing. They were born to shop for shoes.

Beneath the pile of shoes something caught Mick's eye; a white address label on a brown box shipped by UPS from—Mick took a closer look, pushing aside shoes—from Saigon via San Francisco to li'l ole Carbondale. Hmm, what could this be?

He cleared away more shoes. The top of the box was partially open. Through the flaps he saw what appeared to be the points of a star; a yellow one, sown on a bi-colored cloth of red and blue. Curious he thought. He struggled to pull the box free of the shoes, opened it further and unfolded the cloth and in his hands he held a Viet Cong flag.

So this is where they're coming from; Mae's closet of all places. Mick glanced over his shoulder at her sleeping soundly on the bed. He put the flag back, folded the same way he found it, and buried the box again, beneath the shoes. They had been in disarray anyway so he doubted she'd be able to tell they had been moved.

Mick checked on Mae again, being paranoid about her waking up, even though David had assured him she'd be out cold for a least six hours. He then sat down in the living room on the couch and helped himself to a little more rice wine, feeling unnerved by the discovery of the VC flag.

The perfume, he tried to rationalize, not wanting to believe that Mae was the spy. It could be nothing more than a coincidence. Hundreds, probably thousands of women wear the same kind, but how many women in the US of A keep VC flags in their closets—who aren't Communists, unless, unless it's a souvenir captured by someone she knows. Mick felt some relief in contemplating this possibility. And just because Mae had voiced some reservation about Vietnamization, and was apparently inclined to accept a coalition government for South Vietnam if it led to peace, that didn't make her a Communist, much less a Communist spy.

It would take concrete proof to convict her of something like that; like photographs of the files which David was convinced had been taken based on the clicking noise Mick had heard following the opening of the file cabinet drawer.

"It's the common m.o. of most spies of course …," he had said, "… who want to lift information from a source without having to remove it from the premises."

Mick knew she had a camera somewhere; why else a receipt for film being developed? Despite the late hour, Mick called David at home to report on his findings; the perfume, the flag and the receipt.

"Take the receipt and pick up the photographs before she has a chance to, as soon as K-Mart opens. When again, the day after tomorrow? That's Thursday, Thursday morning."

Thursday morning Mick stood right outside K-Mart's doors waiting for them to open. When they did he made a beeline to the camera shop, presented the receipt, paid for the photos and walked out, but before he got to his car someone grabbed him hard by the arm. It was Mae.

"Mick, how the hell you get that receipt? I thought I had lost it. When I came to pay anyway they pointed to you walking out the door, and said you had the receipt. What did you do, take it when I passed out the other night? Why? Why do you want my photographs of me and friends on vacation in Los Angeles?"

Mick sheepishly opened the envelope and sure enough it contained photographs of Mae in front of the famous Brown Derby restaurant with Vietnamese people happily posing.

"Mae, I uh, I…."

"You what?"

"Let's talk, over here in my car, Mae."

They got in and Mae was breathing so heavily with anger the windows fogged up.

"David interrogated you the other day because he suspected you of sneaking into his office and going through some top secret files and photographing them."

"Yes, and you believe that his suspicion is correct? That I am some kind of spy?" she asked nearly shouting, and nearly crying. She had a very hurt look on her face.

"I didn't know for sure. He didn't know for sure. We needed evidence, so he sent me to your house to look for some."

"When I was not there you break into my house?"

"No, you were there, passed out on your bed."

"Passed out or knocked out, Mick? You give me a drug?"

"A little powder that's harmless, like a sleeping pill."

"Okay, so now you have your evidence, in your hand."

But there was still the question of the perfume and the flag.

"The night of the break in, Mae, I was doing research at the Center in the library unbeknownst to the intruder. After I heard whoever it was leaving David's office I followed her down the stairs, but by the time I got to the door she was gone."

"Why do you suspect a she?"

"Because the intruder wore perfume. I smelled it in the stairwell. The other night when I was at your house I smelled it again, on you."

"So what does that prove, Mick, I know many Vietnamese women who wear it. It's called *Lotus Mist*; very popular in Saigon. David's wife wears it too."

"David's wife is Vietnamese?"

"Of course, you did not know this?"

"No, no I didn't. He's never mentioned it."

Mick was beginning to feel quite foolish having jumped to conclusions based on photos of files she didn't possess, at least as far as he knew right now; there could be another roll of film somewhere. And the perfume; that was now explained, sort of. The flag though, how could she explain that.

"A good friend is an officer in the South Vietnamese Army. It was taken in a battle," she said. A souvenir after all.

"Mae, I just don't know what to say."

"You could start with 'I'm sorry.'" She said softly, her anger having subsided some.

"I'm sorry."

"Did David tell you about my alibi?"

"Yes, but you don't have to explain that."

"Thank you."

"I hope we can still be friends." Mick said.

"More than that—partners," Mae replied.

"Partners?" Mick asked, wondering in what way.

"Yes, in trying to find out who this spy is, along with David of course. Hopefully once you've told him about the photos and the flag and the perfume, I'll be vindicated despite me not wanting to name the other person who could collaborate my alibi on the night in question."

"I'd have to say, based on what we know now," David said with apparent relief when Mick met with him that afternoon, "Mae is no longer our number one suspect. I'm willing to give her the benefit of the doubt regarding her alibi. I'll call her and let her know ASAP. However, and I'd bet the farm on it, photos of the fiscal files do exist, which is especially dangerous for you if they fall into the hands of Stuart. And if the press gets a hold of them too, then we'll be shut down for sure, as a result of the public outcry over the Center being connected to that agency of which intelligence is central of."

"So then, David, since Mae is no longer the leading candidate, who is?"

"I haven't a clue now, although I still suspect it's a woman, unless Nguyen Lu wears perfume. I have noticed that his wrist tends to be a little limp at times, and he walks a bit on the tips of his toes. Seriously, though, again, perhaps we can get some hints as to who it might be through Stuart by asking questions about his intelligence source, but not too many. We don't want to arouse his suspicion, he's paranoid enough already. Remember, we've still got a bomb to deliver with his prints on it, and you're the delivery boy. When? Around the first of September?"

"As far as I know right now."

"This is August 30. You have told him what nights I usually work late, right, Tuesdays and Thursdays till at least midnight? That should narrow it down some if he is really intent on killing me."

Mick met with Stuart that night at Mr. Natural's, and any fears of him knowing were immediately put to rest. He seemed genuinely excited to see him.

"Count down three days, Man!" and he smiled. "Let's go to my house."

They rode together in Stuart's van, and Mick immediately noticed behind the driver's seat, lying in a brown box of the postal type, like the one he had recently seen in Mae's closet, a VC flag. It was Stuart of course, who was the source of the god damn things that were showing up at the demonstrations. The hair on the back of Mick's neck stood up. He was in the presence of the enemy.

When they got to Stuart's house they went straight to the basement, and approaching the workbench like a father creeping up on his sleeping baby so as not to disturb it, Stuart pointed proudly to the finished bomb.

"It'll fit quite nicely in your backpack, Mick, don't you think?"

The thought of handling the thing made his scalp crawl.

"Pick it up at nine o'clock Tuesday night. It'll be set to go off at ten."

After Stuart dropped Mick off back at Mr. Natural's, he drove home and called David.

"It's a go; Tuesday night. I pick the bomb up at nine at Stuart's house. It'll be set to go off at ten."

"Perfect. He picked one of the two nights you told him I'd be working late. That's intent to commit murder. The state police bomb squad will be waiting. It'll be defused, dusted for prints, and then we'll bust the sonofabitch."

Chapter 30

Tuesday night Mick arrived at Stuart's around 8:30 p.m.. They went to the basement.

"She's set to go off at ten," Stuart reiterated.

He took Mick's backpack, unzipped it and sat it on the workbench next to the bomb, which he picked up gingerly and placed oh-so-carefully in the backpack. He slowly lifted it off the bench by the straps and handed it over to Mick.

"Walk softly, you're carrying a big stick."

It felt heavy as an iron pipe packed with explosives would, and Mick's legs felt shaky as he walked up the steps holding the backpack away from his body so as not to bump it. He was just as careful not to bump it on a step or against the wall. Stuart followed him to the front door.

"Drive slow, watch for pot holes, don't go over railroad tracks or speed bumps. In an hour that right wing propaganda center will be dust and smoke," he said. "With a little blood mixed in."

Mick forced a grin and nodded in response. He walked to the car and put the bomb-laden backpack on the front seat and drove off very slowly, both hands gripping the steering wheel tightly. Breathing did not come so easy. He felt light headed and numb, in fact so numb he couldn't feel his foot on the gas pedal. It was as if he were floating down the street, until suddenly, about halfway to the Center, a dog darted out in front of the car. Mick instinctively broke, without thinking about the bomb, to avoid it, but too late. The dog ran off limping and yelping into a nearby grove of trees and sat down licking at one of its hind legs. Mick got out and went to see how badly the dog had been hurt. As he approached, the dog, a beagle, cowered and whimpered, but it appeared to be okay—no blood at least.

Just as Mick leaned forward, hand extended to comfort the dog, in a thunderous flash like a lightning hit, the car, about thirty yards away, exploded. Mick, reacting as he did to incoming mortars and rockets in Nam, laid out flat and covered his head with his arms as shrapnel-like pieces of the car ripped through the trees, and debris, some flaming, showered down all around. Miraculously, none of it hit him. He didn't know about the dog; it was long gone.

Soon there were sirens and the police came, followed by a fire engine, along with an ambulance. A cop spotted Mick on the ground and came over to him.

"You okay?"

"Yeah, I think so."

"Was that your car?" the cop asked.

"Yes it was."

Mick looked at what was left of it being hosed down by firemen. Aunt Jenny's cherry, aqua and white, '58 Chevy Impala was now nothing more than a charred hunk of junk yard scrap.

"What the hell happened?"

"I don't know. I hit a dog and came over here to see if it was okay and boom."

"Were you smoking?"

"No."

"Strange that it would just blow like that all of a sudden," one of the cops said. "You weren't hauling any kind of explosives were you, like dynamite?"

"Yes sir, as a matter of fact I was."

"What?"

"If we could go to the Vietnamese Studies Center on campus I'll explain."

But Mick couldn't explain it to himself. Had braking suddenly caused the bomb to go off? If so, why the delay? Had the timing mechanism malfunctioned? Or, had it been purposely timed to go off before he got to the Center?

After a wrecker came to tow Mick's former car away, two of the cops escorted him up to David's office where he and the state police bomb squad were waiting.

"Where's, what the...."

David was confused seeing Mick with police and without a bomb.

"It went off on the way over here. Didn't you hear it?"

"So that's what that was. We thought it might have been a sonic boom."

Mick explained what had happened, and David explained as briefly as possible to the two Carbondale cops the reason for the bomb squad being there.

One of the bomb squad said if braking for the dog would have caused it to explode it probably would have happened immediately, not a couple minutes later.

"Yes, the timing mechanism may have malfunctioned, or it had been set to go off at that time," he said.

"In which case," David said, "it was probably because Stuart knows about you, and with a little intense questioning," he looked at the cops and grinned, "we can find out from whom. That would be our spy. And even without fingerprints on the bomb, or the bomb itself, we know he built it and gave it to Mick to transport to the Center. You've got what was said when he handed the bomb over to you on tape, right, Mick."

"Yeah, unless my heart pounding drowned it out."

"It's time to bring this guy in," one of the cops said. "Where's he live, Mick?" David asked.

"1010 Mill Street."

Chapter 31

With Stuart busted and behind bars (no bail—risk of flight) in Carbondale awaiting extradition to Chicago for a federal trial for conspiring to bomb a government building and attempted murder, Mick's services were no longer needed by the Center except for appearing at the trial as the prosecution' key witness, so he was paid in full—ten thousand dollars—for having successfully infiltrated the Weather Underground faction of SIU's SDS. He was now free to simply be a Vietnam vet going to school on the GI Bill again.

Regarding the spy, since David had cleared everyone whom he originally suspected, the trail went cold.

"But I still think it's a woman, and a Vietnamese, because of what Mae said about the perfume you smelled being popular among them. She may be able to help us, that is help me since you're no longer on the payroll. She knows most of the Vietnamese around here, although there aren't that many."

While Mick was no longer employed by the Center as it were, he continued to hang out there doing research for his thesis, which Mae sometimes assisted him with. She seemed to have gotten over her resentment for being suspected of being the spy, but the nature of their relationship had changed. It was strictly friendship now, as she admitted to Mick that she had fallen in love with the professor of her alibi fame. His name remained anonymous.

At the same time, Mick renewed his ties with the Club the first Friday night the fall semester began.

As soon as he walked in John spotted him through the crowd and pointed to a booth. From where Mick stood he could see Reggie and Trudy sitting in it. He hadn't seen them in months. When they saw him they whooped and hollered, got up and hugged him and each planted kisses on his cheeks. He felt embarrassed to arouse such a commotion.

"Where ya been ya sonofabitch. Why haven't you come by the house to see the baby? He looks just like you ya know."

"Reggie, shut up," Trudy said. "Sit down, Mick, I'll get another pitcher and a glass."

"Seriously, where ya been, Man?" Reggie asked, settling back down in the booth. Something Mick was glad to see him sitting in instead of the wheelchair.

"John hasn't told you?"

"Only that you went back to Springfield for awhile. You're aunt was sick, right?"

"Yeah." That explained it for the moment. He'd tell him the real reason later perhaps.

Trudy came back with the beer and a glass for Mick.

"The baby looks exactly like Reggie," she said, countering Reggie's snide remark about it looking like Mick. "Handsome as can be. You'll have to come and see him."

"I will as soon as I get another car."

"Another car? What happened to the one you had?"

"Small accident."

"Mines for sale," Trudy said.

"That yellow VW bug?"

"That's the one."

"Looks too much like a lemon. I'm thinking about getting a truck."

"You, a truck?" Reggie laughed.

"Hey, they come in handy," and Mick proceeded to tell them about the land he planned to buy, with financial assistance from his Aunt Jenny he told them, at Lake Wells, and the stone house he wanted to build, where he'd write his book.

"Sounds pretty ambitious to me," Reggie said skeptically.

"Like you learning to walk again?" Mick countered.

Reggie laughed. "Touche."

So how you doing with that anyway, Reg?" Mick asked, referring to Reggie walking again.

"Getting stronger every day."

"Good, I could use your help building that house."

"Fine, but I'm not sure we'll be staying around here after I graduate in December. We love it here, but there just aren't enough good paying jobs. I've got some pretty good prospects in Chicago. Well, we've got a baby sitter waiting."

"Love ya, Mick, bye, you know where we live," Trudy said.

"Yeah, love ya, Mick." Reggie fluffed Mick's hair, chugalugged what was left of his glass of beer, and they left, and Mick went up to the bar and drank until last call. Back to old habits again.

Chapter 32

Most of the classes Mick took in the fall semester of 1970 related to the broadcast journalism curriculum. He had gotten away from it the past two semesters taking political science courses to make Stuart think that was what he was in to.

But broadcast journalism was not without its politics. In fact, as was Mick's contention, it had become quite politicized by anti-Vietnam War, left-leaning editors and reporters who wore their sentiments on their sleeves, like Walter Cronkite and others on national TV. That was something a pure journalist whose job it is to report the news, should not do, Mick contended. His feelings irked his fellow classmates who were left-leaning wanna be journalists, as well as his professors who were has-been left-leaning journalists.

No doubt the press had sway over the American people's opinion about the war, and consequently had influenced political as well as military decisions in conducting it.

Beginning with Johnson, then Nixon, our presidents felt the press-induced pressure to end US involvement in it, which Nixon was now trying to do with Vietnamization. To Mick, that meant we were no longer committed to helping keep South Vietnam, and perhaps the rest of Southeast Asia, free of Communism. It would be left solely up to the South Vietnamese now, something that didn't sit well with Mick. He saw this as an abandonment of the original commitment we had made to them.

After the success of the Cambodian Raids of '70 however, Vietnamization looked promising, so an emboldened Washington and Saigon decided to follow them up with a similar campaign into Laos at the beginning of 1971. The goal of which, David informed Mick, was to occupy and destroy North Vietnamese Army base areas in southern Laos, and to interdict the Ho Chi Minh Trail there.

"But no U.S. ground forces were permitted to participate," David said, "because the Church/Cooper Amendment that was passed after the Cambodian Raids forbids them from setting foot in that country again, or Laos.

"The amendment also prohibits American advisors and forward artillery and air controllers from accompanying South Vietnamese soldiers into Laos, which greatly diminishes their access to superior fire power," David told Mick.

To make matters worse, he said, it was learned through intelligence that the NVA had discovered details of the operaton from press leaks, and from agents working within ARVN, so the enemy had prepared for it by bringing in more troops and artillery and tanks.

Despite all of this the operation was launched the first week of February. By the last week of February, under a relentless enemy onslaught of infantry, artillery and tanks from an estimated four divisions, the South Vietnamese (outnumbered by approximately 40,000 to 8,000) withdrew back into South Vietnam, and a major test for them in fighting the NVA on the ground on their own (without U.S. air support) had failed miserably and Vietnamization suffered a severe setback.

"From the outset the operation was doomed when once in Laos the South Vietnamese stopped their advance," David said.

"Why'd they do that?" Mick asked.

"Because Thieu told his commanders to cancel the operation once they had taken 3,000 casualties—dead and wounded. With a national election coming up in the fall, heavy casualties would be detrimental to his candidacy. This is what happens, Mick, when you've got a politician medaling in military affairs, and his desire for votes dictates battlefield decisions. There's no doubt in my mind it's influencing Nixon's decision to Vietnamize, which is nothing more as far as I'm concerned than a veiled retreat."

Despite the failure of the Laotion raids, some of which could be blamed directly on Thieu, he was re-elected President in August of '71 in an election that raised questions about the validity of its democracy. The crafty Thieu forced the other two leading candidates to the sidelines by ram rodding a law through the National Assembly that drastically restricted the number of candidates eligible for election. Consequently he ran unopposed garnering more than 90 percent of more than six million votes cast by the South Vietnamese people.

The Laotian Raid, like the Cambodian Raids of 1970, stirred up the antiwar movement again. It had picked up momentum over the last two years, and had grown to include, in addition to the typical draft-dodging, leftist, radical students, a coalition of Blacks and Hispanics. They opposed the war on moral grounds, but also because it diverted huge sums of money from LBJ's Great Society programs.

There was also a new group called the Vietnam Veterans Against the War who caught Mick's attention at the Club one night. They were there to recruit fellow vets to join them on a bus trip in April for a big demonstration in Washington, D.C. He was asked to go by one of the VVAW guys, Bobby West, who knew Mick's name and was aware of the letters-to-the-editors Mick had written, which in reality had only been a stratagem to convince Stuart that he was against the war. His support for it had been waning of late, yes, but he certainly wasn't ready to publicly demonstrate against it. Besides, weren't we in the process of getting out anyway? It had to be a process. We couldn't just, in one fell swoop, pull the rug out from beneath the feet of the South Vietnamese.

"Hell no, just a few good tugs at a time will do," Mick said to himself while sipping a beer as he watched these vets-turned-peaceniks passing out fliers promoting the bus trip to Washington D.C. to protest the war. "A little too late isn't it, the war is over, we've botched the god damn thing. The Laotian Raid made that plain. It had exposed the Thieu government and its army's ineptitude.

"Vietnamization; what a sham. It's just a euphemism for a U.S. retreat."

Mick became more and more disgruntled as he drank. "What a waste. All those GIs who had died, for what, to leave Vietnam in disgrace?" Mick got drunk again.

Chapter 33

At the end of June in 1971 the expected happened. David got a call from a reporter at the *Southern Illinoisan* newspaper saying she had received information from an anonymous source in the form of photographs of financial records linking he and the Center with the CIA. She wanted to talk with David and university officials about it before doing a story.

"And she also wants to know if we infiltrated the SDS," David said as the two sat in his office. "All I can do is deny, delay, deny, delay."

"Deny the authenticity of the photos?" Mick asked.

"That's right. But she may try to invoke the Freedom of Information Act to get the real thing—the files themselves. She'd have to go through the university's public information office. But she won't find them, they no longer exist in my files. If she's dogged enough though, she might be able to request the originals that would be on file at headquarters in D.C.. By the time she got through all the bureaucratic red tape and obfuscation though, this war will be over and the Vietnamese Studies Centers will be closed down anyway."

"Or, David, maybe you could convince the reporter that the fiscal files were phony too, and were being used as bait. Like that invasion shit you contrived, to entrap the mole who we think is an enemy agent working for Hanoi in conjunction with the SDS in an attempt to show that the Center, and others nationwide, are funded by the CIA through the host universities, which will invariably cause them to be shut down."

"Hmmm." David lifted an eyebrow and rubbed his chin. "That's a thought. I'll sleep on it, in the meantime I'm going home for one of those delicious little TV dinners. Get Smart is on tonight. Love that shoe phone."

"TV dinner? Doesn't your wife cook?"

"She's gone back to Vietnam to visit old friends for awhile. First time since we've been married and she came to the States with me."

"Where were you married?"

"Saigon. She worked as a secretary for the agency there. That's how we met."

"Is that where she's from?"

"No, in fact she's originally from North Vietnam—Haiphong. Like many she fled there because of Communism."

"Did she know you were destined for cosmopolitan Carbondale, Illinois?"

"Oh yes, she was eager to come. She wanted to see what life was like in middle America. Little did she know that Carbondale was more like Berkeley than Midwestville. Well, good night, Mick."

"Yeah, see ya later, David."

Mick went home to eat too, and to feed Jazzpur. On the way he saw a dog trotting with a limp down the sidewalk. It looked like the one he had hit. He pulled over in his truck, which he had recently bought to replace the Impala, and got out and called to it. The dog stopped, looked around and perked up as Mick whistled for it to come. It came, head lowered, wagging its tail furiously. Mick pet it on the head and in return the dog licked his hand.

"Don't know what your name is, Boy, but you're Lucky to me. Hitting you saved my life ya know. You look hungry. Are you hungry, Lucky, huh? Get in the truck let's go."

Mick opened the door, picked the dog up; not too big of a dog, and sat him on the seat and took him home.

Jazzpur was not pleased. He hissed and spit, and humped up sideways with his tail looking like a bottle brush. Lucky backed up and sat down, his head cocked looking at the cat. Being a stray he no doubt had seen many before in the alleyways posturing like this. Enough to know that some meant business, judging from the long scratch scar on his nose. He kept his distance and Jazzpur his. Mick fed Lucky two cans of cat food and he wolfed them down in short order and looked for more.

"No more yet, Lucky. So I guess you're the one I hit, huh?"

Mick examined the leg the dog limped on, and he felt a knot on the hip.

"We'll have a vet look at that. Probably too late to do much about it now, though."

Jazzpur was perched on a table scowling, not at all enthralled with the attention Lucky was getting from Mick.

Chapter 34

It took a few weeks for the check of $10,000 Mick had been given for infiltrating the SDS to clear. Even though it was a government check, the bank in Carbondale had difficulty tracking it through the various agencies who passed the buck in accounting for it. Finally a small, obscure bank in a Virginia suburb of Washington, D.C., the Truman Bank & Trust, vouched for it. This money trail would be damn hard to follow for that reporter at the *Southern Illinoisan*.

Mick then contacted the realtor, Sheila, in Murphysboro, who had been handling the land he wanted to buy. Happily he found out it was still available, but she said that Mick wasn't the only one interested. A woman from Carbondale had also inquired about it.

"A woman?"

"You sound surprised," Sheila said.

"Yeah, I am. I don't know too many women who are into the woods."

"Around here with all these hippies, surely you know some," Sheila said. "Anyway, I don't think Mr. Wilson cares about the gender, only who bids the highest. He'd like to meet with you both. So far you are the only two. I'll call you back with a time. Hopefully it'll be convenient for you. Will you be home tomorrow morning?"

"Yeah, sure."

"I'll give you a ring then."

The phone rang at nine. "Mick, this is Sheila. Can you meet Mr. Wilson at the property around two this afternoon?"

"You bet."

"How'd ya like to go for a ride, Lucky. Haven't met a dog yet who didn't like to go for rides. I know you wouldn't Jazzpurr. Cats are too damn skittish."

Lucky bobbed his head and wagged his tail as if he knew what Mick had proposed. He followed him to the truck and hopped in and sat pretty as you please on the seat next to Mick. As soon as they took off though, Lucky gravitated to the passenger window which was already rolled down. His head was outside, ears flapping, tongue lapping at the pleasantly warm, early summer breeze.

Mick felt about as anxious as he ever had about anything, anticipating finally buying wooded land on a lake. But it was a nervous anxiousness; someone else wanted it too. Mick reached over and pet his new-found friend.

"Be lucky for me again, Lucky."

At the country road sign where Mick usually parked by the big old cedar tree, Sheila and a man were waiting. Even there she still wore high heels and a business suit. The man, a short, older gentleman, wore work clothes, a billed leather cap and boots. They shook hands when introduced.

"Mr. Wilson, this is Mick Scott."

He smiled. "Good meetin' ya, Mick. Call me Jack." He sounded southern.

"Jack, same here."

"The plot I've got here for sale is ten acres. I'm asking $150 per acre bottom line. There's one other person in the running. Whoever offers the most over that gets it. Cash on the barrel head no questions asked. Its been marked at each corner with stakes and red flags. Nice piece of land for someone who likes to hunt; there's squirrel, rabbit, deer, geese, duck, good fishin' too. Got some lunkers in that lake. Hope ya ain't too scared of snakes. There's a cottonmouth or two around. For such ornery varmits though, they're pretty shy, unless ya step on one." He laughed.

Sheila cringed and looked around on the ground where she stood.

"Well, that's about it. Like I say, whoever makes me the best offer over 150 an acre. Now why some gal would want a piece of land like this, ten acres no less, is beyond me, but these days ya never can tell. Sometimes ya can't tell the difference between fellas and gals up there in Carbondale. That's okay though, like I say, it'll go to the highest bidder."

Mr. Wilson was pretty windy, and before Mick could get away the other interested party arrived. Mick recognized her right away as one of the women who worked at Mr. Natural's, the red-headed one who didn't shave her legs. He didn't know her name. She didn't act as if she recognized him when he nodded. He waved goodbye to Sheila and Mr. Wilson and drove away.

"Where in the hell did that hairy-legged hippie chick waitress get enough bread to buy land on with her salary, Lucky? Ya say at least she's got a salary, Boy? Hey, I damn near got killed earning mine."

Mick called Sheila at four that day and offered $175 per acre.

"Okay, I'm waiting for the other party to make an offer. She said she'd call sometime tomorrow, and then I'll call you."

Around noon the next day Sheila called.

"It's yours."

Elation rushed through him. This was a dream come true. He could hardly contain himself. He resisted shouting yippee, and instead opted for "Great, wonderful, great."

"We can close on it in about two weeks. It'll take that long to dot all the i's and cross the t's," Sheila said. "Say on the 23rd."

"Okay."

"I'll call you when everything is ready to sign."

On the 23rd Mick got a call from Sheila saying they could close on the property anytime at her office in Murphysboro.

Mick went to his bank and that afternoon the deed was in his hands. It was the happiest moment of his life. Then as a friendly gesture when Mick got back to Carbondale, he went to Mr. Natural's to see the woman who had also bid on the land. She smiled good-naturedly and offered her hand in congratulations.

"I'm Anna."

"Mick."

It wasn't very busy so they had time to talk some.

"You know, I really don't need all ten acres," Mick said. "I could sell you, oh, I don't know, two or three. I could use some of that cash back. That is if you're not planning on cutting down the trees and building a K-Mart there."

She laughed. "Are you?"

"No, I'll be building a stone house on it someday though."

"Interesting. Actually two acres would be ideal for me. That's all I wanted in the first place really, but he wouldn't sell less than ten. I'm just wanting a place to get away from the lights of town. I'm a stargazer."

"With the naked eye?"

"No, I have a telescope."

"I'm kind of a stargazer too, the naked eye kind," Mick said, looking at her gleaming green eyes, which was like stargazing. "I've never seen them so bright as they look out there. It's like you can reach up and touch them they seem so close."

"I know. So how much would you want for two acres then?" she asked.

"A little less than one-fifth of what I paid for ten."

Mick did the math on a napkin.

"Cash on the barrel head no questions asked. All the acreage looks about the same topography-wise. Half of them front the lake. You could have one of the acres on the lake, and the other back through the woods at the east end of the parcel which can be accessed by County Road 7 North. Mine can be accessed by 8 North, so we wouldn't be running into each other all the time. If that sounds okay to you I'll have a surveyor plot it out and we can split the fee."

"It's a deal," she said. "Can you come back tomorrow about this time. I'll have the money then."

The surveyor marked off the two acres—one fronted the lake—with red flags on stakes at the corners. Then with Anna's permission, Mick replaced them with stacks of stones to blend in more with the environment; subtle reminders of their property boundaries between which ran imaginary fences. Good enough for friendly neighbors who had agreed not to infringe on each others' space.

That settled, Mick went about reading up on building stone houses in an old issue of *Mother Earth News* that he found at the library, and throughout the summer he occasionally visited his land. He loved the way that sounded—his land.

When the fall of '71 came he was back in the classroom, the first semester of his senior year, and at the Center keeping abreast of the war, where he got the inside scoop because of David' intelligence connections via the teletype he had installed.

While negotiations continued and then unceremoniously collapsed in late '71, the North Vietnamese began an unprecedented build up of an estimated fourteen divisions with tanks just north of the DMZ. In response, the day after Christmas, Nixon reinstated the bombing of North Vietnam south of the 20th parallel (the DMZ being the 17th). This resulted in a resounding outcry that he was again widening the war, when in fact the bombing was intended only to impede the menacing build up of enemy forces for what the Pentagon contended was a prelude to an all out invasion of South Vietnam. Washington anticipated a large scale offensive would be launched against the south sometime in the spring of '72.

It was speculated that Nixon ordered the bombing around Christmas when students were away from the campuses so there'd be no demonstrations against it. Again, apparently, the antiwar movement was dictating the Administration's strategy regarding the conduct of the war.

Mick had planned on staying around Carbondale during the break, in fact he did for Christmas, but the day after he got a call informing him that his Aunt Jenny had died after a short illness that he hadn't known about. But Mick knew it wasn't really the result of a short illness, but an acute and chronic one called alcoholism. For years she had been drinking herself to death.

Mick was a pallbearer, along with some distant relatives from Indiana—cousins who he hadn't seen since he was little. After the funeral, New Year's Eve, in the old family tradition the cousins went to Aunt Jenny's house to drink, and he went to Tommy Seno's Tap to drown his sorrow. It didn't take long. As soon as he got there, Tom Burk, who he hadn't seen in more than two years, bought him a shot, which he chased with a beer, then another, and he in turn bought Burk a shot, who returned the favor, again.

Burk had always been a hero of Mick's; since the night he saw him intervene when two notorious greaser hard guys were picking on a little Barney Fife-type at a street dance. He politely asked them to stop, to which they said, "Fuck you." Being a Golden Glove champion boxer, Burk whipped them both as the band played on. Not once did he ever brag about it. Nor did he talk about being in Nam in the infantry where he saw considerable action—enough to win a Purple Heart, and enough to make his hand shake when he drank. He used to have kind of a deceptive choir boy's face, but not anymore. He looked old around the eyes. That's where having seen combat always seemed to show.

They did talk about sports and pussy and other nonsense though, which they were forced to do practically shouting as the closer it got to midnight the more crowded the place had become—elbow to elbow, butt to butt, chests to breasts. When the climatic moment came Mick found himself kissing a strange woman, and they wound up together at a disco called the Opera House dancing beneath a crystal ball to the Bee Gees. It all made Mick quite dizzy, and he staggered outside and threw up in the snow.

He slept it off at Aunt Jenny's house where his cousins had crashed too, having had a party of their own there, and then he returned to Carbondale. He had a cat and dog to feed, and some college holiday bowl games to watch, still being somewhat interested in football, his favorite game.

Chapter 35

Entering his final semester as a senior, Mick hit the books hard wanting to graduate in June. Then he'd go on to graduate school, which he had a head start on having already begun his thesis on Vietnamization. At the end of March in '72 Vietnamization was confronted with one of it's biggest challenges when, as the Pentagon had predicted, based on the big Communist buildup of forces at the DMZ, the enemy sprang a massive offensive against South Vietnam. They employed twenty divisions, amounting to around 125,000 men who were supported by hundreds of tanks and artillery pieces.

Newspapers gave a running account of what would be a three-pronged offensive beginning March 30 around Easter. In fact the press called it the Easter Offensive.

The initial NVA attack came across the DMZ and out of Laos. It caught the greatly outnumbered 3rd Division completely off guard. After three days of fighting elements of South Vietnamese Marines nearby managed to stave off further NVA assaults. They inflicted heavy casualties on the Communists, thereby managing to prevent them from taking Quang Tri, which had appeared to be their primary objective on the northern front. But the enemy counter attacked, and again the South Vietnamese soldiers fled with their families (an old South Vietnamese Army bugaboo—families on the battlefield) and refugees to the south. NVA tanks and artillery ruthlessly fired into the mass exodus, killing an estimated 20,000 civilians. A horrendous atrocity that the world press paid relatively scant attention to. The North Vietnamese then attacked Hue, but they failed to take it while Quang Tri remained contested.

On the central front the NVA routed South Vietnamese forces defending Kontum Province, and if they took all of the province they would in effect be cutting South Vietnam in two. They attacked Kontum City, but the Allies had received advanced warning, and U.S. chopper gunships, artillery and tactical air repelled it initially. They attacked again and took the northern sector of the city but American B-52s wiped them out.

Meanwhile in Binh Dinh, the South Vietnamese took back three district towns in Kontum Province that had been lost in April and May, and the enemy's offensive on the central front also ended in failure.

The southern offensive involved three reinforced NVA divisions and remnants of various VC divisions attacking Loc Ninh and An Loc with infantry, heavy artillery and tanks. They overran Loc Ninh and surrounded An Loc but the seige was broken with help once again from American air, and the first attempt by the Communist to take An Loc had failed.

Another enemy assault on the town was attempted, and another, and they also failed as US C-123 and C-130 air drops kept the defenders well-supplied with food, medicine and ammunition. The elite 81st ARVN Airborne Ranger Group was inserted in anticipation of yet another attempt.

It came May 11, preceded by the standard artillery barrage, but in an awesome display of air power, USAF fighter bombers and B-52s laid waste to the attacking enemy. An entire regiment caught in the open literally vanished. What was left of the NVA regrouped the next day and attacked again and again, and again and again they were beaten back, and then they were counterattacked by the 81st who retook the northern sector of An Loc.

The Easter Offensive had for the most part ended in failure, although Quang Tri City remained contested. The South Vietnamese Army had fought well and in some cases gallantly, which bode well for the success of Vietnamization at this juncture. But in all of the battles the deciding factor, unquestionably was U.S. air support, and not just the bombers. The cargo planes had kept the South Vietnamese defenders well-supplied, especially at An Loc. Would they in the future survive without it?

US air power had also been brought to bare on North Vietnam while its army invaded the South. But the bombing wasn't restricted to below the 20th Parallel anymore. Nixon ordered the bombing of Hanoi and Haiphong too, in April, over the objections of course of the doves in Congress, who again accused the President of escalating, and risking nuclear war with the Soviet Union since their ships were in Haiphong Harbor supplying the north with weaponry—namely tanks, surface-to-air missiles and anti-aircraft artillery.

The newest phase of the bombing of the north had begun when it appeared the NVA invasion of the South would succeed. A strong and bold message had to be sent to Hanoi that Washington would not tolerated the invasion. So in addition to the bombing, Haiphong Harbor was at last mined, and sea traffic in and out of the harbor ceased, shutting off a main war supplies line to the North Vietnamese Army from the USSR.

Hanoi came to realize that a quick end to the war might not be so near. They thought that perhaps now negotiating in earnest would be advisable just to get the U.S. out of the way so they could have at the South Vietnamese Army again someday when American air power would no longer be a factor.

When the Easter Offensive appeared to be succeeding early on in late April and early May, Hanoi had shown little interest in negotiating, why should they have, another 70,000 US troops had been withdrawn, with another 20,000 scheduled to leave in June. And they had been winning on the battlefield against the South Vietnamese at the time, but when the tide began to turn in favor of the South Vietnamese, the North Vietnamese changed their tune. "In addition to their fading military fortunes, North Vietnam's superpower allies, the Soviets and Chinese were leaning heavily on them to negotiate," David said when Mick asked him for some background information on the negotiation situation.

"Why?" Mick asked.

"Because the Soviets have their own needs and agenda, namely credit, wheat, arms agreements and detente. All of which are dependent on improved relations with the United States, which had suffered because of Moscow's cozy relationship with Hanoi. Our intelligence estimates that total military and economic aid from Moscow to Hanoi amounted to about $775 million with China contributing around $75 million."

"Is it expected to continue at that level since they're wanting to improve relations with us?" Mick inquired.

"Well, we know that the Soviets have pledged to continue with it through 1973, even while they're urging North Vietnam to negotiate. And as an indirect result of Nixon's visit to China in February, Mao Zedung himself, we have learned, is trying to get North Vietnam to be more flexible in negotiations for the sake of continued dialogue with Uncle Sam. Plus, it's believed that their respective economies can no longer afford to finance Hanoi's war." David paused long enough to light his pipe and he smiled. "Through a stroke of ingenious detente, it seems, Nixon and Kissinger have succeeded in driving a wedge between Peking, Moscow and Hanoi. Without the level of military aid the North Vietnamese had been accustomed to receiving from their two big allies, coupled with the impact the bombing has had on the movement of war materiel, and the defeat their armed forces suffered as a result of the Easter Offensive, Hanoi will be inclined now I believe to negotiate in earnest. As earnestly as their belligerent Communist attitude will allow.

"And to be quite honest, Mick, my sources tell me Nixon is anxious to reach an agreement too, before the ever-growing number of doves in Congress, who are in a tizzy over the bombing and mining, manage to legislate us out of the war instead of negotiating an honorable exit."

To help clarify the very complex negotiating situation for anyone who would be interested, David conducted a rather brief, but succinct lecture on it at the Center. Mick attended, along with a number of other people, including students, a couple of faculty members he recognized, a townie or two, Mick judged, based on the way they were dressed; rather formally, and a reporter whose mug shot he had seen on the editorial page on Sundays in the *Southern Illinoisan*.

"The North Vietnamese," David began, "have decided, so it seems, to begin negotiating once again, thanks in part to a few well-placed smart bombs, one of which downed the vaunted Thanh Hoa Bridge, cutting a key link in the war-supply chain coming in from Red China to Hanoi, in addition to what the B-52 and fighter-bombers have done to their troops in the South during the Communist's Easter Offensive.

"An old war eagle general I once knew said, 'when lightning bolts are brought to bare by those who have the most, an olive branch is oft returned by those who have the least.' The North Vietnamese have gotten fewer and fewer from the Soviet Union, their main supplier of high-tech weaponry, since we've mined Haiphong's harbor.

"Ironically, in January of '72 we surprised North Vietnam by offering them an olive branch of our own in the form of an 8-point peace plan which one might characterize as concessions. It requires the total withdrawal of U.S. troops and the resignation of South Vietnamese president Thieu."

David elaborated on the various points especially the most contentious one demanding that Thieu resign.

"Thieu of course sees this as a complete caving in to Hanoi's constant demand that his government be dismantled in favor of a coalition government that would include the Communists, namely the Viet Cong.

"'All the North Vietnamese want is for South Vietnam to surrender unconditionally,' Thieu has said. Standing firm in his opposition to the so-called peace plan, Thieu has reiterated that there will be no abandonment of territory to the

North Vietnamese, and no coalition government. And he adamantly demands the total withdrawal of NVA troops in direct reciprocation to the U.S. troop withdrawals.

"Nonetheless, presently, Henry Kissinger, America's chief negotiator, while continuing to meet behind the scenes with Le Duc Tho, is trying to get Thieu on board, but it may not be possible as the President I am told, views negotiations in their present state as a sinking ship for South Vietnam.

"The date of the next lecture is dependent on any note worthy breakthroughs in negotiations. Thank you all for coming. I hope we've been able to clarify what has become an extremely complex issue, at least as complex as the war itself. Good night."

Mick had taken notes on David's lecture, and after the other attendees left, he went to the Center's little library and expanded on them for his thesis, as negotiations were an integral part of Vietnamization. They would go along way in determining the political fate of South Vietnam if it survived as such.

When he had finished and walked down the hall to leave, he saw David through the open door of his office sitting at his desk, face in hands.

"David, you okay?"

"Oh, Mick, you're still here. Yeah, I'm okay I suppose, as good as a man can be whose wife is missing."

"Missing?"

"You know she went back to Vietnam for a visit. I haven't heard from her for nearly two weeks."

"My God, you mean she just up and vanished?"

"That's about it. The Saigon police have been looking for her, without any luck. She was last seen by someone who knows her, dining with a Vietnamese man at a restaurant downtown. Since then no trace."

Mick didn't know what to say except, "I'm sorry."

"I've got some friends with the agency in Saigon working on it too. I'm hoping to hear something soon."

"Well, goodnight, David. Oh, I meant to ask, heard anything about Stuart."

"No, but I'll let you know when I do. I think it'll be awhile before he goes to trial though."

"Has there been anymore activity around here that would indicate the spy is still operating in our midst?" Mick asked.

"No, not at all. It's as if she just dropped off the face of the planet," David said with puzzlement. "Hopefully Stuart, with a little friendly persuasion, will be able to tell us something about that. The two obviously had a working relationship. How else would he have known about you? He must have; he tried to kill you."

"Is the *Southern Illinoisan* continuing with an investigative story about you and the Center?" Mick asked.

"They're trying, but I've told them that the fiscal files they apparently have photos of are fake, and were used as bait to snare the spy, which they'll have to take my word for."

"What choice do they have?" Mick added. "Like you said before, they can't prove otherwise unless they can track down the originals at headquarters after going through all of the bureaucratic red tape, even if they are armed with the Freedom of Information Act. The war will be over by then. Let's just hope it doesn't end on Hanoi's terms."

"The whole god damn war is being fought on Hanoi's terms, Mick, and judging from the way negotiations are going it'll end that way too. Hey, it's time to close up shop. I've got another one of those delicious TV dinners waiting for me in the fridge," David said dejectedly. Mick didn't like seeing the man who was normally high-spirited down like that.

"Okay, David, good night," Mick said with a tone of condolence.

CHAPTER 36

While hitting the books hard his last semester, wanting to graduate on schedule, Mick cut back considerably on his drinking. However, once in awhile on weekends he indulged a little, but not at The Club. A bad kitchen fire had forced it to close for more than a month, which forced Mick to find another place to socialize—a place called PK's, short for Pizza King. But the pizzas were of the frozen variety—Tombstones—and were baked in a portable stainless steel oven on the back bar.

PK's was primarily a hippie juicer hangout, although plenty of marijuana was smoked too, in the little beer garden out back where Mick partook now and then, providing it at times. He always kept a stash on hand, harvested from the wild stuff that came up every year in his jungle-like back yard where Jan had grown it before he died.

Actually the clientele was fairly mixed. There were pool tables to cater to the sharks, some of whom were women, and women drank there in about equal numbers. There was a fairly wide age-range too, but most were young and hip-looking.

One of the guys Mick toked up with occasionally, had introduced himself as Gary. Mick had noticed him for the first time when he walked into PK's one night. Actually it was hard not to notice him. Although he was not especially tall he stood out, because of his build, and the way he carried himself. He had medium-length black hair, and a neatly trimmed mustache and closely-cropped beard, covering but not concealing his square chin and jaw. He wore cut-off blue jeans and leather sandals, and his stout, muscular legs bulged as he walked with a confident stride. His shoulders and arms were muscular too; a tight fit for the black t-shirts he usually wore, and his waist was trim. But Mick admired him only as a man admires another man for his athletic appearance and nothing more. And he admired the women Gary attracted. He had seen them leaving with him on occasion after long, intense conversations. He was a rapper for sure.

On one of the nights they toked up together out back in the beer garden, Mick told Gary about his plans to build a stone house, and he offered to make Mick a stained glass window for it, for a price of course.

"Let's go to my pad, I'll show you what I do."

Mick followed him in his truck. Gary drove a VW bus like Stuart's. He lived in a typical college town apartment complex, but the inside of his apartment belied what Mick thought was typical for a typical college student, which he would soon find out Gary wasn't.

The decor looked like what Mick perceived to be sort of Americana 1930s. There was an old, ornate, stand up lamp with an old fashioned yellow shade casting soft light on the back and arm of a stuffed, maroon felt chair that blended perfectly with a maroon rug whose green vine leaves and yellow flower pattern were highlighted by the splash of golden light the lamp provided.

"Have a seat," Gary said.

The couch, which matched the chair, looked inviting.

Gary put a record on—The Doors—and lit a candle that sat in a saucer on an antique travel trunk that served as a coffee table which looked more hippie 1960s than 1930s. On the trunk Mick noticed a paperback book by Jack Kerouec entitled *Darma Bums*.

"Beer?" Gary asked.

"Sounds good," Mick said, being one who rarely turned down such an offer.

Gary left and came back with two green bottles of beer—a German bock. He sat in the chair and began to roll a joint over a wooden tray after sorting the seeds out on it.

"When will you be building this stone house?" he asked.

"I've already started actually; gathering the stones for it on the land I just bought."

Gary looked impressed. He lit the joint and they passed it back and forth between tokes.

"So, you do stained glass, huh?" Mick asked.

"Yeah, come on in here."

Mick followed Gary to another room.

"This is my studio."

Scattered about on a large table in the middle of the room were pieces of stained glass and strips of lead, a variety of small tools, a soldering gun, a roll of solder and a partially completed window. What really caught Mick's eye was an elongated, octagonal stained glass enclosed lamp comprised of red, yellow and blue diamond shaped segments hanging from the ceiling on a brass chain in a corner of the room.

"I could make you a window like the one I'm working on here. This one is going to my mother for the landing of a staircase. One this size; a 2-by-4 foot rectangle would run you around two hundred, two-fifty."

"Yeah, well, I'm not sure what size I would want. I haven't even drawn up the plans for the place yet."

"*Fox Fire* probably has a book on how to build them," Gary suggested.

"*Mother Earth News* has an issue on it. Sounds easy enough, but I know it won't be; labor-wise for sure."

"Nothing that durable would be," Gary said.

"I noticed you have a book out there by Kerouec called the *Darma Bums*. What the hell is a Darma Bum?"

"*Darma* is basically a Buddhist term for truth. The book is about the Beat Generation trying to find it," Gary explained.

"The truth about what though?" Mick asked.

"Life, what it means, how to live it. It's all pretty subjective really. Life has different meanings for different people. Charles Manson sees it one way, Billy Graham another way."

"My girlfriend in Vietnam was a Buddhist, but I didn't learn much about it from her. Only the difference basically between the squat, pot-bellied, smiling figure like that big one inside the entrance to the Emperor's Palace Chinese restaurant uptown, and the slender, more serious one you see in pictures of pagodas and temples. Happy Buddha she called the fat one. Represents the care-free attitude in taking life in stride. I think she called the skinnier, contemplative one Siddhartha."

"That's right, Prince Siddhartha," Gary said. "He's the true Buddha."

"So then Buddha really did exist. I've always thought he was just a mythical figure, you know, like a Greek god."

"No, Man." Gary frowned. He seemed perturbed at Mick's ignorance. "Siddhartha was born in the 6th Century B.C. in northeast India; the heir to the ruling royal family there. He left that life in search of something more spiritual and the secret to the end of suffering. At the age of 35 his pilgrimage took him to the *Bodhi* tree. *Bodhi* meaning enlightenment, which he attained there, and he spent the rest of his life teaching those drawn to the Path of Enlightenment that leads from suffering and dissatisfaction to spiritual fulfillment. In other words Buddhism."

"And that's what you're in to?'

"I'm more into the Zen form of it really," Gary said.

"What the hell is Zen, anyway?" Mick asked.

"The word itself is actually Japanese for meditation, but I don't get hung up on actually meditating. You know, like lying on my back and closing my eyes and tuning everything out; that takes too much of an effort which defeats the purpose as far as I'm concerned. I do it passively by simply trying to be aware of life as it exists in the present moment, because that's all that's really real, at any given moment; the here and now. In other words, this is it."

"Far out. I just got a rush when you said that," Mick said.

"You got a rush from realizing it's true; the moment of knowing, or the knowing of the moment; a *satori*. It comes naturally if you just let go of worrying about the past and the future and instead focus on the present."

"Yes, but don't we have to plan for the future?"

"What we do each moment contributes to that," Gary said. "It's like when I'm working on a stained glass project. I have a plan, but I don't worry about when I'll complete it. It's a work in progress and I focus on each moment that naturally leads to its completion."

While Gary spoke he tugged and twirled strands of his hair as if it stimulated his brain. Apparently it did, for words of wisdom flowed from his tongue.

"The process itself is rewarding and free of the anxiety associated with worrying about when I'll be finished, which is suffering, and suffering is what Buddhism seeks to relieve us from. That's the purpose of practicing the religion."

"How do you define suffering, Gary? I mean if you've got a tooth ache you don't need Buddha, you need a dentist."

"I'm talking about mental and emotional suffering, which comes mostly from dissatisfaction about things not being the way we want them to be. You may be dissatisfied with your truck let's say, for arguments sake, and I don't blame you," Gary joked and he laughed, "because it's old and it rattles. You want a newer one but right now you don't have the money to get one, and so you agonize about that instead of being satisfied at the moment with the older one, which, despite the squeaks and rattles, provides you with adequate transportation. It got you here."

"So what's wrong with striving for something you want that's better?'

"To want is to desire," Gary argued, "and desire leads to frustration when we can't have what we desire. You desire a new truck, again for arguments sake, but you can't afford one, consequently desiring the new truck is an unrealistic expectation that can't be fulfilled at the moment, which leaves you frustrated and even depressed. Desiring immortality, for example, is an unrealistic expectation, yet people get depressed about dying—the underlying sadness in the transitory nature of existence. Desiring some beautiful woman who is involved with someone else is another example. Suffering results from unfulfilled desires and unrealistic expectations. Letting go of them relieves us of the suffering and brings us peace of mind. Let go of unrealistic expectations, like expecting people to behave in a way that pleases us, let go of possessions; 'cling to nothing for its loss is pain,' Buddhists say. Let go of the egotistical self which constantly desires to be fulfilled in one way or another. Let go of ones self, ones body, in other words ones life without mourning for ourselves. Buddha taught that removing such attachments will give us contentment and peace of mind, and ultimately leads to *Nirvana*—Buddhism's heaven. Now, do I practice all of this like a good Darma Bum should? Hardly, I have too much of a desire for these." Gary held up his empty beer bottle and grinned.

"Yeah, me too," Mick said. "And it usually leads to suffering in the morning. I better go, we'll talk more sometime about a stained glass window for my stone house, if I ever get it built. See ya at PK's sometime."

Chapter 37

Mick continued to keep track of the Vietnam War for the sake of advancing his thesis on Vietnamization, whose advancement depended in part on the progress of negotiations.

The concessions the U.S. was willing to make to the North Vietnamese, namely that their troops could stay in the South while US forces were required to leave, and our apparent willingness to abandon Thieu, sorely disappointed Mick. He couldn't help but think, despite the fact that the American military had soundly beaten the Communists on the battlefield, we were at last losing the war regardless—and not just at the negotiating table, but on the home front. The antiwar movement and the mass media and Congressional doves held sway in influencing the Nixon Administration's decisions regarding the war. Decisions that had boiled down, in Mick's estimation, to a complete abandonment of our original commitment to, "… pay any price, bear any burden … oppose any foe to assure the survival and success of liberty," as articulated by JFK in reference to our escalating involvement in Vietnam in the early 1960s.

In the earlier years of the war, after Diem was assassinated and others were deposed by coups, we stood by Thieu, and despite the headway he had made through pacification in winning the confidence of the South Vietnamese people at last, it seemed now that we were quite willing, at the insistence of Hanoi, to abandon the commitment we had made long ago to him and to the South Vietnamese.

And again, what had so many South Vietnamese soldiers and American GI's and their families given up so much for—to placate the god damn dissidents in the U.S.?

Mick felt anger, disappointment and even guilt and shame, prime ingredients for a good drunk, or a bad one.

He started off drinking at home, and the more he drank and the more he thought about the direction the war had taken, not just recently, but since Nixon had announced Vietnamization, the more frustrated he became.

He needed to talk with someone about it—someone besides Lucky who laid at his feet and Jazzpur who was perched on the back of the chair where Mick sat. Another vet would do, but The Club was closed. No, better yet, a Vietnamese—Mae; she'd drink with him too.

Impulsive as he was inclined to be, especially when drinking, Mick didn't call, he just drove straight to her house. It wasn't too late—about eight. The lights were on. He knocked on the door. It took her a bit to come. When she did she was barefooted and wearing a terry cloth robe and her hair was wet.

"Mick. I just got out of the shower. Come in, I'll get dressed. Want a beer? I've run out of rice wine."

"Okay."

"Help yourself, I'll be out in a moment."

Mick went to the fridge. "Christ, leftover Buckhorn. Oh well what the hell." He opened one and paced around as he drank. His heart pounded. There was a lot he needed to get off his chest that had been building up ever since Nixon announced the U.S. was getting the hell out of Nam. Ironically, instead of feeling relief though, Mick felt like the weight of the entire free world had been placed on his shoulders—a burden that he and thousands of other Vietnam vets had been willing to shoulder. But apparently not the American people anymore despite JFK's urging. And Mick felt compelled to apologize on behalf of them to Mae, a South Vietnamese, for his country forsaking her's and leaving it to fend off the Communists without us, the vanguards of world freedom.

"Mick, why you look so sad?" Mae asked when she came out still barefooted, but dressed in short shorts and a tank top.

"I look sad? Huh. I'm thinking more like pissed off."

"You are pissed off? About what? The kind of beer I've got?" she joked.

"Nah, any kind of beer's all right with me as long as it's cold. Who am I kidding, I'll drink it when it's warm. We did in Vietnam. That's what I came here to talk to you about, Mae; Vietnam."

"Let's sit down, here, on the couch. That's what you're pissed off about Mick, Vietnam?"

"Aren't you?"

"Why, because U.S. is leaving?" she asked, somehow knowing what was on his mind.

"Yes, because the Communists demanded that we do without them reciprocating, and we're giving in to their demand that Thieu must go too. Hell, we're kowtowing to their every whim. Why not just give the South to Hanoi now and save a lot more bloodshed."

"You have no faith in Vietnamization Mick?"

"Do you?"

"The South Vietnamese Army performed well in the face of the Easter Offensive."

"Yes," Mick agreed. "But what would have happened without U.S. air support? When it's gone so goes South Vietnam I'm afraid."

Mae became solemn. "Yes, Mick, I must admit I'm afraid you are right," and tears welled up in her eyes.

"I'm sorry, Mae." He put his arm around her.

"Me too," she said. "Sorry for everyone concerned. This has not been good, if a war can be."

"It looked encouraging in '68 right after the Tet Offensive. If only Westmoreland had been granted his request for more troops. It was misrepresented by the press as desperation. They thought we were reeling from the magnitude of the offensive, when in fact it was the Communists who were reeling, particularly the Viet Cong. They were decimated and Westy simply wanted to finish them off along with their NVA comrades once and for all while they were on the ropes. We could have won the war then, in '68, but our leaders didn't have the backbone to grant Westy the troops, and the American people didn't have the stomach, being fed casualties every night on the tube, to see it through."

"Don't blame the American people, Mick. They were not sold on the war as LBJ should have done. As any president must do when his country is at war. He sat back and allowed the journalists to turn American people against the war after Tet. They misrepresented the results of it. It had been a devastating defeat for the Communists no doubt, as you said. The press played right into the hands of the Politburo's *dich van* strategy by fueling antiwar sentiments in the U.S., especially among the impressionable, young radical dissidents, and it spread across American campuses like wild fire, literally. You've witnessed it right here at SIU—Old Main burning, American flags and draft cards burning. Yes, I believe you are correct in your assessment that the Allies could have won the war in 1968," Mae said.

"So then, do you believe the Communists will win?"

She sighed. "Yes, I'm afraid so. It is just a question of when now. I think the Center will be closing in the near future too, Mick. I'll probably move to Los Angeles then; there are quite a few Vietnamese moving there. Soon there will be many more."

"I wonder what David will do."

"You know his wife is missing in Vietnam," Mae said.

"Yeah, very mysterious."

"Not so much to me."

"Really? Why?" Mick inquired.

"You must keep this strictly between us," Mae said, looking intensely into Mick's eyes. "I believe she is the spy."

"What?" Mick was shocked.

"Yes, and I believe that she has probably gone back to North Vietnam where she is originally from."

"But that's not so unusual, is it? It's my understanding that many fled the North to come south when the Communists took over up there. You did, right?"

"Yes. My mother did anyway, with me in her womb, but I don't believe David's wife fled. I think she was sent south to Saigon by the Politburo to spy. David met her at a CIA office in Saigon. She was hired to work there by a Mr. Ivan Johnson, but that was his alias. He has since been found to be a Russian, and an agent of the KGB."

"How do you know this, Mae?"

"I did a little checking with a friend of mine who works at the US Embassy in Saigon. My suspicions were first aroused when you revealed that the person who had gotten into David's secret files was wearing *Lotus Mist*, a perfume that's sold only in Saigon, which meant that the person in question had to be a woman and Vietnamese. It wasn't me and I knew it wouldn't have been Su Vinh and Tran Le. They are staunchly anti-Communist. I know of the work they have done with pacification around Pleiku. Their parents are rather high up district officials. And Nguyen Lu, as effeminate as he is, does not wear *Lotus Mist*; *Chanel No. 5* maybe." Mae laughed. "Just joking."

Her laugh was short-lived.

"I thought and I thought, then it came to me; who else would have known for sure that David wasn't in the office that night, and who else would have known exactly where the fiscal files were kept—David's wife. She could have known the combination to the safe too. On occasion she helped him when he worked late, typing and filing and such, like she had done for him as his secretary at the CIA office in Saigon. I've not shared with him my suspicions of course. I'll let him sort it out if he hasn't already. If he has though, I doubt he'd let on. I'm sure if he does know his heart is breaking.

"Yeah, if all that you suspect is true I would imagine it is."

A moment of silence followed before Mae changed the subject.

"Are you still planning to go for your masters, Mick?" Mae asked. "It would be a shame to see all that preliminary work you've done toward a thesis go to waste. The last chapter of Vietnamization will probably be written around the time a thesis would be due; in two years or so if you get into graduate school soon. You will have tracked it from beginning to end."

"And your book. Have you started on that yet?"

"Not yet, but soon."

"Mick," Mae took one of his hands in hers and held it on her knee, "since you've apologized to me for the US pulling out, which wasn't at all necessary, it's certainly not your fault, I'd like to thank you for your service to South Vietnam."

They hugged, but that was a far as it went. Mae had another lover now.

Chapter 38

Strange bedfellows an alliance between the U.S. and the U.S.S.R. did make in May, when Nixon visited Moscow, the first such visit by an American president, while Soviet-built tanks were spearheading the North Vietnamese's Easter Offensive, which were no match for American B-52s.

Better to battle by proxy though, through third world allies, than to have a direct nuclear confrontation between the two mighty adversaries, as out of Nixon's visit, detente kept the Cold War from turning hot. He and Leonid Brezhnev signed an agreement to officially begin talks on the Strategic Arms Limitation Treaty.

The treaty allowed each country to deploy only two anti-ballistic missile defense systems. Thus, each side gave up attempts to achieve immunity, and the "balance of terror," with its promise of "mutual assured destruction," would remain as a deterrent and principle guarantor of peace. And the treaty froze the number of intercontinental missiles for the United States at 1,764 and for the Soviet Union 2,568. The Russians were allowed more because the American missiles were known to be technologically superior.

In addition, Nixon announced an agreement under which the Soviets would purchase at least $750 million worth of US grain over a three-year period. And a joint agreement was also reached that involved technology and scientific cooperation, which included the two nations' space programs.

All of which put even more pressure by the U.S.S.R. on the North Vietnamese to negotiate an end to hostilities so the Kremlin could get on with forging a more congenial relationship with the U.S. in hopes of avoiding mutual destruction.

Building fallout shelters was not such a paranoid endeavor during these times, as paranoia is often delusional. The threat of nuclear war was real.

Detente between the world's two super powers, and an emerging third—Red China—overshadowed for the moment the discord that prevailed at the Paris Peace Talks over how the conflict in Vietnam should be resolved, giving hope that an earth-destroying nuclear war could be avoided in the future after all.

Chapter 39

When the summer of '72 came, after receiving his B.A. in Communications, with a minor in Literature, and before going on to graduate school, Mick spent most of his time on his land at Lake Wells gathering stones for the house.

On one particular night when camped out he noticed far off through the trees a faint light. He went to investigate. The moon was bright enough to see to walk without a flashlight. Soon he came upon one of the small piles of stones he had used to mark the boundary of his land and Anna's. He stopped there, but he was close enough to tell that the light came from a kerosene lamp sitting on the ground, and near it he saw the shadowy figure of someone standing near it peering at the sky through a telescope. It was Anna. Brave woman, he thought, to be alone at night in the woods, but it had become a brave new world for women these days.

Mick watched his new neighbor for awhile, then he returned to his camp site and sat by the dwindling fire, which he didn't bother to rekindle. He liked watching camp fires die down from crackling infernos into soft glowing embers. It was soothing to the eyes and prepared them for sleep, which is what Mick did soon after crawling into his sleeping bag. In the morning, after a quick cleansing, eye-opening dip in the lake, he fried bacon and eggs and potatoes over a new fire and spent the rest of the day gathering stones. In two days he had gathered enough to go all the way around the planned foundation one level high. At this rate, by fall, Mick reckoned he'd be able to go several levels high, at least up to where the bottom of the windows were to be. Maybe one could be stained glass as his new-found friend Gary had proposed.

But of course each level of stone would have to be mortared together which Mick would learn to do as he went, with the article in *Mother Earth News* on how to build stone houses as his guide. Some carpentry would be involved too, in putting down a floor and framing windows and doors, and building a loft and the roof. He had yet to buy the necessary tools and wheelbarrow to haul the sacks of mortar mix from his truck to the site, and more stones from the farther reaches of the property. The wood beams for the loft and roof could be dragged, but not easily, from the truck with a good rope. Mick shook his head thinking of all the hard work he'd have to do. He could sure use some help, and hopefully he'd get some from John. They had informally agreed on some kind of arrangement.

Back in town, after two days and a night in the woods by himself, Mick was ready for a little socializing again. After feeding Lucky, who had been kept outside tied up with plenty of dry food in a bucket while he had been gone, and Jazzpur, who had access to a bag of it, and a litter box in the basement, he smoked part of a joint, rolled another to take with, and headed out to PK's for a beer. It would be happening even in the summer because the regular clientele were primarily, but not exclusively, non-student hippie-types who stayed in Carbondale year round, and a few guys like Gary who attended summer school.

Mick had begun to feel more comfortable hanging out a PK's since The Club had temporarily closed. His hair had gotten longer again, and he was letting his beard grow, and since graduating, he too had become a non-student staying in Carbondale, although he would be going to graduate school in the fall.

Gary wasn't there yet. He usually didn't come until late, but to Mick's amazement he saw Anna there, sitting at a table with a female friend drinking beer. He had always had this pre-conceived notion that she was a health nut since she worked at Mr. Natural's, and not someone who would be inclined to drink alcohol in a smoke-filled place like PK's. He did not impose, instead he went to the bar, ordered a beer and drank it there. Once in awhile he glanced over at Anna, but she didn't seem to notice him. Surely she had seen him come in though; she sat facing the door. Maybe not though, she appeared to be immersed in serious conversation with her friend. Mick turned on the stool and watched a pool game. Gradually the place grew more crowded and noisier with pool balls colliding and being racked, players shouting, the juke box blaring, and people conversing loudly, trying to be heard over the general clamor.

As expected Gary came in relatively late, at 10:30, and he made his way to the end of the bar, the only place left to stand. After a moment he spotted Mick and smiled and waved, and soon he made his way around to him.

"What's happening," he asked.

"This place tonight, right here, right now, this is it," Mick said, in mockery of the little Zen Buddhism lesson he had gotten the other night from Gary.

Gary nodded and grinned. "You learn well. Wanna go out back and smoke a joint?"

"I was about to suggest the same thing," Mick said.

They made there way through the crowd to the little beer garden out back, and lo and behold, Anna was there with her friend toking up. Mick nodded and she said hello, and he and Gary stood not too far away and lit up. Soon more people came outside to smoke too, and before long at least three joints were floating around a circle that had formed; a '60s social phenomenon that surrounded the smoking of grass, like the passing of a piece pipe at a powwow as it were.

Mick introduced Gary to Anna, and she in turn introduced her friend Eve to them. Once back inside the four of them sat at a table together, and Anna and Gary soon were locked up in an intense conversation about astronomy. That was something that was totally Greek to Mick, so he struck up a conversation with Eve, which wasn't so easy. She immediately took offense to him referring to her and Anna as "… you guys." He had apparently been paired up with a women's libber who had a chip on her shoulder big as an ice block, and everything he said she picked apart as being chauvinistic, like when he stupidly said Anna was an interesting chick.

"Chick? I don't see any feathers."

Soon Mick stopped talking and he excused himself and wedged into a narrow space at the bar. Later he noticed the three were conversing freely and happily so, it appeared, and they got up and left together. Just before walking out the door behind the two women Gary made a special effort to make eye contact with Mick. He smiled and shrugged his shoulders as if to say, "hey, what can I do, they find me irresistible," or something like that.

"The rapper," Mick muttered to himself with some resentment.

He looked around for a familiar face, but saw no one he knew. How's that old jazz song go—Saturday night is the loneliest night of the week? But it wasn't too late for a Saturday night thing with Mae—she'd still be up.

Although Mick didn't think of her as one of those so-called "old reliables," whose doors drunken, horny guys knocked on in the middle of the night knowing they'd easily be opened, he expected she'd be open to, if nothing else, a friendly little nightcap or two. Mick drove to her house and in the driveway was another car parked behind hers. All the lights in the house were out. Guess maybe it was too late.

Mick went home and settled for a nice, quiet nightcap with Lucky at his feet and Jazzpurr at his shoulders on the back of the stuffed chair, his usual perch. All old reliables in their own little ways.

Bright and early Monday morning, Mick went about buying the tools he thought he'd need for his project, and a camper top for the pickup to keep them, and him, out of the rain when it did while he worked at the site. He also began to accumulate the necessary lumber. Then he went to The Club that afternoon, which had reopened, to recruit John to help with the building. He said he would, but only on Sundays when he wasn't bartending.

"I know it's a little early, John, but I guess I'll have a beer."

John winked. "Comin' right up. You know Reggie and Trudy have moved to Chicago," John informed Mick when he brought the beer.

"What, damnit, without telling me? Hell, I never did see the baby."

"Trudy left you this, Mick."

John handed him a sealed envelope and went about stocking coolers. Inside the envelope was a photo of the baby; a red-cheeked, blue-eyed, blond baby. Nice looking kid, but, but, Reggie is Mexican and Trudy's natural hair color is black, bleached blond. She couldn't hide the roots.

"God damn, is Trudy trying to tell me something here?" Mick pondered. Hell yes, you stupid sonofabitch, you didn't wear a rubber that night, remember?"

Mick put the photo face down—on the back was a note.

"How could I have aborted something as beautiful as this?" it said. "Reggie knows but he doesn't care, Mick. He loves the boy; he loves you. Besides what happened between you and me happened before he and I fell in love and decided to get married."

"Fucking fly-by-night sex." Mick cursed to himself. "No strings attached my ass. Christ, were there others, in Vietnam? You didn't wear rubbers there either, when you and Tron got it on."

Mick remembered well, Mae's condemnation of such careless behavior by GI's. Had he fathered a child over there too. Who would be taking care of that one for him?

Unprotected sex when you're drunk, that's the problem. Anything when you're drunk is a problem. Mick beat himself up badly over being an irresponsible, baby-making drunk, but it didn't stop him from drinking, in fact he drank more to drown the guilt.

In the morning he swore off it again, of course, which lasted as long as it took for him to feel like partying again, less than a week later after he had worked up a sweat and a thirst one day hauling stones.

But the guilt he felt for fathering a child with the wife of one of his best friends, even though they weren't married at the time, and the thought of perhaps having fathered a child in Vietnam too, caused him to drink even heavier. But after a couple of hard drinking bouts he allowed that they had simply been youthful indiscretions, and he went on with the carefree life of a soon-to-be graduate student, hopefully, whose biggest worry would be finishing his thesis. He had started it way ahead of time using the resources of the Vietnamese Studies Center.

That source would dry up soon though. The last of the U.S. combat troops were due to leave Vietnam in August, and with that, the Center would surely close. But until it did Mick would take full advantage of what information it had to offer, particularly that which pertained to Vietnamization.

Its progress, or lack thereof after Uncle Sam's departure, would have to be tracked after the Center closed through newspapers and magazines.

Chapter 40

The last time Mick saw David at the Center he had told him about his wife disappearing in Saigon, and since then Mick had had a conversation with Mae about her suspecting that David's wife was the spy, and she had laid out why.

It had all sounded convincing enough for Mick to suspect her too. When he met with David again, he immediately inquired as to whether she was still missing in Vietnam.

"Yes," he said, and he quickly changed the subject.

"I tried to call you this morning, Mick, to tell you Stuart's trial starts next month in Chicago. You'll be expected there as the prosecution's key witness. They'll put you up in a hotel for three or four nights. I'll let you know about a week in advance. Hope it won't interfere with your graduate work too much. You're going to graduate school this fall, right?"

"Yeah, I've officially been accepted."

"I'm anticipating that the Center will close down this fall when U.S. involvement in Nam ends once and for all."

"Is the *Southern Illinoisan* still trying to connect the dots between the Center and that agency which intelligence is central of, and you and the university?" Mick asked.

David smiled. "Yes, but by the time they do the Center will have long been closed and any story would only be after-the-fact; not exactly what journalists shoot for."

"What will you do when the Center closes, David?"

"I'll be going back to Vietnam to try to find my wife myself, but not until Stuart's trial is over. I'm a witness too of course. It won't take too long to convict that sonofabitch with all the evidence we've got."

"Well, then, just give a me a call when I'm supposed to go to Chicago," Mick said.

As the summer of '72 wore on, in Vietnam the Communist's Easter Offensive at last began to succumb to the South Vietnamese Army's counteroffensive, aided greatly by U.S. air power, which at the same time was having a tremendous impact in North Vietnam on the importation and movement of war materiel over land routes from China. In addition, the mining of Haiphong Harbor cut off the shipment of supplies flowing in from the Soviet Union. This resulted in Hanoi coming to the conclusion that it would behoove them to negotiate seriously with the U.S. in an attempt to end our involvement in Vietnam totally, including the bombing of the North.

So, partly because of behind-the-scenes pressure exerted by Mao Zedong on the North Vietnamese to be more flexible in negotiating, Le Duc Tho met with Kissinger once again in Paris on July 19. But just like before that meeting failed, as did the ones scheduled for August. They were undermined, and understandably so, by Thieu who feared that his government would be left out in the cold, even though Le Duc Tho had indicated Hanoi might be willing to accept a coalition government that would, in addition to the Viet Cong and South Vietnamese neutralists, include Thieu's. This was a definite softening in their previous position that totally excluded Thieu.

Despite the failed meetings in July and August, Tho and Kissinger agreed to meet again in September. Meanwhile, in August, the last U.S. combat troops left South Vietnam as U.S. air forces unleashed the heaviest bombing raids ever over North Vietnam.

And throughout the summer of '72 in Carbondale, since the Club had reopened after closing because of the kitchen fire, Mick found himself going back and forth between there and PK's, his new haunt. Going back and forth as it were between his old Vietnam vet friends and his new juicer-hippie friends. In the process he discovered they both had a lot in common these days in that many Vietnam vets had become hippies of sort because of their disillusionment with the way the war was turning out. Disillusionment with the political leadership of this nation who had gotten us involved in a war they were apparently willing to let North Vietnam win.

This had become apparent, ever since Congress refused to give General Westmoreland the troops he wanted, the troops he needed, to drive the last nail in the Communist's coffin after the Tet Offensive in '68.

Mick's best old Vietnam vet friend had become John, since Reggie had moved to Chicago. John was no longer just a bartender at The Club. He had become part owner, and he remained true to his commitment to help Mick with the stone house on Sundays and any other day that he could, in exchange for all the ice cold beer he could drink, and the biggest T-bone steaks Mick could find to feed him, which they grilled on a grate over an open fire of hickory wood. The beer was kept in a tub full of ice to be drunk after the day's work, while the steaks cooked, and after they were devoured. And in the dog days of August, when the high humid heat of southern Illinois rivals that of any place in the tropics, they worked up quite a thirst lifting, and mortaring stones in place, laying down the wood floor, putting in the windows and doors, and digging a trench for a pipe from the well to where the pump would be in the kitchen.

John wired the house for the electricity that would be run from a utility pole on the county road. After several Sundays of 12-plus hours of work a day, in addition to the week days Mick worked there by himself, enough stone had been laid high enough above the windows and doors to put up the beams to support the loft and the roof. The fire place would then be built in the middle of the circular house with two hearths at floor level on opposite sides, and one at loft level. The stained glass window Mick would have Gary make, Mick decided, would be in the roof of the loft as a skylight.

All the while a stone outhouse was being built too, around a big hole they had dug. After all, Mick couldn't do what bears do in the woods every day.

Mick was anxious to come up with a design for the skylight, so he went to PK's one Monday night in hopes of running into Gary to get some ideas. Mick hadn't seen him since the night he left with Anna and Eve, but he wasn't there. He was there Wednesday night though, with Anna. Mick asked him if he had a design in mind.

"Yeah, I do, let's go to my studio."

Mick met them there. Gary presented him with a sketch of a circle with what looked like an S drawn through the middle of it. There was a dot in the middle of each curve of the S. One side of the S was shaded, indicating the circle would be two-toned. The circle was set in the center of a triangle.

"This is the sign of the TAO; the symbol of Zen," Gary said. "It represents the totality of the paradoxes of existence; yin and yang, black and white, day and night, good and evil, etc. etc. But it can be in whatever color scheme you'd like."

"Cool," Mick said. "I like it. The frame could be the triangle. A triangular skylight. It would be in the roof of the loft."

"How big do you want it to be?" Gary asked.

"Oh, I don't know; 3x3x3 feet."

"Okay, what color?"

"Hmm, how about green and yellow for the Tao sign, and clear glass for the triangle background?"

Gary nodded. "I'll work up an estimate this week. Meanwhile, wanna try one of these?"

He dangled a baggy containing what looked like pieces of moldy dried apples in Mick's face, but that's not what they were.

"Psilocybin. Magic mushrooms," Gary said.

"So that's what they look like," Mick said. "Not too appetizing."

"You don't eat them for the taste," Gary replied, somewhat annoyed.

"Yeah, so I've heard. I don't know, Man, that's new territory for me. Where'd they come from anyway?"

"My closet. I grew them in pressurized jars of fermenting brown rice. In the wild they grow on cow shit. Don't worry, it's not like dropping acid, they're organic. The trip is more mellow, I think; not so noisy, and it lets you down easier when it's over. You don't crash as hard. Anna, how about you?"

"Sure."

She picked one out and ate it, and Gary followed suit.

"Try one, you're among friends," Gary assured Mick. "Nothing bad's going to happen. Just kick back and enjoy the ride."

Mick took one and chewed it and swallowed. It tasted like, well, like dried mushrooms, but bitter.

Gary got up and went to the kitchen and came back with three green bottles of imported beer, his trademark German beer: Beck's.

"Here, wash it down with this."

At first Mick felt like he was just getting off on grass; light-headed, light-assed, a quivery sensation in the stomach. He felt a little hot, then chilled, and the hair on the back of his neck bristled. His scalp crawled. The saliva in his mouth thickened and was hard to swallow. He took a swig of the cold beer. Soon his entire body seemed to be levitating off the chair.

And the music they were listening to, Pink Floyd's *Time,* driven by the tick-tocking of a clock, sounded louder and clearer than he had ever heard it before, as if the clock were in his head. and the lyrics, *Every year is getting shorter never seem to find the time. Plans that either come to naught or half a page of scrib-*

bled lines, made Mick think about the book he planned to write and how he kept putting it off, and he vowed to start on it soon. Maybe tomorrow or the next day.

It appeared to Mick that Gary and Anna were getting off now too, judging from the smiles on their faces, and the sparkle in their eyes.

Mick began to see strange things. The wood grain in the arms of the chair he sat in seemed to be moving like liquid beneath his hands. The vine design in the rug looked alive and appeared to be growing all around Gary and Anna's sandal-clad feet. The multi-colored paisley patterns on Anna's long, linen skirt moved about like little creatures in a sea; the folds of the skirt looking like waves. In a way Mick felt like he was floating in a sea.

The fantastic painting hanging on the wall that Gary had informed Mick was Horatio Bosch's tri-canvassed *Garden of Earthly Delights* had become a motion picture telling a rather nightmarish story. The wall itself, of swirling stucco plaster, seemed to be breathing and pulsating with the music.

Everything looked to be connected by molecules, and he could see that everything consisted of them, and Mick saw, as a result of eating the mushrooms, that there was more to life than meets the eye in our normal state of consciousness; something below the surface—the underlying current of existence—that certain hallucinogens allow us to tap in to.

Mick shared his revelations with Gary and Anna, and they shared theirs in return, which were eerily similar to his. Were their minds connected too, by this underlying current, as in extra sensory perception, or was it just the result of the commonality of their experience of tripping on magic mushrooms together?

Whatever it was it elevated Mick's thoughts and his ability to articulate them to new levels, particularly in the realm of Zen, which he, thanks to Gary's interpretations, came to realize wasn't so esoteric a religion after all, but one that simply teaches us that the time to live our lives is now before it slips away—*and then one day you find ten years have got behind you,* the lyrics of Pink Floyd's song said.

"Wow," Anna exclaimed out of the blue, "Now I get it. This is it!"

And that's the way it went for the rest of the night, one revelation after another, until the birds started chirping as the sun crept up in the east, and Mick went home and slept most of the rest of the day.

CHAPTER 41

The first of September, two weeks before Mick entered graduate school, he got a call from David telling him Stuart's trial would begin in a week.

"You'll be staying at the Hilton on South Michigan Avenue for three nights and three days. Check in next Tuesday. Everything has been arranged. Just sign your name for meals. If you drive they'll give you mileage, or you can take the train or fly."

"I'll take the train, I like the club cars."

"Okay, your ticket will be waiting at the station Tuesday morning. The Chicago train leaves at six. "I'll be driving up, Mick, but I'm not due to testify until sometime next week. Let's go over what your testimony will basically entail. It'll mostly be a confirmation of what we've got on tape, which you've heard first hand of course. The anti-American, pro-Communist diatribes, Stuart's participation in the Weather Underground's war council in Austin, where their alliance with the premier of North Vietnam was confirmed by the telegram they received from him congratulating them on their antiwar activities. His participation in bomb-making workshops, and his subsequent threat to use them against university buildings, particularly the Center, and his threats against me."

"We've also got him on tape trying to recruit others and me, don't forget, to participate in the Days of Rage riots in protest of the Chicago 8 conspiracy trial, and his expressed intent to commit violence against the police there," Mick added.

"Right, and most importantly, Mick, we have you as an eyewitness to his actual making of the bomb he planned to use to blow up the Center, presumably with me in it. Instead though, after finding out from a yet-to-be identified spy who infiltrated the Center that you were a spy for the Center who had infiltrated the SDS, the bomb was timed to go off in your car while you were transporting it to the Center. This of course might be difficult to prove though, because it may have gone off as a result of you stopping suddenly to avoid hitting that dog."

"One thing for sure though, David, that workbench in his basement is loaded with evidence—scrap bomb parts with his fingerprints all over them, and on the blueprints too."

"Okay, Mick, as long as we've got our ducks in order. Good luck."

Mick arranged for a neighbor to feed Lucky and Jazzpur while he was gone, and then it was off to Chicago again, to testify at Stuart's trial.

The train left Carbondale at six a.m.—much too early to drink anything but coffee in the club car. He had a Danish with it, then he opened the newspaper he bought at the station and was shocked to read the headlines—**ISRAELI ATHLETES MURDERED AT OLYMPICS.**

> *Sept. 5, Munich*—On this day of terror, eight Palestinian guerrillas, apparently affiliated with the Black September movement, scaled a wall in the Olympic Village and forced their way into the quarters of the Israeli Olympic team. Moshe Weinberg, wrestling coach, and Joseph Romano, a weight lifter, resisted and were killed immediately. Nine other Israeli athletes were held hostage while West German authorities surrounded the building. The terrorists demanded the release of 200 Arabs being held in Israeli prisons, and an air plane to fly them to safety. About 10 o'clock P.M., believing they had reached an agreement the terrorists led their bound and blindfolded hostages from their quarters into buses that transported them to waiting helicopters. The helicopters lifted them to Furstenfeldbruck Air Base, 20 miles from Munich, where West German police were lying in ambush. Two terrorists descended from a helicopter and walked to inspect a Boeing 727 jetliner they expected to use for their flight to the Middle East. West German sharpshooters fired upon them. One Arab tossed a grenade at one of the helicopters killing all the Israeli hostages onboard. By the time the shooting was over, all nine hostages were killed. The 20-hour ordeal resulted in the death of 11 Israelis, one Munich policeman, and five terrorists. Three were captured. For the first time in history the Olympic Games were suspended for 24 hours so memorial services could be held for the murdered athletes.

Christ, Mick thought, the Jews and Arabs will never be at peace. He returned to his seat and read the book he brought on how to build fireplaces.

Around one in the afternoon the train arrived at Union Station in Chicago. Mick took a cab to the Conrad Hilton and checked in. A message from the federal prosecutor's office was waiting: *Please meet with us in Room 313 at the federal court building at three p.m. today to go over your testimony. The trial begins at eight in the morning. Thank you.*

Mick enjoyed his plush digs on the 17th floor of the hotel with its panoramic view of beautiful Lake Michigan, with Soldier's Field in the foreground;, the hallowed home of Dick Butkus, the great Chicago Bear. Before Nam that was his hero. In Nam he had met many more.

He had a little time to kill before meeting with the prosecutor, so he took a walk around the Loop, bought a hot dog from a street vendor for lunch, then moseyed through Grant Park to beautiful Buckingham Fountain. The wind sprayed his face with a light mist, and through it and the cascading water he noticed on the other side of the fountain, sitting on a bench, the man who had bought a hot dog right after he had at the stand in the Loop. He remembered him because of the way he was dressed—military-like, in a clean, and neatly-pressed green Army fatigue jacket, and new-looking blue jeans tucked into brown, shined boots. Clean-shaven, he wore his hair in a pony tail. All-in-all a look not so unusual in this day of military-surplus popularity.

What really got his attention though was the look the man was giving him— one of hostility. Mick turned and walked away, but then he heard the sound of footsteps coming up behind him fast. As the man he had seen staring at him through the fountain passed he said, "Testify tomorrow and you're dead."

He continued walking past Mick briskly and darted through the traffic on Michigan Avenue and disappeared down a side street.

"Holy shit, what have I gotten myself into?"

Mick did not take the threat lightly, but by the same token he was not one to be easily intimidated. But was it really just an attempt at intimidation, or did the man mean business?

"I've come this far, I'm not turning back now," Mick resolved, and he began to walk back to the hotel and suddenly he realized just how seriously he had taken the threat. His legs felt hollow and shaky, and his stomach sick. He knew that these guys—the Weather Underground, assuming that that's who the man represented—were quite capable of killing. They had, afterall, tried to kill him once before.

Feeling sweaty, Mick took a shower and put on fresh clothes—nice, conservative clothes to enhance his credibility. He also had trimmed his hair and beard. Then he went to meet with the feds.

The prosecutor, a short, rotund, balding man of about thirty-five or forty wearing a three piece pin-striped suit, greeted Mick with a strong hand shake, but he didn't smile.

"I'm Wilson McCrary. Have a seat," he said rather curtly.

Mick sat in a chair in front of the desk the prosecutor sat behind.

He spoke with a thick Chicago accent, and his voice was surprisingly deep for a little guy. Mick imagined it would carry quite well in a court room. He was glad he wouldn't be cross-examined by this guy, but that's what it felt like he was doing as he quizzed Mick about what his testimony would be. When he was done he smiled.

"I just wanted you to get a feel for how the defense will come across, Mick. They will be very tough. Their client is facing a long stretch. I think you'll hold up well though. The truth is on our side and we've got plenty of hard evidence to back it up; the tapes, fingerprints, the blueprint for that bomb, that telegram from North Vietnam's Premier. This should be a slam dunk. Court convenes at eight in the morning. See you then."

"Sir, there's something I need to tell you. I've been warned not to testify."

"By whom?"

"A man in Grant Park who had been following me. He walked past me and told me if I testified tomorrow I'd be dead, and then he ran across Michigan Avenue and disappeared."

"Well then, will you anyway?"

"Yes."

"Good. We'll provide you with protection, starting now. This time you'll be followed by the good guys, and we'll have someone posted near your door at the hotel."

Wilson then made a phone call to arrange for the detail.

"If you could wait for about 15 minutes before you leave."

"Okay."

"We'll try to squeeze your testimony into two days, Mick, instead of three to get it over with so you can get the hell out of here and back to Carbondale. I'll try to arrange some sort of protection for you down there for awhile too."

In the rush of people going home after work around 5 o'clock, Mick couldn't tell that he was being shadowed by the feds as he walked through the Loop and down Michigan Avenue en route to the Hilton, until he got off the elevator on the 17th floor. A tall, broad-shouldered, stern looking, blond man in a suit who had ridden up with him got off too. He immediately introduced himself as Jack and he told Mick he had been assigned to make sure he got to court and back safely.

"I'll be stationed in the room next to yours—1725. If you need me call the room directly. You don't have to go through the switchboard. Please leave for the courthouse at seven. I'll ride down in the elevator with you, but I'll remain a few steps behind once we've gotten off. Have a nice evening," he said dryly.

They went to their respective rooms and Mick ordered a BLT with fries from room service. He looked over the TV lineup for the evening: national and local news, Laugh In, the Beverly Hillbillies and Carol Burnett, followed by the local news again, and Johnny Carson, what else.

While eating he watched the CBS Evening News with Walter Cronkite, which was dominated by the Olympics—not the games, but the murder of the Israeli athletes. That story overshadowed the terrific news that the South Vietnamese Army had recaptured from the North Vietnamese, Quang Tri which had been lost at the very beginning of the Communist's ongoing Easter Offensive. The South Vietnamese had suffered more than 5,000 casualties in the process. The fighting and bombing almost completely obliterated Quang Tri City, which is what CBS focused on and not the fact that the South Vietnamese Army had prevented an all out invasion by the North Vietnamese Army.

After leaving a wake-up call for six, Mick got ice from the machine in the hall and made highballs with tap water and the little complimentary bottles of bourbon that comprised, along with other kinds of booze, the room's table top bar. Halfway through the Late Show he got sleepy, so he went to the bathroom to brush his teeth before turning in when he noticed on the floor in front of the door a white envelope. He picked it up and opened it. Inside was a note.

"I meant what I said, testify tomorrow and you are dead."

Instead of feeling intimidated though, Mick got pissed. He had grown tired of being threatened.

"I'll be testifying, you bastards, come hell or high water," he grumbled out loud.

Mick went to bed and slept well enough considering that his life that day had twice been threatened.

The wake up call startled Mick and he was surprised to be waking up in a hotel room.

"Oh, yeah, the trial."

He stretched, got up, took a quick shower, dressed and called Jack.

"This is Mick, I'm headed for the elevator."

"Okay, I'll meet you there," Jack said.

It was a crystal clear morning and Mick walked briskly to the federal court house determined to testify against Stuart and the Weather Underground regardless of the threats they had made on his life. In fact he would be testifying about an actual attempt Stuart had made on his life.

"All please rise. The Honorable Judge Richard Cason presiding."

"Please be seated," the judge said as he sat behind the bench.

Being the star witness on this particular day Mick sat at the prosecutor's table with Wilson McCrary and two others whom he had not met.

"The people of the United States of America vs. Stuart Bolshinsky of the Weather Underground," the judge announced. "Proceed."

The prosecutor stood and said, "As the government's first witness I'd like to call to the stand Mick Scott."

Sworn in, Mick sat down on the hot seat. He hadn't felt nervous until then. In response to Wilson's questions Mick explained that he had been recruited by David Gordon, director of Southern Illinois University at Carbondale's Vietnamese Studies Center to infiltrate the local Students for a Democratic Society, and ultimately its radical Weather Underground faction. Initially, he testified, it entailed the taping of the conversations of Stuart Bolshinsky, who had been the leader of that chapter of the SDS before becoming aligned with the Weathermen, who planned and carried out certain activities such as the violent demonstrations in protest of the Conspiracy 8 Trial in Chicago which had been tabbed the Days of Rage by the press.

Stuart Bolshinsky, Mick testified, decided to go the militant route after attending the Weather Underground's so-called war council in Austin, Texas where he participated in workshops and received blueprints on how to build bombs. After which he voiced his intent, on tape, to use them against Southern Illinois University buildings, namely the Vietnamese Studies Center, hopefully, Stuart had said, when the Center's director David Gordon would be present. He then used the blue print to build a bomb in his basement which Mick witnessed.

Mick testified that he was then asked to infiltrate the Center so he'd be in a position to plant the bomb there. In the meantime someone photographed certain top secret fiscal files at the Center that would reveal Mick's role in infiltrating the SDS. Apparently the photos then fell into Bolshinsky's hands, for in the process of transporting the bomb to the Center the night it was intended to blow it up, the bomb went off in Mick's car. Luckily though after Mick had gotten out of the car to check on a dog he had hit. And though it could be argued the bomb went off prematurely as a result of Mick suddenly breaking to avoid the dog, the feds contended it was most certainly built with the intention of harming something or someone—if not Mick, the Center with David Gordon in it. Mick pointed out that Stuart knew what nights the director would be working there late, and he chose one of those nights to plant the bomb there.

Upon cross examination the defense tried to portray Mick as a drunken, conniving, back-stabbing, anti-Communist zealot, and fascist bully who had once been arrested for beating up a demonstrator who was attempting to burn the American flag at an antiwar rally, in violation of the man's First Amendment rights. And he, the defense contended, had secretly taped the confidential conversations of Stuart without his permission also in clear violation of his Constitutional rights. And they asked him, reminding him that he was under oath, if he smoked marijuana, a question the judge permitted over objections from McCrary on grounds of irrelevance, so Mick had to admit that he did. By the time they finished with him for the day it seemed that Mick had been the one on trial.

Drained by the stress of his first day in court, after a meeting with prosecutors who assured him that he did well, and no charges regarding the pot could be brought against him without witnesses, Mick, forgetting about Jack, slipped out the back door of the court house and hailed a cab for Billy Goat's for a beer—or 10. He liked the friendly atmosphere there, something he needed now as much as the beer.

He didn't expect the bartender Fred to remember him, but amazingly he did, although Mick was dressed conservatively, he had trimmed his beard, and his hair was shorter than when he had been there before during the Days of Rage.

"Long time no see." He wiped off the bar in front of Mick, dumped the ash tray and sat it back down. "What a ya have?"

Mick looked up at the revolving lighted Schlitz Beer Globe hanging above the taps.

"That beer that made Milwaukee famous."

"Comin' right up."

Wearing a white shirt and clean-shaven with closely-cropped hair, Fred looked like the consummate beer joint bartender—friendly, smooth, vigilant and fast. Mick quickly finished the first beer he bought, and as soon as the empty glass touched the coaster, Fred came back.

"Nother one?" he asked.

Mick nodded.

He drank this one a little slower, not wanting to get drunk too fast, and he needed to eat, so he ordered a cheeseburger with the next beer forgetting what that combination had done to his stomach the last time he was there. And like the last time he had been to Billy Goat's, around five, the place became crowded and noisy with people who stopped in for drinks after work. It was especially busy being a Friday, and Fred got some help from another bartender who had come on duty. He was fast and smooth like Fred, and he kept a full glass in front of Mick who lost count of how many he had.

Gradually much of the after-work crowd left and was replaced with out-on-the-towners and out-of-towners who stayed in the surrounding hotels while attending conventions as Mick found out when a group of loud men with pronounced southern accents crowded up to the bar next to him. It was obvious they had been elsewhere drinking.

"Any good barbeque joints around here?" one of them asked Mick.

"I don't know really, I'm from out of town."

"Yeah? So are we."

"Where from?" Mick asked.

"Louisiana. We're here for the National Beer Distributors Association convention. Just came from the ball game at Wrigley Field. Lotta a beer gets distributed there."

They all laughed loudly.

"We're pretty good at that here too," Fred said when he came to wait on them. "What a ya fellas have?"

"Old Styles. Give this guy one too," the man who had been talking with Mick said. "So where you from?" he asked Mick.

"Springfield, Illinois originally."

"You're kidding. One of my best buddies in the service is from there—Jan Sanders."

"What? Jesus Christ, I don't believe it," Mick said.

"Don't tell me you know him."

Knew him. Mick didn't have the heart to tell the guy Jan had died, then he'd want to know how.

"Know him? We were roommates in college," Mick said.

"How's he doing?" the man asked.

"Uh, fine, just fine." Mick continued to lie. "You guys were in the Marines together, huh? In Vietnam?"

"Yep."

"At Con Thien?" Mick asked.

"That's right." The guy stopped smiling and took a drink of beer.

"From what I've heard that must have been hell," Mick said.

"You could say that. Jan tell you about it?"

"A little."

"And I'd bet, knowing Jan, that he didn't tell you that he saved my ass and a few others over there."

"No. No, he didn't say anything about that."

"In my opinion he should have gotten the Silver Star for what he did, and he probably would have if, if—you sure Jan is doing okay?"

At that point the other men spotted a table that had just become empty and they went for it, leaving their friend with Mick at the bar.

"By the way, my name is Andrew."

"I'm Mick."

As the conversation continued it centered on Jan's heroics. "Our squad had gone out on recon patrol and we walked into an NVA machine gun nest. Jan had been walking point and when they opened fire he disappeared while the rest of us were pinned down. One by one we were getting picked off until suddenly the machine gun nest blew, and then Jan reappeared. He had rolled around on the ground behind them and dropped a grenade in on their asses. We lost three guys, but all of us probably would have been wasted if it hadn't been for Jan."

Andrew paused to take a drink.

"You sure he's okay?"

"Yeah," Mick reassured him, but Andrew didn't seem convinced.

Being a little drunk he began to talk loosely about how much his friend had changed after he came back from an R & R in Bangkok.

"He got kind of schizo. Sometimes he would be almost giddy, which was totally out of character, and other times he'd be real withdrawn. We stopped having him walk point; he just seemed too distracted for that. And back at base camp whenever the platoon would go to this little bar in the adjoining village, Jan stayed behind. One night I got worried about him and I went back to see how he was and I caught him shooting up. 'Junk, Man, junk,' Jan explained. 'I tried some in Bangkok and now I'm hooked.'"

Mick was surprised at how candid Andrew was being about their friend, but then again, he was pretty drunk.

"I asked him where he was getting it, and he said in the village. He was being supplied by the *mama sanh* who ran the bar there. The shit was coming in across the DMZ from North Vietnam, and apparently there were a few others at base camp who were hooked, which those fuckers up north no doubt intended. I reported it, and the *mama sanh* got busted, and the supply dried up, including the damn beer with her in jail, and Jan kicked the habit cold turkey. When he went through the withdrawals the other guys in the platoon thought he had malaria. The doc knew better, but he let on that's what it was, and I never told them any different. In about a month Jan was walking point again. He's stayed clean back here in the World, right?"

For some reason Mick felt compelled to tell the truth.

"Jan died of an overdose last year. I found him with a needle in his arm too."

"No, no, Man, fuck!" Andrew blurted out loudly, causing sudden silence in the tavern—a moment of silence for Jan as it were, but only briefly as the general noise quickly returned to its previous level.

After that there wasn't much left for the two to talk about, so they exchanged addresses, promising to stay in touch, shook hands, and Andrew rejoined his friends who were leaving.

Mick finished his beer, bid Fred ado, and he made his way upstairs to Michigan Avenue. He took a deep breath of the cool night air, which caused him to swoon, and he felt sick to his stomach. Not wanting to throw up on the street he ducked down under the bridge that crossed the Chicago River. Lights from the buildings along Wacker Drive across the way sparkled on the water. Mick walked to the top of the seawall where he stood staring down at the river. He didn't notice the shadow coming up from behind. The next thing he knew he was being fished out of the river and onto a Chicago Police boat, and a cop straddled his ass while pressing on his back to force water out of his lungs. An ambulance waiting on the shore transported him to a hospital, where, after having been half-conscious, he became acutely aware that he had been hit on the back of the head when a doctor stuck a needle in his scalp in preparation for stitches.

"Fifteen," the doctor said when finished.

After x-rays of his head were taken to determine if he had sustained a fractured skull revealed nothing, he was given the heave ho with the bill in his hand, as big city hospitals normally do to drunks who have been rolled, although the police were curious about why his wallet, still full of money; water soaked money, hadn't been taken. They asked him if he could think of any reason someone might want to kill him, but at that moment, in his foggy state-of-mind he couldn't, until he came to his senses in the cab on the way back to the hotel. He went straight to Jack's room and pounded on the door. Jack answered immediately, apparently not having been asleep. He looked wide awake and angry.

"There you are. Where in the hell have you been, Scott? Why'd ya give me the slip?"

"I'm sorry, Jack. I didn't intend to, but I was a little freaked out by the defense trying to make me out to be some kind of criminal, so without thinking about needing protection, after my testimony I went out the back door and headed for a bar to mellow out. On the way back somebody clubbed me and pushed me into the Chicago River. Luckily some cops on a patrol boat saw what had happened and they fished me out."

"Did they catch the guy who clubbed you?"
"No."
"Are you going to continue to testify?"
"Sure as hell am. What time is it, my watch wasn't waterproof?"
"Almost three-thirty."
"I can still get some sleep. I'll be ready to go again at seven, Jack."
"Okay."

Mick was required to testify for only half of the following day, and then he was whisked off to Carbondale on the afternoon train with Jack sitting in the seat behind him. The prosecutors said they'd provide protection until a verdict was reached, possibly by the end of the following week.

That night in Carbondale Mick noticed Jack parked on the street in front of his house in a rental car. In the morning he saw a different man in a different car. They were shadowing him in shifts.

Since he had gotten back two days earlier than expected, there was a chance he'd be able to touch base with David before he left for Chicago to give his testimony. Mick wanted to tell him about the attempt that had been made on his life for testifying. David was surprised to see him.

"I thought you'd still be in Chicago when I got there. Finished testifying already?"

"They rushed me through it and got me the hell out of Dodge. Somebody tried to kill me."

Mick showed David the back of his head.

"What the hell happened?"

Mick told him all about it.

"They sent a detail down here to make sure it doesn't happen again."

Mick got up and looked out the window.

"See?"

David looked out too, at a man leaning on the fender of a car parked next to Mick's truck, smoking a cigarette with an eye on the front door of the Center.

"That's Jack. His shift starts every night at six."

They both sat down again.

"That son-of-a-bitch'n Bolshinsky will be convicted soon," David said. "Here." He handed Mick an envelope. "This is your bonus for testifying."

In the envelope was a cashier's check for two thousand dollars, half of which would pay for his Chicago hospital bill—at about fifty bucks a stitch plus the x-ray Mick figured.

"That closes the books on your mission. Job well done," David said, shaking Mick's hand. "Want a drink? I think this calls for a little libation. I keep a bottle here in the desk for such occasions. Scotch. You like Scotch?"

"Haven't drunk much of it."

"I'll get some ice from the fridge. It's great on the rocks. Good sipping whiskey, or gulping if you prefer."

David brought back two tumblers containing ice cubes, filled them with the whiskey and sat one down in front of Mick. He torched his pipe, leaned back in his chair, and took a sip of his drink and smiled. The aroma of the cherry blend tobacco and the Scotch Mick sipped gave him a mellow little rush as good smells can do.

"Mick, have you ever thought about pursuing a career with the CIA? They recruit college guys you know. After the outstanding job you did in infiltrating the SDS I'm sure they'd be interested. I'd be willing to sponsor you of course."

"I don't think so, David, I've got other plans, but thanks anyway."

"So what are your plans beyond graduate school? I know you've been wanting to write a book, and you've bought some land to build a house on."

"That, and I'll probably try to find a teaching job around here, or maybe I'll get back into radio. First things first though. I'll need to finish my thesis."

"Well I know this place has been quite useful to you in providing good background information on it that the mass media doesn't have access to. But since U.S. involvement in the war is ending we'll be closing next week, so I'm afraid you'll have to rely on newspapers primarily. They should give you a pretty good day-by-day account of it, albeit somewhat delayed and skewed by the press's largely pro-Commie point-of-view."

"What will you be doing once the Center closes, David?"

"I'll be leaving right away for Saigon."

"Oh, your wife has been found?"

"No, I'm sorry to say." David took a drink. "I'm going there to help look for her. Want another Scotch, Mick?"

"Better not, don't want to keep Jack waiting too long."

"Jack? Oh, yeah, Jack. Well I'm flying to Chicago in the morning. I can't see this trial going on much longer than a couple more days once I've testified. With all the evidence we've got against this guy what else can the defense do but rest and hope for the best."

"How much time do you think he will get?" Mick inquired.

"At least 20 years is my guess. Depends on the judge. Some are pretty lenient these days."

"Well, good luck, David. Maybe I'll see you back here at the Center once more before it closes."

"Hope so, Mick. Be careful now."

Jack tossed his cigarette away and got in his car when he saw Mick coming. On the way back home Mick saw him through the rear view mirror. He went inside and looked out an upstairs window, and there Jack was, parked on the street in front of the house. Having gotten a buzz from the Scotch he was tempted to slip out the back door and walk uptown to The Club or PK's to chase it with some beers, but he didn't want a repeat of what happened in Chicago, so instead he decided to settle in for the night and watch TV stretched out on the couch. After awhile he dozed off but was awakened by Lucky growling. His ears were perked up and he was looking toward the rear of the house. Jazzpur had become attentive too. Mick got up and went through the kitchen to the back door that opened onto the little enclosed back porch.

As he stepped into the back yard he saw it coming at his head from the side—a hand with some kind of big hammer in it. Mick ducked just in time and the momentum of the assailant carried him over the top of Mick who grabbed the man's legs and drove him into the ground, but he was surprisingly strong and he rolled Mick over and sat on him.

"You were warned not to testify you sonofabitch, now you're going to die."

He raised the hammer with both hands and started to come down with it on Mick's forehead, but Mick thrust his hips upward bucking him off and he quickly scrambled to his feet and jumped on the assailant's back. Flattening him, Mick twisted his arm behind him as high as his shoulder blade while keeping him down with a knee pressed hard on his ass. With his free hand Mick took the man's long pony tail and wrapped it tight around his neck and began choking him with the intent to kill, but before it got that far Mick was restrained by someone from behind.

"I'll take over from here," the man said, and he handcuffed Mick's attacker with assistance from Jack who had come running from the front of the house. Mick recognized the assailant as the man in Grant Park who had warned him not to testify at Stuart's trial. They found the assailant's weapon on the ground. It was a big hammer alright; a sawed-off mauling ax that could have killed an elephant. Jack and his partner then marched him off to an unmarked police cruiser parked in the alley and he was driven off to jail. Jack came back.

"You okay?" he asked Mick.

"Yeah, I think so. Who's that other guy?"

"State police stake out. He's been patrolling around the block and through the alley."

"My dog and cat alerted me that somebody was out here. I thought it might be you but I wasn't sure."

"Was he the one who threatened you in Chicago?" Jack asked.

"That's him."

"Looks like you're going to be a witness at another trial now. He'll be charged with intimidating a federal witness and assault at least, I would imagine, and if we can prove somehow that he's the one who knocked you into the Chicago River, maybe attempted murder; two counts. That sawed-off mauling ax sure as hell could have killed you."

Mick shook Jack's hand, which didn't take much of an effort as Mick's hand, along with everything else was shaking on its own. "Wanna come in for a cup of coffee and a bite to eat?" Mick asked.

"Nah. With this guy busted I can go back to the motel and get some sleep."

"Thanks, Jack."

"No problem. Good luck."

Now free to come and go as he pleased without worrying about being attacked, after cleaning up a little and giving Lucky a pork chop bone and Jazzpur tuna oil, Mick walked uptown to The Club. He still had time for at least two or three beers before last call. He hadn't seen John since before he had gone to Chicago. John knew now, about Mick's undercover work, and being the adventurous, macho type, he'd be interested in hearing about what had transpired surrounding his testimony, especially what had just occurred. Mick's adrenalin was still running high over it.

John found it all to be rather amusing really, especially the pony tail choking. "That'll teach 'em to wear their hair like women."

"You know, this is the third time now, John, that these guys have tried to kill me."

"Once in Chicago and tonight, when else?"

"You heard about that car that blew up over on Wintergreen Street last year, right?"

"Yeah, we thought it was a sonic boom, then somebody came in and told us what that some car blew up."

"That was my car. I was transporting a bomb destined for the Vietnamese Studies Center. I hit a dog and got out to check on him and the bomb went off."

"What the hell?" This really got John's attention. He stopped washing glasses, dried his hands off on a bar towel, and poured himself a beer. "Whose bomb was it?"

"Stuart Bolshinsky's. You know, the guy I told you about who's with the Weather Underground. He found me out and we believe the bomb had been timed to go off with me in the car. Problem is, we can't prove it; only that the bomb was intended for the Center. We've got Stuart on tape saying as much. And I'm an eyewitness to him making the damn thing, and he put it in my hands to be transported."

"Sounds like an open and shut case to me, Mick, but let me play the devil's advocate here for a minute; what if this guy walks on some kind of technicality. Won't they come after you again?"

"The only walking he'll be doing is around and around his cell for the next 20 years I'd say, at the least.

"Hey, by the way, can you help me out at the lake this Sunday, John?"

"Uh, sure, yeah, why not. We've missed a couple of weeks. Don't wanna get too out of shape. I guess it's about time to hoist some of those beams up for the roof and the loft, huh?"

"Right, they'll have to be notched though, so we can bolt them down on top of the vertical ones supporting the stone walls. That'll firm up the entire structure so it can support the roof which I'd like to get done before Old Man Winter comes blowin' in."

"Okay, I'll meet you out there about seven Sunday morning. Oh, did you know that the SIU chapter of the Vietnam Veteran's Against the War is sponsoring a rock concert at Giant City Saturday?'

"Yeah, I saw the flier on the bathroom door," Mick said. "I might have to check it out."

"Not me, I don't get along with those guys too well, since that fucking turn coat John Kerry got up with that fucking Hanoi Jane in Detroit at that 'Winter Soldier' investigation and testified that GI war crimes in Nam were more widespread than thought, I said fuck 'em."

John gulped down the rest of his beer and poured himself another one.

"Sure atrocities happen in war, Mick. Always have, always will. War itself is a god damn atrocity when you get right down to it, but GI atrocities pale in comparison to what the Communists are guilty of, and not just in Nam, look how many millions Stalin and Mao Zedong killed. What the hell motivates these guys, anyway, to accuse their fellow soldiers of such things?"

"In my opinion, politics," Mick said. "The politics of the likes of Tom Hayden, Fonda's old man; left wing socialists who embrace the Communist insurgents of the world as some kind of romantic, freedom fighting folk heroes, like Mao, Che, Castro and Ho Chi Minh; the enemies of capitalism which they feel guilty about participating in because of the wealth it creates, while some in third world countries live in abject poverty. They believe the wealth that is achieved by individuals through free enterprise should be pooled and then distributed evenly among the masses. And who do they see as the figurehead of Capitalism? The president of the United States, Richard Milhouse Nixon, a staunch anti-Communist Republican. They won't be happy until he is out of office. They want a left wing socialist dove like McGovern or McCarthy in the White House.

"And yet it's Nixon who's trying to make peace with the Soviets and Chinese, and he's the one who is getting us out of Nam," John added. "Hopefully though, he'll continue with the bombing of North Vietnam to persuade Hanoi that it would be in their best interest to keep their fucking hands off the South after we've gone," John, an unabashed hawk, said.

Mick did manage to get three beers in before last call, and he felt nice and high walking home—his male ego inflated by thinking abut how he had handled his assailant, employing old high school wrestling moves. The pony tail choke hold though was a new one. Mick had to laugh.

Chapter 42

It was Stuart who would get the last laugh, however. Less than a week after David had gone to Chicago to testify he called Mick with the shocking news—Stuart had been acquitted of all charges.

"What?"

David repeated it. "The god damn Constitution protects the wrong people. The tapes, all of those tapes, were ruled inadmissable."

"But why?"

"Because," David said, "according to this god damn judge the recording of private conversations unbeknownst to one of the parties being recorded for the purpose of using it as evidence in a court of law against that party is illegal in Illinois. It's an absolute travesty, Mick, to let this blood thirsty traitor walk. Regardless of the recordings, you were an eyewitness to his making of the bomb. He handed it over to you with the expressed intent to destroy the Center with me in it, or destroying your car with you in it."

"It's my fault, David. The defense managed to discredit me as a witness. They painted me as a lush and a pot head, and a conniving, anti-Communist zealot who had once attacked an anti-war flag burner in violation of his Constitutional rights."

"No. That shouldn't have been enough to discredit the hard evidence we had, like his stinking fingerprints on various scraps left over from the bomb that were found on the workbench in his basement. All hope is not lost though, if it's proven that your pony tail pal is affiliated with the Weather Underground, i.e. Stuart Bolshinsky, they can charge him with conspiracy to intimidate a federal witness, and conspiracy to commit murder in connection with the attack on you in your back yard, and the Chicago River incident."

"A lot of ifs there, David. Meantime Stuart is free to raise hell again."

"Not for long though, if....," David chuckled, "if they can get pony tail boy to sing soon and implicate Stuart as a co-conspirator. Just give him to me in an isolated cell for an hour or less, and he would, guaranteed."

"No Constitutional problem there," Mick said. "If he doesn't sing, David, and they don't retry Stuart I'll be looking over my shoulder again."

"Why, Mick, Stuart won't be around Carbondale anymore."

"True, but I think the Weather Underground, on his behalf, would probably like to exact some revenge for me infiltrating them."

"You could be right, but you seem to be able to handle yourself pretty well. And you could request a continuation of government protection, but since Stuart's trial is over, for the time being anyway, I doubt if that would be granted. Although you'd be a witness against pony tail boy, which might require protection since he is most likely affiliated with the Weather Underground. I'm sorry, Mick, I wish there was something more that I could do, but I'll be leaving for Saigon by the end of the week, after the Center closes."

"Yeah, well, I guess this is the end of the ride for you and me. Good luck in finding your wife."

"Thanks, Mick, and good luck to you. Goodbye."

With the Center closing down Mae would be leaving Carbondale too. She had told Mick she planned to move to Los Angeles. He went by her house to say goodbye, but that professor's car was there again. The frequency of its presence indicated to Mick that their goodbye took precedence, which was okay—he didn't like goodbyes anyway, besides, the last time they were together would more than suffice. So Mick went on to PK's where he saw Gary with Anna and Eve, and he informed them of the VVAW rock concert.

"Saturday afternoon at Giant City State Park. Be there or be square. So how's my window coming along, Gary?"

"It's just about done, and your house?"

"Sometime next summer, unless it's a mild winter, then maybe by spring. Been doing any star gazing out there lately, Anna?" Mick asked.

"Last night. It was crystal clear out. The Big Dipper looked like you could reach up and grab it. We're going out there again tonight to view a special astronomical happening. Wanna come along?"

"Might as well, it's too wet to plow," Mick said.

"Pardon me?" Anna looked puzzled being from Chicago.

"Oh, it's an old farmer's term for, 'sure why not.'"

"Eve?" Anna asked.

"No thanks," she replied, making a face as if she had been insulted. She just didn't appreciate Mick's company, thinking that he was a sexist pig because he once referred to Anna as a chick. Interesting, coming from a chick who was constantly checking her friend's ass out.

Gary, Anna and Mick went in Gary's van, and on the way they stopped by a liquor store and bought a gallon jug of wine.

"Li Po enjoyed viewing the moon and the stars under the influence of wine," Mick informed his friends as they drove off to the lake.

"Oh yeah, Li Po." Gary would naturally know about him. There was little that Mick knew that Gary didn't. "The Eighth Century Taoist poet," he said.

"Yes, one of my English professors turned me on to him. It was once said by one of his contemporaries that for Li Po it's a hundred of his poems per gallon of wine. I don't know that many of them, but I've memorized a couple. They're short but sweet. Wanna hear one of 'em? It's about the Milky Way, or what he called the Star River."

"Sure," Anna and Gary said simultaneously.

DRINKING ALONE BENEATH THE MOON

Among the blossoms, a single jar of wine.
No one else here, I ladle it out myself.

Raising my cup, I toast the bright moon,
and facing my shadow makes friends three,

though moon has never understood wine,
a shadow only trails along behind me.

Kindred a moment with moon and shadow,
I've found a joy that must infuse spring:

I sing, and moon rocks back and forth;
I dance, and shadow tumbles into pieces.

> *Sober, we're together and happy. Drunk,*
> *we scatter away into our own directions:*
>
> *intimates forever, we'll wonder carefree*
> *and meet again in Star River distances.*

"Far out," Anna said. "Let's hear another one."

> *Facing wine, I missed night coming on*
> *and falling blossoms filling my robe.*
>
> *Drunk, I rise and wade the midstream moon,*
> *birds soon gone, and people scarcer still.*

"One more," Gary insisted.

> *We drink deeply beneath dragon bamboo,*
> *our lamp faint, the moon cold again.*
>
> *On the sandbar, startled by drunken song,*
> *as snowy egret lifts away past midnight.*

When they arrived at Lake Wells Anna lit the kerosene lamp to light the way to the clearing where they'd set up the telescope, which Gary carried.

"Oh, Mick, grab those two sleeping bags so we'll have something to sit on, and don't forget that wine," and they traipsed off through the woods with Anna leading the way. When they got to the clearing she set up the telescope, doused the lamp and focused in on what they had come out to see.

"There they are—the three brightest stars in the Summer Triangle, which are still visible enough in early September," Anna said. "Near the Triangle there are four relatively small constellations with interesting Greek Mythological backgrounds. The stars tell stories."

"Like in telestars," Gary joked.

"Something like that. The first constellation I'll be focusing on is Equuleus; the little horse, and just to the west is Delphinus. See Mick, Gary. It represents the Dolphin, which according to the Greeks was created by Poseidon, the god of the sea who had wanted to marry Amphitrite. But she was so repelled by the thought of having to live under the sea she fled to the distant Atlas Mountains. Poseidon sent several messengers after her in hopes that she might return to him.

Only the Dolphin, Delphinus succeeded, and he was rewarded by Poseidon with a constellation.

"And this is Gary's little constellation, Sagitta, the arrow, because many see in it an arrow outburst by the constellations five-point stars. The arrow of Greek Mythology shot by Sagittarius the archer—Gary's birth sign, or if you prefer, the one shot by Apollo to kill the Cyclops, or as I prefer, since Gary is a Sag, to see it, as some do, as Cupid's arrow. See Gary? And finally there is Vulpecula—the fox. This is the constellation that astronomer Jocelyn Bell discovered in 1967 to have the first pulsar—a rapidly rotating neutron star whose regularly pulsating radio signals led some to believe it was a message from an intelligent extraterrestrial civilization. That's it guys. You won't see it any better this late in summer."

To be quite honest, to Mick, under the influence of the wine, it wasn't all that distinguishable from the rest of the Milky Way, or Li Po's Star River. Gary continued to look, and he acted as if he could see what Anna saw. Maybe he could; they were usually on the same cosmic plain.

Let's have a fire," Mick suggested.

Using the kerosene lamp, he and Gary rounded up wood for a fire, and they sat around it on the sleeping bags and drank wine and talked about Greek Mythology and the stars, and other cosmic things, until they got good and drunk, and Gary and Anna snuggled up in one of the sleeping bags and Mick passed out on the other one reciting to himself another of Li Po's drunken poems:

A FRIEND STAYS THE NIGHT

Rinsing sorrows of a thousand forevers
away, we linger out a hundred jars of wine,

the clear night's clarity filling small talk,
a lucid moon keeping us awake. And after

we're drunk, we sleep in empty mountains,
all heaven our blanket, earth our pillow.

Chapter 43

Luckily, the weather the day of the VVAW rock concert was excellent. Mid-September in southern Illinois, when the heat of its semi-tropical-like summer gives way to cooler, early autumn breezes, it couldn't have been sweeter for a rock concert in the park. Some of the leaves on the trees had started to turn red, orange and yellow, but most remained green. And the sky was bright blue like the eyes of the woman who was hitchhiking, Mick thought, when he stopped and she got in. She did look faintly familiar, but he couldn't place her.

"Thanks for the ride. Going to the concert?" she asked.

"Sure am. Good day for it." Mick said.

"Uh huh." She smiled and her eyes got even bluer.

"You a student at SIU?" Mick asked.

"Uh huh. You?"

"Yeah."

"What's your major?" she asked.

"I'm a grad student in communications and journalism. You?"

"Design."

Then he remembered where he knew her from—the Halloween party at Bucky Fuller's three or four years ago. The one who went off on him about Vietnam. What's her name? Katie, Kathy? Something like that. But apparently she didn't recognize him; he had shorter hair and no beard then.

The small talk continued until Mick found a place to park near the meadow where the concerts were held. The woman thanked him for the ride again and they went their separate ways. She quickly crossed the road toward the meadow, while he walked to a nearby stream just to see what could be seen. Mick always seemed to be drawn to water, as Scorpio's are, Trudy once told him, being a water sign.

Seeing nothing particularly interesting though, besides the water pouring over nondescript rocks, he too crossed the road to the meadow where a crowd was growing, and the usual dogs-with-bandanas-around-their-necks-chasing-frisbees-thrown-by-their-hippie-masters-show had gotten underway, as the band sat up in the shelter.

Before the music began, a member of the local Vietnam Veterans Against the War took a microphone and proceeded to explain that the concert was being held to promote peace.

"We were hoping for an F-4 Phantom flyover, but they've all been shot down over Hanoi!" he shouted. And the crowd, which now numbered two thousand, Mick guessed, responded uproariously. The band then launched into a rendition of Woodstock; the anthem of all outdoor rock concerts great and small.

The crowd grew larger and the music louder, and the air smelled of marijuana. Mick had brought some of his and he shared it with whoever was standing nearby, and they in turn shared theirs with him, but he kept his bottle of wine to himself. He had another being chilled on ice in a cooler in the truck. Mick always liked to have something in reserve. The thought of possibly running out always bothered him.

Before long, through the crowd, Mick noticed Gary and Anna standing near the band. He couldn't help but focus on her with that cinnamon red hair glowing in the sunlight. She stood out. And although he couldn't see them from where he stood, he knew that her bright green eyes would be glowing too.

Anna was relatively tall for a woman; about Mick's height, around 5' 10". He liked the way she carried herself, with an air of sophistication, shoulders back, head held high, but not in a haughty way. She usually had a slight smile on her face, exuding good vibrations. Anna was a listener more than a talker, but when she did speak she usually had something pertinent to say. She spoke with a pronounced femininity in the way s's and t's came off the tip of her tongue, giving her speech a subtle sensuality. And he liked the way she looked dancing in place to the music.

When the song ended Mick heard a voice behind him.

"Now I know where I remember you from."

He turned around and there were those big blue eyes again.

"That Halloween party at Bucky Fuller's."

Mick braced himself for the venomous anti-Vietnam War onslaught that he had endured from her before, but it never came. In fact she apologized.

"For being so obnoxious that night. I got a little too drunk. I thought I'd see you again sometime, so I could tell you how sorry I was, but I never did. My name is Kathy in case you don't remember."

"Don't worry about it, Kathy," Mick said. "Sip of wine?"

"No thanks, I don't drink anymore."

"Do you still get high?"

"On life," she said.

"I can't imagine going to a rock concert and not getting off on at least something." Mick said.

"How about the music and the people?" she asked rhetorically.

"I can dig it, but I've gotten so used to drinking and smoking at concerts, I don't know, it just seems to go hand-in-hand with things like this," Mick said, and he took another drink of wine.

"Hey, that's okay. Whatever turns you on," Kathy said. "Is there some way I could get a hold of you sometime?" Mick asked.

"You could call me. Are you good at remembering numbers? Mine's pretty easy to remember. 565-5566."

"565-5566. Got it."

"Guess I'll walk around. See ya," she said.

"Bye."

Mick walked around too, and gradually he wound up with Gary and Anna again. They were higher than Mt. Everest on something, besides wine and grass Mick was sure. He could see it in their eyes and the way they smiled, like they were seeing things not normally seen.

"What's happening?"

"Everything," Gary said.

Yes, they were definitely on a different level than Mick; probably as a result of eating some of Gary's homegrown magic mushrooms, he guessed.

He tried to carry on a conversation with them, but they were just too far out, so Mick continued wandering about with his bottle of wine and one big doobie in his pocket that he'd save for whenever the time was right to light it up. For the moment though, he felt perfectly fine on the wine, and the high that was leftover from the last doobie.

Suddenly the sound of a wailing blues harp caught his attention, and to his surprise he saw that it was Gary playing with the band. Then he remembered seeing a blues harp lying on the trunk/coffee table at Gary's, but he had no idea the man played so well, despite being stoned on what Mick presumed to be mushrooms.

They were doing a rousing Doors song called the *Roadhouse Blues,* which featured a harp. People were dancing all over the place. Mick scanned the crowed and he spotted Kathy talking with someone and laughing. He envied her for having such a good time sober, at a rock concert no less; something he had never tried. It would be like going to a bar and just drinking coke, which he had tried. Being sober around those who were drinking wasn't easy. It was like trying to communicate with people who were retarded, and for about two weeks it was that perspective that kept Mick out of the bars, but he soon missed the camaraderie. Birds of a feather flock together.

There had been some times though, when conversation under the influence had been meaningful, particularly when marijuana was being smoked, but more times than not Mick forgot what lofty things had been said after he sobered up the next day.

For some reason though, he had managed to retain what Gary had imparted to him about Zen Buddhism, and being aware of what's happening in the here and now, a lesson he immediately applied to the present as he tuned into the music and grooved on the scene from where he stood.

Stretched out before him on a slight slope reclining toward the bandstand were the throngs of generally stoned people mingling and dancing on the meadow that was now partially shaded by the tall trees atop the west wall of cliffs the sun had moved down behind.

The air had cooled considerably since early on in the day when the sun beamed down from overhead. Everything then had looked so clearly defined, bright and clean like a photograph, but now in the purple haze of dusk streaked by the scarlet and golden light of the setting sun, there was an oil painting quality to it all, of blurred colors—Van Gogh-like; a perspective brought on perhaps by the wine Mick had drunk and the weed he had smoked. Even the music had begun to sound blurred. He decided the time had come to go, but not necessarily home. He had tired of standing up for so long, and he needed a good ole bar stool at The Club or PK's to sit on. And it would be nice to be out of the wind, which, with the sun going down, had become a little too cool.

Mick went to his truck and he was surprised to see Kathy standing there.

"Could I have a ride back to town?" she asked.

"Sure."

Before they got out of the park Mick pulled over. "Could you drive, Kathy? I think I'm a little too drunk."

She nodded and smiled, and they switched places.

"I know you're not drinking," Mick said as Kathy drove off, "but ya wanna go to a bar with me?"

"No, I don't think so. I'm not that comfortable in bars anymore."

"So then where do ya hangout, anyway?"

"At home, on campus, Mr. Natural's."

"Mr. Naturals, huh. I haven't been there in ages. Not since....," Mick caught himself before divulging why he used to frequent Mr. Natural's. "Not since, I don't know, since last year."

"Really? How come?"

I got a hold of some bad garbanzo beans."

"Oh," Kathy replied, sounding as if she had taken him seriously.

When they got back to town Mick told Kathy to drive to her place from where it would be fairly safe for him to drive on to PK's. Before she turned the wheel over to Mick she asked him to repeat her phone number.

"565-5566."

"Good. Call me sometime, but when you're sober, okay?"

"Okay."

Mick drove to PK's. The place was crowded being a Saturday night with school in session, and it got even more crowded as concert goers came in. Two of them were Gary and Anna.

They saw Mick and motioned for him to join them at a table in a corner which had somehow been overlooked by others who apparently couldn't see the tables through the tables. A waitress came and Mick ordered a pitcher of beer and three glasses.

"Man, you were dynamite on that harp today," he told Gary, who smiled shyly.

"Thanks."

"Is there anything you don't do? I mean like you know, with the stained glass, the music, astronomy, the books you read?"

"I don't know enough about car engines yet."

"And he doesn't dance," Anna said. "But I like the way he moves when he plays the harp," she said, nudging up against him while looking into his eyes.

Gary smiled again even more shyly, and his face turned red.

"And I'd like to learn photography, and another language beyond high school French. How about you, Mick, what are you into? Building that stone house is pretty far out."

"Writing I suppose. I'll be starting on a book pretty soon. And as you know I'm into Li Po, and I've written some poetry of my own. Anybody wanna hear one of 'em? It's pretty short."

"Fire away," Gary said.

> *When sun shafts pierce the chilling dusk,*
>   *and autumn breathes of smoky musk,*
> *I contemplate with abated breath,*
>   *this question of the greatest depth.*
> *When leaves fade they spin, soar, float, dying.*
>   *Is it the whim of the wind, or a niched course*
> *drawn for tracing?*

"Very existential, Gary said.

"Huh? It is? I've never really understood what's existential," Mick said.

"Basically it has to do with the question you ask in your poem. Do we live our lives according to some divine plan—the *niched course drawn for tracing*, or by self-determination or free will, your *whim of the wind*? In other words are we guided by God, or do we guide ourselves, free-wheeling through life."

"Right. That's the point I'm trying to make in the poem, but I've never really thought of it as being an existential question," Mick said.

"I think Jean Paul Sartre probably says it best—besides the creative way you put it in your poem of course," Gary added diplomatically, "in his book *Existentialism and Human Emotions*, which I happen to be reading right now. He writes that atheistic existentialism, which he represents, states that God does not exist, and that there is at least one being in whom existence precedes any kind of God concept, a being who exists before he can be defined by any concept or divinity, and that this being is man, or as Heidegger says, human reality. What is meant here by saying that the existence of man precedes any kind of divine creation, or God? Sartre says that it means that first of all, man exists, turns up, appears on the scene, and, only afterwards, defines himself, and then he becomes something, and he himself will have made what he will be. Not only is man what he conceives himself to be, but he is also only what he wills himself to be. In other words, man is nothing else but what he makes of himself, Sartre contends.

"Then you don't believe in divinity, or God in other words?" Mick asked Gary.

"I didn't say that I don't, I'm saying that an atheistic existentialist like Sartre doesn't."

"And you, Anna?"

I tend to be believe in a combination of the *niched course drawn for tracing*, in other words divinity, and *the whim of the wind*—or existentialism or free will.

"Yeah, that's the way I see it too, Anna," Mick said. "But at times I'm agnostic, unless I've got a hangover and then I'm an atheist because I know that no God would let someone suffer so much."

"But the devil would," Gary said.

"I don't believe in him either," Mick said, "or heaven and hell."

"You don't believe in any kind of afterlife?" Anna asked incredulously.

"Not really: just existence and oblivion, but since with oblivion there is no consciousness, our last second of consciousness, or sub-consciousness in existence becomes everlasting in that we will know of nothing else beyond it since with the oblivion that follows there is no consciousness. Follow me?"

"Uh no, but maybe another mushroom would help, the one I ate this morning is wearing off."

"Not to change the subject," Gary interjected and thankfully so, "but I've written a poem too, anyone care to hear it. It's a little long though."

"That's okay, let's hear it," Mick said.

"An Evening at the Gutter's Feast:

Who rules over this triumph of deceit?
This wasteland of beer stained windows and cheap neon
Smeared with the stench of dying dreams
and a sickly haze of stale tobacco.
A temple with desert floors of sawdust and spit.
Where glittering elixirs are mixed that bleach souls
while saturating stomachs with multicolored syrups,
that children, in their primordial wisdom, refuse to drink.
Elixirs that shroud tortured minds from the unmerciful fact of their own
 finite existence.
Elixirs that make tolerable the slow constant drip of mundane, mediocre
 lives.
An elixir that acts as an unction covering the rot in their souls.

Who worships at this temple to fermented grains, grapes and yeast?
Who are these trembling creatures who nightly claw and scramble to take part in this grotesque masquerade.
Choosing to blanch their bodies as well as their souls
In this sunless tomb made from craving, whoring, jealousy and lies?

Who worship here?
You and I!
We infest the legions that serve this throne to misery.
We are the jack booted mercenaries who demand to feed our lust and egos off of the pain and insecurities of our fellow cripples.
We nightly crawl on this temple's grease covered filthy floor preferring our desperation in heavy doses.

And what of our nocturnal potentate, Our "HIGH" priest.
This pale fleshed demon with his predator's eyes
stands behind his grief scented alter of wood with
its flowing tapestry of spilled whiskey, wine, cigarettes and wet change
and smiles as he anoints our lips with his malignant swill.
This cunning flatterer, who is as ruthless with his honey words as any assassin their knife.
This specter that greases the slope of our downfall and listens without compassion to our desperate screams.
A specter whose limpid gaze disguises an appalling disgust for this
human menagerie which lacks the strength to change and can only wallow in it own stench.
A menagerie of craving, straining, yearning creatures trapped in a world of grey skies with razors touching them on all sides.

Mick found Gary's poem to be a little unsettling. It was an affront to his lifestyle. It made him feel like a fool for patronizing bars, which he had been doing on a fairly regular basis for the last six or seven years.

Mick saw himself in the poem, reflected in the telling mirrors of all the back bars he had stared into, looking for relief from his mundane life while wasting his time, health and money.

And the poem cast aspersions on people like John, his friend the bartender, and his favorite bartender Tommy Seno in Springfield, whom he had always looked up to, albeit from a bar stool. Were they that *cunning flatterer, who is as ruthless with his honey words as any assassin their knife.... who greases the slope of our downfall.... whose limpid gaze disguises an appalling disgust for this human menagerie which lacks the strength to change....?*

Did they really see Mick that way; the way he sometimes saw his blurred reflection in the mirror of the back bar when he was drunk?

When he went to get another pitcher of beer, he couldn't help but see, while watching PK's bartender work, the insidiousness of the process as described by Gary in his powerful and disturbing, yet insightful poem. In his paranoid state-of-mind, being strung out from drinking and smoking pot all day, Mick freaked out and left the bar (without saying goodbye to his friends) swearing he'd never drink again.

Chapter 44

Back on the wagon, Mick focused on writing his thesis on Vietnamization. With the Center closed he relied mainly on newspapers and magazines for resources. The library provided plenty of those. He also tried to keep track of the peace talks, which had been deadlocked, but in early October there was a breakthrough.

The North Vietnamese at last showed a willingness to accept the Thieu government as part of a tripartite governing body for South Vietnam, as opposed to their earlier demands that Thieu be totally excluded, something Washington had steadfastly rejected.

They proposed that there be an immediate cease-fire, a prisoner exchange, a total American troop withdrawal (which was already underway), a cessation of the movement of new NVA troops into the South, and the creation of a "Council of National Reconciliation" composed of three groups; representatives from the Thieu government, the PRG (Provincial Revolutionary Group—basically the VC) and the neutrals. The neutrals would eventually supervise elections. Follow up talks were then held to work out the details, even though Thieu continued to steadfastly oppose the establishment of a coalition government that would include the Communist.

Why were the North Vietnamese so anxious for a settlement at this time? It was speculated that the upcoming presidential election in the United States had much to do with it. The North Vietnamese anticipated that the anti-Communist hawk, Nixon, would win in a landslide over McGovern, the dove, and once re-elected for a final term, he'd hold out for much harsher terms.

Perhaps the most compelling reason the North Vietnamese were anxious to settle before the US presidential election was, that by the first week of October they had the essentials of the agreement they wanted; that being to get the US out. This they had accomplished anyway with help from the antiwar movement and the US press demanding that they do so, and our willingness to allow those North Vietnamese troops who were in South Vietnam to remain. And why not? It would put them in a position to eventually take over the South with us out of the way.

Indeed Nixon was re-elected in a landslide, which Mick had contributed to, although reluctantly. He had in fact been reluctant to vote at all as he had become disillusioned with American politics. He blamed politicians for screwing up the war, and civilians like former Secretary of Defense Robert McNamara who interfered with the military in conducting the war. Worst of all, McNamara had changed from hawk to dove in mid-flight at the height of the war; a turn around that caused much confusion about the mission, all the way down through the ranks from the Commander-and-Chief (LBJ) to grunts on patrol.

Chapter 45

CHARGES FILED IN WITHERSPOON CASE

CAIRO, Illinois—Cairo police have issued a warrant for the arrest of Stuart Bolshinsky of Carbondale in connection with the murder of civil rights activist Gretchen Witherspoon, also of Carbondale, whose body was found by fishermen in Horseshoe Lake in 1969.

Bolshinsky, a member of the militant Weather Underground, was recently acquitted of conspiracy to bomb government buildings and attempted murder. His exact whereabouts are unknown but police believe he may be living in Canada.

Mick was shocked. He had no idea that Stuart had been a suspect in the murder. He had heard that a Cairo red neck was the prime suspect, but that the police were dragging their feet in arresting him. Now he knew why.

In the back of his mind though, Professor Witherspoon had thought all along that Stuart may have done it. He had deduced as much when the police told him they suspected one of the men of the coalition. Stuart, he knew, was infatuated with his daughter, and he also knew that it was unrequited, and he had observed that this caused Stuart to be resentful in regards to relationships his daughter had with others, especially Marcus Jackson. Stuart was always wanting to know what these two were up to outside the coalition, and if he was told that they had gone out to dinner or something he became visibly upset. He was terribly jealous of them. The Professor couldn't help but suspect Stuart, and he expected the police would be arresting him soon, but when Stuart got busted for conspiracy to bomb government buildings and attempted murder he figured the investigation into his daughter's murder would be put on the back burner until the case went cold. Despite halfway expecting it, when Professor Witherspoon got the news that Stuart had actually been charged with his daughter's murder, he snapped. He thought of the autopsy in which the coroner had said her clothes, including underwear, had been ripped from her body so violently it left cuts, and she had been strangled with so much force that her esophagus had been pulverized.

The Professor wanted to kill Stuart, and he would if he got the chance. The chance came when his daughter's killer was tracked down in Toronto and was extradited to Cairo where he was arraigned at the Alexander County courthouse. Professor Witherspoon waited outside. As the police escorted a shackled Bolshinsky from the courthouse to a squad car, the Professor positioned himself among reporters and photographers. Among them was Sam Taylor who happened to see him pulling a pistol out from the inside pocket of his jacket. Sam stopped him with one hand while putting the other arm around the Professor's shoulder, which he held tight while whispering in his ear.

"No, this is not what Gretchen would want, you spending the rest of your life in prison. Think of the scholarship you're setting up in her name; in the name of peace."

Muscles taunt, Professor Witherspoon resisted Sam's interference at first, but then he went limp, pushed the pistol back inside his jacket and he cried.

Sam, with his arm still around the Professor's shoulder, held him tight until Stuart had been placed in the squad car and driven off, and the Professor sighed deeply with relief. No one else saw what he had intended to do, and conventional justice was allowed to take its course, and swiftly so. While the investigation into Gretchen's murder had dragged on for nearly five years, within five months a jury of his peers convicted Stuart Bolshinsky of second degree murder.

In a sense Bolshinsky had convicted himself. When testifying on his own behalf, under an intense cross-examination by the prosecutor regarding how he felt about Gretchen's seemingly close relationship with Marcus Jackson, he trembled with rage, then broke down and sobbed while muttering that he was sorry but the two of them had stepped out of bounds. The jury apparently took this as a confession, and they found him guilty and he was sentenced to fifty years in prison.

Chapter 46

Before the cold weather set in, Mick, with help from John on a couple of Sundays, made major progress on the stone house. They got the roof beams up, and draped a sheet of strong clear plastic over them so work could be done on the interior throughout winter.

In the process, as part of the routine in working with John, Mick started drinking again. On one of the Sunday nights after John left because he had a date, Mick drank by himself at the site by the fire they had made to cook steaks on. When he got up away from the fire to relieve himself he noticed a light in the woods on Anna's property, and he faintly heard voices. It was probably her star gazing with Gary, something Mick had been wanting to do again.

As he got closer Mick could see in the light of the kerosene lamp Anna brought with her to star gaze, that indeed she was with Gary. He hollered at them, and with bottle of beer in hand Mick stumbled toward them, and he tripped on something and fell on the telescope, flattening it on the ground beneath him. The beer bottle broke in his hand on a rock. He struggled to his feet; blood streamed from a cut on his palm.

"God damn, I'm sorry," he apologized profusely, but they paid no attention to him while trying to determine how much damage the telescope had sustained.

Anna set it back up and peered through it.

"I can't see a thing."

"I'll pay for it," Mick blubbered. "I will."

"We'll talk about that later," she said. "Are you okay?"

"I cut my hand."

Anna looked at it holding his hand under the kerosene lamp Gary held up.

"That probably needs stitches."

"No, no it doesn't, I'll be okay?"

"Well we should at least wrap it, it's bleeding pretty good," Anna said.

Mick took off his jacket and extended his arm to Gary. "Here," stick your finger in that hole in the sleeve and tear off a piece," which Gary did, and Anna wrapped it tightly around his hand.

And Mick, feeling terribly embarrassed, excused himself and sheepishly returned to his property, and he drank himself to sleep by the fire.

In the morning when he returned to town he called Kathy asking her for advice on staying sober. She suggested an AA meeting; the one she attended every Friday night.

"AA? I'm too young for that."

"You've got a problem, right? Otherwise you wouldn't have called me for help."

"Yeah, you're right."

"That's the first step, Mick, admitting that we have a problem."

"What's the second step?"

"Doing something about it."

"Like not drinking anymore?"

"That's the idea. But what seems to work best is going one day at a time without drinking. Anymore, again, forever; is a little too much to digest, especially when you're young. That's what the old timers at the meeting say. One day at time is their motto," Kathy said.

"Okay then, I'll start today," Mick said. "Oh, where is this meeting Friday night?"

"In the basement of the First Presbyterian Church on University Avenue, at seven."

"I'll see you there. Thanks, Kathy."

It wasn't that hard for Mick to stay sober for the next four days before Friday night. He wasn't an every day drinker anyway, but a binge drinker who would drink a lot for a night, even a day or two, then he'd get so sick he'd swear it off until be started feeling better again. He felt like he was on a roller coaster at times.

What was hard though, was trying to type his thesis with the cut on his hand; a reminder each day of his embarrassing, drunken behavior Sunday night. And it would cost him to replace Anna's telescope—an expensive one he guessed. He would find out as soon as he went to Mr. Natural's, where she worked, to see her.

Maybe he would even be hanging out there again since he wouldn't be going to the bars anymore.

"No, not anymore," he said to himself, "but one day at a time."

Friday night he went to the AA meeting. Kathy was there and he sat down next to her in a circle of chairs.

"Glad you came," she said.

Mick got nervous as more people arrived, and he was surprised to see that a few were younger like him and Kathy. She however was one of only three women there, and they were older, and most of the men were older than Mick too. Just about everybody smoked, something Mick was certainly used to, being a bar fly.

The meeting began with the moderator saying, "Hello, my name is Jim and I'm an alcoholic."

The others responded in unison, "Hi, Jim."

"This is a twelve step meeting," he said. "Is there anyone here for the first time?"

Kathy looked at Mick.

"Oh, yeah, me. Uh, my name is Mick, uh, and a, I guess I'm an alcoholic."

"Hi, Mick," everyone said.

Jim asked Mick if there was anything he'd like to talk about.

"No, I'll just listen," he said.

Around the circle it went, each person introducing themselves by their first names and admitting that they were alcoholics. Some talked a little about how their day had gone, and how grateful they were to have a meeting to go to that night. One man said that for thirty years, since the age of seventeen, he had lived in an alcoholic fog, stumbling around, blind to reality. But when he got sober because a doctor told him if he didn't he'd die from a pickled liver, he came to realize that life without booze was better, "like when I was sixteen, waking up to each new day feeling pretty good, instead of being sick and tired and depressed."

Kathy was the last to speak. She talked about how both of her parents were alcoholics (something Mick could relate to), and despite the horrors of that, she was surprised, and disappointed in herself that she had become one too. One of the women then offered that alcoholism often runs in families, like a tradition, and some of us are genetically predisposed.

"Okay everyone, let's stand and hold hands and say the Lord's Prayer if you so choose."

With the prayer over, in unison they all practically shouted, "Keep comin' back, it works!"

After the meeting Mick felt like he used to when he had been to church—spiritually high. It had been a powerful experience.

He and Kathy walked out together. "Wanna get something to eat?" he asked her.

"I'm sorry, Mick, I've got a date."

"Oh, okay. Thanks for turning me on to AA. I got a real rush from it."

"Well, like they said, keep comin' back, it works. See ya next Friday night?" she asked.

"For sure," Mick said, fully intending to.

Saturday night Mick went to Mr. Natural's to see Anna and ask her how much he owed her for the telescope.

"I'm sorry, Mick, I paid six hundred dollars for it."

"When do you work next?" Mick asked.

"Tuesday afternoon."

"I'll bring the money into you then."

"Okay. How's your hand?"

"Sore."

"Do you have an aloe vera plant?"

"No."

"You could get one at that nursery out on 51. Pinch off a piece and rub the jell on the cut two or three times a day. It'll heal real fast."

"Thanks, I'll try it."

"I'm meeting Gary at PK's after we close here. Why don't you join us," Anna suggested.

"Yeah, well, I've decided to lay off the alcohol for awhile. I think I'll just hang out at home tonight."

Anna nodded and smiled, then went back to work. It was starting to get busy being a Saturday night. The bars would be hopping too. Mick felt an urge coming on, but he fought it off and went home, ordered a pizza to be delivered, not wanting to go into any place that served beer, and he kicked back and watched a football game on TV.

Sunday he went to Lake Wells to work on the house, by himself, as John had something else to do. With the beams in place that would support the floor joists for the loft, Mick managed to hoist sheets of plywood up a ladder for the floor itself, and he nailed them in place. Job well done, he felt like celebrating. A cold beer would taste great, but again he resisted the urge, driving past the gas station that sold beer on his way back to Carbondale. But there were beers in the fridge. He had forgotten about them. He opened the fridge door. Damn they looked inviting. He reached for one and popped it open. Just before it got to his lips he dashed it into the sink, opened the other four and poured them out too. Close call.

"Sonofabitch, is this what it's going to be like for the rest of my life? Remember, Mick, take it one day at a time," and he made it to the next Friday night meeting where once again he announced, "I'm Mick, and I'm an alcoholic."

But no matter how many times he said it he really didn't believe it, so he blew off the next meeting, and instead went to The Club where the first sip of the first beer he had had in a month tasted like the first sip of the first one he had ever had when he was sixteen; cold, bubbly and bittersweet, and like then, it only took one to get him high because he drank it so fast. One was not enough though, it never was. He drank three more in quick succession while talking with John when he could, about what needed to be done yet at the house at Lake Wells. Then he went on to PK's where he hoped to see Gary, although he still felt a little embarrassed about the telescope incident.

Under the influence again—despite his injury and how much it cost him to replace Anna's telescope—in retrospect, he thought it was kind of funny. Actually, so did Gary who came into PK's right after Mick.

"Anna may not have been seeing stars after it happened, but I sure as hell was," Mick joked.

They both laughed at that.

"Oh, hey, your window is done," Gary said. "Would you like to go see it?"

"Yeah."

"They drank up and went to Gary's.

Mick was blown away by what he saw; a triangular window, 3x3x3 feet, of clear glass, except in the middle where there was a green and yellow sign of the Tao, symbolic of Zen. Gary held it up in front of the light of a lamp and it glowed beautifully, like a large piece of emerald and topaz jewelry.

"That's what it will look like in your ceiling when the sun hits it," Gary said, looking pleased with the finished product.

"Far out," Mick said. "Far out. How much?"

"Three hundred."

"I'll pay you tomorrow." Mick still had plenty of money from being paid to go undercover.

"Okay. Let's smoke a joint," Gary said.

He took the window into the front room and propped it up against a lamp on a table, put some music on, went to the kitchen, brought back two bottles of beer and lit the joint.

"So when do you think you'll be done with the house?" Gary asked.

"By next summer, hopefully."

"Are you prepared for the loneliness of living out there in the woods?"

"I think so. I'm kind of a loner anyway. I'll be staying plenty busy, though, working on my thesis and my book, and when I get my masters I'll find a job."

"Book?"

"Based on my experiences as a combat correspondent for Armed Forces Radio in Vietnam."

"Sounds interesting. What's the thesis about?'

"Vietnamization."

"So where do you think that's headed?" Gary asked.

"Disaster. You know that light at the end of the tunnel LBJ was always talking about? North Vietnamese tank headlights coming down the Ho Chi Minh Trail headed for Saigon."

Gary chuckled. "I know it's really not funny though. All those years of war—what is it now, eight or nine, and it's going to end like that?"

"Maybe I'm being too pessimistic," Mick said. "Since we've withdrawn our combat troops the South Vietnamese Army has fought pretty well. If we can keep them well-supplied while bombing the communist supply lines up north then-"

"But we've been bombing the shit out of the Ho Chi Minh Trail for years and it's sill being used as their major infiltration route," Gary argued, indicating to Mick that his friend had been keeping up with the war some, although he hadn't talked about it until now.

"That's why we need to continue to cut it off at its source by bombing the shit out of Hanoi. Meanwhile we'll continue to negotiate with a lighting bolt in one hand and an olive branch in the other as we try to convince North Vietnam to keep their fucking hands off of South Vietnam," Mick continued.

"Some would argue that we should have kept our hands off of the South because it's basically a civil war, or a revolutionary war really, resulting indirectly from Ho Chi Minh revolting against France," Gary said.

"You know a little more about it than the average Joe, Gary."

"I've got a B.S. in history. We touched on Vietnam's a little."

"And now you're working on a masters in human development counseling? Why the switch?" Mick asked.

"Psychologists make more money than history teachers."

"I think I could use a psychologist right now," Mick said.

"How so?"

"I act pretty crazy sometimes when I'm drinking."

"That's not you, that's the booze," Gary said.

"You drink quite a bit, Gary, but I've never seen you drunk and acting stupid."

"I don't like losing control to the alcohol. I impose my will on it. Before I drink I have a little talk with myself. 'Gary, be cool, don't be a fool.'"

"I've tried that, but sometimes it just doesn't work. The alcohol takes over," Mick confessed.

"Then you could be an alcoholic," Gary said candidly. "Some people can drink, and some people can't. I think a lot of it has to do with emotional maturity and psychological tranquility. When someone is troubled by something it may result in negative behavior when under the influence of alcohol. Anything in particular that's bothering you, like what you experienced in the war maybe? Writing that book might help out therapeutically speaking."

"Yeah, there is a lot about that fucking war that's bothering me, now that you've mentioned it; haunting me to be more exact."

"Like what?" Gary asked, looking and sounding genuinely interested.

"Well, I was scheduled to go on a reporting assignment into A Shau Valley. The Ho Chi Minh Trail runs right down the middle of it. There had been a tug-of-war over the valley between the US 1st Cavalry Division and the NVA. Sometimes the enemy held it, and sometimes we did. In April of '68, after two years of ferocious back and forth fighting, we finally gained control of that segment of the Trail, including the airstrip A Loui. I was to be on the first Allied plane to land there since 1966; a C-130 loaded with ammunition. Like a fool, I got drunk the night before I was to fly in, overslept and my best friend over there, Bruce Samuels went in my place. The plane was shot down on approach and everyone on board was killed. As a result, the next plane going in would still be the first one, and I was on it. This one made it in obviously. As soon as we landed everyone was asked to help retrieve the dead from the ill-fated plane that Bruce had been on. Being military foremost over being a correspondent, I participated.

"The wreckage, along with the bodies were strewn out all over a field of brush, elephant grass and scattered trees. I stumbled on what I at first thought was a log, when I looked back I realized it was the charred torso of a man. A wallet lay next to it. I opened it and inside, protected by the thickness of the leather, was a photograph of Bruce, and his wife and little boy. That torso should have been mine. But because I had gotten drunk the night before and missed the plane, it was Bruce's. Strange, when I left A Shau the next day, I had kind of an out-of-body experience as I looked back down on the valley. It felt like I was leaving a part of me behind, as if through Bruce's death I had died some too, since I was responsible for what happened to him because of my god damn drunkenness. You'd think I would have stopped drinking after that—instead I drank more, and continued to do so. Recently I stayed sober for a month, and when I worked undercover I didn't drink either, not much anyway."

Mick let it slip. Gary hadn't known about that.

"Undercover?" He looked alarmed.

"I uh …"

"You're a narc?"

"No, hell no. If I were I'd have to bust myself. No, I uh," Mick felt like he had to explain now that the cat was halfway out of the bag.

"You're not a member of the SDS are you?" Mick asked.

"No, I'm not very political."

"I was hired by the Vietnamese Studies Center to infiltrate them," Mick said. "That's how I got the money for the land I bought at Lake Wells, and my truck and the materials for the house, and the skylight and the telescope."

"I've always wondered about that. I thought maybe you were from a rich family or something. You must have been successful then, if you got paid."

"I was successful up to a certain point. We managed to get the leader of the SDS, a guy named Stuart Bolshinsky, who went radical and became a member of the Weather Underground, behind bars and charged with conspiracy to bomb government buildings and attempted murder, and we got him to trial."

"Oh yeah, I read about all of that in the newspaper," Gary said.

"And despite all the evidence we had, one god damn juror voted for acquittal, so he walked."

"Does the Weather Underground know you are the one who infiltrated them?" Gary asked.

"Oh yeah, they've tried to kill me three times. First this Stuart guy tried to blow me up in my car, then one of the Weatherman's henchmen clubbed me on the back of the head and pushed me into the Chicago River when I had gone there to testify at Stuart's trial. The cops fished me out before I drowned. Then I was attacked again in my back yard, but I got the best of the guy, and now he's in jail awaiting trial for intimidating a federal witness and attempted murder."

"Won't they try to kill you again?"

"The feds don't think so since they've failed three times, and in the process they've compounded the original charges against them," Mick said. "It's like they've gotten themselves in quicksand, and the more they struggle to get out the deeper they go. Anyway, back to this drinking problem I have. After Bruce got killed because of my drinking, you'd a thought I would've quit after that, but like I said, I just drank more."

"Alcoholism can be a vicious cycle," Gary said. "Some people drink to forget about the very problems that are caused by their drinking."

"And the only way to break that cycle is to stop drinking, but I'm not ready to do that yet, I guess," Mick said.

"In that case, let's have another beer," Gary said, not thinking perhaps that Mick' problem was that serious. Most people didn't think of a little youthful drinking to be a serious problem. Deep down inside though, Mick knew that it was, for him anyway, yet he continued to imbibe.

Chapter 47

A new round of peace talks between the U.S. and North Vietnam opened in Paris in late November, but they soon deadlocked, primarily over Hanoi's backtracking on previous agreements, in addition to making new demands which Washington found unacceptable. So, in order to get the Communists to negotiate sensibly, from a U.S. standpoint, President Nixon sent them a note demanding they do so within 72 hours or we would renew the bombing of North Vietnam and remine Haiphong Harbor. Hanoi ignored Nixon's ultimatum, and by Christmas the bombing and mining began. The results were spectacular. At the completion of the twelve-day campaign North Vietnam's industry and economy lay in ruins.

Hanoi, fearing the Red River dikes would be bombed next, flooding vast areas of the North (something the U.S. had long-considered), indicated they would negotiate in earnest, and the bombing ended, and Mick was reminded of what David's general friend had said about lightning bolts and olive branches. Negotiations were scheduled to resume in January of 1973. An agreement was ratified in Paris on the 23rd. The highlight for the Allies was the stipulation that no more NVA could enter South Vietnam, although those who were already there were allowed to stay, which kept them in position to attack Saigon later on.

Chapter 48

Mick got an early Xmas card from David, postmarked Saigon, saying he had not been able to find his wife there, and that he now suspected she had vanished on her own.

> *Kidnappers, killers, usually leave something behind like blood; the victims or even theirs, or displaced furniture and what have you, because in most cases there has been some kind of struggle, but when someone chooses to disappear, especially a woman, they take their toothbrush and makeup. Hers were missing from the hotel she was known to have stayed in last. At first I was inclined to let her go if she wanted to leave me so badly, but when I found out who it was that she was last seen with—a North Vietnamese spy the agency was on to, I knew where she had to have gone—to Hanoi. Mick, we were man and wife for six years—for six years she faked it. She faked her loyalty to me and to the South Vietnamese. I'm certain now that she was the Center's spy. She exposed its connection, my connection, to the CIA to the press and the SDS and the Weather Underground, which in turn exposed you, and it nearly got the both of us killed. I can't let her get by with this, Mick, she's going to have to pay. I'll be going to Hanoi myself to track her ass down. I'll be posing as a Soviet journalist. I speak Russian, as well as Vietnamese, the northern dialect, fluently.*
>
> *If our friend Stuart is retried I'll see you in Chicago. I'm being kept apprized of all of that.*
> *Merry Christmas,*
> *David Gordon.*

That was the only Christmas card Mick got, but he did get a phone call from Kathy, New Year's Eve day inviting him to an AA meeting that night.

"I haven't seen you at any of the meetings for awhile. How are you doing?" she asked.

"Okay. I haven't been staying sober though. Have you?"

"Of course, one day at a time. Don't give up, Mick, sometimes it takes several tries."

"I'm really not trying anymore. I'm just not convinced that I'm an alcoholic."

"But you have admitted that you've got a problem with drinking," Kathy said, not letting Mick off the hook.

"Sure," Mick conceded, "I probably drink a little too much at times, but that doesn't make me an alcoholic, a lush maybe, but not an alcoholic."

"Well, okay, I wish you the best then."

"Thanks, Kathy, bye."

Mick sure as hell didn't stay sober that night. He had been invited to party at a bar called Merlin's, where Gary would be playing harp with the band he had played with at the Vietnam Veteran's Against the War's concert last fall.

Mick started New Year's Day off early, drinking at home by himself. He had purchased the stained glass window Gary made for him, which he sat on the sill of a window in the front room to admire.

Mick felt excited about how far he had come along with the house at Lake Wells, with John's invaluable assistance of course. Without him it would have been much more difficult, if not impossible, especially when it came to getting the beams up in place, and wiring the house and running water to it from the well. Mick had known nothing about electricity and plumbing, except how to use it. In the spring he would need John's muscle and expertise to get the roof on too.

On his way to Merlin's he'd stop at the Club to reiterate how much he appreciated all of this, and when he had gone to the bank to get money to buy the window, he got enough to pay John a little something for spending his days off helping Mick out. A few beers and steaks were hardly worth his trouble.

John resisted taking the money, so Mick stuffed a goodly wad of twenties into the pocket of his shirt. Knowing Mick meant business John smiled and winked and said, "Okay, you sonofabitch."

"Expecting a big crowd tonight?" Mick asked.

"No, not really. Not with all the students away, but I guess Merlin's is having a big party anyway. They'll draw a lot of townies and university hangeroners; you know, the ones who flunked out as freshmen and sophomores and don't have the nerve to tell mom and dad yet."

"Guess that's where I'm headed next," Mick said, "to Merlin's. That guy Gary I introduced you to awhile back at PK's is playing with the band."

"Don't have a date, huh?" John asked.

"No. The chicks I get to know always seem to find somebody else."

"How about a shot of peppermint schnapps to go with that beer," John asked.

Mick gladly accepted, then he drank two more of that combination, told John he'd see him next year, and he went across the street to Merlin's. It was 9 o'clock and the place was crowded and noisy already. He saw Gary on the stage with the band tuning up.

"Mike check one, check one, check two, check check. Check mike three, check, check four."

Thumpity, thump thump, the drummer tested his.

Guitars and keyboard tuned, they started, rocking hard right away. Gary soon joined in with the harp, and people began dancing in front of the stage.

Mick hung loose for awhile, leaning against a brick wall at the back of the bar, bottle of beer in hand.

On the other side of the rectangular bar that was situated in the center of the room, at one of the tables along the wall, Mick noticed Anna and Eve. He enjoyed Anna's company, but with Eve there he'd keep his distance. He didn't need some bitch bummin' him out on New Year's Eve.

From where he stood he had a good view of the band, being elevated on the stage well above those dancing in front of them. The band sounded better than they did at the outdoor concert, acoustically, in the more confined space of the bar which had been designed specifically to accommodate rock bands. That was Merlin's bread and butter.

Gary played good; real good, and Mick felt proud to know him. They weren't really friends yet though; more at acquaintances. Mick found Gary to be rather aloof at times, and a little arrogant. When one is as accomplished as he is though, it's understandable, Mick thought. He exemplified what was meant by being a Renaissance Man—but a down-to-earth one. He didn't mind sharing his weed and beer, and his knowledge, whenever Mick went to his pad. It was always an adventure going there. His artwork, his books, his music, his philosophical discourse inspired Mick. In a way Mick thought of him as kind of a guru.

When the band took a break Mick went to the stage to congratulate Gary on a great first set.

"Thanks, Man," he said somewhat shyly. He also could be quite humble at times.

"Can I buy you a beer?" Mick asked

"Sure, but I drink Beck's." Gary said, not in the least bit shy about discriminating at Mick's expense, but Gary had always been generous when it came to sharing his beer with Mick; the foreign stuff which he had to admit tasted better than the bland domestic brands.

"No problem," Mick said.

He bought them both a Beck's, and they went to where Mick had been standing along one of the brick walls.

"Are you a full-fledged member of the band now?" Mick asked.

"If I want to be. They're talking about going on tour as a front band for a new group out of Champaign called REO Speedwagon. They want me to go along."

"You going to?"

"I think so, but I'd have to quit grad school. I could always go back though, if it didn't work out."

"What about you and Anna?" Mick nodded toward her, still sitting with Eve on the opposite side of the room. They looked to be engaged in an intense conversation.

"You guys tight?"

"Sort of. Sometimes I think she's closer to Eve though."

"Huh?"

"We're a threesome, but at times I feel like the odd man out."

"A threesome? You mean like in menage e trois."

Gary grinned and nodded.

"I must admit, I kind of wondered about that," Mick said. "There did seem to be some sexual tension going on there between the three of you. How does that work anyway, I mean, never mind."

"Use your imagination, Mick. Maybe you could take my place while I'm gone," Gary said, his grin widening into an ornery smile, and then he chuckled knowing how unlikely that would be.

"Yeah, I'm sure Eve would love that, as much as she hates me. Besides, I find it difficult enough to satisfy one woman at a time. They take so damn long to get off."

"You'd only have to satisfy one while she's satisfying the other. Anyway, thanks for the beer. Time for the next set. Oh, by the way, there's a party after the gig at the sax player's house—211 W. Gates. Maybe I'll see you there," Gary said.

"If I make it that long. I started partying pretty early."

At midnight, with revelers hooping and hollering in celebration of another year of their lives gone, Mick found himself suddenly being hugged and kissed by a stranger, and he returned the favor. When they parted, and he focused on her face, especially her big, bright, blue eyes, he realized she wasn't a stranger after all. It was Kathy.

"What are you doing here?" Mick asked in an admonishing sort of way.

"Same thing you are, getting fucked up," she said.

Disappointed, yet selfishly delighted at the same time knowing he was not alone in finding it difficult to stay sober, he offered to buy her a drink, which she gladly accepted, and the two cozyied up together at the bar.

"I thought you were going to an AA meeting tonight, Kathy?"

"I was but the beast got the best of me."

"The beast?"

"That insidious little voice in the dark recesses of the alcoholic's mind saying, 'it's New Year's Eve, you've got to drink.'"

"Yeah, I heard it too," Mick said.

"I thought you didn't think you were an alcoholic, Mick."

"Sometimes I have my doubts, but right now I really don't care. I'm having a good time. I know that guy playing harp up there. He invited me to a party tonight. Wanna come? Of course the last time we went to a party together we had a fight," Mick said.

"What about? I don't remember."

"Never mind," Mick said, not wanting to get her started on Vietnam again, especially when she was drinking.

The band was so loud they stopped trying to talk over it. Kathy took Mick by the hand and dragged him to the dance floor where they squeezed into the crowd. It was the last set and the band left nothing in reserve in doing their signature Doors song, *Roadhouse Blues*, featuring Gary on harp. Mick couldn't keep up, so he left Kathy on the floor dancing with two other women, and he returned to the bar.

When the band said goodnight the crowd responded wildly demanding an encore. When they finished, the diehards clamored for more, but were ignored and the band disassembled. Kathy came back sweating and panting, and she quaffed the beer she had left.

"All right, so where's this party?" she asked.

"211 W. Gates."

They arrived in separate vehicles at about the same time. A few people were already there, in the kitchen around a keg.

As was Mick's habit when going out on the town, he kept a bottle of wine on ice in a cooler in the car, which he brought into the party.

Soon Gary, Anna and Eve arrived, followed by the band members who were greeted like stars by a couple of the women who latched on to them right away.

Gary came across as a little standoffish at first, so Mick left him be and wandered about the party with Kathy. They weren't the only ones of course who had drunk a lot; just about everyone looked pretty ripped, but after a couple or three joints made it around, things seemed to mellow out some, except Kathy. She became her old obnoxious self again, that is her old obnoxious, under-the-influence self again, like she had become at that Halloween party at Bucky Fuller's with Mick, only this time she picked on somebody else—the saxophone player who's party it was.

"Isn't it really a sexaphone?" she said to him loudly. "I mean aren't you trying to turn the women on with that long shiny gold thing between your legs while moving your hips around and around like you're fucking?"

"Some women, yes," he said smiling, "but not you."

Her belligerence had backfired. She stormed out of the party; staggered to be more exact.

"Where'd you find her at?" Gary asked, finally talking with Mick.

"She fell off of the wagon."

"The kind Anheiser-Busch Clydesdales pull? Man, that chick is juiced."

Mick felt some embarrassment for having brought Kathy to the party, while at the same time he felt sorry for her too. He knew how hard she had been trying to stay sober. She had tried to help Mick stay sober. Could he help her now? Hardly. Not if he didn't stop drinking, which he had no intention of doing for awhile. Presently he was enjoying it thoroughly, and he had gotten a second wind from smoking grass, and the cool wine tasted good going down, and he enjoyed meeting a different crowd of people—the musicians and their friends.

Mick had long admired those who played music because of the discipline it took to practice, and practice while others like himself were running around and goofing off. Although Mick did participate in sports in high school—football, which entailed practicing a lot also. But unless you went on to play in college or the pros, learning music would be longer-lasting and more fulfilling for virtually a lifetime.

Mick remembered looking down his nose at those who played in the marching band at halftimes. His football playing days relatively short-lived and insignificant, he now found himself looking up at the guys in the band. He tried to imagine what it would be like on a stage in the limelight making music so good it moved people to dance to it; so good it moved women to seduce you.

Actually the guys in this band proved to be pretty cool. They all got as fucked up as Mick, but not just on booze or pot. Some were doing lines of cocaine, an activity Mick had never witnessed before.

They formed lines of the coke on a mirror with a razor blade and snorted it up their noses through a tightly rolled dollar bill. The sax player offered Mick a line. Curious about the legendary drug, he snorted one too. It tasted somewhat like aspirin.

It didn't take long for him to feel the affect. He got a rush that felt like he was taking off in a jet fighter (something he had done in Nam), and a tremendous feeling of euphoria came over him in warm rushing waves, and he began communicating with the others rapidly, as they did in return, on what he thought was a high intellectual plain. And he couldn't stop clinching his teeth so much that his jaws got tired, but that didn't keep him from talking; he talked even more. He talked Gary's head off, which may be why he and Anna and Eve left.

By daybreak only he and the saxophone player remained, and Mick talked him to sleep. Wide awake at six in the morning, Mick still wanted to party. He had beer in the fridge at home. When he got there he was shocked to see Kathy sitting on his front porch shivering and crying. She had remembered where he lived she said, because the night they had gone to the Halloween party at Bucky's dome he had called her attention to black Jazzpurr sitting by a jack-o-lantern on the front porch of his house directly across the street. She had never forgotten that.

Mick led her inside, sat her on the couch and wrapped a blanket round her shoulders. She continued sobbing.

"Shit, I was sober for almost a year, Mick."

Mick no longer wanted to drink that beer. He suddenly felt sober despite all that he had drunk. Although he was a little wired from the coke.

"Start again today," Mick said, "the first day of the new year."

"Tomorrow. I've been drinking today. God, what a fool I made of myself at that party."

"You weren't that bad," Mick said.

"Don't enable me, I acted like the stupid, loud mouth drunk that I am."

"Join the club," Mick said.

"No, that's not a club I want to belong to."

"Hungry?" Mick asked.

"I don't think I could keep anything down."

"How about some scrambled eggs and toast. That'll soak up the alcohol."

"Okay, I'll try some."

"Oh, by the way, that's Jazzpur the cat, and Lucky the dog," Mick said.

Like with Mick, Jazzpur perched himself on the back of the couch behind Kathy. Lucky laid at her feet. She patted him on the head.

Mick went to the kitchen to make the eggs. When he came back out to the living room he found Kathy passed out on the couch, so he ate the eggs and toast himself and went upstairs and laid down. When he awoke several hours later around sundown, Kathy was lying next to him reading a book.

"Do you mind if I hang out here tonight, I don't want to be alone right now?" she asked.

"That's fine. I know you must be hungry by now. I sure am. Like spaghetti?"

"Love it. I'll make it though," Kathy insisted.

"Okay. I'll make a salad and some garlic bread."

While preparing the meal they talked about alcoholism and how their parents' had affected their childhoods, and after eating they went upstairs again and laid down together and they began kissing. Mick's hand found Kathy's braless breasts beneath her blouse which he unbuttoned and his mouth found them too. He flicked her nipples with his tongue and she moaned while running her fingers through his hair, and she guided his head further down and he kissed her stomach while pulling her panties off of her hips. She removed them the rest of the way while Mick discarded his underwear. He resumed kissing Kathy around her stomach and on the inside of her thighs breathing her womanly taste, her womanly smell, and she writhed with pleasure moving her hips up and down and around and around against Mick's face. Sensing she was on the verge of an orgasm Mick slid his hips between hers. She felt like warm silk. They moved to the rhythm of their mounting passion, and after Mick got off Kathy came. Afterwards they fell asleep and didn't wake up until mid-morning the next day.

Kathy got out of bed, got dressed and kissed Mick goodbye.

"Back to my regular routine," she said. "School, yoga and AA on Friday nights. That's where you can find me, Mick. I hope you'll go back too. Call me sometime if you'd like."

Mick needed to get back to his regular routine too—working on his thesis, and he vowed to start on his book, soon.

Chapter 49

She had slipped out of Saigon late at night on a motorbike with a VC courier who was delivering a message to an enemy command post in the tunnels of Cu Chi below the infamous Iron Triangle, a complex myriad of passageways that ultimately led to the Ho Chi Minh Trail. From there she went north on the Trail with an NVA courier in a small truck bound for Hanoi. She being David Gordon's lovely wife, Le. At least that was the role she had been playing for six years. She had played many roles since going south, and eventually to the United States.

In Saigon she had played the role of a secretary working for the CIA where she cozied up to David and made him her husband. That had been the plan from the very beginning. North Vietnamese intelligence had learned that he talked top secret in his sleep from a Saigon bar girl he slept with on occasion who was actually a Viet Cong. And when he was assigned to the Vietnamese Studies initiative stateside it had put her in a position to undermine the pro-war agenda of the Vietnamese Studies Center he was assigned to direct in Carbondale at Southern Illinois University by exposing, to the local antiwar movement and the press, its affiliation with the CIA. If such a connection were established, this Center, all of the Vietnamese Studies Centers in the U.S., would probably be shut down because they were located on university campuses where student activists would riot against them demanding they be closed on the grounds that the CIA was an agency that committed political assassinations and instigated coups in the third world. She exposed the connection by secretly photographing certain top secret fiscal files and turning the photos over to the antiwar movement, a.k.a. the Students for a Democratic Society. In the process she had managed to expose Mick Scott, who had been paid by the CIA through the Center to infiltrate the SDS and its more militant Weather Underground faction, which resulted in attempts on his life. But before it was determined that the spy was none other than David Gordon's wife, she returned to Hanoi where she was welcomed back with open arms by Vu Trong Thanh, head of North Vietnam's Office of Intelligence.

Thanh knew of course, by monitoring U.S. Armed Forces Radio broadcasts throughout the western Pacific, and the BBC in Hong Kong, that the American antiwar movement, hyped by the American press, was having an impact on the moral of the American people and their politicians, including the president of the US himself—two presidents actually. The antiwar movement indirectly influenced Congressional decisions that were detrimental to the Saigon government and its armed forces, mainly as a result of the withdrawal of U.S. combat troops.

But Thanh was anxious for a first hand account as to the impact the antiwar movement was having on the morale of the American people and their politics. This Le could provide. They met at a café in downtown Hanoi where they sat before a steaming pot of tea at a small table beneath a poster of Ho Chi Minh. His likeness was everywhere, like Mao's in China, and Lenin's in the Soviet Union. Although Ho was deceased, he was remembered fondly as the father of Vietnam's revolution.

Before the conversation got very far, an air raid siren went off; the American bombers were coming. They scrambled, along with many others, to a nearby shelter beneath the street. Soon the muffled sound of bombs exploding, and the rapid firing of anti-aircraft guns could be heard, and the light bulbs at the end of cords dangling from the ceiling flickered as particles of dirt came sprinkling down. The earth shook. The bombs were falling close by. Le's legs shook. She hadn't been in an air raid for years. The others, including Thanh, remained calm. They were accustomed to it.

"Nixon is very angry," Thanh said. "It is not going well for him in Paris. It is not going well for him at home, all of which makes him especially dangerous. I fear that he may resort to doing something drastic, like bombing the Red River dikes which would flood much of our nation. Worst yet, he could resort to using nuclear weapons against us. The conventional bombing has impacted us enough. You see, here we are now, cowering in this hole. But we shall not be discouraged." The round faced Thanh whose belly spoke of being well-fed despite general food shortages smiled. "We will win this war."

"Yes, it is our destiny to become one Vietnam independent of the West," Le said, "as we were long before the French and Americans came. In the meantime the Americans are planning something big to try to prevent that from happening.

This I discovered when I accessed the top secret files at the Vietnamese Studies Center in Carbondale."

Thanh looked intrigued.

"So tell me, what are they planning?"

"To invade our nation. Perhaps you already know this. The troops Nixon is withdrawing from the South are being reconstituted on Guam from where the invasion will be launched just north of the DMZ when the monsoons pass."

"No, I did not know this, but it would be a big mistake on Washington's part. We have a heavy concentration of troops, tanks, artillery and anti-aircraft weaponry positioned along the DMZ poised for an assault on the South. They could easily be re-positioned along the coast and reinforced. I will pass your information on to the Ministry of Defense immediately."

For her accomplishments in espionage, Le was awarded by the Politburo with an apartment and a job with Radio Hanoi, which was beaming propaganda broadcasts throughout Southeast Asia to counter Armed Forces Radio and the Voice of America. She wrote scripts for the infamous Hanoi Hannah because she was familiar with what was going on with the antiwar movement in the US, something Hanna used news about to demoralize what remained of US forces in South Vietnam. However, news of what was happening in North Vietnam in late 1972 (the Christmas bombings and the mining of Haiphong Harbor) dominated the broadcasts, not only of Radio Hanoi, but radio and television and magazines and newspapers all over the world. Not so significant because of the time of the year, but because of the time of the war—after thousands of US troops had been withdrawn. But Nixon felt the North Vietnamese were not negotiating in Paris in good faith as they continued to invade South Vietnam. Bombing the hell out of Hanoi, in addition to mining Haiphong Harbor might convince them to do so before we went even further and bombed, as Thanh feared, the Red River dikes which would turn much of North Vietnam into a massive rice paddy.

To get to Hanoi from Saigon, the week before Christmas David Gordon flew to Hong Kong on Flying Tiger Airlines, then connected to Canton, and from there he flew on to North Vietnam's capital on an old Chinese Airways twin engine propellor-driven plane. He arrived early in the morning in a misty ground fog. To get to downtown from the airport he'd have to take a ferry across the Red River because all of the bridges had been bombed down. While crossing he could see a tower of one of them, the vaunted Paul Doumer Bridge, protruding through the fog. The spans had long been blown into the water. David couldn't see the opposite shore until they came right up on it. The chugging old tug pushed the ferry close enough for him to jump out without getting wet above the knees. He asked one of the other passengers for directions to the Hotel Metropol where most of the world press and other foreign visitors stayed.

"Now called Hotel of the Reunification," he was told. "Only about six blocks."

David would walk. His wet feet squished in his wet shoes. The morning traffic consisted mostly of bicycles with an occasional Russian Moskvich automobile mixed in. Something very peculiar along the street in the sidewalks caught David's eye; a series of one person bomb shelters that looked like manholes deep enough to stand down in. Concrete lids lay ajar on top. Presently they were not being used. Too foggy, perhaps, for the bombers to come, but he saw the results of a recent bombing—a block of houses that had become rubble. This was disconcerting to David. He didn't like to think that anything but military targets had been bombed. But apparently this was not the case.

Soon he came upon the hotel—its classy French colonial architecture looking incongruent among the common Vietnamese buildings in the block. Armed with fake Soviet press credentials and a visa, he sauntered through the vast lobby to the desk and checked in, using his fake name—Vladimir Mantolnikov. He was then escorted by a bell hop to his second floor room. Upon entering the room, the bell hop, an older man, smiled and put out his hand expecting a tip. Even though he was posing as a Russian, David obliged—modestly.

The room was spacious, sparsely furnished and sparkling clean. On a table sat a bowl of bananas and grapefruit and a vase with flowers—large red and white ones.

"Nice touch for Commies," David thought.

Having been awake for the better part of three days making connections on planes—the last one being a rickety old affair that was noisy, shaky and cold, making it impossible to sleep. After devouring one of the bananas and a grapefruit, David laid down for a nap. Around four o'clock he was awakened by a call from the desk clerk who said a man from the Politburo's Foreign Ministry Press Department was there to see him. David wondered how it was known that he had arrived.

"He would like for you to meet him shortly in the hotel bar," the clerk said in Vietnamese.

"Hmm," he thought, "I could use a drink right about now."

He freshened up a bit, put on clean clothes, his shoes had dried some, grabbed his pipe and a pouch of tobacco; a Vietnamese blend that he bought at the airport, and went downstairs through the lobby to the bar. It reminded David of the cocktail lounge at the Caravelle Hotel in Saigon—not so large, rather quint and pleasantly lit by sconces on the walls and little lamps on the bar. There were a half dozen or so tables with white table clothes that were also lighted by little lamps. A thin, middle-aged man in black trousers and a white shirt sat at one sipping tea. When he saw David come in he got up, bowed slightly and offered his hand asking if he was Vladimir.

"Yes, yes I am."

"My name is Nguyen Duc Kinh of the Foreign Ministry Press Office."

"How do you do."

They shook hands.

"You are here to do a story on the bombing for Pravda? I believe it is being called the Christmas bombing by the press."

"Yes, that's right."

"Please, have a seat," Kinh said.

"I'd like to order a drink if you don't mind," David said.

"No, of course not, please do."

David signaled for the waiter. He ordered a vodka on ice. David hated vodka, but Vladimir would drink nothing else.

"I will provide you with a guide to view the destruction wrought by the bombing," Kinh said. "Will you be taking photographs?"

"It's my understanding that your office has a pool of photographers I may use."

"Yes, this is true. I will assign you one. The photographer will also serve as your guide. When would you like to begin your tour?"

"Tomorrow morning," David said. "Say 10 o'clock?"

"Very well. The photographer will meet you here at the hotel in the lobby at 10 o'clock. Now I believe I will have a drink too. Warm rice liquor with a twist of lime. The house specialty."

Kinh went to the bar and soon returned with the drink. The waiter had been busy serving others who had come into the bar. The place had gotten crowded and noisy. David could hear the language of many countries being spoken; Vietnamese of course, French and Russian and even English. All of them David understood.

The conversations centered on the bombing which had lasted virtually non-stop, weather permitting, for the past two weeks. It had, according to what was being said, exacted a terrible toll on North Vietnam, something that David was not sad to hear. But as Vladimir he would have to appear that he was while viewing the destruction tomorrow, after all, he was a Communist reporter in Hanoi to do a story on the barbaric American bombing.

In reality though, he had gone there to try to find his wife to exact some revenge for being the spy who had sold out the Vietnamese Studies Center by exposing its connection to the CIA, which exposed his connection to the CIA, making him a target of the Weather Underground. All of this while she had been playing the role of his loving wife. Betrayal was at the heart of the matter—deadly betrayal. To find her though he'd have to make some inroads into the Politburo, for since she had worked as a spy in the US, a rather prestigious position in espionage, she'd surely be known there. Perhaps Kinh could help him in this regard. The name his wife had come to the South with before changing it when they got married was Le Tran Nhu. She had changed it to Lee Gordon. Surely since she had returned to the North she had gone back to using her original name.

"Mr. Kinh, I'm also interested in doing a story on the role women play in North Vietnamese intelligence. Through the KGB I've learned of a particular one who had worked with them in infiltrating Saigon's CIA office seven years or so ago. Her name is Le Tran Nhu."

"Oh, I'm afraid that would be quite difficult, Vladimir. Intelligence is a very sensitive area."

"I assure you, her name would not be used in the story."

"I'm sorry but-"

David took a wad of Russian rubles from his pocket and placed them on the table in front of Kinh.

"Twice as much if you provide me access to this woman."

There was silence as Kinh looked at the stack of money. He twisted his mouth and raised an eyebrow.

"Le Tran Nhu you say?"

"Yes."

"Okay."

Kinh scooped up the rubles and put them in his shirt pocket.

"One hundred more you say?"

"If you deliver."

"Okay, I know who she is. She works at Radio Hanoi. I will arrange for her to come to the hotel tomorrow evening after you've returned from your tour of the bomb damage. Your room?"

"That would be fine," David said.

"The number?" Kinh asked.

"210"

"At 8 o'clock?"

"Eight o'clock," David concurred.

Kinh stood up, bowed slightly and left.

David got up and started to leave too, for his room, just as an air raid siren went off. The other bar patrons and the bartender and the waiter, knowing where to go, scurried through French doors that led to a courtyard. David followed them across the courtyard and down into a shelter. Everyone seemed to sober up quickly. There was no chattering. David sat with the others on wooden benches along the walls. The shelter was lit by two yellow bulbs on the end of cords hanging from the ceiling. The concussion of anti-aircraft guns being fired could be heard, along with the periodic muffled boom of what David presumed to be bombs exploding. He felt it through his feet and bottom, and up to the top of his head. His scalp crawled with fear. The bombs were falling close. He looked at the people sitting across from him. They all looked terrified as he was. He anticiapted that at any moment a bomb would hit directly on top of them. And when one of the explosions sounded especially loud he hunkered down. There were gasps and explanations in various tongues. "Shit!" David heard in more than one. And he realized he had said it in English not Russian. In this moment of terror he had reverted back to what came natural.

When the all clear came there was a general sigh of relief, and everyone made a beeline to the bar for more drinks. David's spontaneous slip of the tongue nearly compromised his cover. An English woman asked him if he was an American. "I thought I detected an accent," she said.

"Oh no, I'm Russian," he said in Russian, not daring to reveal anymore of an American accent. She understood and that was the end of the conversation.

He finished his drink and went to his room. It was late enough now to go to bed. He needed a good night's sleep.

David awoke in the morning with the sun beaming through the window. At first he didn't know where he was, then he remembered the air raid. Hanoi. He looked at his watch.

"At 10 o'clock meet the photographer in the lobby for a tour of the bomb damage. You're doing a story for Pravda, remember?"

Then he remembered that at 8 o'clock that night Le would be coming to his room, that is if Kinh came through. What would he do though when she arrived? Kill her, then fly back to Saigon via Canton and Hong Kong. By the time they discovered her body he'd be long gone.

David went down to the bar, which also served as a restaurant, and had a breakfast of grapefruit, sliced bananas, a poached duck egg, French bread and coffee, then he went to the lobby, sat in a chair and smoked his pipe while waiting. At 10 straight up a man in khaki clothes with two cameras on straps draped over his shoulder came through the door. David got up and approached him.

"I'm Vladimir Mantolnikov."

The man, who was relatively young and handsome with thick shiny black hair, smiled and extended his hand.

"I'm Vu Thuy Binh. Just call me Binh."

They shook hands.

"First I will show you the damage from yesterday evening's bombing. I saw it coming to the hotel."

David followed Binh out to the street where his Russion-built car was parked. They drove two blocks and around the corner onto Sweet Potato Street, and David saw the damage. All the houses on one side of the street the entire length of the block had been wiped out. People were sifting through the rubble of bricks, concrete blocks and twisted metal looking for bodies, and hopefully survivors. Four bodies were on the sidewalk covered with blankets. Binh took pictures.

"You see, not all bombs hit military targets," he said. "Many civilians have been killed."

Acting as a reporter, David wrote down what Binh said on a note pad.

On the way out of Hanoi, all along the streets, David saw wall murals and graffiti saying **DA DAO NIXON GIAC MY**, in other words, *Down with Nixon, the American pirate*. The "x" in Nixon's name came in the form of a swastika.

Anti-aircraft guns could be seen everywhere protruding from the tops of buildings and trees. This city and Haiphong had the reputation among American pilots of being more heavily defended than Berlin at the height of World War II.

Binh drove a few miles out of Hanoi to the Catholic hamlet of Phu Xa to show David a monument in the village square that had been erected in remembrance of twenty-four people who had been killed in an air raid there in 1966.

Now, in 1972, the bombers came again: three of them flying in a V-formation, high and far away. The sirens went off and the peasants came running out of the rice paddies toward a long, deep trench. Those who had been in the village, including Binh, ran for the trench too, amidst the chickens, pigs, dogs and goats who were cackling, squealing and barking, and scurrying about. Yet there was order in the chaos. Everyone had been given a job to do. Little boys and girls, looking no older than five or six, ran around picking up chicks and piglets. The older children went after the pigs and goats, while teenagers scrambled into the fields to get the bullocks. They corralled them into other trenches cut into the rice paddies. Mothers took care of the toddlers. Militia men and women grabbed their rifles and took up positions in the fields. They'd fire at the low-flying jets hoping for a lucky hit.

Shocked by what was happening, David stood and watched the planes at first as they broke formation and followed one another in a long sweeping turn, then he finally realized they were diving straight toward him and the village. But because he had hesitated he didn't have time to reach the trench so he just laid flat on the ground and covered his head. He heard the whistling noise of rockets shooting through the air. He peaked out from beneath his arms and saw two or three impact a rice paddy. Then he heard the roar of the engines as the planes pulled up and away, their afterburners glowing.

"What the hell was that all about?" David wondered aloud as he stood up and dusted himself off.

"Terror bombing," Binh said as he walked up from the trench.

Soon they were joined by a village official, a Catholic Communist who explained that not all of the terror bombing has resulted in a couple rockets landing innocently in rice paddies.

"They've bombed our churches," he said. "We celebrate mass in farm huts late at night now, when the bombers rarely come."

He said there were 23 villages in the district and that they all had been bombed regularly since 1965.

"One raid at Phat Diem killed 72 people and wounded 46 in one of our churches on a Sunday morning at the hour of Vespers," he said. "More than 8,000 families have been evacuated from Phat Diem and dispersed throughout the countryside."

They drove to Phat Diem where David was shown the damage; the craters around the canals, dikes and dams of the irrigation systems. He was shown the ruins of the church, the shops and homes; the graves. David took notes and Binh pictures. And in his mind David visualized how such an article would look to the world; like the American bombing targeted civilians. He wanted to see the damage that had been done to the military targets, but Binh said they were off limits. He'd see only what they wanted him to see.

On the way back to Hanoi they came to a river where the bridge had been blown out, but it had been ingeniously replaced by floating flat-bottomed sampans lashed together with pontoons laid over with wooden planks.

The cars were going in single file, each waiting for the one ahead to get over before moving onto the makeshift bridge. There was a long line of bicylists with baskets of supplies resting on boards on the back fenders, and peasants on foot loaded down with baskets suspended on the ends of long, flexible bamboo poles. Despite the bombing, life in North Vietnam went on.

Back in Hanoi, Binh dropped David off at the hotel. "I will develop the film and provide you with the photos for your story at eight o'clock tomorrow morning," Binh said before driving away.

David said okay, but he would no longer be at the hotel then. For shortly after eight o'clock p.m., when Le came to his room, he will have killed her and fled Hanoi.

At eight o'clock there was a knock on the door. It was Le. When she saw that it was David she started to scream. He put his hand over her mouth and grabbed her by the back of the neck and yanked her into the room and kicked the door shut behind her.

"I'll break your neck if you scream," David said.

She went limp and nodded. David slowly removed his hand from her mouth, and he let go of her neck. He could have killed her right then and there, but first he wanted to hear her explanation for betraying him.

"Surprised to see me?" David asked.

"Surprised? More like terrified. You've come here to kill me no doubt."

"You betrayed me, Le. You were a US citizen, you betrayed your country. That makes you a traitor."

"David, you must try to understand what motivated me. My family was killed in the bombing of our village in 1965, while I was away at school in Hanoi. It angered me so I vowed to do whatever it took to make the Americans pay. I joined the army, and because of my advanced education and mastery of English I was trained in intelligence by the KGB who had an agent working in the CIA office in Saigon. I was sent south to be hired by him as a secretary there."

"And to woo me."

"That was not part of the original plan, but when we learned that you would be going to the U.S. to direct one of the Vietnamese Studies Centers I was given the assignment of seducing you, yes, and making you my husband so that I'd be in a position to undermine the mission of the Centers by exposing their connection to the CIA."

"Yes, I know all of this now. That's why I'm here to make you pay for your betrayal."

"What is that saying, David? All is fair in love and war? I'm sorry, David. Please, you must try to understand what this war is really all about. It is not about the spread of Communism beyond Vietnam. We have no desire to conquer others, we only wish not to be conquered by someone else. It's about imperialism versus freedom and independence. We won our freedom from the French; not just for northern Vietnam, but for all of Vietnam. The DMZ was to be a temporary divide until a Geneva-mandated unifying national election could be held, but because the US feared the popular Communist Ho Chi Minh would win they propped up a puppet regime in the South—Diem, the zealot anti-Communist—and he saw to it that no election was held. And because Diem was so unpopular among the southern Vietnamese, including his own generals, he was assassinated and Thieu was installed in his place. All of this you know, of course, but perhaps you don't know how determined the Vietnamese people are to unite this country under one flag, be it Communist or otherwise. That would be our choice. This is what true democracy is all about, although it may not be the kind the US prefers. And since this choice was not allowed through the ballot box, it will be decided on the battlefield between the armies of the people and the army of the puppet Thieu."

Disarmed by Le's compelling argument, David reconsidered killing her, but he was in a predicament now. She could reveal to authorities before he had a chance to get out of Hanoi that he was not a Russian journalist, but a CIA agent. If he didn't kill her he'd be at her mercy. He placed a hand over her mouth again and grabbed her by the back of the neck, one powerful jerk and she'd be dead. But looking into her eyes he couldn't bring himself to do it, instead he bound and gagged her with socks tied together, wrapped her body up tight in a sheet like a mummy and placed her in the bathtub.

"Goodbye, Le."

He quickly packed and left the hotel for the airport.

Chapter 50

The bombing of North Vietnam above the 20th Parallel ended December 30, 1972, and the White House announced that private peace talks would resume in Paris January 8, 1973. They began on schedule after a bitter denunciation of the bombing by the North Vietnamese's chief negotiator Le Duc Tho. But by January 13 he and Kissinger had come to a basic agreement. Nixon approved it on the 15th, and on the 16th Alexander Haig arrived in Saigon with the unenviable task of trying to get Thieu to go along with it. South Vietnam's president responded by calling it a "surrender agreement," and at first refused to sign it. But Nixon, through Haig, promised he'd retaliate strongly if Hanoi took advantage of the agreement, and he assured Thieu that he would push Congress to continue aid (other than troops) to South Vietnam. At the same time he let Thieu know that the US would sign the agreement whether Saigon did or not, and if they didn't all aid to South Vietnam would stop. Thieu signed, and on the 28th of January the agreement went into effect. It called primarily for a cease fire, the withdrawal of US troops, a POW exchange, and it prohibited the US and North Vietnam from sending more troops into South Vietnam.

Despite reaching an agreement, according to a Washington insider who wrote an anonymous story for *The Wall Street Journal* that Mick read, the Nixon administration had no illusions that North Vietnam would give up on forcing South Vietnam into the Communist fold.

First of all the agreement left an estimated 200,000 North Vietnamese troops in the South. And the article quoted unnamed intelligence sources in Saigon as saying that in the first four or five months of 1973, North Vietnam sent south an estimated 5,000 administrative personnel to assist in governing the Communist-controlled regions of South Vietnam. It was also reported that the 200,000 NVA soldiers who stayed in the south after the Agreement was finalized were being told that they would not be returning home, but that young women were to be coming soon from the North with whom they were to establish permanent communities.

And despite having been dealt a devastating blow by the tremendous casualties of the Easter Offensive of 1972, and the beating Hanoi took from the Christmas bombings, the North Vietnamese went on another land- and people-grabbing expedition the night before the Paris Agreement went into effect on the 27th of January, 1973. The infiltration of men and equipment into the South continued. Seemingly endless convoys carried them down on an expanded and hardened Ho Chi Minh Trail, and on an additional 12,000 miles of new roads within South Vietnam, one running 175 miles from the DMZ to the Central Highlands.

Additionally the North Vietnamese refurbished or built landing strips at approximately thirteen locations in South Vietnam. A large field capable of handling transport planes and MIGs was developed at the former US Marine base at Khe Sanh, and the base itself was developed into a major military complex. Truck parks were built to accommodate the 4,000 to 5,000 vehicles that had come in through the Communist supply system (i.e. the Ho Chi Minh Trail) in the northern part of the country. And again, in blatant violation of not only the Geneva Accords of '54 and the Laotian Accords of '61, but also the Paris Agreement of 1973, Hanoi boldly infiltrated 75,000 more NVA troops into the South in addition to hundreds of tanks and numerous artillery pieces, antiaircraft guns and surface-to-air-missiles.

All of this in clear violation of the Paris Agreement. Small wonder that Thieu, who had called the Agreement a "surrender," was so reluctant to sign it. He did so only because the US threatened to cut off all aid to South Vietnam if he didn't.

Meanwhile, President Nixon had signed a bill that prohibited direct or indirect combat activities over, in, or near Laos, Cambodia and both Vietnams after August 15, 1972. It was just a matter of time now before Southeast Asia's shaky House of Dominos fell. The United States, handcuffed by its own government, did nothing to stop the continuous influx of supplies moving into South Vietnam through Laos and across the DMZ in direct and clear violation of all the accords that had been reached relative to the Vietnam War, especially the Geneva Accords of 1954 and the more recent Paris Agreement.

Chapter 51

"Well, John, it's official now," Mick said with indignation as he moseyed up to the bar at the Club. "We've cashed it in."

He plopped a handful of assorted change down and ordered a beer, which would be half price for the next two hours; from four to six. John sorted out what he needed and poured Mick a glass.

"Cashed it in?"

"The war, John."

"Oh, yeah, but didn't we reach some kind of mutual settlement with that Paris peace agreement?"

"The only thing mutual about it was that we both signed it. Hell, North Vietnam violated it before the ink dried. Remember Khe Sanh, John, the base you helped build, the base where I almost got my ass blown off by North Vietnamese artillery? Well it belongs to them now."

"Say what?" John's eyes flashed.

"You heard me. And they've turned the Ho Chi Minh Trail into a regular highway that handles more trucks, Good Buddy, than I-57. And what are we doing about it? Nothing, absolutely nothing, because we've negotiated and legislated ourselves into a position that won't allow us to because our word is good and the god damn Communists are stinking liars and cheats, and because the American people and their representatives in Congress were convinced by the antiwar movement and the press that the war was unjust, unwarranted and unwinnable."

John became as indignant as Mick.

"Damn right a war is unwinnable when you're forced to fight it with one hand tied behind your back like we were. We weren't given the troops we needed to mop up on 'em right after the Tet Offensive, and we weren't allowed to go after the bastards in Cambodia after 1970 because of that, oh, what was that bill Congress passed?"

"The Cooper-Church Amendment."

"Yeah, that's it. Those fucking politicians. They sure know how to start wars, but they sure as hell don't know how to fight 'em or finish 'em."

"Oh, they knew how to finish this one, John, on the enemy's terms. Like Thieu said, the Paris Agreement is tantamount to surrender. In all fairness to the South Vietnamese Army, it's not over yet though. They did very well in fending off North Vietnam's Easter Offensive, and Thieu has shown strong leadership in not giving in to pressure from us to accept every demand the Communist put on the table in Paris. He's proven to be anything but a US puppet for sure. If we'd a gotten the same kind of leadership from our presidents during this war it would have been won three years ago. Instead that talking head up there on the tube, Walter Cronkite, took the bully pulpit from LBJ and used it on the evening news to convince the American people that the war was winnable."

John reached up and turned the television off.

"Fuck it, Man," Mick said, "I'm ready to go back to the woods. It's supposed to be mild this weekend. Wanna work on the house, John? We could be done with it by the end of spring, basically. Just need to put the roof on and build the front porch. Most of the interior work I can get done while I'm living there."

"Sure," John said. "I'll meet you there Sunday morning around eight."

It was a chilly mid-March morning, but the weatherman had promised temperatures would reach the upper 50s or even low 60s by afternoon. Mick got there early and built a small fire to brew some coffee on while waiting for John. He sat facing the lake which sparkled from the rising sun. Some of the trees were beginning to bud, giving them a faint tint of green. Mick sensed the slightest hint of spring in the air; a subtle, underlying warmth in the cool breeze coming off the water as the sun got higher in the sky which had grown from a misty gray to blue.

The coffee perked Mick up, and he was anxious for John to arrive so they could get started on the roof. And Mick was anxious to see how the stained glass skylight would look in it. He would invite Gary out to see it whenever he got back from being on tour with his band. In fact, he would have a big house-finishing party once the porch got done. That would be the last thing he and John would do.

John would be the toast of the party for sure. Without him the house couldn't have been built. The steaks and beers, and the money Mick had given him were a mere pittance of what his help had been worth. Mick would do something else in honor of him, like, he chuckled, naming the outhouse for him with a sign over the door that simply said, JOHN.

John arrived about nine and they had a cup of coffee before starting work.

"I didn't bring any steaks today," Mick said. "Thought we could do some fishing. They'll be biting now that the water is starting to warm up a little."

John laughed. "I've never caught anything bigger than my bait."

"No sweat, Man. I've got a couple lures that are guaranteed to bring in the lunkers, and this lake is loaded with 'em."

"Better be," John said. "Alls I had for breakfast at Mary Lou's Diner was a three-egg Denver omelet, hash browns, sausage and a short stack."

Despite John being weak from a lack of nourishment, by three the plywood for the roof had been nailed down on the eight beams that ran up at 45 degree angles from notches in the top of the circular stone wall. The roof beams had been bolted, the ends being mitered at 45 degrees, into the outside faces of each of the four vertical beams that rose from footings in the center of the house, up the corners of the chimney that they were mortared into for added support.

Then they installed the framed, stained glass window skylight in the triangular hole Mick had cut for it in the plywood roof. They gingerly put it in its place and screwed it down. From the outside the colors and design were barely discernable, but inside, with the sun shining through the yellow and green glass, the window glowed beautifully, filling the house with golden light, like a church, although the window's design symbolized Taoism. Nonetheless, it had spiritual implications and it gave Mick a feeling of peace. He stood there in silence, absorbing the moment. This would be his home soon.

John, who had been on the roof caulking the skylight, got down and came to the door.

"How's it look, Mick?"

"Come in and see for yourself."

"Wow!"

John stood in awe of it just as Mick had.

"This calls for a drink. I brought some wine this time, especially for the occasion. This basically finishes it John, except the shingles and porch. The interior work I'll finish after I've moved in."

Mick took the bottle of wine and two glasses from the cooler and sat them on a makeshift table that consisted of a piece of plywood spanning two saw horses, and poured.

"Gotta get a nice old round oak table for this place," Mick said.

John nodded. They clanked glasses and drank.

"You know you're welcome to come out here anytime you want, John. I'll be getting a fold-out couch, you can crash on that."

"I'll take that hammock outside, weather permitting," John said.

"If I'm not in it," Mick retorted.

"Oh, they turn upside down quite easily," John said with a good natured wink and smile. "Hey, let's see if we can catch some of those lunkers you were talking about, Mick, I'm getting hungry."

"Okay, I'll get the tackle.

They cast their lines and switched to Hamm's Beer, *".... the beer refreshing, from the land of sky blue waters,"* only this wasn't Wisconsin or Minnesota, but beautiful southern Illinois.

It didn't take long for Mick to land one—a bass—about three pounds he guessed. Then John reeled in a nice one, and they had more than enough for supper.

Mick scaled and gutted them, coated them with flour and fried them in an iron skillet to a golden brown. That was all they needed; fresh fish and a couple of cold beers, and a rekindled fire to take off the chill of the evening as the sun went down behind them.

John looked at Mick and smiled. "You're turning hippie on us ain't ya, Mick?"

"I am? How's that?"

"The long hair and beard; living out here, you know, like a back-to-the-lander."

"I don't know, John. I'm not even sure if I know what a hippie is anymore. Seems like there are so many different kinds."

"Where'd all this hippie shit get started at anyway, Mick, San Francisco?"

"Well, according to a course I took in English called the Beats and Beyond, that's were it's flourished. But actually the hippie movement, as we know it, began in the late '40s and early '50s in New York City at Columbia University. Jack Kerouac, William Burroughs and Alan Ginsberg were students and writers there. They smoked weed and did other kinds of drugs, hung out in coffee houses, and by-and-large just snubbed their noses at conventional society and the traditional values of previous generations. Then they took it on the road to San Francisco in the early '60s where they congregated with other writers and intellectuals at poet Lawrence Ferlinghetti's City Lights Bookstore. In '67 Ginsberg, antiwar activist Jerry Rubin and LSD guru, Timothy Leary, a Harvard professor, joined thousands in what was called a "Gathering of the Tribes," at Golden Gate State Park. They celebrated love, peace and all that shit, with Leary advocating the use of acid to open the mind up to it all, and to '…. turn on to the scene, tune in to what is happening and drop out.' And Rubin hoped to persuade the 'culturally alienated' there to engage in political activism.

"And then that summer at the Monterey Pop Festival, thousands danced in the sun with flowers in their hair. Jimi Hendrix went ballistic with an irreverent version of the Star Spangled Banner on a flaming guitar that he smashed on the stage, symbolic, I guess, of America crashing and burning, or at least its traditional values.

"Word of the Gathering and the Summer of Love spread across the nation like pollen in the wind, and a new generation of hippies known as flower children, born of the beats, flourished, not just in places like Haight-Ashbury, but in relatively obscure little places like Carbondale too. But I've discovered that not all the children of the flowers are of the same petal."

"Boy that's for sure," John said, "around here you'll see umpteen different kinds. You've got your good time rock 'n roller types who dress like they're members of a band. Then you've got the more serious kind who are into yoga, yogurt and transcendental meditation. Then there's the communal types who are into group sex, and the back-to-the-lander Mr. Naturalites living in the country growing organic veggies and their own weed."

"And the political types," Mick added, "who are influenced by the likes of Rubin, Hoffman, Hayden, Marx and Mao, who are members of the SDS, Weather Underground, and Youth International Party (Yippies), and some the Communist Party. Some of these are actually professors who use lecture hall podiums as bully pulpits to espouse their left-wing politics. They expound on the teachings of Thoreau, Gandhi and King, yet they condone violence if it serves their purpose, that being the dismantlement of Capitalism and the US government, if it's Republican.

"Oh, and the occultist types like the Manson Family, who some call hippies just because Charlie has long greasy hair, and they indulge in group sex."

"Don't forget about the hippie soldiers, Mick, the kind that were in Nam," John said. "The kind who had marijuana leaves and 'make love not war,' and 'peace' scribbled on the canvas covers of their helmets."

"Now that's a pretty bizarre paradox, isn't it, John, protesting the war, in a sense, while fighting it."

"So then where do you fit it here, Mick?"

Mick stared at the fire and poked at it with a stick.

"I guess you could say I'm kind of a peacenik now. I've turned against the war, the way it's ending up anyway. And I've become disillusioned with American politics because of the way our politicians got us involved in South Vietnam without any honorable exit strategy, at the expense of about 50,000 American GI lives, not to mention all the Vietnamese who have died. And now I suppose you could say I'm kind of dropping out by wanting to live out here in the woods."

He looked around and out at the lake.

"But I prefer to think that I'm more of a back-to-the-lander than a drop out. I'm not sure I fit in anywhere really. Since Nam I've felt kind of lost at times. And you, John, do you feel like you've readjusted since coming back to the World?"

It was John's turn to stare at the fire and stir. A glint of the flames were reflected in his light brown eyes.

"Not always. I find that I'm pissed off at times, about the war, for the same reasons you are. Because of the way we basically just quit in the middle of it before we got the job done like Americans are supposed to do. But I really don't have time to think about it all that much, running the bar and all."

He looked back at Mick and smiled. There was always something reassuring about the way John smiled. Maybe it was the handlebar mustache.

"Do yourself a favor, Mick, don't you think so much about it either. It's too god damn frustrating.

"Well," John said, "I better head back to town now before I get too drunk to drive."

"Yeah, me too. I've got a dog and cat to feed. And I've got to get up early to meet with a professor to discuss the progress of my thesis. Thanks for all your help, John."

"No sweat."

Chapter 52

▼

Professor Miller looked a little older than most faculty Mick knew; with his gray, thinning hair. His gray mustache was thick though. He wore those Western-style string ties, and Western-style shirts and slacks and boots. He raised horses on the side. Mick liked him because he was more down-to-earth than the ivory tower types.

The Professor was surprisingly open-minded too, Mick thought, compared to most of the others he had had, particularly in regards to the Vietnam War. Surprisingly because he had been a journalist before entering academia, and normally those who did that brought to the classroom their left-leaning attitudes, but not Professor Miller. He made no political judgments about the subject of Mick's thesis—Vietnamization. He judged it only on the merits of research, continuity and interpretation of its significance relative to current world affairs. The latter of which was obvious. The results of Vietnamization's success or failure would impact relations between East and West for years to come.

"It has reached its most critical moment now, hasn't it, Mick?" the professor asked smiling.

"Yes it has."

"Do you think the situation over there will be resolved before or after your thesis is due, which would be in December, correct?"

"Correct. No, I don't think it will be resolved by then," Mick said. "I think it'll probably be another year and half, two years."

"Well maybe by December we'll at least have some indication as to Vietnamization's success, or lack thereof; enough anyway to draw a conclusion. Although if you'd like, we could extend the project. I think this thesis would be quite publishable if it were expanded into a book, but it would have to include the actual conclusion of the war. Have you thought of that?"

"Well, I have intended to write a book about Nam, but one based on my personnel experiences as a reporter there, back in '67 and '68."

The professor sat back and rested his hands, folded, on his stomach, and he sighed.

"Yes, I too contemplated writing one based on my experiences as a reporter in the Korean War for the Pacific Stars and Stripes Newspaper, but I kept putting it off, and putting it off. Before long I won't remember enough about it to write anything. Don't make that mistake, Mick."

"I'm curious about something, Doctor. As a former journalist why do you think the mass media, particularly TV guys tend to lean so far to the left in the political spectrum?"

"Oh, I have a long-held theory about that, but I seldom share it with anyone. It sounds a little too simplistic."

"I'd be interested in hearing it."

"Very well, then. I think it's because it's the popular way to be in high school and college, especially among young, starry-eyed idealists who think of themselves as inordinately intelligent and compassionate. Particularly the boys who want to be popular with the bleeding-heart liberal girls of the class who say they are antiwar, and who think it is wealthier people's fault—i.e. successful Capitalists—that other people are poor. They believe that socialism and welfare, in other words government handouts, are the answers to all of society's woes.

"You see, popularity is very important to these people, Mick, especially to the talking heads who want their handsome faces to be seen closeup on TV every night for the nation to admire, while they interpret the news, from the liberals' point-of-view of course. They want to show everyone how bright, compassionate, hip and insightful they are, especially in the eyes of the bleeding heart girls of the audience. And just like at school, they want to be popular among their colleagues—other reporters, editors and producers, who of course are liberals too. Same thing applies to academia, with the podium up on the stage in front of the lecture hall being the anchor's desk."

"Hmm, interesting, Doctor."

"Yes, well, as I said at the beginning, perhaps it is a bit too simplistic, and conjectural on my part, yet it may not be more complicated than that after all."

"What about print guys, Doctor?"

"Same theory applies, basically, except their liberal hearts bleed ink."

"You were a print guy, what kept you from going left? I'm assuming you haven't anyway. You seem too open-minded for that."

"My mother ran a small town newspaper in western Illinois. She taught me early on that personal politics have a place in the editorial pages, but not on the front page. The news she said, should be reported straight, like an arrow guided by the quill. In fact that was the name of her paper, *The Arrow and the Quill*. Big papers like the *New York Times* would do well to take her advice.

"Well, Mick, it looks like you're making good progress with the thesis. Let's meet again in September."

He looked over a calendar in a small black book.

"How about the 13th; same time, same station."

"Sounds good. See you then, Doctor Miller."

Chapter 53

The campus was in full spring bloom, especially the magnolias, and their scent filled the air. It made Mick feel high. He spotted a sunny spot on a grassy knoll overlooking one of the main walks. A good place to sit and watch students going back and forth between classes. They looked even younger to him now than when he first came to school four years before. Being a veteran, and now a graduate student, he surely looked older to them, especially with the beard. He had first grown one for his undercover role, then shaved it when that was over. He grew it back again, admittedly because they were in style, and vainly, because with his sandy red hair he thought he resembled a lion in a way; with his mane-like beard. He often thought of himself as cat-like, like a jungle cat—a survivor. He had survived a rough childhood, a tough neighborhood, the war. He had survived three attempts on his life. Mick felt kind of proud. He smiled to himself watching the others go by down below. But when he saw Kathy coming down the walk he was suddenly reminded of his drinking, which had been somewhat of problem at times, he had to admit, and it brought him down a bit.

"That's the first step," Kathy had told him, "admitting that we have a problem."

Mick had been wanting to talk to her again. He called out her name. She stopped and looked around, then she spotted him. She smiled and came up the knoll.

"Mick." She seemed glad to see him. "I was hoping you would have called me by now. I owe you a spaghetti dinner."

"I'm sorry, I...."

She interrupted him. "Would you like to come over and collect this weekend?"

"Uh, well, yeah, sure. What night?"

"How about Saturday?"

"Great. Where do you live?"

"Chateau Apartments. Number five."

"Yeah, I know where they are. What time?"

"Seven."

"Okay."

"Gotta hurry, I'll be late for my next class. Bye."

"See ya Saturday night," Mick said.

Mick watched Kathy as she hurried away, almost trotting. He had not seen her from that vantage point before, and he was pleasantly surprised to see how shapely she looked in the lacy, white cotton dress she wore; the way it clung to her hips, and for the first time he noticed how nice her legs were, and for the first time he felt genuinely attracted to her, even though they had made love before. But it had been when he was in an alcoholic fog—like in a dream. It didn't seem like it had really happened.

Mick rested his back against a tree, closed his eyes and took a deep breath of the sweet spring air, and it did seem to make a young man's fancy turn to love, or lust at least. He looked forward to Saturday night, but he cautioned himself against looking forward to it too much. He was somewhat wary about getting too involved with Kathy. At times she had proven to be a little unpredictable.

"And the same could be said about you too, Mick," he muttered to himself, "when it comes to your drinking for sure."

He didn't like thinking about that, so he blocked it out of his mind and replaced it with more positive thoughts about his stone house; it had a roof on it now. He anticipated moving in by June, or July at the latest. It would take at least until then to nail the shake shingles on.

"Better get started on that pretty soon, Mick, time is a wasting," he said to himself.

He had also been putting off telling the landlord that he'd be moving out of the house in Carbondale soon. Today would be as good as any day to do that. Mick went home and called him, and he told Jazzpur and Lucky to be prepared to move into a different kind of neighborhood. One without an ally for Jazzpur to prowl in, but he assured Lucky there'd be plenty of squirrels to chase at the new place. They seemed okay with it.

Mick decided to start packing well in advance. When the time came he wanted to be able to move right away.

While packing his books he came across Li Po's poetry, which he hadn't read in some time. Mick related to Li Po's descriptions of nature, particularly the night time sky which the Chinese poet often viewed lying on his back drunk with wine.

Mick had done that plenty of times on his property at Lake Wells. He planned on continuing the practice occasionally as a source of inspiration for his own nature poetry. In fact he planned on doing it Friday night, beginning in the early evening just before sundown, lying in his hammock with a bottle of wine.

He loved the transition the sky went through at twilight. Sometimes a ghostly moon appeared in the east accompanied by the Evening Star. And when today gradually becomes yesterday before a new tomorrow dawns, in the firmament one has a view of eternity, and the birth of stars that occurred billions of light years away. Mick laid in his hammock all night and drank himself to sleep until awakened by the sun. He then went back to town to feed the cat and dog and himself. After sleeping some more, until mid-afternoon, he sat down at his desk and began to write a poem about his heavenly observations of the night before, but the words came slowly, so he drank more wine in the spirit of Li Po, thinking that would get his creative juices flowing, and it did, so he thought, enough for several verses. But by the time he was supposed to be leaving for Kathy's he had gotten good and drunk again. Should he go anyway?

His judgment clouded he went with poem in hand to show Kathy. She was not impressed. In fact, she promptly told him to leave.

"Don't ever come over here, Mick, if you've been drinking."

"I take it that means it's okay if I'm sober?"

"When are you going to get sober?"

"I don't know, maybe never."

"You might want to reconsider before it kills you like it did your parents. Goodnight," and she shut the door in Mick's face and turned off the porch light. He stood there in the dark feeling very lonely, and too drunk really, to even go to a bar, yet he did not want to go home. He needed to talk with someone besides a cat and a dog. He drove uptown, risking a driving-under-the-influence, to a liquor store by the train station, and he bought a bottle of *Mad Dog 20/20* wine, and when he saw a wino he knew by the name of Jesse go behind the store, he followed him.

"Hey, Jesse, want a drink?"

"Sure, Buddy, Jesse always wants a drink."

They sat down on an old railroad tie facing the tracks with their backs against the liquor store wall. Mick took a drink and offered the bottle to Jesse, who drank a hefty swig and handed it back.

"You from Carbondale?" Mick asked.

"No, Mississippi," he slurred. "But I've been up here since I uz thirteen years old. How about another drink?"

Mick took a swig and gave the bottle back to Jesse. "So you went to school here?" he asked.

"Didn't go to no school. My pappy and mammy was share croppers. Had to work on the farm, then my Mammy she died and my Pappy he up and left, and I went to washin' dishes in town so I's could eat. I slept right over yonder in that shack across these here tracks. Still do, yep. Give me another drink."

The bells of the nearest crossing began to ring, and soon a southbound freight train came rumbling by blowing its horn. A light across the tracks that blinked between the cars passing, shown in flashes on Jesse's black face. One of his eyes drooped, and it looked like there was a tear coming from it, rolling over his cheek. He wasn't crying Mick didn't think; just an old injury seeping he thought, like the kind old alley cats get. Jesse no doubt had been through a lot, but there wasn't any meanness in his voice. He sounded gentle.

"How's come you're sittin' here sharin' your wine with somebody like me?" he asked Mick after the train passed. "You don't look like no bum."

"I might not be a bum, Jesse, but I'm a drunk."

"Folks call me a wino. Guess that's what I am alright. I sure do like that wine you got. Can I have another drink?"

"Sure, Jesse."

Mick watched him as he drank. Some of the wine ran from the corner of his mouth and dripped off his chin and onto his soiled, once-white shirt that was missing a couple of its buttons. Mick noticed that his filthy pants were half unzipped, and his laceless leather shoes were barely still attached to their worn soles. The way Jesse sat Mick could see a hole in one. Must have hurt when he walked, at one time, but maybe not now, to a man so callused to the world, living his life on the streets in search of that next drink of wine.

Mick felt deeply sorry for Jesse, and he began to feel sorry for himself. Was this how he would end up someday? Someday hell, he was there now, wasn't he? Sitting behind a liquor store alongside the railroad tracks, sharing cheap wine with one of Carbondale's winos. What the hell are you doing, Mick? Give the bottle to Jesse and go home for God's sake.

He handed it to Jesse, who drank lustfully, without seeming to notice Mick's departure.

Feeling low down, both physically and psychologically, after this particular binge, Mick stayed at home for three days to recover. Having Jazzpur and Lucky as companions seemed to help with his recovery; their occasional antics lightened his mood, and by Wednesday Mick felt good enough to go back to the library to work on his thesis. When he tired of that he read some from Walden Pond thinking Thoreau's way of communing with nature might be a little healthier to emulate at the this time than Li Po's.

As far as he knew, Thoreau did it sober, something Mick hoped to be on a continuous basis once he moved to Lake Wells, which would be soon, as it was now late April. Mick liked what Henry David had to say about why he went to live in the woods at Walden Pond.

> *I went to the woods because I wished to live deliberately, to front only the essential facts of life, and see if I could not learn what it had to teach, and not, when I came to die, discover that I had not lived. I did not wish to live what was not life, living is so dear; nor did I wish to practice resignation, unless it was quite necessary. I wanted to live deep and suck out all the marrow of life, to live so sturdily and Spartan-like as to put to rout all that was not life, to cut a broad swath and shave close, to drive life into a corner and reduce it to its lowest terms, and if it proved to me mean, why then to get the whole and genuine meanness of it, and publish its meanness to the world; or if it were sublime, to know it by experience, and be able to give a true account of it....*

"The library will be closing in fifteen minutes. If you have material to check out please do so now," someone on the PA announced.

Mick didn't realize it had gotten so late. He had walked to the library because he enjoyed strolling home across campus, especially on soft spring nights.

As he crossed the street into his neighborhood he smelled the smoke. When he turned the corner on his block he saw the firemen rolling up the hoses down at the end of the street. He couldn't tell from where he stood what house they were in front of, but when he got closer he could see it was his, what was left of it. The site of it put Mick into a state of shock. He walked up to one of the firemen and muttered something, which the fireman somehow interpreted to mean Mick lived there.

"Darn good thing you weren't home. One of your neighbors said she heard an explosion before it became engulfed in flames. Gas leak is my guess. We'll know more tomorrow when we've had a chance to check it out."

"Did you, is there, did you see a cat and a dog?"

"No, Buddy, if they were inside I'm afraid they'd be gone. It all happened so fast, and it got so hot so fast because the house is so old. It was a tender box. I'd be surprised if they could have escaped. And as hot as it got I doubt if there'd be a trace. Sorry."

Mick's heart was broken. Nothing in the house mattered more than those two. Sure, they were just animals, but some animals he had learned were better than some people. He loved them as if they were his children. Losing them left Mick heartbroken. He shivered from the pain, and he cried.

"Got someplace to stay tonight?' the fireman asked.

"Huh, no, no I don't."

"We'll contact the Red Cross. They'll put you up in a motel or something."

Waiting with the firemen for the Red Cross to arrive, Mick finally came to the realization that his utilities weren't gas at all, but strictly electricity. He told the fireman who looked puzzled.

"So then what the hell caused the explosion?" he pondered. "And you know your neighbor said something else that's kind of curious. She said she thought she heard glass crashing just before the explosion. This'll be a good one for the arson squad."

The Red Cross came, checked Mick into a motel, gave him some cash for food, and told him to come to their office in the morning to discuss replacing his clothes, for all he had left he wore. But Jazzpur and Lucky couldn't be replaced.

Instead of buying food Mick impulsively bought beer to help him numb the pain, and to help him sleep. It worked, although he had a nightmare about fires, and being trapped in one in a house, but at the last moment escaping it, and when he looked back at the house he saw Jazzpur and Lucky looking out a window, flames behind them.

Mercifully, he was awakened from the dream by a knocking on the door.

"Will you be staying another night?" a woman, who's voice was barely audible through the door, asked.

The clock said eleven. Must be check out time.

"No, but I'm not quite ready to leave yet," he shouted. "Can you give me another fifteen minutes?"

"Okay."

Mick laid there for a moment thinking about the loss of his pets, and what he'd do next. First he'd be moving into his house at the lake; ready or not. Thank God he had kept all of his money in the bank, except for the small amount he had on him.

He got up, dressed, and drove to the Red Cross office to thank them for their help, and to decline any further assistance.

With nothing left to his name to pack, Mick bought groceries and drove to his new home, but in a state of deep gloom, as he had expected to be taking Jazzpurr and Lucky with him. And he expected that finally moving into his stone house would be a joyous occasion. He tried to make it that by transcending his sorrow by sitting in the middle of the round house with a view of the skylight and meditating on that. The symbol; the sign of the TAO, Gary had informed him, represented the paradoxical totality of life, the good and the bad, light and dark, it's ups and downs, and being able to accept them both as we live would give us peace of mind. At least that's how Mick saw it.

This was his home now, not some landlord's. He had built it with his own two hands, with a tremendous amount of help from John, of course. He thought about all of those Sundays they had worked on it together, and the other times too, when he had worked on it by himself. He remembered the very first stone that he had left in its place on the ground; a corner stone, and from it the others were placed up and around. In retrospect he envisioned it growing, like through a time lapse camera over a period of three years becoming this, his stone house in the round, surrounding the stone fire place and chimney rising up through the lofty ceiling. It was like a little lodge.

Although it was a mild spring day, Mick started a fire in the hearth; a house warming as it were, but in the process of watching the wood burn, he rekindled his grief, and instead of meditating as before, he impulsively fell back into the old habit of drowning it with alcohol again. John had left a bottle of Jack Daniel's there, on the counter in the kitchen. He dashed a shot into a glass of water, the only way he could stomach whiskey. Hesitating to drink it for some reason, he stared at the crackling fire, and suddenly it popped like a small explosion.

An explosion; the fireman said a neighbor had heard an explosion before the house quickly went up in flames. What could have caused it, the fireman wondered, since gas was not used to heat the house and the stove was electric. Mick wondered too. Then it hit him, a bomb, or a Molotov Cocktail thrown through the window. The neighbor also said she had heard glass crashing too, just before the explosion. The bastards were still after him, even though Stuart was in prison, and that other goon who attacked him in Chicago in his backyard in Carbondale was locked up too.

Mick splashed his drink, which he still hadn't tasted, on the fire, and drove into town to talk to the police. "Who do you suspect?" a detective asked.

"Individually I couldn't say, but in general, the Weather Underground."

"Yes, Mr. Scott, we are familiar with your past connection to them."

"I thought since Stuart Bolshinsky had been put away, and the guy who accosted me last year in my backyard had also been incarcerated, that would be the end of it. Guess they, that is the Weathermen, won't put it to rest until I'm dead."

Chapter 54

After eating a greasy breakfast of bacon and eggs at the Varsity Grill one morning, on the way back to his truck Mick saw something that made his heart stop; a flier tacked to a telephone pole that said: **FOUND—BLACK CAT, SMALL SPOTTED DOG LOOKS PART BEAGLE. CALL 232-4543 OR COME BY 615 CEDAR ST. APT. 2.**

Could it possibly be Jazzpur and Lucky? Mick drove straight to the address on Cedar Street and knocked on the door of Apt. #2. A young woman answered.

"You found a dog and cat?" Mick asked.

"Sure did. There they are," she said, opening the door wider.

They must have recognized Mick's voice as Lucky came running, tail wagging wildly, with Jazzpur following meowing.

The shock Mick felt from finding them was as great as that which he had felt when he thought he had lost them in the fire, but it brought him great joy instead of deep sorrow.

"That's them alright. I thought they had died in a fire."

"Oh, that house that burned up a couple of weeks ago around the block?"

"Yeah," Mick said.

"They did smell smokey. I gave the dog a bath. The cat took one on his own, naturally. Well, they're yours again." The woman sounded disappointed that she'd be giving them up.

"I'd like to give you something for taking care of them."

"That won't be necessary. It was fun having them here."

"Oh. Well, okay then, thanks a lot. Come on boys, let's go. Thanks again."

They followed Mick to his truck. He opened the door and they hopped in. Lucky sat in Mick's lap with his head out the window, and Jazzpur cowered on the floor when they took off.

Mick wondered how they would take to their new environs. "Not very well if you don't get them some food. Right boys?"

He stopped at a store and bought big bags of dried dog and cat food, and a few cans of tuna, which oddly enough Lucky liked too.

Lucky adapted to his new home readily—nose to the ground sniffing after rabbits or whatever. Jazzpur was a little more tentative. He just hunkered down and looked around acting scared. Finally though, he got up and sprayed a tree to mark his new territory.

Mick hadn't adapted totally yet. He was without furniture, with only his sleeping bag for a bed, and the hammock. First thing the next day he would go in to the Salvation Army Thrift Store and buy some, and some pots and pans, plates, dishes and bowls and cups and utensils, a typewriter and maybe a TV, and a new radio at K-Mart where he'd also buy one of those little refrigerators and a hot plate which would be good enough for his food preparation needs. Good thing he had a truck.

After he got settled in he'd have John out for a party, and Gary when he got back in town from being on the road with his band, and Anna if they were still hangin' out. What about Kathy? Not if there would be drinking, and there would be.

"I thought you were going to quit, Mick," he said to himself.

"After the party."

"Sure, then after the next one, and then the one after that," he said, continuing with the soliloquy. "God damnit, Mick, when's this shit going to stop? Right now, today, this is it."

Chapter 55

Mick got a nice little stretch of sobriety going throughout the long hot summer of '73. And as anticipated, the interior of the stone house kept relatively cool.

In the mornings, after a couple of jolts of java and toast with peanut butter and honey for energy, before it got too hot outside, he went about exploring the surrounding woods for exercise. He hoped to find a set of deer antlers to hang above the front door. He had heard they were supposed to be good luck, but he didn't have any luck in finding one.

In the evenings Mick sat by the lake and fished, or he'd kick back in the hammock and watch the sky turn black and fill up with stars until the mosquitoes got to be too much, then he'd retire to the house and read, or work on his thesis.

He seldom went to town, except to get groceries, or to stop by The Club to say hello to John, but he didn't drink anything but Cokes.

Although he was isolated, Mick didn't feel that lonely at first. In fact, in the solitude he got in touch with himself in a way he hadn't felt since his early youth, before he started drinking. He recalled those soft summer days of innocence when, to escape his tumultuous home life he went to the woods where he always felt at peace.

At night Mick enjoyed reading Walden while sitting in his stuffed chair beneath an old stand up lamp, and like they did at the house in town, Lucky slept at his feet and Jazzpur lay curled up on the back of the chair.

While reading, in the background he semi-consciously heard the sounds of the night; a whippoorwill and the wind as it sang through the trees. Without trees, the wind could only be felt, they gave it a voice. Like the sun and the moon and the sky give the lake its reflection. Without actually seeing the lake at the moment, Mick envisioned what it looked like in the moonlight. He envisioned what his stone house looked like in the moonlight, nestled among the trees under a starlit sky, his reading light shining through the window, and what he looked like through the window sitting alone (save for Jazzpur) in his chair in the lamp light reading, but he didn't feel lonely. He found companionship in Thoreau's insightful words, especially when he came to the section in the book entitled SOLITUDE. Thoreau wrote:

> *I have never felt lonesome or in the least oppressed by a sense of solitude, but once, and that was a few weeks after I came to the woods, when, for an hour, I doubted if the near neighborhood of man was not essential to a serene and healthy life. To be alone was something unpleasant. But I was at the same time conscious of a slight insanity in my mood, and seemed to foresee my recovery. In the midst of a gentle rain while these thoughts prevailed, I was suddenly sensible of such sweet and beneficent society in nature, in the very pattering of the drops and in every sound and sight around my house, an infinite and unaccountable friendliness all at once like an atmosphere sustaining me, as made the fancied advantages of human neighborhood insignificant, and I have never thought of them since. Every little pine needle expanded and swelled with sympathy and befriended me. I was so distinctly made aware of the presence of something kindred to me, even in scenes we are accustomed to call wild and dreary.... Men frequently say to me, "I should think you would feel lonesome down there, and want to be nearer folks, rainy and snowy days and nights especially." I am tempted to reply to such,—This whole earth which we inhabit is but a point in space. How far apart, think you, dwell the two most distant inhabitants of yonder star, the breadth of whose disk cannot be appreciated by our instruments? Why should I feel lonely? Is not our planet in the Milky Way?.... I find it wholesome to be alone the greater part of the time. To be in the company with even the best, is soon wearisome and dissipating. I love to be alone. I never found the companion that was so companionable as solitude. We are for the most part more lonely when we go abroad among men than when we stay in our chambers.*

Weary-eyed, Mick closed the book on that chapter, not the least bit longing to be downtown at The Club or PK's with the drunken crowd.

By August though, after weeks of solitude, he had to admit that he had grown lonely, and he thought about contacting Kathy again. With Mick being sober now, maybe she would be open to having dinner somewhere, or she could come out to Lake Wells for a day and evening. He didn't have a phone so he would have to go to the gas station on the way to Carbondale to call her.

"Hello."

"Kathy?"

"Yes."

"This is Mick."

"Oh, hi, Mick, how are you?" she asked half-heartedly.

"I'm doing fine. Takin' it one day at a time," Mick said, using the code words drunks use to tell each other they're sober, for the moment anyway. "I have been for several weeks now."

"Working the program?" Kathy inquired, referring to AA.

"My own. A lot has transpired since I saw you last. That night when I came to your house drunk and you shut the door in my face, leaving me standing on your porch in the dark. But I don't blame you. Would you like to get together over dinner and talk?"

"Okay, now that you're sober."

"Would you like to come out to my place at Lake Wells?"

"You're living in that stone house now?"

"Yes. A little sooner than I had planned."

"Do you have anything to cook with?" Kathy asked.

"Of course, and I've got all the ingredients for spaghetti."

"Sounds good. When?"

"Sunday night, I'll pick you up."

"That's okay, I have a car now. Remember? How do I get there."

"It's pretty easy really."

Mick gave her directions to where the county road came to the lane that became the path that lead to his house.

"It takes about thirty or forty minutes to get here from Carbondale. I'll be waiting for you by a big, old cedar tree at 5 o'clock if that's okay."

"See you then," Kathy said. "Bye."

She arrived a few minutes after five, dressed very summer-like in sandals, shorts and tank top, and who could blame her for not wearing a bra on such a hot day. They hugged, and then Mick led the way down the path toward the house. On the way she marveled at the beauty of the lay of the land; the way the path meandered through floral and fauna, stones and trees, until it came to the grassy clearing at the edge of the lake. The view Mick had from the house, of the expanse of deep green water rippling from the breeze.

Kathy sighed. It's so cool here."

"It's even cooler in the house." Mick nodded toward it about twenty yards back in the woods, shaded by oaks and hickories.

"Far out," Kathy said. "With the stone and those wood beams it blends in so well with the surrounding environment you can hardly see it. It looks like one of those old post cards of a lodge in the north woods."

Mick smiled. It was all by design. They walked to the house and went inside, and immediately Kathy noticed the skylight.

"It's beautiful. Did you make that?"

"No, my friend Gary did. You met him at that party New Year's Eve, or should I say New Year's Day."

"I did? I don't remember much about the party, except accosting that saxophone player. What I remember most though was how sweet you were to me later that morning when you found me sitting on your porch, and that night too."

Kathy smiled and put her arms around Mick. He returned the favor and they kissed, and except for going back to town to get her clothes, she stayed at the lodge with him for the rest of the summer. And like with most flowering relationships, at first they were inseparable, doing everything together—cooking for each other, paddling around the lake together in the canoe Mick rented at the marina, hiking, swimming, star gazing, reading to each other at night, he from some of Hesse's and Hemingway's works and she from Anais Nin, a nice blend of yin and yang. And most importantly they stayed sober together.

After awhile they naturally began to indulge in some things separately. Mick resumed working on his thesis, while Kathy, as a result of reading a *Fireside* book, began building a stone sauna bath house, which gave them each some space by day, making them appreciate even more what they shared in the loft at night. And occasionally a little afternoon delight in the hammock, or anywhere else an extemporaneous moment of playfulness might take them.

It had been the sweetest summer Mick had known, but one early fall day, Kathy flippantly informed him when he asked her if she was okay after she had returned from town not looking too well, that she had just had an abortion.

"My God, Kathy, how long have you been pregnant?"

"Three months."

"Why didn't you tell me, we could have discussed it?"

"Discuss what? It's my body, it was my decision to make," she said. Her blue eyes didn't look so pretty anymore.

"Not entirely, Kathy, that baby was part mine." Mick was angry too.

"What would we have done with a baby, Mick?"

"Raise it."

"In other words we would have gotten married?" Kathy asked with an incredulous smile.

"That's what most people end up doing when they love each other," Mick said.

"I thought we loved each other like lovers do, not as man and wife. There's a difference you know," Kathy said condescendingly.

"There is?" Mick knew of course that there was, but he wanted to hear Kathy make the differentiation.

"Yes. Man and wife, that's supposed to be like forever. Lovers, well that's a little more transitory."

"That's how you've viewed our relationship?"

"Yes, Mick, I thought you did too."

"I thought we had something special, but evidently I was wrong. I think you better leave, Kathy."

"Just like that? Right now?"

"Yes, please leave, now."

Kathy cried as she gathered up her things, which required making two trips to her car. Mick cried too, inside. It felt like something had been torn out of him, and he wanted to drink to kill the pain. He remembered John's bottle of Jack Daniels. After Kathy left he got it and a glass and sat them on the table in front of him and poured, but before he got the glass to his lips he stopped, thinking about all the months of sobriety that would go down the drain if he drank.

"But I'm hurting, Man, I'm hurting. Wouldn't it be better to be drunk and feeling no pain, than to be sober and hurting?

"Coward. You don't have the guts to deal with life's problems without getting drunk?"

Mick didn't like thinking of himself as a coward, so he got up and poured the drink down the drain, and he endured the pain of his breakup with Kathy and losing his child without anesthetizing with alcohol.

Above all though, it was the abortion of his child that troubled him most. How could human life be discarded so easily. He couldn't blame Kathy entirely though; she was a child of the '60s, a time when many things had become expendable—like the unwanted children of free love and the lives of GIs in that fucked up war.

Mick went outside to watch the sun set. With its normally blinding light being refracted by the curvature of the earth, it was possible to look directly at the flaming red ball going down beyond the golden horizon, and higher in the darkening blue sky wind-swept pink and purple clouds looked as if they had been brushed there by the hand of God.

Twilight, the most peaceful time of the day, Mick had always thought, when it slowly faded into night and the world rested, save for its nocturnal creatures, which Mick had been when prowling the streets and drinking.

On this night though he'd only drink camomile tea, and go to bed sober. But despite the herbal teas somnolent properties, he could not sleep. The smell of Kathy lingered in the loft. He tossed and turned trying to get her out of his mind, but he couldn't.

Had he been too reactionary in telling her to leave? They could have talked it out more. But what else was there to say? The cold indifference she had shown about the abortion had thoroughly pissed him off. Mick had always thought of her as a more caring person than that. Apparently she didn't really care that much about him; not enough to have his baby anyway.

Maybe he had jumped to conclusions about their relationship. She had distinguished between the kind she thought they were having—the kind lovers have, not man and wife. Ergo the difference between fly-by-night fucking and marriage. In all honesty though, the more he thought about it, Mick had to admit that the former appealed to him more at the moment than the latter, and he couldn't blame Kathy for feeling the same way. But the next time he'd make damn sure that he and his lover, whoever she might be, took the necessary precautions to prevent having to deal with the abortion issue again.

Chapter 56

One cool October evening Gary showed up at Mick's door. He looked fifteen pounds lighter and tired.

"Just get back?" Mick asked.

"About a week ago. Thought I'd see you down at PK's, but Wynn the bartender said you hardly come in anymore, so I thought maybe you had finished the house and moved in."

"A little sooner than I expected to, but yeah, here I am. Come in."

Immediately the skylight caught Gary's eye. He looked pleased.

They sat down at the round oak table Mick had lucked into finding at a used furniture and junk store in Makanda, a quaint little town in the hills near Giant City State Park.

Mick was in arm's reach of a dwindling fire in the hearth, which he stirred with an iron poker, causing it to flare up again, sending off a wave of warmth and the pungent, but sweet smell of wood smoke.

"Nice," Gary said, his chiseled face flushed by the crimson light of the fire.

"I've got some whiskey, want some?" Mick asked. "Jack Daniels."

"Uh, yeah, sure, why not. Drank a little of that on the road. Actually more than a little. Those rockers drink hard, Man."

"How do you want it? Straight up, with water, on the rocks, a shot?"

"On the rocks will do."

Mick fixed Gary the drink and poured a cup of coffee for himself.

"On the wagon again?" Gary inquired.

"Yeah," Mick said, and he didn't like the sound of disappointment in his own voice, and in his attitude of resentment. Was he not resolute in his abstention anymore? It didn't take much, like an old drinking buddy showing up, to waiver.

Gary took a sip from the glass of whiskey and ice which glowed a reddish golden brown. With his eyes reflecting the fire light too, and with his black hair, beard and mustache, and black turtle-neck sweater worn under a black and red plaid Pendleton shirt; stone wall in the background, he looked like a model in one of those whiskey ads in an outdoor magazine. And like they are designed to do, it made Mick want to partake in the product. But not wanting to get drunk because that's what it would lead to—he resisted.

"Still smoke pot?" Gary asked, taking a joint from his shirt pocket.

Actually Mick hadn't for awhile. His stash burned up in the fire in Carbondale and he hadn't gotten around to buying more. He declined Gary's offer, remembering that marijuana often made him nervous and somewhat paranoid, and he would drink to take the edge off. It was kind of his "gateway drug" to the use of alcohol.

"No thanks, but feel free, Man."

Gary lit up and Mick took a drink of coffee, satisfied enough with the rush he got from the caffeine.

"So tell me, how was it on the road?" Mick asked.

"Grueling. At first it was great, but then it got to be a chore."

"What, dealing with the groupies?"

Gary smiled. "That too. What was really difficult though, was keeping the creative juices flowing night after night while playing the same old songs over and over again. Now I understand why cocaine is so widely used on the rock n'roll circuit. It keeps you going at a pretty high level of intensity when you're performing, but it's real easy to get strung out on. I think if I saw one more line of that shit I'd puke. I got a good taste of it, but the rock n'roll road life just isn't for me."

"So what's up with you and Anna now, since you were gone for so long?"

"Oh, we're okay, in fact, being apart made us realize how close we really were, even with the relationship we had with Eve."

"Where is she now?"

"Colorado."

"Where's Anna?"

"She's over there on her property plotting out a site for the teepee."

Mick laughed. "Teepee? What teepee?"

"The one we're planning on living in next spring. I ordered it though *Mother Earth News* from a company in Oregon. We'll be cutting the poles for it this week from some farmer's stand of pines down by Cobden."

"Far out. I'm going to have white Indians for neighbors. Go get her, Man, we'll have a little party."

"Sure, okay. Mind if I get the wine I've got in my van?" Gary asked. "I can only handle so much whiskey."

"No, go ahead."

"Be back in about twenty minutes."

While Gary went to get Anna and the wine, Mick went outside and got some wood from a stack of it for the fire. He prepared a plate of cheese and sliced summer sausage and crackers, and he lit a couple of candles and an incense stick. Gary soon returned with Anna.

"Hey, Mick, haven't seen you for awhile."

"Hi Anna."

She was dressed warmly in a golden sweater and green corduroy jacket, blue jeans and boots. She smelled of the outdoors. Her red hair was mussed by the breeze just enough to give it a teased look, and her face was flushed from the brisk autumn air, bringing with her an invigorating breath of freshness into the room. She glanced about smiling.

"Wow, your house looks fantastic. It's so, I don't know, what's the word, rustic?"

"I think that says it," Gary said. "All he needs now is a cross-eyed moose head hanging over the fireplace."

"I'll settle for one of those big bass out of the lake."

"Okay Hemingway, got glasses for the wine?"

"Sure. Oh, here, have some sausage and cheese."

Mick offered the plate to his guests. They each sampled some and Gary poured wine for himself and Anna.

"So, Anna, Gary tells me you guys are going to put up a teepee next door."

"Yes, in the spring. We're just prepping the land for it now and acquiring the poles."

"And I thought I was being bold building this house out here. Tell ya what, I'll let you use the privy for twenty bucks a month."

They all laughed.

"Seriously though," Mick said, you'll need a place to go."

"This is true," Gary said.

"What's that other little house out there?" Anna asked.

"Sauna bath. You guys can use that too if you'd like, but I won't charge you for that."

"Tonight?" Anna asked

"Sure. I'll go out and get it going. I could put some music on for you, but sometimes it's nice just to listen to the sounds of the night; the whippoorwills and hoot owls, and coyotes and the breeze blowing through the trees, and the water lapping at the rocks on the shore."

"That's music," Anna said.

"I'll be right back."

Mick went outside to the sauna, got it going, then returned to the house.

"It's ready, come on."

He took a candle with him, and placed it in a pool of wax he dripped on a rock, and at the door of the sauna he stripped. Gary and Anna followed suit. They were used to being naked by threes, but not Mick, and he felt a little self-conscious about it.

Anna sat down on the bench between Gary and Mick. Mick sat back and closed his eyes, resisting the temptation to steal a glance at her body, but soon he gave in. He opened his eyes and looked at her sweating breasts gleaming in the glow of the candle light. She inhaled deeply and rose on her buttocks, while arching her back and thrusting her chest out.

"Oh, this is so nice," she said softly, exhaling with a long sensuous sigh.

Mick couldn't help but feeling aroused, which for men, when naked is difficult to hide, and for women too, when bare-breasted, as was the case so it appeared, with Anna.

Feeling a little fidgety about what he perceived to be some sexual tension in the air, on his part for sure, Mick got up and splashed water from a container onto the bed of hot rocks causing it to hiss and steam, and the sauna became even hotter.

After a few more minutes they were all sweating profusely and straining to breath. Mick had had enough. He got up and went outside, and Anna and Gary followed. The chilly autumn night air cooled him off instantly, giving him the most delightful rush, and it made his head swim as he looked up at the moon. Judging from the smiles on their faces, Anna and Gary must have been experiencing something similar. Soon though they were shivering so they returned to the house and got dressed.

"That was great, Mick," Gary said.

"Sure was," Anna concurred. "I think I'm going to build one of those."

"You've got access to plenty of stone."

"Right. I just hope I don't stub my toe on another one."

She showed Mick her foot. One of the big toe nails was black, but that didn't detract from the beauty of her foot. Everything on Anna was well shaped.

"Guess we better head back to Carbondale, Anna," Gary said

"Wanna flashlight to find your way back to the van?" Mick asked.

"No," Gary said, "the moonlight will do. Thanks."

Mick watched them walk away holding hands. Lucky man, Mick thought. And like an image that lingers after one closes one's eyes, the image of her naked body gleaming with sweat in the candle light in the sauna stayed with Mick well into the night as he lay in the loft fantasizing what it would be like to make love with her. No doubt Mick had become infatuated with Anna, but there was no way with Gary in the picture that he'd ever act out on it. Besides, he just couldn't imagine that she'd be attracted to him, beyond friendship. She was just too damn beautiful. At times Mick suffered from low self-esteem, although when he was drunk he experienced illusions of grandeur—the schizophrenia of alcoholics, he had learned from those who admitted to the same problem, at the AA meetings.

CHAPTER 57

▼

As Mick had hoped, the heat from the fireplace kept him warm enough through the winter. It helped to have a hearth at loft level. He utilized the sauna often, and once in awhile so did John, Gary and Anna, although not all at once. Gary and Anna did together mostly, but without Mick. He just didn't feel comfortable in that situation; lusting for Anna the way he did, especially in the presence of Gary.

It had been a short winter. Spring came early, and in the early spring, around the first week of April Mick went about the woods hunting morel mushrooms, the thick, golden, sponge-like, cone-shaped fungi prized for their delicious, juicy, nutty taste. And prized enough by some to pay five to ten dollars a pound for. When floured and fried they rivaled bluegill fillets, or they could be eaten sauteed with onions, celery and peppers served on a bed of wild rice with wild asparagus on the side; a menu Mick had discovered in a Euell Gibbons book.

And as much as he loved finding them, Mick enjoyed the hunt itself. It gave him a good excuse to experience the woods in the spring before they became overgrown with poison ivy, briars and cottonmouth snakes.

The trees had barely begun to bud, giving them a faint green tint with lovely lavender red buds mixed in. There were patches of May apples growing here and there—their solitary yellow flowers blooming beneath their umbrella leaves would produce fruit that tasted of citrus. There were violets, and tiny ferns uncurling in the sun, where before long they'd be in their preferred shade of fully-leaved trees. And there were the succulent purple-green spotted trout lily leaves, with their spindly-stemmed white bell flowers, and baby red poison ivy sprouts showing through the fallen brown oak leaves that a robin scurried through looking for grub worms.

A light breeze underlain with the cool warmth of early spring blew ever-so-slightly through the budding trees, and Mick swore he could detect the moist, earthy smell of fresh morels, like one smells the scent of coming rain.

He followed his instinct, treading lightly as if he were afraid to scare them off. A rabbit suddenly darted out of a thicket giving him a start. He caught his breath and moved on, and he came to a little stream and leaped across it, and nearly landed on a morel. He paused to savor the sight of it. The first one he always paid homage to before picking it; a ritual he swore brought more, and it did, many of them of various sizes scattered about.

He harvested them delicately, and placed them gently in the flannel shirt he had taken off so they'd remain as whole as possible for the pan. And after he found a handful or two of wild asparagus growing along the county road, he partook of his spring feast, and not one drop of blood had been spilled. This was the kind of hunt that no critter had to pay for.

Something else sprang up that spring like a mushroom, overnight it seemed; a large tepee on Anna's land. Mick was invited over to see the inside. Ducking through the door he was immediately struck by how spacious it was, both in circumference and height, fifteen to twenty feet high, Mick guessed, and bright because of the way the light outside shown through the teepee's white cotton cloth.

The ground inside was covered with straw mats, except in the middle where they had built a fire in a shallow pit, surrounded by stones, to cook with and to keep the tepee warm when necessary. The smoke rose naturally out the opening at the top. To keep the rain out, Gary showed Mick, flaps were put in place at the top with moveable poles.

At the moment Anna was cooking soup in a kettle suspended over the small fire on a spit.

"Have a seat," Gary said, pointing to a bean bag chair. "They're perfect for in here."

Mick settled into one, and Gary into another. There was one for Anna, but she remained standing seasoning and stirring the soup.

Gary offered Mick a peace pipe, as it were, but he graciously declined, still abstaining from any kind of substance but caffeine.

"So what a ya think?" Gary asked. "Pretty far out, huh?"

"Yeah. It's amazing how bright and spacious it is in here. It's been pretty chilly at night. Do you stay warm enough?"

"We've got plenty of blankets."

Gary nodded at a pile of them on a mattress.

"Winter might be a different story though. We'll see. Of course we could always move in with you if it gets too frigid. Just kidding, but that does bring up something we'd like to talk with you about—the use of your outhouse and water supply, until we have our own, if we decide to stay out here for awhile."

"Soup's on," Anna said.

She ladled out three bowls of it thick brown rice and bean soup with onions, celery and carrots. It was more on the order of stew, and as they ate Anna agreed to pay a nominal fee to use the outhouse, but the water table Mick's well tapped into ran beneath her land too, so he wouldn't charge anything for the water. However, the only pump was in his kitchen. To minimize disturbing him too often for it they agreed to get it twenty gallons at a time in four, five gallon buckets; each carrying two. This, they determined, would last them awhile, as it would only be used for drinking, cooking, the washing of utensils, and face, hands and feet. Full body bathing would be done in the lake, weather permitting. As a matter of practicality they'd wash their clothes at a laundromat in town. The three also agreed to give each other plenty of space, which there was plenty of.

Occasionally their paths did cross. Mick encountered Anna one day when she came over to use the sauna, and she asked him if he had ever seen some guy in a fishing boat peering in the direction of his house through binoculars.

"I've seen him twice now, in the last week or so," she said.

"Maybe he's scoping out the deer. There's a small herd that comes to the shore to drink near here," Mick said.

"Yeah, that's probably it. Oh, by the way, Gary's playing with a band at Merlin's tomorrow night. Why don't you come?"

"I just might. It's been awhile since I've heard live music, except my own, if you can call it that. I've been trying to teach myself how to play a recorder."

"I know, I've heard you."

"Sorry."

"Oh no, sounds like you're making some progress with, what is it, *Pop Goes the Weasel?*"

They both had a good laugh.

"Maybe we'll see you tomorrow night," Anna said, and they went their separate ways.

The following day Mick dropped his updated thesis off at Professor Miller's office, then he went on to the library to read a recently published book the professor told him about on the Tet Offensive of 1968. It brought back some memories. Mick had been in the middle of the offensive the night it erupted. He had just returned to Saigon from a reporting assignment at Khe Sanh, when he was immediately thrown into the Battle of Tan Son Nhut at the sprawling air base on the northern outskirts of the Capital with a loaded tape recorder and M-16 rifle. As a military correspondent for Armed Forces Radio he had been trained to use both. Hopefully he wouldn't be in a position where it would be necessary to use the latter.

Mick wound up riding to the front lines on the perimeter of the base in a jeep with two US Air Force Security Police Officers, but the enemy's small arms fire became so intense they were forced to abandon the vehicle and take cover in a ditch. Bullets zinged overhead, and Mick's escorts returned fire. Mick turned the recorder on and began to give a play-by-play account of the battle as the Viet Cong attacked Tan Son Nhut. The airport's defenders had been caught off guard, not so much by the attack itself, as it had been expected, but by the number of enemy and their tenacity. It quickly became apparent that Mick's weapon would be needed—to be fired by him.

He couldn't make out individual enemy, but he saw the muzzle flashes of their weapons and he directed his fire toward the flashes with his weapon on semi-automatic. Simply by squeezing the trigger the bullets flew almost as rapidly as if the weapon were a machine gun. Every seventh round was a tracer which allowed him to see his line of fire in the dark. The flash of one of the enemy's weapons he was shooting at ceased. Maybe he had taken him out.

Everything happened so fast that Mick really hadn't had time to think about how utterly terrified he was until the security policeman next to him, a lieutenant, had his helmet shot off. The bullet only grazed his scalp, but Mick reckoned the enemy had a bead on them and he was about to suggest to the lieutenant and the other officer, a captain, that they move, when a Cobra helicopter gun ship swooped in and rocketed the Viet Cong's position. But there were plenty more where they came from as numerous Viet Cong penetrated the perimeter having overrun one of Tan Son Nhut's main guard posts. The Cobras kept them at bay though, long enough for reinforcements to arrive, although some VC with satchel charges managed to get to some of the old DC-3 airplanes parked near the runway and blow them up. They also shot down a couple of Cobras. It had turned into a pitched battle, and Mick went back to being a correspondent in describing it for use as a special feature to be played on Armed Forces Radio as soon as he could get it to the station. That's what he had been sent there to do. With reinforcements, his weapon was no longer needed.

He described how one of the DC-3s that had been parked among those that had been destroyed, got airborne, and circling high above the battlefield firing its two electric Gattling guns, pouring endless streams of tracer-laced .60 caliber bullets down in laser-like beams into the advancing enemy lines, resulting in a massive slaughter. When the sun rose in the morning, hundreds of dead and wounded Viet Cong littered the battlefield. Their attempt at overrunning Tan Son Nhut had failed miserably.

Later that morning, when Mick got the tapes to the station, he learned that the battle he witnessed was only one of many throughout South Vietnam, as the Communists had launched a nationwide offensive against numerous cities including Hue, DaNang, Nha Trang, Pleiku, Can Tho and others. All of them had resulted in a dismal failure for the enemy as the VC particularly, were virtually decimated resulting in a tremendous victory for the Allies in the Tet Offensive of 1968.

But America's nay-saying mass media didn't report it that way. Especially Walter Cronkite, who on national television in front of an audience of millions, portrayed the offensive as a Communist victory and the American people, including of all people their president, LBJ, became convinced that the war was unwinnable.

This is what pissed Mick off the most. A television newsman had convinced the President of the United States—not his advisors, his cabinet, or his generals, but a journalist, had convinced him that the war was unwinnable simply because Communist forces had launched a nationwide attack, which in fact, had ended in a dismal defeat for them.

General Westmoreland knew this of course, and he had requested more troops to put the final nail in the enemy's coffin, but his request was misinterpreted by many in Washington, including LBJ. They thought it meant that the General thought the situation in South Vietnam had become desperate given how the media had characterized Tet as a success for the enemy, which couldn't have been further from the truth. If they had listened to the general the war might have been won by '69 or '70, but because they chose to listen to what the defeatist press said, the war lingered on. The American people lost patience with it, the antiwar movement gained momentum, and the US Congress, dominated by doves, legislated the country out of it. It outlawed any further options in helping to keep South Vietnam, and probably Laos and Cambodia from succumbing to Communism.

Some of the leaders, no doubt, lacked the resolve—the backbone—to finish what others, namely JFK, had earnestly started out to do. In the process, they abandoned an allie. The world was watching alright, and all of its upstart tyrants liked what they saw—a paper tiger. Still, in the beginning American soldiers, airmen and sailors had proven to be a ferocious foe in combating the Communists on the battlefield.

Thinking about all of this stirred Mick's emotions. He felt anger, sadness, frustration and disappointment in his country and its leaders.

"Fuck," he blurted out, having forgotten that he was in the library staring out the window reflecting back on all of this.

Awakened from the daydream by his own sudden, angry outburst, Mick looked around to see if he had freaked anyone out, but he was the only one remaining in the periodical section, and as far as he could tell on that floor of the library, except for a librarian, who had probably heard Mick's profane exclamation, but acted as if she hadn't.

Of course he'd be the only one there. It was Friday evening. Only nerdy bookworms hung out at college libraries past four on Fridays, especially at SIU. Mick left and headed uptown to catch Gary's gig at Merlin's.

When he got there he looked in the window through the purple haze of the smokey neon light glow, and he saw his friend on the bandstand blowing harp. He could faintly hear the music through the glass, but when someone opened the door to go in it came out loud and clear.

Mick wanted to go in, but he was nervous about it because of his state-of-mind—the negative emotion he felt over reminiscing about Nam. He was in the habit of wanting to drink when he felt like that. But he also had something else on his mind—like meeting a woman maybe. It had been awhile, a little too long in fact for a man his age. Was this the place for a man who was going through recovery to meet them though? Mick stood there debating whether to go in or not.

"You don't have to drink alcohol. Just have a Coke."

Mick went in, ordered a tall Coke at the bar and found a place to stand with a view of the band. He took a big drink of the Coke before he realized it had rum in it—bartender's mistake, and soon he got a buzz from it, and he liked it. Next time he ordered the Coke that way, and a year of sobriety went down the drain, into an empty stomach, and the alcohol rushed straight to his brain, and before long he found himself dancing with a strange woman out on the floor. When the song was over they went their separate ways, but Mick found other women to dance with between numerous drinks. Then, in a display of bizarre behavior Mick got on stage, took a microphone and began to sing a relatively obscure song by Quicksilver Messenger Service called *Whatcha Gonna Do About Me*, but he soon forgot the words and he began to "scat" through it, like jazz singers do when they forget the words to the songs they're singing, but not so terribly slurred and off key like Mick.

The band graciously tried to go along with it as best they could, but when the crowd starting booing, Gary, as kindly as he could, ushered Mick off stage, and a bouncer escorted him to the door.

In the morning he awoke lying on the front seat of his truck with the sun beaming down on his face through the windshield. He sat up and was surprised to see that he had made it to where he always parked by the old cedar tree at the edge of his property at Lake Wells. He didn't remember driving there. He got out and stumbled through the woods to his house. Over a cup of coffee he began to remember what he had done the night before at Merlin's. It was like a bad dream; not so much that he had made such a scene, but the fact that he had gotten drunk again after so many months of sobriety. It depressed him deeply. But instead of hiding from the world for awhile, like he had done after the binge that resulted in drinking with Jesse the wino by the railroad tracks in Carbondale, Mick went to an AA meeting that very night and confessed to his fellow alcoholics what he had done; one of them being Kathy. She approached Mick after the meeting.

"I'm sorry, Mick."

"About what."

"About what happened between us," Kathy said. She laughed. "I'm working on Step Nine, you know, making amends to people we've harmed."

"You're a hell of a lot farther than I am. I'm back at Step One," Mick said.

"No, you're past that, Mick. That's why you're here tonight at a meeting."

"I've been to meetings before, only to get drunk again."

"Me too, remember? For some people sometimes it takes several tries," Kathy said. "The important thing is not to give up; keep trying."

Jumping ahead to Step Nine, after the meeting Mick went to the teepee to apologize to Gary for disrupting his gig.

"Yeah, well, maybe you should take some singing lessons, or just stick to that recorder then step up to the flute. We could use a flute in the band."

Gary had gone easy on Mick, almost to the extent of enabling him by not saying anything to him about his drinking, but Mick wasn't about to go easy on himself, this time. He went to meetings at least three nights a week. Kathy attended the same ones usually, but they didn't rush back into a relationship again. They played it cool.

Mick recovered from his relapse quickly. One of the old timers advised him not to beat himself up over it too much, and to move on again, relying on the trite, but tried and true motto of "one day at a time." He liked the simplicity of that philosophy. It made the problem more manageable, instead of thinking in terms of never and forever.

Chapter 58

Mick had almost forgotten what Anna had told him before his last drinking bout at Merlin's about the man she had seen in a fishing boat on Lake Wells peering ashore through binoculars, and the fear he had had that it could be a Weatherman still wanting to exact some revenge for him infiltrating them. Or was he being paranoid? Maybe the guy really was just an outdoors man observing wildlife.

In any case, he occasionally kept an eye out for the guy, and one day he did appear again looking ashore through binoculars in the general direction of Mick's house. The deer herd, which Mick reckoned the man might have been observing before, hadn't been around for awhile. Lucky's barking had kept them away no doubt. So then what the hell was he looking at? Trees? There certainly were some impressive ones on his land, but to come and look at them several times from a good distance with binoculars? No, that just didn't compute.

Mick went inside and got his binoculars, and through the smallest of an opening in the trees he focused in on the man in the boat. He saw that the man was black and he looked vaguely familiar.

"Where have I seen him before?"

The man must have seen Mick peering at him through binoculars too, because he suddenly put his down and sped away.

Mick started looking over his shoulder again, everywhere he went, and he always kept a wary eye on the lake. Being paranoid he concluded that the man out there was a Weatherman.

Mick thought hard about where he had seen the man in the boat before, and suddenly one night it hit him. Marcus. Marcus Jackson, leader of Carbondale's

Black Panthers, and member of the locally-formed, radical coalition that included the Weather Underground. He's out of jail after serving a stretch for shooting it out with Carbondale police.

God damnit. How long would they be seeking revenge, Mick wondered. Hell, Stuart Bolshinsky had escaped conviction for his antiwar, anti-American, anti-social activities, and his attempt on Mick's life, although he was now in prison for murdering Gretchen Witherspoon. And the fucking war, the Weather Underground's biggest excuse for indulging in anarchy, was over with, at least as far as our involvement in it was concerned. So what more did the bastards want? Surely those with such lofty goals as overthrowing the U.S. government weren't so petty as to spend so much time getting even with an insignificant individual like Mick. But then again those who would bomb buildings with people in them, while proclaiming to be antiwar would not take too kindly to having their hypocritical, sociopathic asses exposed without exacting revenge, sooner or later. And apparently now it was later.

From the beginning, Marcus had suspected Mick of being a mole. After one of the very first coalition meetings at Mr. Natural's, he had followed Mick, who had walked to the meeting, on foot, but Mick gave him the slip and actually turned the tables on Marcus, boldly following him for a short distance. Mick thought Marcus knew that he was being followed judging from the way he constantly looked over his shoulder, and the pace of his walk—almost a trot, and judging from the attitude of intense animosity he displayed toward Mick after that. A man in his position, a street smart revolutionary, did not take too kindly to being outfoxed.

And Mick had also heard through the grapevine that Marcus thought he had tipped off the Carbondale police that he'd be running guns in Stuart's van the night of the shootout, because Mick had been present when the two arranged it. Little wonder he would be on Marcus's shit list.

Mick tried to go about his business and leisure normally, without worrying too much about being stalked by Marcus, but he thought a lot about what he could do to get the jump on him, before Marcus got to him first. He wrote to his mentor, David, for suggestions.

> *"Play frogman and slap a bomb on the bottom of the bastard's boat and blow his ass to hell and back,"* he promptly wrote back.
> *"Seriously. I've enclosed a Navy Seal's handbook on underwater demolition. Get yourself a wet suit, tank, snorkel, mask and fins, get in shape, and the next time you see him out there, swim up underneath him and blow his shit out of the water. The cops will just think the gas tank blew."*

Mick liked the idea. After thinking about it for awhile he ordered the necessary diving equipment through a marine supply magazine he found in the library. It came soon, then he enlisted the assistance of John, who had done some diving in the Navy as a Sea Bee constructing docks for seaplanes. The instructing took place elsewhere on the lake to avoid being seen by Marcus on the waterfront of Mick's property.

What Mick didn't like though was the idea of handling explosives. Especially after the bomb Stuart made, that supposedly was destined for the Vietnamese Studies Center, had blown up in his car "prematurely." That's what he hated the thought of most; the prospect of a premature explosions. As a kid, while lighting a firecracker once, it blew up in his hands and face, causing him temporary blindness and deafness, and stinging and bloodied fingers. He ran around the yard yelping like a dog.

First he would practice, using the Navy Seal handbook David sent him, making the bomb with putty or play dough. He would obtain the real ingredients in due time, when he had more confidence in handling them. But that confidence would have to be gained quickly if he wanted to strike before Marcus did. Knowing that Marcus was good with guns, Mick thought that he might try to strike long distance with one. He'd have to be very good, though, if he shot from a boat floating on a lake, although Viet Cong were known to pick off swift boat sailors from sampans before. Or would it be a Molotov Cocktail again, or maybe a satchel charge like VC commandos used? Had it been Marcus who torched his house in Carbondale with a Molotov Cocktail? For that he would have to come ashore, and at night probably. It was doubtful he'd come through the woods by day; too easy to be seen. Either way, Mick knew that Lucky's barking would alarm him. Perhaps Marcus knew that too by now.

But Mick didn't want to wait for either, or other scenarios to develop. He was damn tired of being a sitting duck.

"Understandable," John said. "So we'll wire your truck too, before they do."

"Wire my truck."

"Yeah, so if they try to install a bomb in it, as soon as they touch it they'll get a shock that'll fry their balls. Something we did in the Philippines at a construction site after some locals made off with one of our bulldozers. We wired the other one, and that was the end of that. I'll run a wire down from the utility pole on the county road where you park and connect it to the chasis of your truck. You'll know if it's been messed with if you hear a loud scream. You'll be able to turn it on and off with a switch at the base of the pole. It'll be kind of a pain in the ass, but better than what you'd get if you turned the key on and boom!"

Marcus probably launched his boat from the public marina on the opposite side of the lake from Mick. He'd camp out near there waiting for him to launch, then he'd swim after him at an angle below the surface, and at mid-lake he'd strike.

The swimming and diving he mastered rather quickly. The explosives he procrastinated on, until one fateful afternoon while in the house he was startled by Lucky's louder-than-usual barking, followed by the unmistakable crackling echo of rifle fire, and a short-lived yelp. He went outside to investigate and found his beloved dog dead with a bullet hole in the chest. Mick looked out on the water and he saw Marcus speeding away in the boat.

"That son-of-a-bitch, I'll kill him now for sure."

Heartbroken and trying to fight back the tears, unsuccessfully, Mick wrapped Lucky in a sheet, dug a deep hole, and buried him beneath the sunny, grassy spot where he often rolled around snorting with pleasure.

Mick took Lucky's killing as a forewarning that he would be next, but he wasn't about to stand around and let it happen. He'd make that bomb as soon as he could assemble the necessary components. The Navy Seal handbook listed what he needed, primarily a block of C-4 plastic explosives, and a C-4 detonator whose wire would have to be attached to some kind of timing device to set it all off, all of which would be contained in a waterproof container that could be attached to the boat. John, having worked construction in the area, knew exactly where to find the explosives and detonator; at a construction supply company in Marion, which Mick readily purchased—no questions asked.

He remembered what Stuart had used as a timing device to set the detonator off at a particular time—a little state-of-the-art, battery-powered clock radio the size of a paperback book. He found one at K-Mart where he also bought a tight-lidded lunch box that would work perfectly as the waterproof container that could be attached to the boat by, by an industrial strength magnet. He found that at a hardware store.

Then, using the Seal book as a guide, he assembled the bomb simply by shoving the detonator into the puddy-like plastic explosive, which, in-and-of-itself, when combined, could be volatile enough to cause at least a relatively minor explosion. He removed the battery from the radio and unscrewed the back panel that had a drawing of the circuits on it, which identified the alarm mechanism. He attached the detonator wire to that with a paper clip. He'd put the battery back in when he was ready to set the alarm for whatever time he'd want the bomb to explode. Timing would be of the essence. If Marcus went in a straight line from the marina toward Mick's property his path would, Mick estimated, take him 75 to 100 yards out from where he planned to enter the water. But it would also be necessary to determine approximately how long it would take for Marcus to reach that point after leaving the marina, in addition to how long it would take Mick to swim to that point.

To estimate, John rented a boat at the marina and took off directly toward Mick's house at medium to top speed, the speed the marina's 10-horse fishing boat motors would allow, while Mick timed his swim with his waterfroof watch to where they'd meet. It took them eight minutes to rendevous. He'd set the bomb to go off at 13 minutes. If Marcus went too slow though, Mick might have to abort the mission because the bomb could go off before he was in a position to attach it to the boat.

If he aborted, Marcus would have unencumbered access to Mick's house, thinking that at this time of night he'd be in it. He was sure that was his intent, having blown up the one in Carbondale thinking that Mick had been in it.

Yes, rather presumptuous on Mick's part, but he wasn't about to give Marcus the benefit of the doubt since he had killed Lucky for the purpose, more than likely, of eliminating an alarm so he could come ashore undetected while Mick slept. If he and Marcus didn't rendevous within eight to ten minutes, twelve minutes tops, then Mick would drop the bomb and let it sink to the bottom as he swam away as fast as he could.

Mick anticipated Marcus would be coming at night, but when? Of course he didn't know, so he'd have to go to the spot he'd be swimming out from, every night.

Before sundown the first night he gathered up his diving equipment and put it in the bed of his truck, gingerly wrapped the lunch box containing the bomb in a sleeping bag, and stuffed it into a backpack which he placed on the front seat, and he drove off slowly to the marina. He parked there and hiked through the woods with his stuff for about fifty yards around along the shoreline to the spot he'd be swimming in from, which afforded him a good view of the marina's slips. He put on his wet suit, fins and tank (which was strapped to his back by a harness) and sat on a large rock like a frog ready to leap, but Marcus never showed, nor did he on the second night. The third night, throughout early evening, several boaters came and went until the sun went down and things got very quiet after dark, then Mick heard the sound of a boat motor starting up. Because of the light of the full moon he could see through binoculars well enough to determine that the man in the boat was Marcus. He quickly inserted a battery into the clock radio and set the alarm to go off in thirteen minutes. He had already connected the detonator to the alarm mechanism. He shut the lunch box tightly and hung it on the belt he wore, put his mask on, put the regulator that was attached to the air tank by a hose in his mouth, and slipped into the water. He skimmed the surface so as to keep an eye on Marcus as he timed his swim with his watch. It appeared Marcus was going slow. Maybe too slow to meet Mick within the eight to ten minute window, twelve at the very most. Twelve would put him a minute beyond Mick when the bomb blew, enough distance, hopefully, for Mick to be safe while he swam away in the opposite direction. Time would tell.

At eight minutes Marcus still wasn't very close. At nine a little closer, and closer yet at ten; at eleven he was there and Mick slapped the bomb on the bow. That would put the explosion at two minutes away at mid-lake where the water would be deepest. But Mick hadn't counted on the moonlight reflecting off his tank in the crystal clear waters of Lake wells. Suddenly he sustained a tremendous blow to his back. He blacked out for a few seconds. When he came to he was floating on his back (the tank providing buoyancy) about twenty feet from the boat, and Marcus was standing up in it pointing a rifle at him, then the boat blew and Marcus disappeared in a flash while the explosion sent Mick head over heels through the water. He wound up on his stomach. His legs were totally numb so he used his arms to drag his body to shore.

Although unable to move from the waist down he managed to remove the tank which had a bullet hole in it. He could hear the bullet rattling around inside. That's what had caused the tremendous jolt to his back. It hadn't gone all the way through into his body, but apparently the impact had done something to his back—his spine. It burned and throbbed with pain. Mick laid there for the rest of the night, happy that he had taken care of Marcus, but distraught about having no feeling in his legs.

Christ, was he doomed to be in a wheelchair now, for the rest of his life? He remembered trying to imagine what that would be like when his old friend Reggie was confined to one. He worried—as a young man would—about whether or not he'd ever be able to have sex again. He touched himself. Nothing, save for the feeling in his fingers. His penis did not return the favor. But then again being in this situation—cold, wet, exhausted and wounded, lying on the hard, rocky ground, would hardly be conducive to arousal.

He fell in and out of sleep until dawn when he heard someone talking nearby. Legs still paralyzed, he pulled himself over the ground toward the sound, and he saw two men fishing on the shore.

"Hey, over here, help!" Mick shouted.

They rushed over to him. "What the hell," one of them said, wondering about the frogman his unbelieving eyes beheld.

"Can you get me to the hospital in Carbondale? I can't walk."

"Why sure, yeah."

One guy picked him up under the shoulders and the other one held up his legs. It was the strangest sensation Mick had ever known, seeing his legs in the guy's hands but not feeling them being lifted.

The men were strong and they got Mick to their truck fast. They laid him down in the bed and got one blanket under his body, and one folded up under his head, and off to Carbondale they went, to the hospital. When the doctors and nurses learned that he had suffered a spinal injury, carefully strapped him down tight on a gurney, and rolled him in to emergency.

"What happened?" the doctor asked.

Mick came up with something off the cuff.

"I don't know really. I was putting on my diving equipment when, wham, something hit the tank and knocked me flat on my face. That's when my legs went numb. I managed to get the tank off my back and discovered what looked like a bullet hole in it. Actually, I could hear the bullet rolling around in the tank. I don't know where in the hell it came from. I don't remember hearing a shot."

"You've probably sustained a damaged vertebrae," the doctor said. "We'll take some X-rays to find out to what extent. The police will have to be notified about this. We're required to report all gun-related injuries."

After the X-rays they put Mick in a room by himself to wait for what they revealed, and again, Mick's thoughts turned to the possibility of having to live in a wheelchair. How in the hell would he wheel himself through rugged, rocky woods from where he parked his truck, to the house? Truck? How in the fuck would you be able to drive a truck? You won't be able to live out there anymore. He was crushed. He couldn't help but cry. When the doctor finally came in, Mick expected the worst—paralyzed for life.

"You're a very lucky man, Mick. The paralysis should only be temporary. You have nothing more than a badly bruised vertebrae and nerve, caused by the impact of the bullet forcing the tank to smash against your spine. You should start regaining some feeling in your legs in a day or so, if not sooner. Oh, the police are here to speak with you."

A uniformed cop and a "suit" came in. Mick knew the suit; Lt. Ramsey, the detective who had worked on the case of the Weatherman who had attacked him in his back yard when he lived in Carbondale. He reminded Mick of Jack Webb of the old TV cop series *Dragnet*; the way he talked, so matter-of-factly, no nonsense, just the facts, Man.

"How's it goin', Mick. Doc tells me you'll be okay. Did this have anything to do with the Weathermen ya think?"

"No, I don't think so. I was just putting on my diving gear, it's a hobby I picked up since moving out to Lake Wells, when bam, a bullet punctured the tank knocking me flat on my face. It must have been an errant shot fired by someone target practicing. I've heard them shooting out there before. Must be a range somewhere."

"Think it could have been a sniper?" Lt. Ramsey asked.

"Sniper?"

"The Weathermen. They've tried to kill you before, maybe they're still trying."

"Could be, I guess," Mick said.

"It's my understanding that the tank kept the bullet from going into your back, Mick."

"Yes, Sir."

"So then, would the bullet be in the tank?"

"That's right."

"In that case, we'll be able to determine what kind of gun fired it; the target practice kind, you know, like hunting rifles, or an assault rifle," Lt. Ramsey said. "Either one could be used by an assailant though, or a target shooter for that matter. Of course we'll try to find out who it is that's shooting out there at the lake and see if the bullet in the tank came from one of their guns, then we'll know it wasn't a sniper. If we don't come up with a match, then there is the possibility that it was a sniper."

"Sounds good to me, Lieutenant."

Mick would let them play their detective game, but sooner or later pieces of boat and the body, or remnants thereof, of Marcus Jackson were bound to turn up, or wash ashore, which Mick hoped could be explained by the gas tank exploding, for some reason.

"We'll let you rest now, Mick. Hang in there. We'll find out as much as we can as soon as possible."

But Mick was hoping it would take them a long time to find out as little as possible. One thing for sure, in reality, no one had been shooting at any target range. The only gun that bullet could me traced to would be lying on the bottom of the lake—hopefully.

Mick was kept in the hospital for another night and day. A physical therapist helped him walk up and down the hallway now and then while he was there. He was wobbly at first, but soon he regained full strength in his legs, and because of the therapist's good looks and the way she touched him while assisting him, he knew that he was now functioning fully below the waist, one of his first and main concerns after being injured. His back remained sore, however, so they prescribed some pain medicine, made an appointment with the doctor for later in the week, and then he was released. On the way out he tried to make an appointment with the therapist for the next night, but she turned out to be engaged.

Continuing with his therapy, Mick walked to The Club to hitch a ride home with John when the place closed. On the way back to the lake Mick told him about what had happened. It called for a drink or two; after all, John had trained Mick in diving. They finished off the bottle of "Jack" John had left at the house before.

In the morning though, Mick wasn't so celebratory. He began to feel pangs of guilt for killing a man, even though that man had intended to kill him, and had killed his dog. Sometimes in life though, isn't it necessary, Mick rationalized, to take matters into one's own hands, like Raskolnikov did in Dostoyevsky's *Crime and Punishment* when he axed the old vulturous pawn broker woman to death for taking advantage of the desperate and poor.

In the end Raskolnikov was punished for his crime, but should Mick be punished for his, if enough evidence turned up, even though he had acted preemptively in self-defense? It was a question that worried him, mostly at night, while trying to sleep. Often, as with Raskolnikov, sleep did not come easily, if at all, and when it did it was full of nightmares about his deed. Worry, fear and feelings of guilt are sometimes punishment enough, and the torture of insomnia; tossing and turning, looking at the clock tick-tocking away the long, long hours one slow second at a time, counting them like sheep over and over again. But sleep never comes, and the restless mind begins wandering in the black night. Void of the light of reality it begins to imagine things, worrisome things that through the imagination, in the dark are magnified by a mind made paranoid by sleep deprivation.

But in fact Mick's paranoia was based in reality. He had good reason to worry that Marcus Jackson's body, or parts of it, could possibly surface, which would raise many questions by the police.

When Mick did manage to sleep he had nightmares about such a possibility; Marcus's body parts washing ashore one-by-one over a period of several days or weeks, until a complete cadaver appeared, like the many pieces of a jig saw puzzle coming together to form a complete picture.

In fact, a detective did come to Mick's house to question him about a man (and a boat he had rented at the marina) that was missing and presumed drowned.

"An abandoned car was found in the marina parking lot," the detective said. "Its ownership has been traced to a Carbondale man who can't be located. The marina's proprietor says he heard an explosion the night he rented the boat to the missing man. Recall hearing anything like that late last week, on a Thursday night?"

"No," Mick said, "but it's pretty hard to hear anything through these stone walls."

"Okay. Well keep your eyes peeled for a boat or a body surfacing. They've done some dragging, but they came up empty handed. If the gas tank blew, like we suspect, the guy could be in pieces."

Chapter 59

▼

In the fall, just as the cold weather hit, Anna contracted walking pneumonia and she and Gary were forced to move back to town. They planned to return to the teepee in the spring.

Mick had become accustomed to having neighbors; at first he missed them, but it didn't take him long to get used to living alone out there again. He wasn't entirely alone though, he still had Jazzpur to keep him company, and a new addition to the household—a twelve-week-old golden retriever pup Mick had found advertised for sale in the paper. Of course Lucky couldn't be replaced. There would always be an empty space in Mick's heart for him.

The little pup, that Mick called Carmella because of her color, true to her breed, immediately took to the lake, with some encouragement from Mick who threw sticks out on the water for her to retrieve in a beautiful display of canine athleticism. She loved it, despite the fact that the water, with winter coming, had turned fairly cold. It was a pleasure to watch her warm up again while snoozing by the fireplace, although Jazzpur, the jealous type, didn't appear to be so pleased with the new pup making herself at home in his territory with so much ease.

Mick kept his eyes peeled on the lake a lot thinking that Marcus might show up again, in one form or another, but certainly not alive.

He was confident Marcus had acted on his own, and not in concert with the Weather Underground, as they were virtually defunct now—around Carbondale anyway—since the war, or at least American involvement in it, was over. Much of the radical, revolutionary activity that Carbondale had become famous for in the late '60's and early '70's had diminished considerably since the draft and the U.S.'s involvement in Vietnam ended. It was replaced with a well-earned reputation for being one of the nation's top party schools, according to *Playboy Magazine*.

Students no longer had anything to protest, generally, so they settled back into the traditional collegiate lifestyles, which entailed not demonstrations as such, but demonstrating the ability to drink as much and as often as one could for an entire semester without flunking out. This was something Mick had demonstrated a tremendous amount of ability in throughout his collegiate career. Yet he had somehow managed to earn a B.A. in Communications, and he was in graduate school where he only needed to finish his thesis to get a master's degree. But because of the subject of his thesis—Vietnamization—he could not finish it until the verdict was in on it's success or failure, in other words, would South Vietnam be able to fend off North Vietnam's attempt to conquer it without U.S. help?

Mick tried his best to keep up with it, but news coverage was limited because of a lull in the action—the calm before the storm actually. What coverage there was of the ongoing war was relegated to the tail end of newscasts, and the back pages of newspapers and magazines, which provided little material for his thesis. Luckily though, because of David's position with intelligence at the US Embassy in Saigon, he was able to keep Mick abreast of what was happening in South Vietnam through letters. Together with what Mick gleaned from news sources, he managed to move his thesis along rather well. Unfortunately, Vietnamization itself was not moving along so well.

In January of '74 Mick received a lengthy letter from David informing him that Thieu's army was performing fairly well. Except they had lost some isolated posts and fire support bases to the North Vietnamese, mostly in the western highlands. But David expressed reservations about how well the South Vietnamese would continue to perform in the face of the massive build-up by the Communists south of the DMZ, coupled with the fact that the US had not only withdrawn all of its combat forces, including air support, from the fray, but we had drastically cut military equipment and financial aid to South Vietnam thanks to Congress.

> *For the last ten years they relied on these resources in fighting an American-style, high-tech, expensive war which required helicopters, cargo planes, jet fighter-bombers, ammunition, medical supplies and replacement parts. They cannot maintain this level of warfare without such, and the North Vietnamese know this, and they'll take full advantage of it in the weeks to come. And the already pathetic salaries of the soldiers have been reduced even more, resulting in plummeting morale. A stunning 15,000 to 20,000 South Vietnamese Army soldiers have deserted per month to take care of their families because the military pay is so low.*

Another 100,000 have been granted permission to work instead of fulfilling their service duties, and graft and corruption, and theft of equipment is becoming widespread among the ranks. All the while the enemy is getting stronger as they build up their forces in preparation for another all-out offensive. Thieu foolishly thinks the US will step in then, but we won't, because Congress, as you know, has legislated us out of that possibility once and for all.

On top of all of this, Mick, the South Vietnamese economy, in the absence of U.S. dollars (both in aid and GI spending) is collapsing, and so goes the morale of the civilians. They are suffering from massive unemployment, and their confidence in the Thieu government has dwindled considerably. I believe they sense the army can no longer stand up to the enemy, and goodness knows these people are sick and tired of war.

And sadly, Mick, as the South Vietnamese Army deteriorates, the NVA, as I said, is solidifying. Several divisions in northern South Vietnam have withdrawn to above the DMZ where they are being reinforced and re-equipped with more tanks, artillery, anti-aircraft guns and missiles. A wide, hard-surface road has been built running down the backbone of South Vietnam from the DMZ to Loc Ninh, along with a gasoline pipeline and thousands of miles of telephone lines. In Laos, Cambodia and the South, they've established giant depots, training centers and hospitals, and repair facilities. It sure as hell doesn't take a Sherlock Holmes to detect a build-up for a final invasion. As a prelude though we speculate they'll attempt to isolate Saigon with a series of strategic raids before the grand finale.

In the meantime, I believe I'll go for a steam at that bathhouse you told me about, "The Blue Chiffon Mist," and whatever else they have to offer, since I'm no longer a married man. So long, Mick.

Chapter 60

Early in 1974 the North Vietnamese Army succeeded in isolating Saigon by taking various South Vietnamese Army outposts northwest, north and east of the city, which put them in a position to attack the Capital full force later on. Simultaneously they captured outposts in the Central Highlands, and along the coast between D Nang and Nha Trang, and they isolated Hue.

Overall in 1974, Hanoi had accomplished its goal of putting NVA forces into strategic positions throughout South Vietnam in preparation for the final assault on Saigon. These forces consisted of those who had been allowed to stay in place per negotiations, and those (in violation of the Paris Agreement and the Geneva Accord of 1954) who had infiltrated the South from Cambodia, and from the North down the Ho Chi Minh Trail.

In March of 1975, Da Nang and Hue finally fell to the North Vietnamese, who had captured most of South Vietnam from the coast to Cambodia above Saigon. The DMZ in effect had disappeared and soon, it seemed, Saigon as its capital would be replaced by Hanoi as the capital of one Vietnam; the dream of Ho Chi Minh.

The defeats in the north and on the coast had thoroughly demoralized the South Vietnamese people from the presidency on down to the peasants. NVA victories had come relatively easy and fast, and they were now bearing down on Saigon with an estimated thirteen to twenty divisions whose morale could hardly have been higher. By the 21st of April South Vietnam's Capital had become encircled and President Thieu resigned and fled to Taiwan. Soon after, South Vietnam's Congress in one of their last official acts, selected former president General "Big" Minh to succeed Thieu, because, ironically, he admitted to the long-time suspicion of having Communist ties, and it was hoped that this would be advantageous in negotiating peace with Hanoi. But this was only hopeful thinking—the Communist had no need or desire to negotiate.

On the 26th of May in 1975 they began their final assault on Saigon. By the 30th NVA troops hoisted their country's red banner with yellow star over Independence Palace and the late Ho Chi Minh's dream of independence for a united Vietnam had finally come to pass. Saigon, the former capital of the former South Vietnam, the key domino of Southeast Asia, fell.

Shortly thereafter Mick received David's final letter describing the panic and chaos that occurred as he and the last Americans, and a few chosen South Vietnamese officials, tried to get out of Saigon on choppers with the Communists nipping at their heels.

> *We literally had to fight our way up the stairs of the U.S. Embassy, Mick, to get to a chopper on the roof as hysteric South Vietnamese civilians and soldiers were literally clinging to us in hopes of being flown out too. As I climbed on to the chopper I had to violently shake a woman off of my leg. It's heartbreaking, Mick, what we have done, abandoning them like this, leaving them to the mercy of these Communist dogs, who are anything but merciful. They'll execute and imprison thousands. This is truly an American defeat, not in a military sense of course. When we were involved in the war we were very successful, for the most part, on the battlefield, but we, as a nation, as a people, failed in our resolve to live up to our original commitment as articulated by JFK when he said we must bare any burden, pay any cost to keep the South free of Communism.*
>
> *We cruelly set the South Vietnamese up for a crushing defeat, and our credibility as vanguards of world freedom will be compromised for years.*

David's last words left Mick feeling empty inside, and he wanted to fill that emptiness with booze, but he had a thesis to finish about the failure of Vietnamization, which ultimately was the failure of the United States to live up to its original commitment to help keep South Vietnam and the rest of Southeast Asia free of Communism.

Working diligently at his typewriter at home every day and night, Mick wrapped it up and took it in to Professor Miller just in time to finish grad school in June.

"I'll look it over right away, Mick," the professor said, "and based on what I've seen so far; your writing ability and the amount of research you've done on it, I'm sure it's quite good. Too bad it has such an unhappy ending—for the free world anyway. So what will you do now, Mick?"

"I'm not sure yet. I've got enough savings to tide me over for awhile, then I might try to find a teaching job at the high school level, or get on with a radio station as a newsman. In case you haven't noticed I don't have the face for TV."

"No you don't," Professor Miller joked back. He winked. "Maybe behind the beard you do. What about the book, Mick?"

"I'll be starting on that pretty soon. Maybe tomorrow."

"Don't procrastinate, Mick, if you don't mind a little advise from an old man. Time passes swiftly. You don't want to be lying on your death bed wishing that you had written it."

"How about you, Professor Miller? Started on yours?"

"Last year. Now I'm one year closer to finishing it."

"Yeah, well maybe I'll start on mine today," Mick said. "Guess I better go, Professor, see ya."

"Okay, Mick, take care."

Chapter 61

Except for the stifling heat, Mick liked the laid back southern feel of Carbondale in the summer, when the throngs of students were away. You could even get breakfast at Mary Lou's Diner on Saturday mornings without having to stand in line for an hour.

One Saturday morning there, Mick ran into Kathy who had become a "townie" too. She worked at the Phoenix House; a drug and alcohol counseling center; something that was badly needed in Carbondale, where so many were walking around with their heads in the clouds, high on one thing or another—everything from booze and grass, uppers and downers, acid, angel dust and even heroin, Mick knew. And when they crashed and burned they'd need help rising from the ashes again.

Mick had been one of them, with alcohol his primary drug of choice, and apparently Kathy thought it still was.

"Haven't seen you at AA for awhile," she said with a tone Mick interpreted as admonishment. "If you need to talk come and see me at Phoenix House."

"Thanks, but I'm doing okay," Mick said a little annoyed.

"On your own? Hmm, that's hard to do, but more power to ya, Mick."

"Oh, I've been wanting to tell you, Kathy, that sauna bath you started out at my place; I finished it. Come winter if you ever want to use it feel free," Mick said, sub-consciously leaving the door open for a resumption of their relationship.

"Shwooo, I feel like I'm in a sauna right now. Not even ten o'clock and it's 90 already," Kathy said, blowing the bangs of her hair up with her breath while looking at the thermometer hanging outside near the front door of Mary Lou's.

"Lake Wells is always cool. Come out for a swim."

"I might do that, meanwhile I've got to go to work. I'll see you, Mick. You know where I can be found."

"Yeah, same here. See ya."

Yes, they had left the door wide open.

It would be nice to be with a woman again, Mick thought as he walked away. No doubt he and Kathy had made some mistakes in their relationship before. Perhaps they had learned from them.

He hoped she would take him up on his invitation to come out for a swim soon; a midnight swim, like they had done before in the moonlight. Mick remembered full well how she looked when she got out of the water and stood naked on the shore; wet body shining; sleek and shapely; a beautiful femininity that the unisexual clothing she often wore belied.

To Mick's delight she took him up on his invitation sooner than expected; the next afternoon in fact, and the sunlight had the same affect on her wet, naked body as the moon's had. Her less than buxom, but lovely breasts felt warm and firm pressed against his chest as they stood on the shore wrapped in each other's arms, thighs against thighs, precariously close to intercourse. Mick pushed away not wanting to make the same mistake they had made before that led to an abortion. He wasn't prepared for so much passion so fast.

"It's okay," Kathy said, "I'm wearing a diaphragm."

"Let's hold off for a little while and see if there's anything between us but sex," Mick suggested. "We had a misunderstanding before, I think, about the nature of our relationship. You saw it one way and I saw it another. This time maybe we could develop more of a friendship first. I know that must sound weird coming from a man."

"Weird? I don't know," Kathy said. "Maybe more like unique. Sure, why not, let's give it a try. So I guess we better get dressed then. But could we lie down together in the hammock? It's in the shade and there's a nice breeze blowing now."

"Sounds good to me," Mick said.

Yet he did feel weird choosing to cuddle instead of having sex. What kind of man had he become, anyway?

Soon he and Kathy dozed off with the breeze, cooled by the lake, blowing over and under them; the advantage of lying in a hammock on an otherwise very hot day. Little wonder it was the bed of choice for many who lived in the tropics.

After awhile Mick was awakened by the sound of whimpering underneath the hammock. It was Carmella. He reached down to pet her and he felt something soggy, like a water-logged limb. He looked and saw, lying at her feet, a badly decomposed human arm.

THE END

978-0-595-42572-3
0-595-42572-0

Printed in the United States
94686LV00002B/544/A

978-0-595-42572-3
0-595-42572-0